C000174903

The children who'd been bu
water's edge—one of them
The other was screaming. She
of something from a nightmare. The creature waved
and forth in the air like a trophy, before cutting her in half. Her
innards spilled out across the sand and her blood splattered
against the thing's shell. The monster paused in its frenzy to
slurp up her intestines and organs. The girl's lifeless body still
dangled from its claw.

Milo bent over and retched.

An overweight, middle-aged sunbather who, remarkably,
had remained asleep while chaos erupted around him, now
woke up as one of the creatures loomed over him. He yelled,
more in disbelief than fear. The monster's stinger darted forth,
stabbing him in the chest. His eyes rolled back into his head.
His body began to shake on the sand. The creature's tail pulsed,
pumping venom through the appendage.

Milo turned and fled.

More of the crab-things reared from the waves, feasting and
maiming as they scuttled ashore on their insect-like legs. Their
claws rasped together, and the noise almost drowned out the
shrieks of the wounded and dying.

Click-click. Click-click.

The Clickers crawled onto the beach, and the sand turned
red.

Copyright ©2008 by J. F. Gonzalez & Brian Keene
ISBN 978-1-63789-692-1
Macabre Ink is an imprint of Crossroad Press Publishing
All rights reserved. No part of this book may be used or reproduced in any manner
whatsoever without written permission except in the case of
brief quotations embodied in critical articles and reviews
For information address Crossroad Press at 141 Brayden Dr., Hertford, NC 27944
www.crossroadpress.com

Crossroad Trade Edition

CLICKERS II

THE NEXT WAVE

J. F. Gonzalez
&
Brian Keene

Authors' Note

Although many of the places and locations in this novel are real, we have taken certain fictional liberties with them. So if you see your favorite beach or river herein, run and hide. There's a storm on the horizon and the menu features surf and turf.

Acknowledgments

Both authors would like to thank Shane Ryan Staley, Dave Kendall, David J. Schow, Bob Ford, Mark Sylva, and Tod Clark.

J. F. Gonzalez would like to thank Brian and Cassi, Cathy and Hannah, Mom and Dad, Mary Wolf, Dirk Wolf (RIP), Janice and Jeff Strand, Bob Strauss, Garrett Peck, Mark Sieber, Dave Nordhaus, Mark Williams's ghost, and all the fans of Clickers. Who the hell knew there'd be a sequel?

Brian Keene would like to thank Jesus and the entire Gonzalez family, Cassandra and Sam, those crazy fuckers on my message board, and the security guard at Baltimore's National Aquarium who threw me out when I was doing research.

For our good friend Gene O'Neill, with respect and admiration … but next time, don't let that damn Canadian eat all the food.

Prologue

FLOYD DEATH TOLL EXPECTED TO RISE

Ben Murdock
Associated Press
October 31, 1994

A grim Halloween morning greeted members of the Maine National Guard, American Red Cross, and officials from the Federal Emergency Management Agency as the death toll from Hurricane Floyd continues to rise.

Floyd's powerful category five winds wreaked havoc on Maine's northern coast, with over 1,800 deaths reported. The heaviest damage occurred in the town of Phillipsport, where the previous death toll of 500 has now risen to almost 700. Survivors indicate that Phillipsport, which relied primarily on the lobster industry and tourist dollars, may never recover. The Bangor News quoted one survivor as saying the town was "just wiped off the map. It's all gone." A large swath of destruction, extending from the south of town all the way to Route 193 in the north, was decimated, including the power plant, which supplied electricity to roughly 75,000 customers.

During an interview at the Red Cross emergency station in nearby Cherryfield, U.S. Army Colonel Augustus Livingston stated that there was no truth to rumors that widespread looting and lawlessness preceded the storm, despite eyewitness accounts that many of the dead were armed, or firearms were found near their bodies. He refused to comment on reports that the streets were littered with the carcasses of a species of giant crab, unbeknownst to science. Two researchers from Boston University also refused comment, nor would they verify reports that they'd taken a sample of one of the creatures.

Meanwhile, Hollywood's glitterati are doing their part for relief efforts. Musicians and actors are joining forces, and a benefit extravaganza is planned for Saturday night at Madison Square Garden in New York.

The event, which will be broadcast live on all three networks, is hosted by Chris Rock, and features such musical talents as Soundgarden, Your Kid's On Fire, Sheryl Crow, Suicide Run, Garth Brooks, and multiple Grammy-Award winning hip-hop artist and Nobel Prize nominee Prosper Johnson and the Gangsta Disciples. All proceeds will go to ...

AUTHOR FEARED DEAD
IN HURRICANE'S AFTERMATH

Matt Urich
New York Times
November 05, 1994

As clean-up and relief efforts continued in Northern Maine, after Hurricane Floyd cost the lives of over 2,000 people and over two billion in damages, New York-based publisher Diamond Books said yesterday that it fears author Rick Sychek may have been among the casualties. A Diamond spokesperson said the company reported Sychek missing on Tuesday.

Sychek, known as "the Stephen King of Generation X," and author of such best-selling page-turners as Baron Semedi, Night, Shadowbeast, and Night of the Devil, was last heard from on October 21st. He was staying at the home of a friend in Phillipsport, according to his agent, Cynthia Jacobs. Phillipsport received the heaviest damage during Floyd's assault.

Sychek had just signed a six-figure, two-book hardcover deal with Diamond, and was in Phillipsport to work on his next novel. The winner of the Bram Stoker Award, Sychek was ...

RELATIVES DEMAND ANSWERS

Robert McGavin
The Washington Post
October 26, 1995

To hear Gayle Lee tell the story, there was something else amiss the night Hurricane Floyd raged into greater New England and decimated large swaths of beachfront property, including the complete destruction of Phillipsport, Maine.

"We knew Floyd was coming," she said. Gayle Lee, a forty-year-old high school history teacher from Binghampton, New York, had spoken to her brother, Gary, hours before the storm hit. "The government says a few people got out of hand and were looting," she says. "That's their way of explaining why some people were found holding firearms when they died. But I was talking to my brother hours before Floyd hit, and he said the trouble started much sooner than that. He was in his basement when he called and said he could hear gunshots outside, like there was a war or something."

While it's true that many of the deceased were found clutching firearms, the official explanation is that the local sheriff had organized a posse to prevent looters. Gayle Lee isn't buying it.

"I've been in contact with a lot of folks who lost loved ones in Phillipsport," she said. "And we want answers! It is unacceptable that an entire town was just destroyed like that when other towns of similar size or even larger survived. Something else happened and nobody is talking about it."

When asked to comment on Gayle Lee's accusations, FEMA refused to comment, citing their ongoing investigation. Meanwhile, economists predict that the storm's impact on the insurance sector could …

BODY FOUND ON BEACH

Staff Reports
Bangor Daily News
November 28, 1996

The partial remains of an unidentified human being were found along the rocky cliffs near Falmouth yesterday afternoon, the Coast Guard reported.

"This was possibly a suicide victim," a Coast Guard spokesperson said. The condition of the body and its location, at the foot of the fifty-foot-tall cliffs that overlook the ocean, suggest the individual jumped to his or her death. "Those rocks are really sharp and a jump from that height will really cut you up."

The remains appear to be that of a male or female between the ages of 18 and 30. A size ten black hiking boot and a torn piece of corduroy were found near the body. Anyone with any information is urged to call the Maine State Police at ...

MODEL FEARED DEAD IN DROWNING ACCIDENT

Jessica Andreas
Boston Globe
July 10, 1997

Fast-rising supermodel Jasmine McDonald is feared dead today after a purported drowning accident off a remote stretch of beach on Martha's Vineyard. The incident was reported late yesterday.

The twenty-three-year-old model was vacationing in a beachfront home when, according to her boyfriend, she was overcome by severe abdominal pain while wading in the ocean at waist level. "She screamed that her stomach was hurting," Robert Mills, aged 25, told investigators. "Then she fell in the ocean. I tried to wade out and save her, but the tide carried her out."

Police will not comment on whether foul play was involved. "Right now we're investigating an accident," a police spokesperson said. "Nothing more, nothing less."

Police also refused to comment on an earlier 911 call made by Mills in which he screamed at the dispatcher that his girlfriend was "being eaten alive by a monster!"

"Mr. Mills was obviously very frightened and very panicky and he probably mistook Ms. McDonald's thrashing in the water as something far worse," Officer Harry Atkins reported. "We have a strong undertow all up and down the east coast this week. Ms. McDonald was obviously trying to fight her way out of a strong riptide."

Mills has a history of drug and alcohol abuse, and has had several run-ins with the law.

McDonald had just signed a five-million-dollar deal with Lee Jeans and appeared in advertisements for several cosmetics companies. She was a recent guest on *The Tonight Show* with Jay Leno and *The View*, as well as having numerous appearances on Howard Stern's radio program. The search for her continues.

SURFER MISSING, PRESUMED DEAD

Reuters
North Carolina
June 3, 1998

A twenty-four-year-old man was reported missing by his friends yesterday after surfing off the Barrier Reef Islands.

The surfer, identified as Mark Hansen, was twenty yards away from his friends and about two hundred yards from shore, when he suddenly vanished.

"We thought he'd caught a wave," Allen Minafee, one of his friends, reported. "But he was nowhere to be seen. Even his board was gone."

The Coast Guard is conducting an extensive search along the North Carolina coastline.

BOAT MISSING, FATE OF CREW UNKNOWN

Samuel Singleton
Little Creek Ledger
September 22, 1998

The crew of a missing recreational fishing vessel is feared dead, after a second day of searching by the Coast Guard and other authorities turned up nothing.

The Vanilla Sunshine departed from Virginia Beach two days ago. Onboard were the captain, John Rogers; first mate Steven Andrews; and Frank and Stella Laughman, on vacation from Ohio. The Laughman's had chartered the boat for half a day ...

EXCERPT FROM CRYPTOZOOLOGICAL WEBSITE

September 8, 2000

... likewise, the town of Phillipsport, once a sleepy village on the U.S.A.'s Northern Maine Coast, is now a virtual ghost town. Even now, nearly five years after the devastating hurricane that swept through the greater New England region, whispers of a government cover-up run wild among the locals.

"My brother told me some weird giant crabs or lobsters were all over town," one resident of a village fifty miles north of Phillipsport recalled. "He called me right before they lost power. Said he was going out with a hunting party to nab some and that's the last I heard from him."

Details of the crabs are scant. Scientists who were reported to have been in Phillipsport shortly after Hurricane Floyd blew over have refused comment, and recent reports indicate they have taken remains from at least two unidentified animals, heretofore unknown to modern science ...

ANNOUNCEMENT FROM SAME
CRYPTOZOOLOGICAL WEBSITE

September 9, 2000
From the Webmaster—

We regret to inform our readers that we suffered a severe server crash and have lost the contents of our entire website, as well as backup copies of all data and articles. Please be patient as we slowly begin the task of rebuilding the site. We apologize for the inconvenience.

BODY FOUND

Staff Reports
Delaware Herald
April 3, 2001

The remains of a twenty-two-year-old woman were found on the beach south of Dover by two joggers. The victim is described as a white female. Identification is being withheld pending notification of her family ...

SWIMMER MISSING

Mark Westin
Myrtle Beach Gazette
August 18, 2001

A fourteen-year-old boy was reported missing today and is feared drowned. Aaron Severin was treading water fifty yards from shore with playmates when he suddenly went under. Despite attempts from an experienced swimmer to locate him, he remains missing.

Lifeguards evacuated the beach and a search is now underway by the Coast Guard.

The lifeguard had reported strong rip tides one hundred yards offshore, and the Coast Guard had been monitoring them when the boy disappeared. A spokesman said ...

SCIENTIST CLAIMS FOSSIL CATEGORIZED INCORRECTLY

John Burnham
Science Today
June 13, 2002

A mysterious fossil, discovered in Argentina twenty years ago, and once thought to be the biggest spider to ever walk the earth has been reclassified by a University of Manchester scientist, who claims the specimen is more likely a prehistoric crab.

Plaster casts of "Megarachne Servinei" are exhibited in museums worldwide, and it was even recognized by the *Guinness Book of Records* as the "World's Largest Spider." Arachnid researcher Dr. Ian Sinclair, however, insists that its origins must be reclassified. In a report to appear in a scientific journal next month, Sinclair states the creature is more of a cross between a giant crab and a sea scorpion, than a spider. He believes the fossil may be a relative of the giant eurypterid (sea scorpion) and the Woodwardopterus, an invasive species from the Carboniferous Period, originating in Scotland with relatives in South Africa, including the extinct "Homarus Tyrannous"...

SCIENTIST DIES IN FIRE

Tim Clark
Manchester Herald
June 27, 2002

Dr. Ian Sinclair, renowned scientist and expert on prehistoric arachnids, died Sunday when his flat caught on fire. Sinclair, who was to report his findings on "Megarachne Servinei" next month, was asleep when the blaze erupted, according to investigators.

"It's a total loss," said one official, who spoke on condition of anonymity. "Everything was incinerated, including his research ..."

COUPLE FOUND DEAD,
AUTHORITIES REFUSE TO DISCLOSE DETAILS

Nancy Kress
Ocean City Times
March 19, 2003

Authorities remain tight-lipped regarding the identities of and circumstances surrounding the death of two beachgoers found Sunday night. One eyewitness, who asked to remain anonymous, stated that, "the bodies were sliced up. Looked like crabs had been at them." The witness professed that a cover-up was involved and declined further comment …

FEARS OF "NORTH ATLANTIC TRIANGLE" JUSTIFIED?

Bradley Tate
Boston Daily Herald
December 27, 2003

While it may sound like something out of a science-fiction movie, paranormal investigators, fishermen, and even seasoned commercial mariners are saying that the legendary Bermuda Triangle seems to have moved north.

In the past five years, over 200 vessels, everything from fishing boats to a Coast Guard cutter have vanished in the coastal waters of the northern Atlantic Ocean, stretching from the Bay of Fundy in Maine to Cumberland Island, Georgia. Very little debris has been found, and the internet is rife with cover-up speculation and talk of conspiracies …

MARINE LIFE THREATENED
BY INCREASED GLOBAL WARMING

Frieda Sanchez
The Washington Post
May 18, 2004

Accelerated global warming, along with continued over-fishing and coastal pollution, now poses an immediate threat to many marine species, two major environmental organizations reported yesterday (one of which is sponsored by former Vice-President and former Presidential Candidate Al Gore).

Scientists have documented worrying declines in all forms of marine life. The threat extends from coral reefs to polar-ice communities, and from tiny zooplankton to whale populations. They warn that the steadily warming waters could wipe out entire species, and that other species may migrate to oceanic areas where they are not normally found.

The report, released yesterday, was based on studies by some of the world's leading marine researchers. It said that warmer surface air temperatures were also warming the world's oceans. Human activities such as over-fishing have also contributed to the collapse, and destructive practices like bottom trawling have devastated the habitat of the sea floor.

Reef fish and inter-tidal invertebrates such as anemones, crabs, and snails are migrating toward the poles and coastal areas in response to ocean warming, the report said …

MAJOR HURRICANE
COULD HIT AMERICA'S NORTH-EAST

David Burks
CNN.com
January 4, 2005

The 2005 United States hurricane season, which runs from May to November, will be more active than normal, experts announced today. The 2006 season is expected to be active as well, according to recent simulations.

Hurricane watchers from AccuWeather.com, based in Pennsylvania, also projected that the Northeastern and Mid-Atlantic coastal regions will be hit by a major hurricane within five years. John Solow, senior meteorologist and director of forecast operations at AccuWeather, said that portion of the United States was "long overdue for a powerful hurricane" and the ocean's weather patterns made it a question of when, not if.

"It's a fact," Mr. Solow said at a Philadelphia news conference. "Current models and statistics lead us to believe this event will happen within the next five years ..."

BIOLOGIST DOWNPLAYS INVASIVE SPECIES CONCERNS

Sarah McCoy
Baltimore Sun
August 3, 2005

As evidenced by the recent Asian northern snake-head population found here in Maryland two years ago, and the European zebra mussels found in the Gulf States last summer, invasive aquatic species from across the world are moving into North American waters.

Central European freighters pump their internal ballast tanks full of water from their homeports, drawing in potentially invasive life forms. When changing water at ports in North America, the invasive species are released. But the fear of these species is being overblown by the media, according to one marine biologist.

"If you're asking me if we should take it seriously, then yes," said Dr. Jennifer Wasco, a marine biologist and researcher working at the National Aquarium in Baltimore's Inner Harbor. "But it's not the doomsday scenario that the media suggests. When a species such as the northern snakehead manages to successfully invade an ecosystem, the ecosystems' native species are usually already in decline ..."

HURRICANE WARNING IN EFFECT

Associated Press
July 1, 2006

The National Weather Service and Hurricane Center have issued a hurricane warning from the Florida Keys to the coastal areas of Georgia. A hurricane warning means that hurricane conditions are expected within the warning area, generally within the next twenty-four hours. A hurricane watch remains in effect from South Carolina to Morehead City, North Carolina.

At 4 PM, the eye of Hurricane Gary was located about 370 miles south-southeast of Florida. Gary is moving north-northwest at 18 mph, and this general motion is expected to continue for the next 24 hours. Maximum sustained winds are near 140 mph, with occasional higher gusts. Gary remains an extremely dangerous Category 4 hurricane. Hurricane-force winds extend outward up to 100 miles from the center, and tropical storm-force winds extend outward up to 250 miles. Rainfall amounts of 9 to 14 inches can be expected in association with Gary, along with the added threat of flash floods and mudslides.

Evacuation procedures have begun in the affected areas. Florida State Police have implemented the contra-flow of traffic out of the coastal cities. All lanes on all highways move traffic west. Coastal residents in both states are heeding evacuation orders. Many are taking to the roads, and long lines are reported at gas stations. Flights at most metropolitan airports have been cancelled …

Part One:
The New Wave

1

Robert Fegley stood at the window in his corner hotel room on the seventeenth floor of the Resorts Hotel on Atlantic City's boardwalk, looking through his binoculars at the hotel room across the street. Last night, the young couple staying in the room directly across from the room he and his wife were vacationing in were fucking like bunnies. He'd watched them go at it for over an hour, totally absorbed in his own private porno movie. It was the number one reason why he brought the binoculars with him whenever he and Carol went on vacation. You never knew what people were going to do.

Robert was trying to get a good view of what might be going on in the couple's room this morning when he heard a noise outside.

He trained his binoculars down on the beach, looking out over the sunbathing people lying in the sand. He couldn't place the noise; it sounded like a scream, but that couldn't be right. People came to Atlantic City to gamble, get shit-faced, and get laid and they were doing it now, even while Hurricane Gary threatened the southern part of the country. Why should they worry? That was the south. This was the north. It was far away. No reason to let a hurricane get in the way of fun.

Robert had been coming to Atlantic City every summer for more than fifty years. When his wife was at the pool or at the beach or in the casino playing slots, he was usually either at the bar or the roulette table. But last night he had been looking through his binoculars, trying to see if there was some action going on in one of the other hotel rooms along the Boardwalk, when he'd seen the young couple screwing their brains out in their well-lit room, the drapes wide open.

Carol had a new name for him now: a dirty old man. She'd always called him a dirty pervert, but now that he was officially a senior citizen, with the wrinkles on his face and his hair snow white, that moniker was of no use. A dirty old man was what he was, and it tickled the shit out of him. As long as people were going to do shit like what the young couple in the room across from him were doing, for everybody to see, Robert felt he had a right to watch with his binoculars. There was so much you could see. People did all kinds of crazy shit. Mostly what he saw was people fucking in their rooms without a care in the world that they could be spied on from the hotel across the street. Just because they were up ten stories or more didn't mean they had privacy. The dumb fucks. It amused the hell out of Robert, hence the binoculars.

Robert adjusted the vision on the binoculars and scanned the beach. One time he was scanning the beach and came upon a little take-out restaurant with a little patio. Robert had watched as a young couple ate their meal on the patio, then the woman had stretched her leg out and started rubbing the guy's crotch with her toe.

They'd carried on as if everything was normal. Robert had giggled, amused.

"Nothing going on here today," he said. It was true. Nobody was doing shit. Nobody was getting or receiving a blowjob, nobody was playing with themselves, and nobody was getting laid. He moved the binoculars away from his face, wondering where to look next. Carol was at the beach with their daughter and grandchildren. His son had gone to the store for more beer, and Robert was bored as shit. Now what?

"What's with you people?" he said to himself, putting the binoculars to his face again. "Come on, let's have a little action. It's only twelve o'clock. People fuck at noon, you know. They're called nooners. Hell, if Carol was here, I'd be getting laid now.

Old people fuck, too, you know. That's why God created Viagra."

He made another sweep of the boardwalk. Nothing.

Then he moved the binoculars back up the beach.

Something made him stop and adjust the vision. He squinted, trying to get a clear picture. "What the hell is going on out there?"

Just as it became clear to Robert what the hell was going on out there, he heard the sounds again—yes, they were most definitely screams—and then he saw people running away from the ocean, their features contorted in fear, and then he saw the things coming out of the ocean, running up the beach after the people. He watched, momentarily spellbound, not knowing how to comprehend the scene below him. It almost looked as if some of the things—they looked like fucked up crabs or lobsters or something—were actually attacking people.

"Jesus Christ, what the hell are those things?" Robert exclaimed. He zoomed in for a closer look. "Am I really seeing this shit?"

The screams grew louder and the pandemonium spilled out onto the boardwalk.

Yep. He was really seeing this shit.

And they really were crab-lobster-scorpion things ...

Jerry Barker was on his lunch break, enjoying a plate of *tacos al carbon* at Baja Fresh along the Shops On Ocean One when the shit hit the fan.

He'd just taken a bite and was savoring the spice-marinated steak, onions, and corn tortilla when screams interrupted his thoughts. He looked up, still chewing, wondering if the local security guys were finally doing something about the crazy homeless woman who had been causing so much havoc for the various small businesses that operated on this little strip jutting out into the ocean. Jerry had chased her out of the Sam Goody store he worked at twice this week when customers complained to him that she smelled, and she'd screamed at him like this, too.

He heard the shriek again and looked around, still chewing his food. Other Baja Fresh patrons who were enjoying their lunch looked around at the sound, too. A couple of people who were calmly walking along the boardwalk paused, looking around, trying to determine where the sound was coming from. And then a guy ran out of a T-shirt shop, his face white. "Oh my God, you gotta see this, you gotta see this, there's some fucking shit going on down on the beach!"

Jerry put down his taco and frowned. A woman ran out of the T-shirt store, dragging a five-year-old girl behind her. A young woman ran out after her, screaming. A guy dressed in cook's whites ran out of the hamburger joint at the end of the pier, followed by what looked to be the entire kitchen help. Their panic-stricken faces and screams spoke volumes to Jerry. He got up and turned around, wondering what was happening.

A mass of people ran out of Baja Fresh, pushing past him, and their fear spilled over to him. Jerry rushed over to the edge of the pier and looked at the beach.

He stood watching for a moment, his jaw agape, not believing what he was seeing.

Some fucked-up-looking things that reminded him of giant scorpions or lobsters were literally streaming out of the ocean. There had to be dozens—no, hundreds—of them. They were coming out of the ocean and running up the beach on giant legs, chasing people and fucking eating them!

Jerry didn't know how many people were lying dead on the beach. The entire beach was utter pandemonium. People were crashing into each other, stampeding over each other to get out of the way. It was chaos.

Those that had stopped to look out over the pier to see what was going on started running back toward the boardwalk.

Jerry almost ran himself, but stopped. He looked down at the end of the boardwalk. Some of the things were already there, skittering around, their scorpion-like tails jabbing at people.

"Holy fucking shit," Jerry said.

Then he turned and headed back into the Sam Goody store he worked at and sought refuge in the rear storeroom.

Officer Lyle Strong had his firearm out the minute he saw the things—whatever the hell they were—and started shooting. He hit four of them, missed two, and then ran out of bullets. He dived for the front seat of his squad car, which he'd left running when he stopped to investigate why everybody was running the hell away from the beach, crowding en masse along the boardwalk, and grabbed the shotgun. He raised the weapon and took aim at one of the things, which looked somewhat like a cross between a giant scorpion and a lobster and was the size of a large dog, and pulled the trigger. Its upper half exploded into mush.

He ejected the spent shell and chambered another round and was about to take aim and fire again, when he heard dispatch calling him on the radio. "Unit ten, come in, unit ten."

Realizing this shit was big and getting worse by the second, Lyle was in his vehicle in a flash, locking the doors and rolling up the windows. He laid the shotgun across the front seat of the car and started driving away slowly. He picked up the mike. "Unit ten here. We have a situation at the Boardwalk from South Florida Avenue and up past Belmont Avenue, probably even farther north. I need backup now!"

A trio of shirtless men flung themselves against his squad car, screaming in unison. "There's a bunch of monsters eating people on the beach!"

Officer Strong activated his siren once to scare them away from his car, and they scattered. The boardwalk was so thick with people falling all over themselves to get away that it was hard to move the car forward through them without hitting anybody. He activated the siren again, hoping the sound would be enough to part the crowd to enable him to drive away, but nobody paid attention. For the first time in his ten-year stint as a cop, Lyle Strong was afraid.

A young girl who appeared to be no older than fourteen stumbled in front of him. Her face was streaked with blood. A lumbering fat man tripped over her and fell, sprawling face down. The girl climbed on him, using the hood of his car to hoist herself up. Somehow through all the noise of people screaming and yelling in their mad dash to flee, he made out what she was saying: "Something's eating my boyfriend!"

Officer Lyle Strong stopped the car and got out. He went

to the young girl, trying to make some sense out of what was happening, paying no heed to the mass confusion around him, when suddenly it was on him. There was no time to run or draw his weapon. He saw the segmented tail jerk forward; felt the impact of its stinger jabbing him in the abdomen like a punch in the gut. The force of the impact sent him crashing against the squad car and he barely had time to scream before the thing snapped his head off with one blood red claw and began to feast.

Bobby Duncan was ten thousand dollars in the hole at the poker table and was trying to win it back, but he finally threw his cards down in disgust when the dealer left the table. "Aw, Jesus man, it's probably just a bunch of fucking kids stirring shit up!" Bobby had been aware that something was happening outside for the past ten minutes, but he hadn't gotten up from his game. The dealer had dealt him cards and chips and Bobby had been involved in his own little world, not even thinking about the screams and running feet of people outside, the sirens and the honking horns of vehicles echoing in the casino. Goddamn kids, probably. Maybe it was the god-damned Arabs finally starting shit over here again. Fucking towel-head motherfuckers blowing themselves up in the Sin Capital of the East Coast next to New York City, of course. Bobby didn't give a shit if the entire September 11th scenario was being replayed three times worse.

He had to dig himself out of this hole, had to at least double that to throw Eddie Marino some money so that crazy wop wouldn't come sniffing around when Bobby wasn't expecting it. And then when Marino was temporarily satisfied with ten Gs, Bobby was getting the fuck out of Jersey. Maybe even out of the country.

"Walk away from this table, I'm just grabbing chips and cashing shit in!" he called to the dealer. The dealer wasn't listening. He was looking outside one of the large plate-glass windows at whatever was going on outside.

Bobby watched him for a moment, and then looked around at the now empty casino. The place had literally emptied out within the past five minutes as people began to be drawn out by the frenzied sounds from outside. The hardcore gamblers like Bobby had stayed behind, but eventually they, too, had been drawn away. Now it was just Bobby and a couple of guys in suits wandering around the casino floor—security probably. Bobby looked around, trying to see if anybody was watching him. If the dealer wasn't coming back, then fuck him. Bobby was going to nab a couple of thousand-dollar chips and see if he could cash out.

He was just about to do it when there was a sound of shattering glass. Bobby looked toward the front of the casino. "What the—?"

The dealer was on the ground, covered in glass, and a large black guy was on top of him. Some large red thing was on top of him, and Bobby sat there staring at the scene, trying to comprehend what was going on. For a minute he thought he was trapped in one of those CGI things in movies—Jurassic Park or some shit like that. It looked like some creature with claws and a tail like a scorpion was eating the black guy, and the dealer of his poker table had been unfortunately pinned beneath them as the creature and its meal sailed through the plate glass window. Time seemed to crawl for Bobby; he saw more people screaming, running back into the casino; he saw quick glimpses of more of those crab-things chasing people; he saw an old lady stagger inside the casino, her belly ... well, the only word he could think of what was happening to her belly was that it was melting. She fell face first on the carpeted floor of the casino and that's when Bobby's paralysis broke and he turned and almost ran straight into Eddie Marino.

Eddie Marino grabbed him. He looked past Bobby at the havoc unfolding behind them. "What the fuck's going on here?"

"Let go of me!" Bobby yelled and kneed Eddie Marino in the balls.

Eddie howled, clutching his groin. He tumbled to the floor, his face ashen, as Bobby ran toward the rear of the casino, once again survival kicking in as he pushed past people in his mad haste to get the hell out of the casino.

Tony Genova and Vince Napoli were sitting in a beachside café, waiting for Frankie Spicolli to show up so they could make the exchange. Tony watched his obese partner shovel a chicken wrap into his mouth, and then inhale a second one. They'd been partnered for over six years now, and Tony was still amazed at how much food Vince could eat.

He squeezed his feet together, making sure the briefcase was still between them under the table. Wouldn't do to lose it now; not with all that junk inside. When Spicolli arrived, he'd give them another briefcase, this one filled with money. Tony preferred the latter. If the cops pulled you over, it was a lot easier to explain a briefcase full of cash than it was one full of heroin.

"So what are we doing after this?" Vince asked, crumbs dropping from his open mouth. "We got time to hit the blackjack tables?"

Tony shook his head. "Mr. Marano wants us back in York today. We still got to deal with the fucking Greek, and then we'll pay a visit to our friend on Roosevelt Avenue. Drop the Greek off there. Our friend will take care of the rest."

"Yeah, but it's the Fourth of July weekend." Vince wiped a blob of mayonnaise off his chin.

"We don't get vacations." Tony sipped his espresso. "You know that. Not in this line of work. Besides, the Greek is going to the fireworks. That's where we'll do it. They only got fireworks once per year."

"Won't be no fireworks if it rains."

"You a fucking weatherman now, Vince? You want a job on the Weather Channel? The fuck you know about when it's gonna rain?"

"That hurricane. I saw it on the news. Said we could get over twelve inches of rain."

Tony sighed. "That's down south, Vince. Hurricane Gary ain't supposed to make it this far north."

"But it could still make it rain here, and if it did, there wouldn't be no fireworks. What will we do then?"

Tony sighed. "Lock the Greek in a room with you and let

the two of you discuss the weather for an hour. That's enough to kill any man."

"You ain't got to be mean, Tony. I'm just saying."

Pouting, Vince picked up a pastry. Before he could eat it, someone screamed. Both men glanced out the window, their senses instantly aware, and hands automatically reaching beneath their suit jackets.

"The fuck?" Tony gaped, processing what he saw in the street.

Tony Genova had seen some weird shit in his lifetime—stuff he didn't tell the other guys about (except for Vince, who'd been with him on many of those occasions). But what he saw now took the prize. The monster was the size of a VW Bug. He knew that because it was facing off against a VW Bug. The girl inside was screaming, pounding on the horn. The creature looked like a cross between a crab, lobster and scorpion. It had flattened the car's front tires with its massive claws and was now smashing the windshield with its tail. Another crab-thing scuttled down the sidewalk, stinger lashing out and impaling fleeing pedestrians. More of the creatures followed along behind it, stopping to feed on the bodies. The air was filled with shrieks, tires screeching, horns blaring, alarms—and tearing sounds. Horrible tearing sounds.

One of the things weaved towards the café's storefront, waving its claws in the air.

"Fuck this." Tony grabbed the briefcase and stood up, knocking his chair to the floor. "Drop the Danish and move your fat ass, Vince. We're outta here."

Vince stared out the window in horror, the forgotten pastry still clutched in his fingers. "But what about Spicolli? What about the drop?"

"Fuck Spicolli. Take a look outside. You think he's really gonna show now?"

The crab thing drew closer, only a few feet away from the large glass windows. Vince sprang to his feet, quick and graceful despite his prodigious bulk. He drew his Kimber 1911, and Tony pulled his Sig Sauer. The other patrons cried out at both the things in the street and the two men with guns. Tony and Vince ran for the kitchen, hoping the things outside weren't lingering around the café's rear exit. Glass shattered behind them.

"Not for nothing," Vince panted as they raced through the back door, "but I'd rather be in Vegas right now."

Linda Young was stressed. She was a police dispatcher for the Atlantic City PD, and since shortly after twelve hundred hours, the radio had been jammed with distress signals from officers down at the Boardwalk. Linda had talked to one of them—Burt Young—before communications were cut off abruptly. It appeared that the rest of her cohorts were going through the same thing. Her entire team had been briefed on the possibility of Atlantic City being in the path of Hurricane Gary. Over the last twelve hours, the storm had changed course. Some meteorologists were predicting the storm would veer off into the North Atlantic while others believed it would still hit the south. Still, some computer models hinted at the remote possibility it could veer yet again and make landfall along the Chesapeake Bay, plowing into Baltimore and Washington, D.C. Nobody seemed to be taking those models very seriously, but after New Orleans, it was good to be prepared in any event. They'd been briefed on procedure and protocol, and things had gone on normally until just a moment ago. Now phones were ringing off the hook and their supervisor, Ben Cordway, was huddled with the senior dispatcher, Ken Brown, both with worried looks on their faces. Linda moved her chair out of her cubicle into the middle of the room. "Has anybody talked to anybody else about what's going on out there?"

Ben Cordway looked at her and held his hand up. Linda could make out a voice on one of the frequencies that carried messages from the feds. She tried to make out what was being said. "… I can assure you that we'll have the National Guard out as soon as—"

National Guard? Linda stood up and took a step further into the middle of the action. Her co-workers were in various states of holding the fort down; some were actively talking to officers, others were on the phone with 911 dispatchers. All of them looked nervous and scared. Burt Young hurried past her, his face white. "We're going on lockdown," he said. "We're under attack."

"We're under attack?" Linda was instantly scared. Like millions of other Americans, she'd been transfixed with a mixture of awe and terror on September 11, 2001, when Islamic Terrorists had attacked New York City and Washington, D.C. She was at work that day and had pulled a sixteen-hour shift. For the first time since her career in law enforcement started, she'd been in lockdown that day for the first eight hours until they got a handle on what was going on. Linda wondered how broad in scope the attack was this time. "Where?" she asked. "Is it airliners again? A car bomb?"

"It's nothing like that," Burt said. He picked up the phone at his desk and dialed a number.

"Well then what is it?" Linda asked.

Burt looked at her, holding the phone to his ear. "Something's coming out of the ocean ... a whole bunch of them ... and they're ... *eating* people!"

When Channel Four News Anchor Mike Baker and his cameraman arrived at the Boardwalk just south of Florida Street, he saw right away that this was a story that could make his career. He instructed his driver to pull in as close as possible, and when that proved to be fruitless they stopped in the middle of the street. Mike hopped out of the passenger seat and craned his neck to see what was going on. What they'd heard over the police dispatch lines were ... well, it was crazy. When he saw what was *happening,* he turned and dived back into the van.

"What are you doing?" Mark Adamson, his producer, had already gotten out of the van. Mike's cameraman, Roy Billings, was still in the rear of the van gathering his equipment. "We're the first News Team out here to cover this! Are you insane?"

"Are you insane?" Mike yelled at Mark. "Look at that shit!"

"I don't care!" Mark jabbed his fat little finger at the closed passenger door window at Mike. As usual, Mark was wearing a beige suit that appeared to be two sizes too small for him. He looked like a cheap car salesman. "I'm here to push you, to shadow you on your job due to your crappy performance. You will cover this story, and you will do it now, or so help me God you won't work in this market again!"

Mark wasn't looking at what was going on down the street. Mike could see it clearly from where he was sitting. So could their driver, who turned the vehicle back on and reached for the gearshift. "Oh Jesus," the driver, Julio Romero, said. "We gotta get the fuck out of here."

"Turn the vehicle off!" Mark shouted.

"Mark, this is bad," Mike said, begging his producer to listen to him for once. "This is serious shit, get back in here, or—"

Mark reached for the door handle on Mike's side of the van and tugged. The door was locked. "Unlock this door!"

Mike stole another glance toward the boardwalk. He'd seen people being overtaken by the creatures the minute they got there, and he thought he'd seen a kid crawling between parked cars toward them … it looked like the kid was falling apart. Sure enough, the creatures that were wreaking havoc were now heading straight for them. They were a good twenty yards away.

Mike turned to Mark. "Can't you see what's happening? Just look!"

"Get the fuck out here and do your goddamn job!" Mark yelled, pounding his meaty fists into the door.

The creatures were ten yards away, heading straight for them.

Julio's face grew pale. "Oh shit, man!"

Mike heard the frenzied clicking of the creature's claws; saw them open and shut like double-blade scissors.

Mark pounded the door, so wrapped up in his anger that the outside world was oblivious to him. "If you don't come out of here in three seconds, you're fired!"

Roy Billings finally got a good look at the creatures. "Oh shit!"

"Get us the fuck out of here!" Mike yelled as Julio popped the van into reverse and they sped backward.

After that it all happened so fast that Mike didn't even think of telling Roy to roll the camera. As they sped away from the scene, Mark fell down on the pavement and the things were on him. He caught a glimpse of giant claws dipping forward, deadly looking stingers jabbing downward and then Mark was all but buried beneath half a dozen of the monsters. Julio somehow managed to back the van far enough away to turn it around, and then they got the hell out of there.

Scenes from ground level.

A woman in her mid-thirties who had shown up for a day of sunbathing on the beach with her teenage daughter and her friends lay dead on the sand, already partially eaten, those parts of her that were left now reduced to bubbling flesh as the venom from the creatures did its work.

A twenty-year-old Princeton sophomore lay dead of a broken neck when he was trampled to death in the mad race to escape the beach. He lay on the boardwalk, eyes forever open, so far his body left uneaten and thus intact.

Over twenty squad cars responded to various 911 calls and frenzied distress signals. The creatures killed fifteen of those officers. The five officers that survived fled, some in their vehicles, others on foot. They knew they were no match for the sheer volume of creatures that now littered the entire boardwalk and were now crawling toward the downtown district.

Further inland, along the business district, things turned chaotic. People conducting their daily business began to flee at the sight of the creatures. Vehicles collided with each other as their driver's attention was turned away from the road. Office workers watched in disbelieving horror at the spectacle unfolding below them. Some of those in office buildings were trying to call 911, finding the lines jammed. Others were glued to news websites to see what was happening—so far, the media wasn't reporting on it; that's how fast it was occurring. Still, others called friends and loved ones in Atlantic City, in nearby Baltimore, in New York City, and places even farther away:

"… I'm looking at them right now! These things that look like giant crabs or scorpions are roaming down Florida Street attacking people …

"… oh my God, one of them just … God, what is it doing? Oh my God it's attacking a truck driver and it's—"

"... yes Mom, I've been taking my medicine, but I'm telling you, everybody in my office is seeing the same thing I'm seeing ... no, I'm not! Mom! Mom! No, I'm not doing speed again. I'm not hallucinating!"

"... man, you should see 'dis shit! These fucked up lookin' things are like something out of some fucked up horror movie. They's runnin' up the street snappin' people in half 'n shit and I swear to God, man, one stabbed this muthafucka with this stinga it had on its tail and that nigga was hurtin'! He started swellin' up and shit and he jus' esploded!"

"... just get the baby's things, get my handgun and the ammunition and magazines in the closet and pack the car up and go! I'll meet you at the cabin. I'm leaving now, and don't stop for anybody! I mean it, Suzi! Don't even stop if they say they need help, just keep going, run over them if you have to, fucking shoot 'em if you have to, just get the hell out of ..."

Some people in town on vacations were lucky enough to capture footage on video camera. In the days that followed, their footage would be shown on all the major news networks, much like the video images of the planes that plowed into the World Trade Center towers. Those images would depict horror and widespread panic. They would also provide a first-hand glimpse of the creatures that were invading Atlantic City en masse.

To Robert Fegley, who was still looking out his tenth story hotel room through his binoculars, what was going on below was horrific beyond description.

And it was just beginning.

Robert felt a giant, icy fist suddenly seize his heart and squeeze. His left arm went numb, and the binoculars tumbled from his hand. He clutched his chest and fell to the floor.

What's this, he thought. Heart attack? That's not fair ...

He was dead within a minute.

He was one of the lucky ones. Outside, the carnage continued.

2

The old man watched the skies. The sun was still shining bright as it began its descending westward arc. Sunset was just a few hours away, yet the sun refused to go quietly or gently into the night. The old man respected that—felt a kinship with the orb. It was doing what he could not.

No sense dwelling on it, he thought. And besides, this isn't so bad. It could be much worse.

He breathed deeply, inhaling the aroma of fresh cut grass and hay. The sky overhead was blue and crisp. Bees buzzed in the clover at his feet, and two hummingbirds fought over a red feeder, darting angrily back and forth, trying to get to the sugar water inside.

It was another perfect end to another perfect day.

The old man leaned against the white fence, watching the stallion run. It galloped past him, mane blowing in the warm summer breeze, coiled muscles working like clockwork cogs beneath its skin. The old man envied the horse. His own mane had long since disappeared and his muscles were more rubber than steel these days. He'd grown soft, and this angered and depressed him in ways nothing else could.

He sighed.

Retirement. Day four thousand and eighty-two.

Horseshit ...

These were supposed to be the happiest days of his life—the golden years. Forget what they told you in high school when you were a kid, that those were the best days of your life and you'd never forget them. Hogwash. He barely remembered high school and what little he did remember wasn't happy or joyous. Those memories were filled with a shocked amazement that he'd been that naïve, that stupid and careless. Young men had no clue about the world around them or the things in it. The mysteries of women. The value of a dollar. Respect. Careers. Responsibility. Fear. Wars ...

So, clueless, they ended up getting shipped off to places like Vietnam, and no, those weren't the happiest days of their lives.

They certainly hadn't been his.

The old man had done two tours of duty in Vietnam, as well as participating in Grenada and Desert Storm, all while fighting the Cold War and Congressional overlords between excursions. He'd served many administrations and shaken hands with some of the most important men in the world, and while he was fiercely proud of his service, they weren't the best days of his life. They were days of duty and obligation, of discipline and orders and rules of engagement. And after a lifetime of that, after the final war, when they'd chased the Iraqis out of Kuwait and had been ordered to stop at the border rather than taking Saddam out of commission once and for all when they had the chance—after all of that had come Phillipsport.

The old man shivered in the summer heat. Perspiration beaded on his forehead, and it had nothing to do with the temperature outside. It was a cold sweat.

Phillipsport had been the worst tour of duty of them all. He'd witnessed things there he'd never seen on the battlefield. Things no man, no matter how evil, would do to another human being.

Because the enemy in Phillipsport hadn't been human ...

Part crab, part sea scorpion. Oversized, some bigger than a large dog. Nothing like them in the fossil record, yet the scientists had told him the creatures were millions of years old. Like sharks, they'd been relatively untouched by evolution.

He'd arrived in Phillipsport on October 23, 1994, at the end of a ferocious storm, Hurricane Floyd. It formed late in that year's slow hurricane season and hit New England with a fury. He'd been dispatched to Phillipsport by order of the Pentagon in an effort to oversee operations. Standard homeland disaster ops, buy the book—a nice coda to his years of service. The mission parameters changed while in route, and that was always a sign that shit was hitting the proverbial fan—when peacetime orders became fluid. His troops were now ordered to assist the National Guard and put a lid on the hysteria that was leaking out of the town. Something about creatures coming out of the stormy ocean, ravaging the town, attacking and devouring people. It was unbelievable and his initial reaction was, you're sending me and my men to chase things that don't exist? He'd quickly learned otherwise when he reached the outskirts of the village and saw firsthand the destruction and carnage.

And then he'd seen the things himself.

He'd initially caught fleeting images; large crab-like things with scorpion-style stingers running through town—and hideous amphibian creatures that walked on their hind legs like a human. The old man had been part of the first convoy that made an attempt to get into town. They'd seen the things fifty yards away and the old man had given the order as per the pentagon: shoot first, don't ask questions. His convoy stopped and commenced fire on the creatures, obliterating them.

The next twenty-four hours had passed quickly and even now, reliving it in his mind, it all seemed like a dream. Two thousand troops had been called in and a command center had been set up ten miles outside of town. The storm hampered their efforts somewhat, and the old man had seen some of his men killed by the things they'd been sent in to fight, but he'd lived through it. The nightmares occasionally came back to remind him, but even now, after the mandatory therapy the brass had made him take, all he remembered were brief snatches of the battle that had raged; bursts of gunfire and shattering, scaly skin; visions of dead and dismembered people littering the streets of the quiet seaside town; and the things … the things that had walked on two feet like a man … the creatures that at first glance seemed both amphibious and reptilian by their rough scaled skin, webbed clawed feet, and ugly mouths filled with rows of razor sharp teeth. Their eyes had been the worst. Those cold, black eyes …

The enemy had put up a fight. They were relentless. They seemed to adapt easily from saltwater to freshwater, and infested the local streams and lakes as well as marauding across the land. He'd immediately called in for reinforcements and an additional two thousand troops were on their way up from Boston when the storm abated and the creatures suddenly headed into the ocean, never to be seen again.

He retired after Phillipsport. Bought this farm and intended to breed racehorses. He lost himself in things like bloodstock and genetics and breeding practices, learned how to read a pedigree analysis; hired a staff—everything from a groundskeeper to a biomechanics specialist; surrounded himself with green, rolling pastures in a small, still-rustic region of the country.

These were supposed to be the happiest days of his life.

But then the old man realized that his life had passed before him, and he hadn't been aware.

These weren't the happiest days of his life. These weren't anything.

He was just filling in time, marking off the spaces on another short-timer's calendar. He was bored. And restless. Sad.

Old.

The horse galloped past him again, neighing proudly.

Enjoy it while you can, the old man thought. It'll be over before you know it.

A lawnmower coughed and sputtered to life from inside one of the utility sheds, interrupting his thoughts. That would be Roberts, the groundskeeper, getting ready to cut the grass.

The old man turned away from the fence and walked back towards the yellow, two-story farmhouse. His arthritic knees popped, and he winced. The pain was getting worse. By seven this evening he'd be immobile if he didn't rest now. Maybe he'd check the kitchen, see if May, his cook, would fix him a bowl of chicken corn soup. Then he'd relax in the den for the evening, smoke his pipe and read. Try to lose himself in a book.

So that he wouldn't have to think.

As he approached the house, the screen door banged open. May ran out, her face pale, her eyes wide and shocked, her bottom lip trembling. The old man had seen that look before, thousands of times, in fact. It was the face of terror.

His pulse quickened.

"What's the matter? Are you okay?"

May pointed back inside the house. "The news ... Oh, it's terrible, sir."

His stomach fluttered. "A terrorist attack?"

"No, worse. Come look!"

She dashed back inside, and the old man followed her as fast as he could. His knees cried out as he climbed the porch steps two at a time. He winced again. In truth, he was surprised that May was still here. She lived in the farmhouse, as part of their arrangement, but her plans had been to go see her son and daughter-in-law this holiday weekend. May had a new granddaughter.

The thought of grandchildren made him sad.

The big-screen television was on in the family room (he grimaced every time he thought of that—family room—he had no family, only a bitter ex-wife who'd died of breast cancer ten years before), and the volume was turned up loud, filling the house.

"—numerous casualties, Phil. In addition to the creature's attack, we're now getting reports of looting and other crimes. The scene here is absolute chaos."

Creatures. The old man stopped. Did that reporter just say creatures?

May stood in the family room, staring at the television. The old man joined her, sinking into an overstuffed leather easy chair. The springs groaned along with his joints.

"It's terrible," she repeated. "All those poor, poor people."

The old man shut his eyes to the images flashing across the screen. He'd seen them before. Seen them every time he closed his eyes, in fact, just like now.

"And we're now getting word," a distraught anchorman reported, "that the creatures have come ashore at Rehoboth Beach in Delaware. Again, if you're just joining us, Atlantic City, New Jersey has been attacked by ..."

"What are they, sir?" May's voice trembled. "What in God's name are they?"

Frowning, the old man rubbed his forehead. A headache was blossoming behind his eyes.

"God didn't make those things, May. Someone else did."

"What do you mean?"

"I've—"

The phone rang, interrupting him before he could say more. Sighing, he picked it up.

"Yes?"

There was a moment of silence, and the old man was ready to hang up, convinced it was a telemarketer. Then, there was a series of faint clicks. A voice on the other side spoke—young and hesitant. Nervous.

"Colonel Livingston?"

"Who is this?"

But he already knew. Not the speaker. He didn't recognize the voice, but he knew who the caller represented.

"Are you watching the news, Colonel?"

"I am, indeed."

"Then you know why we called, sir. You reportedly dealt with these things before, though we've been unable to find the file."

"What's your name, son?"

"Lieutenant Harper, sir."

The old man glanced up at May. Her eyes were filled with tears, yet still she did not look away from the screen.

"You can't find the file, Lieutenant Harper, because the brass buried it deep where the sun doesn't shine."

"I understand that, Colonel. I know they gave you a hard time. But we need your expertise now."

"What's the sit-rep, Lieutenant? And don't feed me what I can learn from watching the news."

"We have confirmed sightings all along the Eastern seaboard, from Maine to the tip of North Carolina. The creatures are slaughtering everything in their path."

"Jesus …"

"Yes. It's bad, Colonel."

"Well of course it's bad, son. And there's no need to call me Colonel. I'm retired now."

"Not any more, sir. You're being reactivated. As I said, we need you. Your transport has already been dispatched. ETA one hour and forty-five minutes. We've set up a command center at Fort Detrick."

The old man's joint pain was forgotten. He listened for a while. Indicated that he understood. Then he hung up.

"Bad news, sir?" May asked, wiping her eyes.

He nodded, his eyes not leaving the television.

"Is it … is it because of this?" She pointed at the screen.

"You know I can't tell you that, May."

"Should I be worried?"

He rubbed his forehead. His temples throbbed. "Where does your son live?"

"A few miles north of Virginia Beach. They've got a little place on the water. I was just getting ready to leave—get a head start on traffic—when the news came on."

"Don't go." Livingston's voice was harsher than he'd meant it to be. "It's not safe."

"Why?"

"Because of their proximity to the ocean. Call your son. Suggest they come here instead. Hell, demand it."

"But, sir, we wouldn't want to impose—"

"You won't. The house will be empty. I need to pack a bag. I'll be going away for a while."

"How long, sir?"

He paused. "I don't know. It's possible that I may not be back."

Outside, the lawnmower droned on.

The happiest days of Colonel Augustus Livingston's life had just gotten worse.

3

Several miles off the coast of Little Creek, Virginia
3:30 PM

"This fucking sucks."

Cortez nodded in agreement. "Yeah, it does. But what are we gonna do, man? C.O. wants to play war games before we come in, then we gotta play war games. That's just how it is."

Macker frowned. His creased brow was red from exposure to the sun. "Fucking bullshit, man. We've been playing war games the last four fucking months. That's all we been doing. Fucking North Atlantic cruise. Fucking NATO. Fucking bullshit."

Cortez grinned. Macker was always like this, and their current situation did nothing to improve his mood. The entire deployment had been a bad one for him, from getting dumped by his girlfriend back home via a "Dear John" letter on the night before they left port, to the marijuana bust in Naples, Italy which had sent him to Captain's Mast, where he'd lost two months' pay and a rate, and had ended up doing chow line duty. Macker was in a foul state of mind—and storm clouds were brewing, both on the horizon and on his brow. Once Macker got going, you couldn't calm him down. He ranted until exhaustion or alcohol subdued him into sleep. Cortez decided to wind him up further, because he was bored and there was nothing else to occupy him.

"This is the Navy," Cortez teased. "This is what you signed up for, Macker. Adventure awaits you and all that bullshit. We do more before six in the morning than most people do all day."

He began singing The Village People's "In The Navy." His

deep baritone rolled out over the sea. Macker interrupted him.

"Fuck the Navy. And fuck you, too, Cortez."

"Hey," Cortez jeered, twisting the knife deeper, "don't forget, now that you got busted down, I outrank you, Seaman Apprentice Mack. So show some respect, bitch."

"Fuck you. Fuck your respect. Fuck the Navy. Fuck these stupid-ass war games."

The rest of the sailors onboard the long, squat M-6 boat laughed. There were six of them; Cortez, the boatswain's mate; Macker, the signalman; RM3 DeMars, who was currently napping between two benches; the two Marines, Lance Corporals Leigh and Rabbit (they called him Rude Rabbit); and Ensign Pitts, six months out of the academy and a real pain in the ass—but they'd finally broken him in during this deployment. They were assigned to the U.S.S. Blumenthal, a troop carrier currently anchored several miles behind them, along with the rest of the fleet. The ship was returning from a four-month tour of the North Atlantic, where it had participated in NATO exercises (Operation: Bright Star), and had ports of call in Naples, Italy; Rota, Spain; Dover, England; Haifa, Israel; and Kiel, Germany. They were due to dock in Little Creek, Virginia, after which Leigh and Rabbit would return to Morehead City, North Carolina with the rest of the 24th M.A.U., and the others would see their families and loved ones, all of whom were waiting. And the timing was perfect, too. One mother of a hurricane was churning approximately two hundred miles southeast of them and heading in their direction. Its edges were now expected to hit Virginia, with the worst of the damage further south. The water was already growing choppy from the storm's activity, even though the sky was empty of clouds.

Despite the latest threat from the weather, their C.O. had delayed their arrival, wanting to impress the brass with one more round of war games, this time right off the coast. And here they sat, mere miles from home—all the distance in the world.

Cortez licked his chapped lips. They tasted like sea salt.

"This fucking sucks," Macker said again, just in case anybody hadn't heard him the first time. "It's the fucking Fourth of July tomorrow. The fuck are we doing out here?"

Ensign Pitts stood up and smoothed his khaki uniform. "Quit your bitching, Mack."

The angry sailor fell quiet. He began chewing his fingernails.

A group of dolphins leapt from the water on the port side, chattered in excitement, and then swam towards the shore. The sudden splash woke up DeMars. He blinked in confusion.

"Good morning, sunshine," Pitts said. "Glad you could join us."

Grinning, DeMars sat up and looked around.

"Aren't they something?" Cortez watched the dolphins swim away. "Beautiful."

"Stupid fucking things is what they are," Macker said. "Just another dumb fish."

"They're not fish, you idiot. They're mammals."

Macker shrugged. "I don't care what they are. Bet they taste good just the same."

Leigh pointed at the sky. "Check that shit out."

They all glanced upward, shielding their eyes against the glare. The sky was filled with birds, seagulls mostly, and all of them were heading for shore. There were so many of them that they cast a shadow over the water.

"Well, that's weird," Rabbit said. "What do you think they're doing?"

"Must be the storm." Ensign Pitts shrugged. "They're clearing out."

Rabbit frowned. "But it's not supposed to get this far, is it?"

DeMars suddenly stiffened, sat up, and hunched over the radio behind the cabin. "Sir, the Blumenthal says we can come back now. Operations are over."

"It's about time," the officer grumbled. "Any word on how we did?"

"No, sir."

"Full ahead," Pitts ordered.

Cortez happily complied. The engines roared as he leaned on the throttle. He turned them around in a short arc. The sea was rough and choppy, and the boat's front end bounced up and down on the waves.

Leigh and Rabbit looked queasy.

"Sorry," Cortez apologized. "Can't help it. That Hurricane may still be hundreds of miles away, but shit's getting rough."

Suddenly, the heavy, flat-bottomed boat lurched to one side.

Macker gripped the side to keep from falling into the water. "What the fuck, Cortez? That wasn't no fucking storm swell."

He struggled with the throttle. "It wasn't me. Something hit us!"

Positioned at the rear of the craft, Leigh peered into the sea. "I don't see any—"

A blood-red pincer nearly six feet long, erupted from the water and seized Leigh's head. The marine had time to utter a short, surprised squawk, and then the claw squeezed, slicing his head in half like a grapefruit. He never even had time to scream. His grayish-pink brains, textured like cottage cheese, slipped from the open cavity and plopped into the sea.

The others screamed for him.

The creature thrust itself from the water and into the boat. It looked like a cross between a crab and a scorpion, but it was the size of a horse. The M-6's front end rose from the water with the added weight. The sailors were unarmed. Only the marines carried weapons during these excursions. Rabbit scrambled for his rifle, but it slid down to the crab-thing. The monster grasped it, snapping the weapon in half. Its claws made a terrible clicking noise, like two steel plates being banged together. Rabbit scrambled backwards, but the boat tilted more and he slid towards the scissoring pincers. He shrieked as the creature seized him and began to feed.

Another beast heaved up over the side of the craft and pulled Ensign Pitts into the ocean. It snipped his arm off like he was a paper doll. The foaming spray turned crimson. His screams were horrible.

"DeMars," Cortez yelled, "get on the horn. We need help, goddamn it."

Frantic, DeMars shouted into the radio, but his words were lost beneath the increased clicking sounds as more of the creatures rose from the sea. The cacophony even drowned out the engines.

Click-click. Click-click.

Cortez's lips went numb with shock. "What the hell are they?"

"Fuck," Macker screamed. "Fuck! Fuck! Fuck!"

Cortez cast a quick glance at the ocean's surface, and then he joined his friend. The water was filled with bobbing red monsters, their claws raised above the whitecaps, almost as if they were waving at the sailors.

Laughing, with tears streaming down his face, Cortez waved back at them.

The clicking sounds filled the air. Seawater rushed into the boat, soaking the sailors' pants and boots. Someone's finger floated past. It was Ensign Pitts'. His wedding ring was still affixed to the severed digit.

"This fucking sucks," Macker sobbed, collapsing to his knees. "Jesus Christ, I wish I'd gone to college instead of this fucking shit."

Cortez closed his eyes and began to say the rosary.

The creatures swarmed them, and the M-6 boat sank beneath the water.

Click-click. Click-click.

Ocean City, Maryland
4:01 PM

Yawning, Milo checked his sports watch. Less than an hour to go before his shift ended. Then he'd put up the LIFEGUARD NOT ON DUTY sign, clock out, head back to his apartment, grab a shower, and pick up Sheila. He'd met her at the Bricker's French Fries stand where she was working for the summer. In August she'd head back to college in Pennsylvania, but Milo didn't care. He still had another month to get inside her pants. If she didn't put out by the weekend, he'd cut his losses and grab another one. The beach was ripe with summer help—all of them co-eds.

He glanced to his right. In the distance, the pier jutted out over the ocean, the Ferris wheel turned and the cries from the tourists on the roller coaster echoed out over the water. Seagulls circled like mosquitoes, hoping for a morsel from the fishermen clustered around the end of the pier. To Milo's left, the beach and the boardwalk stretched as far as he could see, bordered by hotels, restaurants, and gift shops selling the same T-shirts, trinkets, hermit crabs, kites, and boogie boards—all of it crap, and all of it the lifeblood of permanent, year-round residents like himself.

Two young girls strolled by his lifeguard stand, their bikinis concealing only their nipples and ass cracks, and leaving nothing else to the imagination. They smiled at him. He smiled back. Giggling, they walked away. Milo eyed them with appreciation.

He loved his job.

It was a perfect summer day. The sky was blue, the air crisp, and the sun warm. The beach smelled of suntan lotion and coconut butter and cotton candy. Nearby, six different radios battled for supremacy, blasting everything from hip-hop to country music. Children shouted happily, splashing in the surf. The waves were large, crashing on the shore with relentless force, thanks to a hurricane that was still somewhere south of them. The size of the waves attracted surfers and boogie borders by the dozens and they were all out there now, bobbing in the roiling surf, catching waves.

So far, the forecasters didn't expect the storm to make landfall this far north. Florida up to North Carolina could see some damage, and Virginia might experience flooding, but here in the upper Mid-Atlantic region, they should just get a little rain—and some massive waves. Not enough to go into emergency mode over, but perfect for attracting even more tourists over the coming holiday weekend. Earlier that morning, he'd watched footage of the evacuations down south. Better there than here.

Milo unwrapped a stick of gum and slid it into his mouth. Of course, if the National Weather Service was wrong, and Hurricane Gary did head this far north, evacuation would be a bitch. The hotels and campgrounds were packed with tourists, and the roads and bridges would be jammed in a mass exodus, all of them moving at a snail's pace, if moving at all.

He glanced back up at the sky. It was cloudless.

"No storm coming," he muttered. "Fucking weathermen don't know shit anyway."

A trio of beauties strolled by, the perfect set—one blonde, one redhead, and one brunette. Milo watched them go, and thought again of Sheila. Maybe he'd bump his deadline up. If she didn't put out tonight, he'd move on.

He turned his attention back to the ocean, watched an airplane fly overhead, trailing an advertising banner behind it. The plane suddenly swerved in mid-air and headed towards town. A moment later, Milo saw why. The sky was thick with birds, all of them fleeing from the ocean. Their shadow hovered over the beach, and their droppings fell like rain. Over by the pier, the gulls that had been badgering the fishermen for random morsels suddenly wheeled and joined in the abrupt migration. Their cries filled the air.

That was when Milo heard the first scream.

Instantly alert; thoughts of Sheila and bikinis vanishing from his mind, he sat up straight and scanned the water. Bobbing heads, kids on boogie boards, people splashing and surfing—but no signs of a troubled swimmer. At the water's edge, two children were building a sandcastle. The scream rang out again, and now others heard it. Sunbathers looked out at the ocean, checking on their loved ones. Those in the water glanced around in confusion.

Milo noticed a red stain on the surface of the water, about fifty yards out. Blood. It spread in a pool, tossed by the waves. A swimmer lay face down, unmoving. Large, dark shapes moved beneath the surface. He watched them glide, unable to tell what they were—just that they were very big.

Sharks?

Someone else screamed. More voices joined the chorus. A swimmer disappeared, yanked beneath the surface. Then another. One of the dark shapes swam beneath a teenager on a boogie board. A cresting wave blocked Milo's vision for a second. When he looked again, the board's two halves floated on the foam.

His heart accelerated. Blowing into his whistle, Milo leaped from the lifeguard stand and ran towards the water, bare feet pounding through the blistering sand.

"Everybody out! Get out of the water! Shark!"

Except that it wasn't a shark. And there was more than one. He didn't know what they were. Something that just couldn't be. One of the creatures surfaced for a brief second before vanishing again beneath the waves. It reminded him of a giant lobster, but that couldn't be right. A wave rolled towards shore, and behind it, he caught a glimpse of something that looked like a stinger.

People rushed towards him, fleeing the water. Milo had to fight his way through the surging crowd. An overweight woman called out for someone named Billy. A man with a broken nose shoved past, dripping blood onto Milo's arm. Two men dragged a woman from the water. Her legs were missing beneath the knees.

Elbowing his way forward through the panicked throng, Milo froze.

The children who'd been building the sandcastle near the water's edge—one of them lay on the sand, unmoving. The other was screaming. She was caught in the clawed grip of something from a nightmare. The creature waved her back and forth in the air like a trophy, before cutting her in half. Her innards spilled out across the sand and her blood splattered against the thing's shell. The monster paused in its frenzy to slurp up her intestines and organs. The girl's lifeless body still dangled from its claw.

Milo bent over and retched.

An overweight, middle-aged sunbather who, remarkably, had remained asleep while chaos erupted around him, now woke up as one of the creatures loomed over him. He yelled, more in disbelief than fear. The monster's stinger darted forth, stabbing him in the chest. His eyes rolled back into his head. His body began to shake on the sand. The creature's tail pulsed, pumping venom through the appendage.

Milo turned and fled.

More of the crab-things reared from the waves, feasting and maiming as they scuttled ashore on their insect-like legs. Their claws rasped together, and the noise almost drowned out the shrieks of the wounded and dying.

Click-click. Click-click.

The Clickers crawled onto the beach, and the sand turned red.

4

National Aquarium
Inner Harbor
Baltimore, Maryland
4:45 PM

Jennifer Wasco was at the Baltimore Aquarium, working in her office, when everything started going to hell.

It had started out as a normal day. Most of the administrative staffers were already gone for the holiday, but the tour guides, operational staff, and a few researchers like herself remained. The aquarium would be busy this weekend, packed with tourists who would point and tap on the glass and fill the place with noise. She was grateful she didn't have to work with the public on a day-to-day basis.

Her morning was spent in the lab researching and making notes on her latest research project. Her specialty was how ecosystems were affected when non-native species were introduced to them. After lunch she accompanied her co-worker, Matt Brewer, to the shark tank and assisted in feeding them as a crowd of tourists ohh-ed and ahh-ed. Matt's usual helper was already gone for the weekend. Jennifer was back in her office, a small cubby tucked away from the tourists and the lab, when the commotion started.

Her boss, Dr. Richard Linnenberg, the aquarium's director, burst in to tell her there was something happening down in Atlantic City. Richard was so stunned he was stammering. His hair was plastered to his head, and his face shone with sweat. He babbled something about giant crustaceans eating people.

Incredulous, Jennifer turned on the small television near her desk and caught the live feed and watched, totally astounded. The implications were mind-boggling. The creatures on the television looked like something out of a science-fiction movie. They showed crustacean traits—lobster and crab, most noticeably. But they also displayed those of an arachnid, especially with the scorpion-like tail. They shouldn't exist. It went against everything she'd been taught, flew in the face of evolutionary theory.

It also intrigued her. The aquarium had never approved of her "side-project" (as Dr. Linnenberg called it) and no grant money was funded towards it, but over the last two years, Jennifer had devoted some of her spare time to tracking down reports of an invasive species purportedly sighted in New England several years ago. What she saw on television matched supposed eyewitness descriptions of that species.

She watched with rapt—and morbid—attention as the things descended on a news van. The camera mercilessly captured it all, even as the cameraman's blood splattered against the lens. The network quickly cut away. The anchorman looked pale. He struggled to speak. Behind it all, the live feed carried the sounds of the creature's claws, clicking like maracas.

Jennifer heard a commotion outside the door.

"These things are hitting Ocean City now!" somebody—it sounded like Mark Kriskee—yelled. She switched channels and sure enough, the same creatures that were attacking people in Atlantic City were now being spotted in Ocean City, right here in their own state, just two hours away by car. She watched in horror. The footage was shaky, as if the cameraman were running while filming it. The monsters had swarmed ashore on Ocean City's nearby Asateague Island as well, and were slaughtering the herd of wild horses that still ran there. Her eyes filled with tears as one of the things stabbed a pony with its stinger. The pony's flesh bubbled and sizzled, sloughing off. She was watching exactly what she spent her time studying—an invasive species and its effect on the local ecosystem—but that didn't lessen the emotional impact.

Jennifer stepped out into the hall and peeked through a

door marked EMPLOYEES ONLY. Strangely enough, business was normal in the aquarium. No one had been evacuated. People moved calmly, staring at the attractions. She wondered what it was like outside along the shops and restaurants that lined Inner Harbor. Had the news spread? Was there mass panic yet?

Dr. Linnenberg hustled back to her office. He looked worried. "I just got off the phone with the Public Safety Director at City Hall," he said. "They're recommending we evacuate the aquarium."

"What?"

He nodded. "Homeland Security agrees. The Mid-Atlantic seaboard is being put on alert."

Jennifer frowned. "Because of the hurricane?"

"No, because of these attacks. We're right on the water."

"They've been sighted in the Chesapeake Bay?"

"I don't know." He shook his head. "I'm just repeating what they told me. President Tyler is supposed to address the nation shortly."

"What are they, Richard? Those things?"

"Nobody knows for sure, or if they do, they haven't made the media's pundit coverage yet, but they sound an awful lot like the species that British scientist, what was his name ..." He snapped his fingers. "Ian Sinclair. That's it. He wrote about a species like this about four years ago; the ones that appeared to resemble something that was thought to be extinct."

Jennifer's mind whirled. Everything was happening so fast. She brushed a strand of auburn hair back from her forehead. "I remember that," she said. "Megarachne Servinei, right? I read about it in Science Today. Wasn't he pretty much discredited, though? He was later found dead before they could publish his report. House fire or something."

"Yeah, that's what they say." Richard mopped his forehead with a tissue. He was a skinny man in dark slacks, a white shirt, and a white lab coat. Even though he had a PhD in Marine Biology, he dressed as if he were an MD. His thick glasses made his eyes appear large and frightened. "And I know what you're thinking, Jen. You can't fool me. News clippings and reports on Sinclair's claims are in that big folder in your bottom desk drawer."

Shocked, Jennifer couldn't reply.

"I haven't been snooping. Was just interested in your side-project. I hate to admit it, but you might have been right all along."

"Thank you, Richard. I appreciate that."

"Listen, I hate to ask this of you, but—"

"I'll stay," Jennifer said, anticipating his request.

His features relaxed slightly in his strained features. She'd just taken the pressure off him. "You're wonderful. You stocked up the other day, didn't you?"

"Yes." A few days ago she'd stocked the living quarters and her office with enough food and provisions to last a few days when she heard about Hurricane Gary, even though meteorologists were predicting the chances of it hitting the mid-Atlantic region were still slim. Still, Jennifer took no chances. There were times when they were involved in marathon research sessions that kept them at the aquarium for days, and during a hurricane two summers ago she and a few other biologists and technicians had weathered the storm at the aquarium. The place was solidly built and could withstand up to a Category 4 storm. Additional engineering and security measures were undertaken after September 11th, and the facility was stronger as a result. "I'm all set. In truth, I'd rather not leave now anyway, especially when we don't know everything that's going on."

"Exactly," Richard said. He began retreating back down the hall toward the aquarium. "We need to be on top of this. Besides, those idiots at the national weather bureau are still arguing about the storm and where it's going to hit. They say it will stay down south, but you know how that goes. I think we should expect the worst and hold down the fort here."

"I agree."

"Good. Start making plans to batten down the hatches. They've already brought the seals in from the outside tanks, and sealed over the rain forest's windows." The aquarium had an actual walk-through replica of an Amazonian rainforest, with greenhouse-style windows facing the sky. "Call around and see if you can get some footage of these creatures. We'll see if we can get a comparison going."

"Comparison to what? You saw them yourself. There's nothing like them in the fossil record. This is an entirely new species we're talking about."

"I know. I'm sorry. I'm just worried, is all."

"Don't apologize. I'm worried, too."

"I'm going to make sure my wife is okay, and then I'll check in with you."

"Go," she urged. "Just be careful."

"You, too."

Richard headed toward the exit and Jennifer Wasco turned her attention to the television. Part of her was excited, but another part was scared to death. And as she started making phone calls to her parents in Hunt Valley to check in with them and assure them she was okay, she couldn't help but think again about the original story that had first sparked her interest in all of this; something that happened off the coast of New England the government had allegedly covered up. It was all rumor, of course, and the official story was that a hurricane wiped an entire town off the face of the earth. But the rumors remained— creatures that were half crab and half scorpion, along with some other species that couldn't be described. She'd always wondered if the stories were true. Her research had turned up nothing.

But now the very subject of that research had turned up along the nation's coast.

She hoped that Richard would make it home okay to his wife, and that he'd find her safe and sound when he arrived. Then she found herself wishing—not for the first time—that she had a family of her own to worry about. Her parents were getting older, but they were self-sufficient and active, a by-product of their generation. They were nothing like how she remembered her grandparents. Jennifer was an only child. No siblings, and as a result, no nieces or nephews. She wanted a child. She loved children, got along well with them. Her friends told her to adopt, or get a sperm donor, but she wanted to go about it the old-fashioned way. She wanted more than just a child. She wanted a family. She wanted a man, someone she could love and who loved her—an equal partner, in both marriage and parenting. But with the demands of her career, Jennifer had little time for a social life. Now here she was, early thirties, and not a single date in the last nine months. Her last serious boyfriend, Stan, had been a risk analyst for the MBNA credit card company and worked at their office in Hunt Valley. They'd had absolutely nothing in common except for sex, and they'd differed even on that. The first time he asked her if they could introduce another partner to her bed, she balked. He broke up with her soon after.

Jennifer's sole companion was her cat, Tucker, and he ignored her most of the time, unless he wanted to be fed. She thought of him, worrying, hoping he was okay. She was sure he would be. She'd left plenty of water in his dish, and if that ran low, he'd drink from the toilet (which he seemed to prefer anyway).

The television interrupted her thoughts. The Breaking News logo flashed across the screen.

Breaking news, she thought. What could be more important than what's happening out there right now?

Jennifer turned the volume up.

"... meteorologists say it defies all logic, but they have confirmed that Hurricane Gary has indeed abruptly changed course. It is now expected to skirt the Carolina and Virginian coasts, shoot up the mouth of the Chesapeake Bay, and make landfall around Baltimore and the nation's capital."

Jennifer gasped. "Jesus Christ. Welcome to life at ground zero."

Sighing, she turned the television's volume down and began leafing through the reports she'd collected over the last several years, trying again to piece it all together, and adding the new information. After twenty minutes, she rubbed her eyes. There were so many unknowns, so much information they still lacked. If only she could see a captive specimen, have an opportunity to view one up close.

She paused in her reading, and smiled. It occurred to her that she did have the opportunity. The creatures were here, according to the news. No deep-sea dive was needed. No rushing to inspect a Japanese fishing trawler's nets. No examining a grainy photo on some half-baked cryptozoology website. They were in Maryland.

And so was she …

Jennifer's cell phone rang—playing her favorite riff by the Dixie Chicks.

"Hello?"

"Jen?" Dr. Linnenberg, his voice almost lost beneath the static. "Jennifer?"

"I'm here, Richard. Where are you?"

"Stuck on 83. I made it about two miles. The roads are packed. Have you heard?"

"The storm changed course? Yes, they just announced it."

"You need to initiate final evacuation procedures, make sure all personnel are gone, and then get out of there yourself."

"Will do."

"My God …" His voice dropped to a whisper. "Unbelievable."

Jennifer grew concerned. "What is it? What's wrong?"

"A bunch of teenagers are looting this tractor trailer. It's sitting in the breakdown lane. I think they might be gang members or something. One of them has a gun just sticking out of his waistband. In broad daylight."

"Lock your car doors," Jennifer said. "Can you get off the highway?"

"No, and I don't recommend you take it when you leave, either. Where will you go? Your parent's place in Hunt Valley?"

"No," Jennifer said, staring at the television. "Actually, a thought occurred to me just as you called. I'm not going to Hunt Valley."

"Good idea. The storm will reach there, too. What's your plan? Head up into Pennsylvania?"

"No. Ocean City."

Richard squawked in surprise. "What? But that's where—"

He paused, unable to finish the sentence. Jennifer's silence was answer enough.

"No," he said. "I absolutely forbid it. You can't—"

"Richard, this connection is really bad. I can't hear you."

"Jennifer, you listen to me and you listen good. I do not—"

"Be careful, Richard. Get home safe. Sarah needs you."

"Jennif—"

She thumbed the off button. Her cell phone went dead.

"Ground Zero," she repeated.

She could stay here and wait for Hurricane Gary to make landfall, or she could head further south, closer to where the creatures had been sighted, and observe them from a distance and try to learn more about them.

"Frying pan or fire," she muttered. "It's not like I had plans tonight, anyway."

Taneytown, Maryland
4:56 PM

Colonel Livingston had his bag packed and was just about to exit the house when the phone rang.

May answered it. "Hello?"

Livingston paused, watching May. She'd called her son, convinced him to come north, and had been glued to the television ever since. Now she passed the phone to him wordlessly. He mouthed, "Who is it?" and she shrugged. "I don't know," she said, and turned back to the TV.

Livingston put the phone to his ear. "Yes."

"Colonel Livingston?" He couldn't place the voice.

"Speaking."

There was a pause. "They're back. They're doing what I told you they would do. Remember? And after they come, then—"

With dawning apprehension, Livingston recognized the voice.

"Sychek?" He whispered. "Rick Sychek?"

The voice stopped. Confirmation.

"My name is William," Rick insisted.

"How did … how …" How did you get my phone number? A silly question, really. Somehow, Rick always found a way to track him down. He'd been doing it for well over a decade now.

"You know what's going to happen next, right, Colonel? You remember?"

"Yes," the old man said, gripping the receiver. His stomach sank.

"Do you know how many times I tried to warn them?" Rick asked. "Sons of bitches. They wouldn't listen to me. Instead, they just wanted to make me disappear. Well, I disappeared all right. And now that the shit is happening right before our eyes again, do you think they're—"

"I just got the call," Livingston said. "I'm being reactivated."

"Reactivated?" Rick paused for a moment. "But you retired."

"Not anymore. They need me. Because of Phillipsport and what happened there. I'm hoping they listened to what I told them in the report I turned in to the Joint Chiefs of Staff eleven years ago. Otherwise, I don't think they would have called me back for service."

Another pause. "I really would like to believe that."

Colonel Livingston's next question was probably futile, but he asked it anyway. "Where are you, Rick? Can you tell me?"

"I told you. My name is William. I don't know who this Rick guy is you keep talking about."

"Sorry, William. Where are you?"

"You won't believe me if I told you, so I won't."

"Try me."

"Haven't you forgotten? They wanted me gone."

"Of course I haven't forgotten. It was me who warned you. If I hadn't, you'd be dead."

Rick's voice was thick with derision. "Only thing keeping me safe right now is that they think I am dead."

"What about Melissa?" Even now, over a decade later, he could still remember Rick Sychek and Melissa Peterson, the only two survivors of the Phillipsport incident. When they'd turned up missing on October 27, 1994, three days after being rescued by Army Reservists and brought to the command post headed by Livingston, he'd been livid. In the weeks that followed he changed his opinion: if he were in their shoes he would have done the same thing. Soon after, he'd learned that several different clandestine government groups had orders to terminate Rick and Melissa with extreme prejudice. He'd warned them when Melissa finally contacted him. At that point, the two were holed up in a motel on the Maine border. Since then, they'd apparently gone their separate ways. Livingston pitied them. Living on the run, under assumed names. Each time Sychek had contacted him, the man had been drunk or panicked.

But Rick didn't sound drunk now. He didn't respond to the old man's question, so Livingston tried again.

"What about Melissa, Ri—William?"

"What about her?"

"How is she?"

"Is this a secure line?" Rick's voice was tinged with suspicion.

"Of course not. Judging by the sound, you're calling me on a cell phone."

"Then I can't talk. Gotta go."

"Wait!"

The line went dead.

Livingston put the phone down on the small end table in the entry hall of the house. May was still glued to the TV. The two major stories were the attacks by the creatures in Ocean City, Atlantic City and other parts of the eastern seaboard, and the anticipated arrival of Hurricane Gary, which had unexpectedly changed course and was now expected to make landfall along the Maryland/Virginia border. In short, chaos. Or as they'd called it in the military, a real cluster-fuck.

Something else was bothering him. Most of the Clickers he'd seen on the news so far were bigger than the last wave had been. The creatures in Phillipsport, for the most part, had been around the size of a large dog. This new wave was much bigger. He wondered what that meant.

Livingston cleared his throat and May glanced up, and then gasped in surprise.

"Sorry. I've never actually seen you in your uniform before, sir."

The Colonel grinned. "How do I look?"

"Quite handsome."

"It's a little snug. Been a while since I wore it. Still, it feels natural. Right."

May's eyes drifted back to the screen. Her hands were curled into fists.

"Has your son called?"

May shook her head sadly. "Not since they left. The news showed some of the roads. It's bad. Congestion everywhere. The traffic isn't moving. What if they can't make it here? What if they run out of gas?"

Smiling, he patted her hand. "Your son is a resourceful young man. He'll be fine."

"And what about you, sir? Will you be okay?"

Touched by her concern, Livingston straightened up and puffed out his chest. "I'm reporting to Fort Detrick. They've set up a forward operating command post there. The base is entirely secure."

"Fort Detrick? That's in Fredrick. Won't traffic be backed up between here and there, too?"

"I'm not driving."

There was a distant roar outside. Startled, May rose from her seat. The noise grew louder, drowning out everything else. Livingston looked out the window. The horse galloped around in fright. Dust clouds billowed across the lawn, and the trees swayed. The helicopter landed in the field, just beyond the barn and the stables. Livingston frowned, anticipating the damage it would do to his pasture.

"Is that your ride?" May asked, her eyes wide.

He nodded. "They're over fifteen minutes late. Not a good start. Take care of yourself, May. Stay safe."

Without waiting for a response, he left the house, wondering if he'd ever see home again.

Philadelphia, Pennsylvania
5:10 PM

The cell phone was registered to a William S. Mark, as were the credit card and driver's license in his wallet, but that wasn't his real name. He still thought of himself as Rick Sychek. Even now, when people called him William, it took Rick a moment to realize they were talking to him.

He'd hung up on Colonel Livingston and was sitting outside of the hospital, scrolling through the names and phone numbers in his cell phone, not even thinking of who he should call next, when he came across Melissa's number.

He'd been thinking of Melissa ever since the Colonel asked about her. He'd been thinking of her before then, as well. In truth, he thought of her every day.

The minute he saw her phone number, more memories came and went, leaving him with a strange sense of sadness. A different kind of sadness than what he currently felt, but sadness nonetheless. He hadn't spoken to Melissa—who was now called Jessica Barron—in over a year, and he briefly considered calling her to tell her he was back on the east coast. His index finger poised over the "Send" button that would put the call through, but then he chickened out. He folded the device up and placed it in the left breast pocket of his shirt and resumed what he'd been doing before he'd gotten the wild urge to call Colonel Livingston: sit on the concrete bench along the walkway that led to the hospital and stare into space, thinking of his mother.

He remembered old faces from Phillipsport—Janice and her son, Bobby; Jack "The Ripper" Ripley, who'd owned the comic book store; Lee Shelby, owner of the local drugstore; old Doc Jorgensen and Deputy Russell "Rusty" Hanks, who'd been a fan of Rick's books; and even that son-of-a-bitch Sheriff Conklin. His expression soured at that last memory. It brought to mind old fears.

It was his mother's grave illness and impending death that had broken through his latest fears—flying and being near large bodies of water, primarily—and brought him back home, to Philadelphia, where he hadn't set foot since he'd left the city for what had then been a temporary move to Phillipsport, Maine to write a novel, the second in a two book deal his ex-agent, Cynthia Jacobs, had arranged for him.

His fingers absently stroked his graying goatee as the memories flashed by. His stomach felt clenched; at times, his hands shook with nerves. He'd gotten completely shit-faced on the plane and somehow made it to the terminal where he'd caught a cab to a motel. His family had wanted him to stay at his sister's house in Lansdale, but he refused. Even now, after all this time, the government could be watching. With the exception of his parents and two siblings, nobody in the family had a clue that he'd survived the hurricane. His parents and siblings had played along over the years, understanding that it was the only thing keeping him safe, keeping him alive. He might as well not have been. It had broken his heart to cut off all contact with them. Twice a year, on Christmas and Rick's birthday, his brother used a pay phone out of town to contact his good friend "William S. Mark" and Rick would catch up on what was happening in his family's lives, but that was it. So when his brother unexpectedly called a week ago, Rick was immediately alarmed. When he got the news that Mom had pancreatic cancer, he'd flipped out.

And now he was here, over a thousand miles away from Fargo, North Dakota, which he now called home, sitting outside the hospital because some of his aunts and uncles were inside and he couldn't risk them seeing him.

He waited.

Waited for Mom to pass on.

The cancer had been detected two weeks ago. His mother had been complaining of severe abdominal cramps for the three weeks prior to finally seeing a doctor. That visit had confirmed everybody's worst nightmare. Pancreatic cancer, the most horrible, most painful, most evil cancer in the world had taken root in his mother and was eating her alive.

His brother, Bob, had bought the airline tickets for him and got him out here. Thank God Bob had pestered him; otherwise Rick might not have bothered. The mere thought of boarding a plane was bad enough; knowing he'd be just miles away from the Delaware River, which fed into the Atlantic, flipped him out. No way was he ever going anywhere within one hundred miles from an ocean ever again. That's why he eventually wound up in North Dakota. The only thing in North Dakota was plenty of open prairies sprinkled here and there with people who talked funny, like in that movie Fargo. It drove Rick absolutely bat-shit for the first year. Now he was used to it.

The only good thing about North Dakota: there was no large body of water anywhere near where he lived. He was smack dab in the middle of flyover country. Nothing could get him out there. No Dark Ones, no Clickers, not even a goddamned sea gull.

A mild breeze lifted his hair from his shoulders, blew it around. The day was warm, the air humid. Rick's hair was pulled back in a ponytail. Everybody in the family commented last night that he still wore his hair long. It was rapidly receding from his forehead so he felt he had to compensate. Shortly after he and Melissa went underground, he'd cut it all off and worn it short for several years. He looked nothing like his former self now; his black hair was graying rapidly, his face had more age lines in it than he ever thought he'd have at this age, and he favored glasses now instead of the contact lenses he used to wear. Where before he'd been somewhat muscular, now he was rail-thin. And then there was the mustache and goatee, which gave him the appearance of a bespectacled college professor.

He felt sweaty beneath the white T-shirt he was wearing. He checked his watch. Five after four. The urge to call Colonel Livingston had hit him the minute he started seeing what was going on in the news that was flashing on the television in the waiting room. Everybody had been glued to it, and Rick had almost screamed in terror and bolted from the hospital. He'd had to fight his nerves not to make a scene, had to bite back the words that wanted to blurt forth in response to everybody in the waiting room wondering, "Oh my God, what are those things?"

(They're Clickers and they're going to eat your flabby asses if you don't get up now and get the hell out of here!)

"They look like some kind of weird-looking crab ... and are those things stingers?"

(Fuck yes, they're stingers, what are you, blind?)

"They're huge!"

(Yes they are—much fucking bigger than the ones I saw before.)

"This can't be happening, this has to be one of those Ashton Kutcher-things ... you know, that show Punked? That's what this is, a joke, right?"

(This is CNN, you shit-for-brains worthless piece of shit who should be in my mother's place, this is not a fucking joke, and if you don't shut the fuck up now, I'm going to drive you down there myself and feed you to those goddamn things!)

And it had went on until Rick finally walked out of the waiting room, telling his brother that "he had to get a breath of fresh air," and made it outside before he could vomit.

He'd started to go back inside and that was when his relatives arrived, so he'd remained outside. He'd caught his breath, fighting the nausea down, and then he'd called Colonel Livingston.

Then he'd sat on the bench for the next five minutes, contemplating his next call.

I've got to tell Melissa, he'd thought. I've got to warn her, hell, she's probably seeing this shit now on the news, it's all over now, CNN is broadcasting and I bet Fox and MSNBC are reporting on it, it has to be nationwide by now, so yeah, she probably knows, besides, she's not going to want to hear from me after all the bullshit that's been happening, she could care less what happens to me anyway, she—

The chiming of his cellular phone startled him. His stomach fluttered and he pulled his phone out and flipped it open.

Jessica Barron. Melissa's new name, post-Phillipsport.

He pressed the connect button and put it to his ear. "Hey."

"Rick?"

He cringed. "No, this is William."

"Right." She paused. "Sorry about that. I'm upset."

"What's wrong … ? Jessica?" He stumbled over the false name, but Rick had a feeling he knew why she was upset.

"Are you watching the news?"

"Yeah," Rick said. "I see what's happening."

"Oh my God, I can't believe it's happening again." He could hear Melissa's son, Jacob, in the background, chortling with other children. Jacob was probably five by now. Melissa had married a guy named Thomas Barron in 1998 and they had two kids, Jacob and a little girl named Stephanie. "This is unreal, this is—"

"I talked to our friend. The old man."

Melissa fell silent. "What did he say?"

"They called him back to active duty. He was just leaving when I called him."

"You didn't—"

"Stay on the phone long? Hell no. You know me better than that."

He could hear her shuffling stuff in the background; she was probably doing housework or dishes or something. Her husband made good money in his job, enabling Melissa to play housewife. "So he knows this is the real deal ... that this is everything you warned him about?"

"I don't know," Rick said. A wave of paranoia came over him. He casually looked around, checked out his surroundings. A couple of people were walking to and from the hospital. Everything seemed normal. "I'd like to think so."

"I just can't believe it," Melissa went on. She was babbling, and while Rick shared her fear he couldn't deal with it. Mom was ten stories above him in the hospital, dying, and he was a thousand miles away from home, near the Atlantic Ocean where all this shit was happening again. "This is just unreal, this is just—"

"Listen, I gotta go."

"—oh ... okay—"

Tell her, he thought. "Mel ... Jessica, my mom has cancer. She's dying, and I'm in Philly now."

Stone silence for a minute. Then, "I'm so sorry."

He closed his eyes, pinched the bridge of his nose. "I got in last night. I ... I can hardly stand being here, being so close to the ocean. I mean, I know it's a good two- or three-hour drive to the nearest beach, but that's too close for me and—"

"I understand," Melissa said, and he immediately knew this to be the truth. In the years that had passed since Phillipsport they'd talked about this fear often. Melissa had developed a fear of the ocean too, but hers wasn't as pervasive as his. Rick couldn't even stand looking at a picture of the ocean. And forget ocean documentaries on TV. Every time he thought of or saw the ocean, he thought of what really lurked beneath it. "If there's anything I can do, please ..."

"I know ... and thank you." For a minute, Rick felt a pang of loss. Melissa was too good for him. Sometimes he wondered why she still put up with him. Eight years after they broke up and she was still putting up with his bullshit dramas, still wanting to help him. Melissa had adapted quite well after they'd gone into hiding.

"How long are you going to be in Philly?"

"I don't know."

"Well ... if you need anything ... call me."

"I will."

"It's a good thing this is on the news," Melissa said. Jacob's voice faded from the background; it sounded like Melissa went into a more quiet part of the house. "You can monitor things better. You'll know when to cut and run if you have to."

"Exactly. Listen, I gotta go."

"Okay. Call me."

"I will." They ended the call and Rick sat on the bench, fighting back tears from his eyes as he wondered how his life could spiral into such a mess.

First Phillipsport and its horrors ... then the loss of his identity, which resulted in the eventual loss of his writing career when he'd been forced to give it up after finishing the novel he had started in Maine in order to keep the feds off his tail ... then the loss of Melissa when their romance, which started shortly after they went on the lam and went into hiding together, disintegrated. What followed were feelings of inadequacy, failure, loss, and fear, and he sought to numb it with a constant flow of alcohol and various affairs with women. The only positive thing in his life the past eight years was his bookstore, which he ran out of a small strip mall in Fargo, and his daughter, Melanie, who was now five and who he had with his ex-girlfriend, Ashley. Naturally, he'd fucked things up with Ashley and she'd left him. If he wasn't such a neurotic freak-show about things like flying and being near water, he'd be fine.

He was seeing a woman named Janet Ellwood now. Janet worked some corporate job in a high rise building in downtown Fargo. She made good money and was very into her career, which suited Rick fine. He considered her a fuck buddy more than anything, while he secretly pined for Ashley.

God he was such a fuck-up!

His cell phone rang. The display lit up, showing that it was his brother, Bob, calling.

Rick flipped the phone open, put it to his ear. "Yeah."

"You better come up," Bob said. His brother sounded awfully numb, like he couldn't believe he was dealing with this. "She's … she's … the doctor's say …"

"Uncle Ted? Aunt Rita?"

"Gone already. They said … they said their good-byes already."

"I'm coming." Rick got up, disconnected the call and headed back to the hospital, wondering how he was going to get through this nightmare.

5

"Hurricane? What hurricane?"

Gary Tucker walked along the beach, enjoying himself. He was completely and totally alone. As far as he knew, everyone else had heeded the evacuation order and bugged out of town. Idiots. Now the storm had changed course, heading farther north. They'd fled for nothing. But not him. No sir. Gary Tucker didn't jump just because The Man said so. He'd been here twenty-two years, operating his kite shop, and he wasn't leaving for nothing.

Besides, the hurricane was called Gary. That had to count for something.

He looked up into the sky again. The wind was calm, and the air was heavy with moisture from humidity. Earlier in the day, the sky had been obsidian, the clouds pregnant and swollen. But not now. Now, the sky was clear. The hurricane had changed course, gone north.

"Good riddance."

St. Augustine was a ghost town. The boardwalk was lonely and sparse. There were still a few people in the water, renegade surfers and beach outlaws, ignoring the National Guardsmen just as he was. He liked it when the beach was deserted like this. Even without the evacuation order, it was like this most evenings. The stragglers would eventually tear themselves away and head off to the bars or back to their hotel rooms to change, leaving the beach momentarily deserted until the teenagers showed up for their impromptu parties. They would arrive by the carload and build bonfires at the campsites and sneak cases of beer in. There would be drunken reveling, loud music, and a couple of lucky people might wander off in pairs to get it on in the dark, away from the bonfires. It would be exciting again. Gary liked excitement, and that's why he lived near the beach. It's why he came out to enjoy himself and feel the essence of the community.

The hurricane would have promised excitement, too, and Gary was mildly disappointed that it hadn't shown.

He'd seated himself at an abandoned snack food stand and was watching the surfers when he saw the giant crab lunge out of a wave. It grasped the surfer, clinging to his back like a misshapen lover. Both man and monster vanished into the surf. More of the creatures scuttled onto the sand.

Gary perked up, heart racing, fear surging through his veins. Of course he'd heard the news. It was all everybody was talking about—these giant crabs or lobsters or scorpions or some weird things that were coming out of the ocean attacking people. It was happening from Myrtle Beach all the way to Boston. They weren't supposed to be this far south, though. He hadn't heard about any attacks in Florida at all.

But now they were coming, and Gary had only twenty seconds to get up to scramble away from the boardwalk and try making a run for it to his car when he was overtaken. The creatures' size belied their speed. Something heavy landed on his back, bringing him to the ground hard, and something sharp jabbed his neck. Both the pain and the pressure were incredible. Gary screamed as his fingers, lips and other appendages began to swell. The weight on his back crushed the air from his lungs. His skin began to sizzle and sloughed off.

Soon, the beach was deserted again.

Fort Detrick
Fredrick, Maryland
7:33 PM

The world was going to hell.

Colonel Livingston stood in a control room half a mile beneath the base golf course. The command center had been carved into solid bedrock during the heyday of the Cold War, and was totally self-sufficient. It had its own power plant, air filtration system, communications network—including radio, phone, internet, and satellite—water and food supplies, and a peacetime skeleton staff that had just been tripled over the last few hours. Along with similar underground bunkers in nearby Camp David and Gettysburg, Pennsylvania, it provided a complete support network and shelter for government leaders in case the unthinkable happened.

Like now, for instance.

The corridors echoed with footsteps and voices, ringing phones and barked orders and grim reports, but no laughter or whispered conversations. This was a moment of national crisis, and Fort Detrick was the center of the storm.

Massive flat screens lined the command center's walls, each one tuned to a different news source—CNN, MSNBC, Fox News, BBC, and local affiliates out of Maryland, Virginia, New Jersey, Delaware, and elsewhere along the Eastern Seaboard. Much like the rest of the world, the military got much of its real time intelligence from media sources on the ground. Other screens broadcast raw data from the National Weather Service, National Hurricane Center, and maritime sources, all keyed in on Hurricane Gary's bizarre change of course. Several monitors displayed websites and internet news feeds, and monitored real time online chats and communications.

None of the news was good and with each passing moment it grew steadily worse.

"So big," he muttered. "Bigger than the ones before …"

The official death toll was thirty-five. That was the number being parroted by the media. The Pentagon and the Office of

Homeland Security had both been quick in putting a lid on press reports and suppressing news coverage now, anxious for their own public relations people to put a spin on things. But the leaks were already starting to pop up, mostly via the internet. Even those leaks were far from the mark in the death toll.

The unofficial death toll was three thousand and rising by the hour.

The National Guard had been called in at every major city on the East Coast and the mayors of New York City, Boston, Washington, D.C., Baltimore, and Norfolk had put their city's police forces on tactical alert. Soon after, the governors of New Jersey, Delaware, Maryland, Virginia, and North Carolina had declared a state of emergency, adding to the states of emergency already declared in the southern states when Hurricane Gary had been hurtling towards them. All the major news outlets were on the story and it had eclipsed the last minute course change and imminent arrival of Hurricane Gary. The Secretary of Defense, Joint Chiefs, and every available cabinet member were in a closed-door meeting with the President at the White House, and the promised press conference had now been postponed three times.

Military and a handful of civilian personnel buzzed around the room monitoring radios and computers. More phones rang. The shrill noise was incessant. In a glass-paneled office, a General was shouting orders over the phone.

Livingston closed his eyes for a second and let the symphony of well-organized chaos wash over him. He felt strangely calm. He had entered this world a soldier; he had a feeling he was going to go out a soldier. This was going to be his last battle. He was sure of it.

He opened his eyes again. A pale-faced corporal thrust a clipboard in his hands. Livingston signed the paperwork without reading it. The frightened soldier hurried off.

Livingston turned his attention back to the screens. The news seemed to have grown worse in the few brief moments his attention had wavered. The creatures had already made their way inland in the major cities they'd washed ashore at and there were more reports of massive casualties and injuries. It was like the Los Angeles Riots, the World Trade Center and Pentagon attacks, and World War II all rolled up in one. Most of Martha's Vineyard was on fire. Police had opened fire on a crowd in Washington. The bottom two floors of Donald Trump's casino in Atlantic City were burning out of control, and many of the other establishments were being looted. Inland areas were no safer. Not only were there the problems associated with an influx of coastal evacuees, but civilians were shooting at neighbors, strangers—anything that moved, convinced they were Clickers. And the latest news from the National Weather Service was that Hurricane Gary had gained strength to a Category 5 storm and was barreling straight for the Chesapeake Bay. That put it on a collision course with Baltimore. It was expected to make landfall by midnight.

Baltimore's Inner Harbor and downtown district were a grid-locked nightmare, and nobody could get in or out, except on foot. Likewise, evacuations had now been ordered for D.C., Roanoke, Virginia, and Philadelphia, Pennsylvania. The Mayor of New York City hadn't ordered an evacuation yet, but all the major tunnels were clogged with traffic heading out. In short, it was a goddamned mess. Add to that the continuing chaos in the south, as residents of the Carolinas, Georgia, and Florida now tried to get back into their abandoned cities—positive that the danger had passed. Livingston had quickly convinced his superiors to put a stop to that. The coastal areas of the south were still dangerous, even without the threat of the hurricane. They were nothing more than oceanfront smorgasbords for the invading Clickers.

Livingston's arthritis was flaring up. He clenched his hands into fists, gritting his teeth against the pain. It helped him focus. On the screen in front of him, a news helicopter was showing footage of a woman being dragged out of her car by two men in the midst of stalled traffic on Interstate 95. Watching it made his stomach ache with helplessness, so he turned away and focused on another broadcast. The logo at the bottom of the screen said it was somewhere in Florida, but that couldn't be right. The Clickers hadn't made it that far.

Had they?

"Sir?" A young corporal named Adams approached him. "They're ready for you in the conference room, Colonel."

Livingston looked away from the television. Without a word, he made his way to the conference room. The vacuum-sealed door hissed shut behind him. The air conditioning was turned up high. A long, oak table sat in the center of the room, stretching nearly from one wall to the other. Plush, comfortable chairs ringed the table, each one occupied by scientists and meteorologists, representatives from the Navy, Army, Marines, Air Force, Coast Guard, and National Guard, as well as the Department of Homeland Security, the Federal Emergency Management Agency, the Department of the Interior, even the FBI, CIA, NSA, and other alphabet soup agencies. Several pitchers of water and coffee had been placed for the meeting, and several videophones were hooked up and functioning as well. On the screens, Livingston saw other officials, including the Secretary of Defense, Donald Barker. The room buzzed with murmured conversation—which stopped when Livingston walked in. For a moment, he expected them all to stand at attention and salute, but they didn't, and he realized just how long he'd been out in the world and away from the game. He knew some of the men and women. Others were strangers. Some looked barely old enough to shave. Others were grizzled veterans like him.

Livingston nodded and shook hands with some of the individuals he knew, then took the last empty seat and poured a cup of coffee.

Corporal Adams, who'd followed him into the room, nodded at the assembled officials and then spoke towards the video monitor. "We're ready to begin, Mr. Secretary."

"Good." Barker's face filled the screen, speaking from his office at the White House. "Thank you, Corporal Adams."

"Yes, sir." Adams turned sharply, pivoting on his heels, and left the room. His demeanor was one of immense relief.

"Gentlemen," Barker said, "ladies. Thank you all for coming. The President would like to know—"

Livingston interrupted. "Where is President Tyler?"

Several people around the table gasped and frowned at

Livingston's insolence. He didn't care. Inwardly, he smiled. Things were off to a good start.

Barker scowled. "The President is currently meeting with a delegation from Saudi Arabia as part of this administrations ongoing effort to—"

"Saudi god damned Arabia? Have you looked outside? You've got a hurricane bearing down and a horde of creatures invading your beaches and coastal cities. Creatures I warned you about twelve years ago! If you people had—"

"That will be enough, Colonel." Now it was Barker's turn to interrupt. "We're all quite aware of your recommendations following the events in Phillipsport. That was a different time and a different administration."

A man sitting to Livingston's left cleared his throat. "If I may, I'd like to remind Colonel Livingston that he is no longer in charge."

Livingston's eyes narrowed. "And you are?"

"I am Jordan Hershey, Department of Homeland Security." He smoothed his tie. His expression was smug. "It's an honor to meet you, Colonel, and I hope you don't take offense, but you should all be advised going into this that we are in charge, under direct orders of the President. We will oversee all operations related to both the Hurricane and these … things. FEMA will assist us, of course, as will the various military branches. We'll try to let you know before we commandeer your forces, but have no illusions. We are in charge."

The military commanders bristled at this surprise announcement and the room erupted with angry shouts and incriminations. Livingston leapt to his feet, intent on leaving the room.

"Enough," Barker yelled through the speakerphone. "That will be enough. We need to focus here, people. We each have a responsibility to our country. Gentlemen, you will be quiet. Colonel Livingston, be seated."

"The hell with you. I'm retired."

"Colonel!"

Livingston spun around and stared at the monitor's camera. "I presented my findings to you eleven years ago and you ignored me. Only thing people like you cared about was manufacturing imagined threats to shore up the bank accounts of your buddies in the military-industrial complex. Didn't want to hear about a real threat like this because you weren't equipped to deal with it. Back then, Secretary Barker, you were still just an underling at the Pentagon. You and your kind—this new breed of yuppie fucks—wanted it buried. You never went to 'Nam. Were never in country. Your daddy saw to that, didn't he? And your staff—these boot camp officers who never grew up with strife or hardship or war. Grenada? Desert Storm? Don't make me laugh. My generation knew hard times. Their generation's biggest hardship was when that long-haired freak of a lead singer quit Van Halen. You wanted Phillipsport to disappear, so you buried my report, swept our warnings under the rug, and started eradicating the witnesses."

The Defense Secretary's voice thundered from the phone's speakers, loud enough that they vibrated. "That's preposterous! The United States government never sanctioned the murder of anyone involved with that incident."

"Bullshit!"

"Really, Colonel." Hershey, the Homeland Security official, sipped his water. "Don't you think we should focus on the matter at hand and leave the conspiracy theories to the folks on the internet?"

"Don't give me that shit. A conspiracy is just the truth without the proof. That's what we always said in my day."

Hershey smiled. "Times have changed, Colonel. Indeed, the world has changed. You're archaic. You're a dinosaur that doesn't know it's extinct. We do things differently these days. My department runs things now. Get used to the idea. Adapt or die, as you people say."

"Changed?" Livingston clenched his fists. "Not a goddamn thing has changed. FEMA couldn't wipe its ass with both hands, a flashlight, and an entire truck full of toilet paper, which they'd never be able to deliver to the correct place on time. And Homeland Security? You're just another bureaucracy. You're like a hydra, except you don't know what your other heads are doing."

"Look," Barker said with a sigh, "I'll admit, we mishandled the intel you gave us. That was a mistake. But Jesus Christ, Colonel, that was twelve years ago. It wasn't my decision. I was following orders, same as you."

"Whose orders?"

"It doesn't matter now. Mr. Hershey is right. Let's focus on the real issues."

Livingston thought of May, sitting back at the horse farm, waiting to hear from her loved ones, waiting to learn of their fate, desperate to see their headlights reflecting in the window, to hear their car rolling up the gravel driveway. He thought of Rick and Melissa, forced into hiding as a result of their involvement with these things, their lives irreparably disrupted and ruined, simply because of what they knew, and the government's insistence that others not know. He thought of today's news coverage and all those poor people, slaughtered like fodder as they swam and played and celebrated their nation's independence.

He thought of Phillipsport, and imagined he heard the sound.

Click-click ... Click-click ...

He sat back down. "Okay. You ignored me then. Why bring me in now?"

"Because you're our expert. We need you."

Livingston suppressed a smile. He'd known as much, but it was important to get them to admit it out loud. It gave him an edge.

He brushed a piece of lint from his uniform. "So here we are, hours into this crisis. What's the President done?"

Livingston glanced around the room, judging reactions. There was a low murmur of consent from some of the others. A woman from the CIA put her hand over her mouth to stifle a giggle. Hershey's expression was unreadable.

"The President was blindsided by this," Barker explained. "You can't have expected him to know this would happen."

"Can the bullshit and tell me what the hell you want," Livingston said. "I'm not here to listen to a political speech. I don't have time for you or Tyler's bumbling idiocy."

There was a pause on the other line. "What is this? Turning against the President now? At this time in—"

"I never liked that son of a bitch and I didn't vote for him," Livingston continued, once again overriding Barker. Fifteen years ago he wouldn't have dreamed of speaking like this when talking to a Presidential cabinet member, but those days were gone. "I'm retired, and he's not my Commander in Chief. And yes, I realize this is going to bite him square on his ass. I don't care. The only thing I care about is the people of this country. You called me because you realize that I've been through this particular fight before. You believe I may be able to use my experience in fighting these things to help with what's happening now. You want to can the bullshit and get down to the business of getting this shit taken care of; then you'd better listen up. Don't discount me again, and don't lie. Do you understand me?"

"You better understand me," Barker shouted. "You will not speak to me like that again!"

"I'll speak any way I damn well please. I have engaged in battle with these things and I'm telling you right now that if we want to survive, if we want to remain a sovereign country in the next twenty-four hours you have to listen to me and do everything I say. If you refuse, I will order any men under my command to disregard any and all orders that come from you and I will alert the media to your indifference to what's at hand."

Barker made a choking noise. Hershey's face was grim. The others in the room stared in shocked silence.

"That's treason, Colonel Livingston." Barker's voice was barely a whisper. "You know very well what the penalty is."

Livingston grinned. "Try me, you fuck."

Barker cleared his throat. "And if we do?"

"You'll regret it. Personally and professionally. And the country will suffer for your stupidity. Do it your way, and this will make the cluster-fuck you made out of the Hurricane Katrina recovery ops look like spilled milk."

Barker sputtered. "D-do you really think that you—"

"You know who I am," Livingston interrupted. "Take a look at my service record. You know what I'm capable of. If you want to try it, then be my guest. But that will be your last mistake. Do I make myself clear?"

Livingston realized that he was so angry his knuckles were white. His face felt hot, flushed. The others in the room stayed silent. He paid them no heed. He had to get through to Barker. Donald Barker had proved to be only one of the dozens of people President Tyler had appointed; who'd done nothing more than fuck things up. When Livingston looked at people like Barker and President Tyler, he wondered how these people could call themselves Republicans. As a life-long Republican and conservative, they certainly didn't represent his party.

He glanced over at the man from Homeland Security. Hershey had stood up again, as if to address the room.

"Sit down." Livingston's voice was like iced razors.

Hershey started to speak, then thought better of it and took his seat.

"Well?" Livingston turned back to the videophone. "What do you think, Mr. Secretary?"

There was an awkward silence on the other end.

"I'm waiting."

The Defense Secretary sighed. "Okay. We'll do it your way, Colonel. But know this. If you screw this up ..."

"Gentlemen," a woman from the CIA snapped, "if you're all done waving your pricks around like sabers, there are people dying in this country. Perhaps we should focus on them?"

"Agreed." Livingston relaxed a little, still tense, ready to get down to business. "Obviously, we need to coordinate our efforts. That's why we're all here. Make sure people continue to leave the coastal cities."

Barker spoke up. "We dispatched the National Guard to open up highways in an effort to ensure that traffic stays moving out of major cities and away from the beach communities."

An official from FEMA raised his hand.

"Yes?" Livingston pointed at him.

"I have instructed my people to help the local authorities of beachfront towns to coordinate evacuation efforts in those communities. I've also instructed them that anybody left behind, for whatever reason, is to remain indoors after night falls. Martial law should be declared, if possible."

"I agree," Livingston said. "Mr. Secretary, what are the President's thoughts on that?"

"Martial law? That's a bit drastic. Under the Emergency Powers act, we can pretty much act as if Martial Law were in effect without actually declaring it. If the President were to go on national television and declare Martial Law, it would compound the situation. We'd have civil unrest, looting, rioting—"

"With all due respect, sir," said the Assistant Director of the FBI, "we already have those things. It's just getting worse. Local authorities lack the manpower to deal with these creatures, the hurricane, and civil unrest."

The rest of the group concurred. Livingston smiled. Biggest dog in the yard. Piss all over the trees and soon enough, the other dogs would fall in line. It worked every time.

"So, we've mobilized the National Guard and Army Reserve Units in the affected states," Livingston said. "We should call up active-duty personnel as well—all branches, including the Coast Guard. Position them in the smaller ports. Dispatch Naval LPDs and LPHs with Marines onboard—I would suggest the 24th MAU out of Morehead City. Send them into the heaviest hit areas. They can engage the enemy before they advance farther into the countryside. Norfolk and Little Creek already fell under attack. I'm sure those men will be anxious for some payback. Get the Airborne in from Ft. Bragg and every other division we can mobilize immediately. Position them further inland, so that they can provide a line of defense."

The discussion proceeded civilly. They were only interrupted once, when Corporal Adams buzzed in to inform them that the Clickers had now been sighted along the southern parts of the East Coast. Livingston suggested using Washington's MCI Center, Baltimore's now derelict Camden Yards, Philadelphia's Verizon Center Arena, and Madison Square Garden in New York as staging areas for the troops and emergency services. All were far enough away from the ocean to avoid storm swell from the hurricane, yet close enough to dispatch personnel and troops quickly to the affected areas. The assumption was that

Hurricane Gary was going to be as deadly, if not more so, than Katrina.

"I'm not going to start another fight about this," Livingston said, "but just clarify this for me. You really didn't read my report on the Phillipsport incident. Correct?"

Barker paused, and then answered with a sigh. "No, I didn't. And I'm sorry."

"That's fine. Have you heard about what it contained?"

"Just that ... the destruction Phillipsport experienced and the loss of life was attributed to ... unnatural forces."

"Unnatural forces?"

"Okay, I might as well tell you." Barker sounded normal now, like the kind of guy Livingston might shoot the shit with at a summer barbecue over beers. "General Hamilton told me about the report shortly after you submitted it and he thought you were off your rocker. Said that you must've been hallucinating or going through some kind of post-traumatic stress situation from 'Nam or something."

"What did he tell you?"

Barker cleared his throat. "He said that you attributed the damage and casualties at Phillipsport to monsters."

"What kind of monsters?"

Barker paused and Livingston suppressed a grin. He knew he had the bastard now. "The very kind that are ... well ... the crab ... or lobster-things or whatever they are ... you know ... the ones on the news ..."

"Correct. Did Hamilton mention others?"

"Something about some kind of lizard things ... crazy shit."

"Do you believe what's happening now?

"Yes."

"Then believe what I tell you now that these things are just the tip of the iceberg," Livingston said, his voice a low growl. "Those so-called lizard-things Hamilton scoffed at are next, and they're ten times worse than these creatures."

"You really saw them?" A slow dawning sense of awe in Barker's voice.

"Yes, I saw them." Livingston closed his eyes for a moment against the memories. "Them and the ... the Dark Ones ..."

"Dark Ones?"

"That's what Rick Sychek called them … he was one of the survivors I mentioned in my report."

"Isn't he wanted?"

Livingston side-stepped that question easily. "Yes. He and another survivor were to be under close guard following the Phillipsport incident but they somehow slipped away. We haven't heard from them or seen hide or hair of them since. The thing to remember is if Rick decided he wanted to capitalize on what happened, we would have found him by now. He hasn't done that, so he's most likely so far underground he'll never be found, or he's dead or left the country."

"He called these lizard-things Dark Ones?"

"Yes." He proceeded to tell the Secretary of Defense and the rest an abridged story of what happened at Phillipsport.

"It sounds too incredible to be believed," Hershey mumbled. "If it weren't for the news footage …"

"You'd better believe it, Mr. Hershey," Livingston said. "That might be the only thing that keeps you alive."

Hershey looked at the CIA official. "Did you people know about this?"

"I'm sorry, sir, but that's classif—"

"They knew about it," Livingston interrupted. "They were on the ground same time we were. Took specimens and photographs, disposed of the rest." He started to add that they'd disposed of the witnesses, too, but thought better of it. He couldn't risk giving Rick and Melissa away and if he admitted his knowledge of the Agency's involvement, then he also risked revealing that he knew about those witnesses still in hiding.

"So why are these creatures resurfacing now?" Barker asked. "What's driving them ashore?"

Hershey spoke up quickly, cutting off the others. "Obviously, it's a direct result of Hurricane Gary. The storm is forcing them inland. The same thing happened in Phillipsport with Hurricane Floyd."

A meteorologist from the National Weather Service murmured something under his breath. Livingston turned to him.

"You have something to add?"

The scientist blushed. "Um … well …"

"What's your name, son?"

"Craley. George Craley, sir."

"And what were you just muttering?"

"Well, that is … Mr. Hershey's hypothesis is ridiculous, sir. The creatures first appeared off Atlantic City, while the storm was still hundreds of miles to the south. They began emerging onto shore long before the hurricane changed course."

Hershey scoffed. "So let me guess … Doctor, is it?"

Craley nodded. "Yes. I was previously with the Oceanic Institute and now I work for the National—"

"Oh, I'm sure your credentials are impeccable, Doctor Craley." Hershey's voice dripped with derision. "But you're not a biologist, are you? And you're going to tell us this is a result of global warming, aren't you? Or mankind's abuse of the environment, and the ozone layer. Or perhaps El Niño?"

"Hershey, quit being a snide little prick," Livingston snapped. Then he nodded at Craley. "Please continue."

"Thank you, Colonel." The nervous scientist sipped water, and then continued. "They're not following a migration pattern. It seems sporadic—just popping up here and there."

"We know that." Livingston was growing impatient. "We're trying to determine why."

"They're being hunted. There's a bigger predator, and it's forcing them out of the ocean. They're seeking safety."

"Hunted," Baker said. "Hunted by what?"

Craley shrugged. "I don't know. Maybe these 'Dark Ones' the Colonel was telling us about?"

The CIA representative nodded. "We were able to confirm the Clickers are a main staple of their diet."

Livingston was taken aback. "And just how did you determine that?"

"We have our ways, Colonel, and you have yours."

Livingston dismissed him with a wave of his hand, and turned back to Craley. "Is that your educated opinion or a guess?"

"A guess—but a logical one. These Clickers are an invasive

species. They're upsetting our ecosystem, possibly because their own ecosystem is being disturbed, perhaps by these Dark Ones. As I said, however, I don't know for sure."

"Who would know?"

"A marine biologist, preferably one specializing in invasive species."

Livingston pressed the intercom and summoned Corporal Adams, ordering the young man to find someone with those qualifications immediately. Before they moved with their planning, Livingston glanced at Craley.

"I hope you're wrong, son. Because if you're right, then things just got worse."

Hershey snorted. "We've got killer crabs swarming our beaches and a category five hurricane bearing down on the nation's capital and some of our most populated areas. How could it be any worse?"

It was a moment before Livingston spoke. When he did, they had to strain to hear him.

"You have no idea."

Baltimore, Maryland
7:35 PM

After nearly two and a half hours of sitting in unmoving traffic at the foot of Interstate 83, Dr. Richard Linnenberg finally decided to walk instead. He'd literally moved less than two miles in the entire time he'd sat there, and was still only blocks away from the aquarium. His car's engine was close to overheating. The temperature gauge edged into the red. He smelled oil and coolant.

His decision to go on foot was helped by the fact that marauding gangs of youths were pulling people from their vehicles and robbing them in plain sight, disregarding the possible repercussions because none were forthcoming. Richard had seen one police officer since getting stuck in the traffic jam, and the man had deserted his own patrol vehicle and headed off on foot, vanishing behind the Port Discovery building. His eyes had looked empty. Haunted.

Richard crammed all of his important belongings into his laptop bag; his satellite radio receiver, insurance paperwork, the car's title, several compact discs, and all of the loose change lying in the console. He tried his cell phone one last time but once again, received a message telling him that it was out of service. He'd watched others go through the same thing over the last hour. All of the networks were down, regardless of the service provider. He'd looked around for a payphone earlier but had been unable to find one.

He shoved the worthless cell phone into his bag as well, then rifled through the glove box and found his can of pepper spray. He'd never used it. Never had a need. It was there more for his wife than himself, something to safeguard her when she was driving alone through the city. He slung the laptop bag's strap over his shoulder, loosened his tie, and rolled up his sleeves. Clutching the canister of pepper spray and his car keys, Richard got out of the vehicle and thumbed the remote control. The car's doors locked behind him with an electronic chirp. Nervous, he glanced around to see if the noise had attracted attention. It hadn't. It was barely audible over the sounds of chaos. Horns blared in futile frustration. Children—and some adults—cried out. Angry shouts rang out, followed by the meaty smack of flesh against flesh. Blows were struck and bodies fell. Glass shattered. A fire alarm wailed in the distance, yet no one came to answer the shrill call. More glass broke as a group of men tossed a newspaper box through a store window and jumped inside. Sporadic volleys of gunfire echoed through the concrete canyons.

There was no way he could walk home, not with the unrest and violence gripping the streets, not with Hurricane Gary bearing down on them, this entire region square in the bullseye. His only choice was to make it back to the aquarium. Hopefully, their landlines would still be functional so he could call Sarah, tell her what had happened. She'd be worried sick about him by now, glued to the television (if there was still power in their neighborhood) and waiting for the phone to ring. She was probably trying to call him, unaware that his cell phone service was out.

He weaved around a burning tire and gripped the pepper spray tighter in his fist. Richard held his breath as a man approached him. It was the middle of summer, but the stranger was dressed in filthy black pants, a ragged pullover sweater, and a knit cap. His body odor hung in the air around him like a thick cloud. When he smiled, his teeth looked like black sunflower seeds.

"Got some Old Bay seasoning?" the vagrant asked, his speech slurred.

Richard was momentarily taken aback. He'd expected the begging plea, the outstretched hand, but he'd assumed the bum would ask for a quarter or a dollar—not Maryland's popular steamed crab seasoning.

"N-no," he stuttered, "I'm afraid I don't."

"Sheesh," the bum wheezed, "that's too bad. There's a bunch of crabs down by the harbor. Was gonna cook 'em up and toss on some Old Bay."

God Bless the homeless, Richard thought. Cops aren't around to roust them from the harbor district, so they're moving in and already thinking about their next meal.

It occurred to him that Jennifer would appreciate the irony—one invasive species—the homeless—invading an area they didn't normally frequent—the Inner Harbor tourist district. Just like the crab-things. He hoped Jennifer was okay. Their last communication had been two hours ago, just after he'd gotten stuck in traffic. She'd said she was going to Ocean City. He hoped that wasn't the case. Certainly she was smarter than that.

Jennifer truly was a blessing to the entire staff. With her background and accreditations, she could work anywhere she desired and he was grateful that she chose to stay with the aquarium. She was a boon, both financially and scientifically, and her enthusiasm, dedication, and skill kept the funds rolling in. In many ways, Richard thought of Jennifer as a daughter. He and his wife, Sarah, had only one child, Susan, who'd passed away when she was fifteen. She'd been electrocuted by downed power lines after a thunderstorm many years ago. Very sudden and very unexpected. As a result, Richard didn't like storms. He still felt the grief each day, and it had changed his and

Sarah's relationship. There was a gulf between them, a void in the shape of their daughter. Jennifer was now the age Susan would have been, had she lived.

The homeless man shuffled away, moving deeper into the city. Richard continued towards the waterfront. The wind picked up and the sky grew darker. A few scattered raindrops splattered against the pavement as the storm's outer bands moved over the city. The last projections he'd heard were that the hurricane would make landfall by midnight, but Richard wondered if perhaps that timetable had been moved forward. Something rumbled in the distance. He couldn't tell if it was thunder, an explosion, or gunfire. None of them were options he wanted to consider, so he picked up his pace.

He spied the Inner Harbor district in the distance; the vaulted glass roof of the National Aquarium towering over the series of shops and clubs, and the giant Barnes & Noble and Hard Rock Café complex and Marriott hotel looming over the aquarium in turn. The World War Two-era submarine and the Coast Guard cutter, both permanently docked at the harbor so that tourists could parade through them, were noticeably absent—taken out to sea by skeleton crews so that they wouldn't be bashed against the concrete barriers as the expected storm surge swamped the area.

He'd expected the harbor to be completely deserted, but it wasn't. Gone were the tourists and shopkeepers, but there were still people—fire and medical emergency crews, public works officials, the homeless, and white-collar employees from the various buildings ringing the waterfront. Richard watched a man in a business suit hurry by. What were they still doing here? he wondered. He understood the presence of the emergency workers, but why were all the business people still here? Maybe they hadn't heeded the evacuation order, or perhaps they'd heard about the traffic jams and the futility of trying to escape the downtown area, and had stayed behind. Whatever the case, they were fleeing now. As one, the crowd swarmed towards him. Their expressions were terrified. Then Richard heard the screams.

What was it the homeless man had said?

There's a bunch of crabs down by the harbor.

"Oh no." Despite his mounting fear, Richard pressed through the onrushing crowd. They battered him back and forth like a pinball, but he kept his footing. He had to see.

He heard the creatures before he saw them, heard their claws snapping together like giant shears.

Click-click … click-click …

All at once, the last of the fleeing pedestrians surged past him, and Richard found himself standing alone in the midst of carnage. The pavement was stained with gore. His shoe slipped. He glanced down and saw that he was standing in someone's intestines. The crab-things were all around him, feasting on their victims or scurrying off into the city, scuttling down alleyways and side streets.

He held his breath and did not move. One of them stood only a few feet away from him. It was approximately twelve feet in length and taller than an average adult man. The thing was busy eating. Its victim, an overweight construction worker, judging by his bloodied and torn attire, was still alive. The helpless man screamed as the monster's claws tore at his flesh, slicing skin and muscle away and shoveling the meat into its beaked mouth.

The rain fell harder, picking up speed. Blood ran through the gutters and into the storm drains. Thunder boomed overhead. His exposed skin stung as the droplets pelted him. He barely felt it—his attention focused on the nightmare in front of him. Cringing, Richard quietly exhaled and took another deep breath. The creature's stench was horrible. It smelled like rotten fish and brine.

Richard licked his lips and slowly backed away.

The beast finally noticed him, stopped eating, and crept forward.

Richard's mind spun. I guess it doesn't matter if Jennifer went to Ocean City after all. She's no safer here than there.

Overhead, thunder rattled the sky. The sound of breaking glass echoed from farther down the street. The wind howled.

Richard took another tentative step backward. The thing followed. For each step he took, it took two, closing the distance between them. Richard knew that if he turned his back to run, it would be on him in an instant. It drew closer. Richard could smell the briny stench wafting off its shell, hear its claws tap against the concrete. Venom dripped from the stinger on the end of its long, segmented tail. The Clicker's serrated pincers were tinted with a delicate crisscross pattern of red and magenta, deepening to a thick shade of black at the tips.

Sweat and rainwater ran into his eyes. Richard blinked and the creature edged nearer still. He took another step and his foot came down in a puddle—water or blood, he didn't know which and couldn't risk looking down.

The thing made a warbling sort of hiss.

Remembering his canister of pepper spray, Richard raised it slowly and depressed the button. The spray hit the Clicker directly in the face, clouding around its black, stalked eyes. They reminded Richard of ball bearings. The creature squealed. Its tail thrashed, whipping back and forth. Then the crab-thing lunged at him.

"Drop," someone shouted from behind him. Richard complied, not out of understanding but because his knees had given out from under him. He tumbled to the gore-slicked pavement and two shots rang out, the blasts deafening in their proximity. Gun smoke tickled his nose, and his ears rang. He dropped the pepper spray, and his laptop bag slipped from his shoulder.

The creature reared back, more startled than injured or fearful. Indeed, even as he cowered on the ground beneath it, Richard could see no wounds on its body. He didn't know if his mysterious savior had missed or if the rounds just had no effect on the hard shell. Probably the latter, given their proximity.

Richard cast a fearful glance up at his rescuer. The man was young, mid-twenties. His hair was buzzed short, and he wore an aquarium security guard uniform. He stood with his feet a shoulder's width apart. A black pistol was clutched in both hands. Richard flinched as the man fired again.

This time, the creature rocked backward. Its eyestalks waved like wheat.

"Run," the man shouted, his eyes not leaving the predator.

"I ... I don't think I can." Richard's entire body trembled with fear. He'd never been more afraid in his life, not even when Susan died. He couldn't stop shaking.

More of the creatures were converging on their position now, attracted by the noise. Hissing, the crab-thing stalked forward again. The guard squeezed the trigger repeatedly, firing three more shots directly into its face.

"This is a fucking forty-five," he yelled. "You better die, you son of a bitch."

The thing responded by leaping over Richard's prone form. He backed away, his eyes glued on the struggle. The man fired another shot. A second later the creature attacked with both its claws and tail. The man sidestepped the first claw, but the second seized his right arm and squeezed, severing the appendage just below the elbow. Blood jetted out around the pincers. The arm fell to the pavement. A fountain of blood jetted from the stump. Screaming, the guard dropped the pistol from his left hand just as the bulging stinger sank into his neck. His cries turned into choked gobbling as venom was pumped into his body. His skin began to bubble and hiss as if he were being cooked from the inside. Blisters formed on his body, swelled, and then burst, oozing fluids.

Overwhelmed with terror, his mind on autopilot, Richard stumbled to his feet. He didn't consider grabbing the discarded weapon. He didn't think about the other Clickers charging him. He let shock override him and just ran. His feet pounded the pavement. His tie fluttered behind him. The rain began in earnest now, falling in sheets, lashing at his skin. Within seconds, his clothes were drenched. He leapt over a dismembered corpse and ran towards the aquarium's employee entrance. Lightning flashed overhead, reflecting off the building's large glass panels. When it flashed again, he saw his pursuers reflected in the panes. At least a dozen of them charged after him. Their clicking claws drowned out both the thunder and his screams.

Jennifer was growing more nervous by the minute.

She was sitting in her cluttered office, her attention focused on the TV. Her office was in the interior of the large structure that housed the aquarium and reinforced with thick, concrete walls. Nonetheless, occasionally she could hear the moan of the wind outside. CNN was broadcasting from several different vantage points, and all the coverage was on the crustacean attacks that were occurring with alarming ferocity along the eastern seaboard. Jennifer took a sip of bottled water. The tuna-fish sandwich she'd purchased from the employee break room vending machine was half-eaten. She hadn't brought much change today, and she supposed if worse came to worse she could break into the machine to get more food, though her hurricane rations she had stocked would last for days if needed. As things turned out, aside from her there were three technicians and a security guard. The rest of the staff had been sent home, along with all the alarmed tourists, who'd fled for the safety of their hotel rooms and vehicles. The Baltimore Safety Director's office had called to ensure the aquarium was being evacuated and that phone call had been an hour and a half ago. The techs had worked quickly to secure the outside exhibits and then they'd retreated inside. They were all gathered together in the break room now, playing a half-hearted game of Scrabble and trying to ignore the approaching storm while she stayed here, doing research. She had no idea where the guard had gone.

The last time Jennifer checked, the outer ridges of Gary were darkening the sky. The wind was strong, blowing rain in fierce pellets. Gary was definitely going to strike them dead center.

Her plan to go to Ocean City and observe the creatures firsthand had been foiled by her responsibilities to the aquarium. It had taken longer to evacuate everyone than she'd thought it would, and by the time they were done it was too late. By now,

Hurricane Gary's winds would be lashing the Chesapeake Bay Bridge mercilessly, and it would be suicide to even attempt to drive across it. Frustrated, she'd called her parents in Hunt Valley and assured them she was fine. The facility had its own emergency generator, but so far the power had remained stable, and they still had phone and internet service—albeit slower than normal and unreliable. There had been sporadic failures of service with both over the last hour. After talking to her parents and calming their fears, Jennifer holed herself up in her office and started researching the creatures that were currently making headlines. The minute she'd first seen them, they sparked some memory of something she'd read a while back. It had taken a good thirty minutes of Google searching, but in time she found it.

First there was Ian Sinclair's research on Megarachne Servinei and the possible links to the giant eurypterid and the Woodwardopterus. She'd taken a keen interest in his research, especially regarding invasive crustaceans. She remembered his initial findings when they first made the news, as well as the fire that claimed his life and destroyed his research. Luckily, much of his research was published and she'd read some of it in scientific journals and online while in college. And it was there where she'd first learned of Homarus Tyrannous.

The journal she'd read about Homarus Tyrannous was one she no longer had access to, and there had been no illustration accompanying the article. From the description, it appeared Homarus Tyrannous was a cross between Megarachne Servinei and the Woodwardopterus and apparently died out two hundred million years ago. Not much was known of them, but images of the creatures embedded in rock had been found along the coast of Greenland, Nova Scotia, and Scotland.

Acting on a hunch, she began researching Homarus Tyrannous on the web. She got very few leads.

Then fifteen minutes ago she'd typed "cryptozoology" and "giant crab creatures attacking people" in Google and the first website was for a site hosted on a server with annoying pop-up windows. Jennifer navigated through the website, which was badly designed, obviously constructed and written by some nut that lived in his mother's basement. Aside from entries on Bigfoot, the Loch Ness Monster, Chupacabra, Moth Man, and other creatures of myth both infamous and obscure, Jennifer came across a brief story on an incident she remembered clearly: Hurricane Floyd, and the destruction of Phillipsport, Maine in 1994.

Reading the article brought the memories back. She'd been a sophomore in college at Penn State. She remembered thinking how horrible it was that all those people had been killed and there were only two survivors.

Now she was reading an entirely different account of what happened at Phillipsport.

And as she read the story, it set her heart racing.

While obviously badly written, the article referenced a self-published pamphlet called Creatures of the Deep, which referenced a story similar to the Roanoke expedition of the early 1700s when an entire British village disappeared, the word CROATOAN carved on a nearby tree. The story in Creatures of the Deep was similar except for the message ... demons from the s—had been painted on a rock. Like Roanoke, the citizens of that settlement disappeared without a trace. The pamphlet theorized that the natives had known what was going to happen and tried to warn the settlers, to no avail. The natives had retreated further inland and something had come out of the ocean and decimated the town.

The writer of the website hypothesized that the same thing had happened to Phillipsport in 1994. Furthermore, he theorized that Homarus Tyrannous was not extinct but still alive, and that every few hundred years deep ocean currents brought them up to the Maine shores to breed. He further theorized that they lived so far beneath the ocean surface and had access to underwater caverns that were unknown to modern man, which was why they were seldom seen and believed to be still extinct.

Jennifer jotted all this down in a spiral notebook, the possibilities swirling in her mind. She punched in the search term "survivors of Phillipsport, Maine disaster" in Google and after a few minutes learned their names: Melissa Peterson and Rick Sychek. A few more Google searches turned up plenty of results on Rick but none on Melissa, so she concentrated on him.

She learned he'd been a writer of cheap paperback horror novels, that he was close to becoming the next Stephen King, and that after Phillipsport he and Melissa had simply disappeared.

There's no doubt about it, she thought, leaning back in her chair and looking at the computer screen. Rick Sychek and Melissa Peterson lived through something awful. They witnessed something that somebody in the government wanted covered up. That was the only thing she could think of. She'd read all the stories she could find on the Phillipsport incident and found hints of a government conspiracy. It was one thing to have casualties during a hurricane the size of Floyd had been … but to have such a wide swath of destruction? With the entire town wiped out? And what about the suggestion that the people of Phillipsport had been not just killed by drowning or being thrown against buildings during storm surges, but actually mauled? And what about the stories she read (however scant they were) that the dead were found clutching weapons, some partially devoured. As one story she read related: "It looked like something ate them."

And then there were the rumors of crustacean shells found littered with the bodies, and more stories that government scientists had whisked them away and after that … well, not so much as a whisper of them.

Jennifer supposed she could spend the rest of the evening doing searches on whether or not the species of crustacean was ever identified, at least until the internet connection failed completely, but she had a feeling it would prove futile. If government scientists really had taken all the specimens at Phillipsport, whatever they'd found out about them was extremely top secret. And with the storm raging outside and the havoc happening right now outside the aquarium, she didn't have the time to spend poking and prodding among the dark corners of the internet to learn more.

The talking heads on the news were calling the creatures "Clickers," and Fox News interviewed a marine biologist in Florida who stuttered and stammered that he had no idea what species of crustacean was currently causing so much trouble.

According to him, it was a species that was completely new. Other biologists were of the same opinion. Jennifer watched the coverage with a feeling of simmering anger. Shortly after she'd decided that going to Ocean City was no longer possible, she'd called the local Baltimore news station to tell their producer that she was available to be interviewed over the phone. She'd done a few interviews with the local media before, and sometimes they came to her to get her perspective on things relating to marine life. Not so this time. Nobody called her back, and when she tried getting in touch with her contacts again, the line was busy.

Fine, she thought, leaning back behind her desk. Screw 'em. It wasn't going to stop her from trying to find out what these things were. She couldn't study them up close, and the internet wasn't providing much help, but she had other resources.

She was just about to flip through her Rolodex to find another contact that might be able to help her when the lights went out.

Then the screams started.

6

Magog Bunker
The White House
Washington, D.C.

7:49 PM

President Jeffery Tyler was holed up in the "Magog" Bunker directly beneath the oval office, on his knees in prayer. He clutched his Bible. The leather binding was worn and cracked, and a broad crease ran down the spine. The pages were dog-eared and many of the verses themselves were circled with red pencil or highlighted with a yellow marker, especially in the Book of Revelation—the book detailing the end of the world. The Apocalypse. Armageddon.

He hadn't removed his suit or his slacks, even when the Secret Service stepped in and forced him to leave the oval office and make his way to the bunker, secreted far beneath the White House and built in the 1950s. It was one of several underground chambers beneath the nation's capital. The room exited into a tunnel network that honeycombed the area beneath Washington, D. C. and Virginia, and eventually, to similar bunkers beneath Camp David; Gettysburg and Hellertown, Pennsylvania; and White Sulphur Springs, West Virginia. The entire maze was built so that key members of the government could get to safety in the event of a nuclear war. To the best of Tyler's knowledge, the evacuation plan had never been used, not even during 9/11. When Tyler became President two years ago, the first thing he'd done was insisted on venturing into the underground rooms for a tour. A secret service agent accompanied him and gave him quite the tour. And when Tyler saw this room, the spirit had hit him. This would be his room, his place to go when things were getting a little too intense for him so he could pray and commune with God in quiet.

He'd been praying for over an hour now, oblivious to the screams of terror and pain outside the White House as giant crab-things chased people down and ate them alive. Tyler wasn't oblivious to it all—the Secretary of Defense and Joint Chiefs had briefed him. He wasn't immune to the suffering of his people, which was why he'd chosen to descend down to his prayer chamber to pray and ask for guidance from his Lord.

He needed guidance now. He was being torn by temptation at every step.

When the Secretary of Defense suggested calling in troops from Fort Bragg, Tyler had balked. The local police force and National Guard can handle things, Tyler had said. The Secretary of Defense had looked at him as if he were off his rocker and Tyler had to remind him how he'd come into this position—by my hand, he'd said. Remember that? Barker had nodded, and then started rambling about something else regarding the monstrosities everybody was so concerned with and Tyler had tuned him out.

But now Barker was in a teleconference with other military and civilian officials, and Tyler knew they'd call for military action as well.

He'd watched some of the coverage on Fox in the oval office and frowned during an interview with a biologist at the University of Florida at Tampa, who said the creatures could be related to Homarus Tyrannous, a crustacean species that some scientists previously thought to be extinct. "It's believed they died off in the Mesozoic Period about two hundred million years ago," the scientist said, looking nervous. "Carbon dating puts them squarely in that period and we have a few reliable specimens embedded in rock that have been found all along the Atlantic region. However, there have been scant reports of alleged sightings of specimens who resemble Homarus Tyrannous in various parts of the world, and—"

Tyler changed the channel in disgust. Fox was degenerating

into a liberal quagmire—a result of sagging ratings and the continuing decline of the nation's moral fiber. Two hundred million years ago? The earth was ten thousand years old, for God's sakes! Didn't these people know their Bible?

The President rose to his feet in the room, wondering what to do now. Clark Arroyo, the secret service agent who'd escorted him to his private prayer chamber, was upstairs waiting for him. Tyler pursed his lips, deep in thought. One can only pray to the Lord for so long for guidance, for strength. He'd been in constant prayer since the first news reports reached his desk shortly after noon today, and he'd been in close contact with his advisors. They were clamoring with him to address the nation, but Tyler had continued his day as planned, and was looking forward to his meeting with Prince Alhazred when he was advised the meeting should be cancelled. "It's not going to look good for you if the meeting goes as planned," his press secretary said shortly before five that day. "The American people are going to expect to see their president do something about this tragedy."

Tyler agreed. It wouldn't look good if he ignored what was going on and continued on with business as usual. He'd learned that by watching the fallout over Hurricane Katrina.

And now something much worse than Katrina was happening.

"Lord, why?" Tyler said, tilting his face up. He brought his hands together in prayer one last time. "Lord give me strength. My closest advisors are telling me I should heed their advice, that I should listen to our scientists who are telling them that the animals ... the things that are beaching themselves and causing so much death and terror are thought to be creatures they thought extinct. They think these things died out millions of years ago. Lord, I know this is impossible. You created the earth in six days and rested on the seventh. According to your word, this earth you created is no more than ten thousand years old, which means those creatures can only be from one thing— your adversary, Satan. I believe that Lord, and I will fight these creatures from hell if you just say the word. But I know I can't sit by and listen to this evolutionary drivel, this ridiculous ... oh, Lord forgive me for saying this but I have to—this horseshit!

Evolution is a trick from the devil, Lord. I know that, and my good friends in Christ know this, but so many of these people, these scientists ... they're not only blinded, they're holdovers from previous administrations. It's making me confused and sick and I don't know what to do. All I know is that I have to trust in you. Which is why I've been here, praying."

He paused, eyes closed. His heart raced. He knew he had to go upstairs sooner or later and face the music. Government sharpshooters were on the roof of the White House and last he'd heard, twelve of those things had been shot. They'd surfaced from the waters of the Potomac, well ahead of the storm. The White House was not only very heavily guarded, it was under lock down.

Key staff members were already in private underground bunkers. Other staff members had been escorted out of the building and others had been sent home. Tyler's closest advisors were telling him he should give the press conference, and then get on board the helicopter that was waiting on the roof and get to higher ground, but Tyler couldn't do that. He had to stay and fight. He had to show his support to the American people. He had to present his strong image to the public that he had things under control, unlike the fiasco of Katrina.

He would not disappoint them.

"Lord give me strength," he said, feeling a welcome surge of strength seep through him. He felt stronger now, more confident, as the pieces began falling into place. "Give me strength to see this through. I'm going upstairs to talk to the American people, to put their minds at ease, to tell them everything will be all right. Most important, I will tell them to put their faith in you, to put their trust in you, to pray. To accept your son, Jesus Christ, into their hearts."

Yes! That was the ticket! President Tyler began to see God's purpose now. God wanted to show Tyler His strength. And He brought these minions of Satan into the world to show the unsaved, the unbelievers, that the powers of Hell were bubbling beneath them. And if President Tyler went on national TV and witnessed to the country—to the entire world—hundreds of thousands of souls would be touched by the Lord and perhaps, just perhaps, some souls could be saved. People would find Jesus. Amen!

"Thank you, Jesus," he whispered. The revelation hit him so suddenly, he was overcome with gratitude. Oh, to be shown Gods' plan! It was so overwhelming, so overpowering, that he felt tears spring to his eyes.

He wiped away the tears, feeling a surge of adrenaline rush through his system. He felt on top of things, in control. He was going to take charge. He knew God's plan now. And he wasn't going to let God down.

He never had before.

After all, he'd managed to be elected President.

Tyler opened a door and ascended a narrow stairway to the main floor of the White House. He opened a door at the top of the staircase and entered a small room that was painted white. He crossed the room and opened another door and Clark Arroyo stood at attention, his features expectant. "Mr. President!"

Tyler buttoned his coat. "Is everybody ready for my speech?"

"Yes sir, Mr. President."

"Lead the way."

"Follow me, sir."

"Do you trust in the Lord, Agent Arroyo?"

The man paused before answering. "Yes, sir."

"Good. May He bless you and keep you."

As Clark Arroyo led President Tyler to the pressroom where the cameras and audio equipment for the occasional televised addresses he made to the nation were housed, Tyler felt more on top of things, more in control, than he'd ever felt. The people who worked in the media room were all waiting; a skeleton crew had remained and would be quickly whisked to safety when the speech was concluded. His speechwriter had already prepared something, complete with last minute additions after conferring with Defense Secretary Barker after his teleconference and it was waiting for him at the console, ready to be recited aloud. All Tyler had to do was smile, put on the charm, and let God work his wonders.

Clark Arroyo opened the door to the media room and President Tyler entered, ready to do business.

8:00 PM

Excerpt from televised speech by President Jeffery Tyler
"... so you should be assured that this government is amassing on two fronts. One, I have ordered and given the authority to state and local governments to enact martial law in their jurisdictions at their discretion, under the Emergency Powers Act. As of now, the states of Massachusetts, Rhode Island, Delaware, Maryland, Pennsylvania, Virginia, New Jersey, North Carolina, South Carolina, Georgia, and Florida are all under martial law, and will remain so until the State of Emergency is lifted. Two, troops have been dispatched on my order to the affected areas including Baltimore, Atlantic City, Roanoke, Myrtle Beach, Norfolk, Long Island, and Boston. Three, because of my giving our local and state governments these powers, those officials in more rural beachfront communities can mobilize more quickly and efficiently. Four, I want to assure the American people that despite what you're seeing on television we have things under control. We are ... we are killing hundreds of these things and we are beating them back. We still don't know what they are or where they're coming from, and we will have the top scientists flown in after Hurricane Gary has passed to collect specimens and study these creatures to determine what they are ..."

O'Mally's Bar
New York City
8:03 PM

"They're giant fucking crabs, you half-wit!"
The comment brought a swell of laughter from the bar and Connie Stewart grinned as she wiped down the bar top. Behind her, President Tyler droned on with the same bullshit on the overhead TV. She was scheduled to work the five to two a.m. shift tonight but her boss, Paul O'Mally himself, told her as she arrived to work that he was closing at eight. "This damn

Hurricane might hit us," he said in his thick Irish accent. "Best you head home, lass."

That was fine by Connie. Despite hearing the rumors that the same creatures that were currently wreaking havoc south of them were spied along the docks and near Staten Island, things were going along normally in midtown. Broadway was a mess as usual, and the streets were clogged with pedestrians and taxis. Despite the dire news, people in this part of town weren't panicky ... yet.

The patron who'd made the witty comment was looking up at the TV bolted behind the bar. His buddies were with him, and they'd all just gotten off of work as day laborers over on Forty-Fifth and Broadway. They wore jeans, dirty T-shirts and heavy work boots and were all nursing pints. Connie knew them well; they were good customers. "One more round for you guys before Paul shuts us down?"

"Why the hell not?" Derek Brubaker set his empty pint glass down and Connie took it and refilled it with Guinness on tap. "You taking off for Westchester County tonight?" Derek asked her. Connie's sister lived in Westchester County.

"To tell you the truth, I was just going to head back home to the Bronx and ride it out." Connie let the pint settle before tapping off the head and handing it to Derek.

"I'm surprised Paul's keeping the place open," one of the other guys said.

"What else can he do? Subways are crowded and the tunnels are clogged with people trying to get out of the city. I wouldn't want to be stuck in the Holland Tunnel if Gary decides to shift to the east and hit us dead center."

Nervous laughter from the guys. "You can say that again," one of them said.

"I heard some of these things were coming up along Long Island," Derek said. He took a sip of his beer.

"I heard a few were spotted along the Hudson."

"No shit?"

"Wonder what they are?"

"It's like something out of some horror movie," Connie said. She turned around and looked at the TV with the rest of the guys. The bar was unusually quiet today; Derek and his co-workers were the only patrons now. The rest had trickled out in the past hour or so. "Scientists don't even know what they are."

"Scientists know what these things are." This came from Bob Ellison. He lit a cigarette, ignoring the No Smoking sign that Paul had posted at the bar. The smoking rules had been ignored on September 11, 2001, too. "You can bet somebody out there knows what these damn things are. We just aren't going to hear about it for days … maybe weeks or months until after this shit blows over."

"What do you think they are then?"

"I think they're some kind of species that's never been discovered," Bob said.

Derek turned to him. "You mean a new species?"

"Nope." Drag on the cigarette. "One that's always been around but we never knew about."

"How can—"

"That sounds plausible," Connie said. She drew up a stool and sat down. "Scientists are always finding these strange things thousands of feet below the ocean."

"There's that jungle somewhere in Asia where they found a whole bunch of shit earlier this year," one of the other guys said. "It was on the news back in February. They went in and found a whole bunch of animals nobody'd ever seen before. Weird birds and reptiles and other critters. They'd been living in this remote jungle for thousands of years."

"I remember hearing about that," Connie said, nodding.

Bob smoked, looking reflective. "Remember that shit from the nineties that happened in Maine? That little town that got wiped out by a hurricane?"

Scattered nods. Connie said, "Yeah, I vaguely remember that."

Bob gestured at the TV. "It's happening all over again only on a much larger scale."

"But that was a hurricane that—" Derek began.

"I've got a buddy that's into all this Loch Ness Monster and Bigfoot and conspiracy theory shit," Bob continued, ignoring

Derek's comment. "And he told me that a lot of people who study that shit think these crab-things," he gestured to the TV where President Tyler was still droning, "were actually responsible for all those deaths. He said they might be a species long thought to be extinct, that there's been legends about them that go way back and that it might have been a combination of the hurricane and under water currents that brought them to Maine that day. I remember when that happened. I remember hearing everybody in that town died except for a couple people, and that scientists found the remains of these giant crabs the government was trying to say washed ashore with the storm surge. Then all of a sudden you didn't hear anything on the news about them. Nothing. Not a word." He drew on his cigarette deeply, dark eyes riveted on the screen. "Now we got this happening. What does that tell you?"

There was silence in the bar as they digested this. Connie shivered. It was warm outside, over eighty-five degrees, but she felt a shiver nonetheless.

"Somebody's been keeping this shit secret for a long time," Bob said, his eyes still focused on the TV. "And I have a feeling the worst is yet to come."

"Hey," another of Derek's co-workers shouted, "everyone quiet down. The President just said martial law's been declared in New York."

"Shit." Derek's face grew pale. "There's gonna be troops on the streets. We can't go anywhere if they lock the city down. Can't leave here. What's that mean for us?"

Connie grinned. "It means that drinks are on the house."

Outside, an armored Humvee raced by. In the distance, a fire siren wailed.

The first fat raindrops hit the ground.

Fort Detrick
Fredrick, Maryland
8:15 PM

"Sir?" Corporal Adams snapped off a salute, but Livingston could see the exhaustion etched in the young man's face.

"Report, son."

"We've been trying to get a hold of all the scientists on the list. Most were unavailable. The few we've been able to reach had no idea what the creatures were or if they could even be properly called crustaceans."

"What the hell else can they be? They look like crabs and they came out of the goddamn ocean! What more do they need? Did you find me anybody useful?"

"Colonel, we found a marine biologist specializing in invasive species. Her name is Jennifer Wasco and she's employed right here in Maryland. She works at the National Aquarium in Baltimore."

"Excellent. Have you contacted her yet?"

"No, sir. Phones are down in Baltimore. We're not sure if it's the entire grid and a result of the storm or those … the enemy. However, Baltimore's FEMA office and the city's Safety Director both confirmed that Wasco was on duty as part of the emergency staff at the aquarium. We know she was still there an hour ago. I've mobilized forces in the area, but they're heavily engaged right now. Baltimore's inner city is overrun with the creatures. Soon as our men arrive at the site, secure it, and confirm Wasco's whereabouts, I'll advise you."

"Never mind that. Can we still get a bird in the air?"

"The hurricane has increased speed again, sir. The outer bands are making landfall already. But yes, we can fly if need be."

"Need be then, son. Get a chopper ready for me. I'm going in myself. I'll lead the extraction team."

"Sir?" Corporal Adams looked stunned. "That's highly inadvisable, not to mention against protocol."

"Fuck protocol." Livingston sighed. Acid churned in his stomach. "If I stay here, I'll end up shooting that officious little prick from Homeland Security. This whole thing—these screens, the chairs—this isn't what I do. I'm a solider. I belong on the battlefield."

"Permission to speak freely, sir?"

"Go ahead."

"Begging your pardon, Colonel Livingston, but with all

that's happening, do you really think this is the wisest choice? We need strong leadership here."

Livingston smiled. "They've got you to lead them, Corporal. You'll do a damn fine job, too, if the last few hours have been any indication."

Adams looked frightened. "M-me sir?"

Livingston nodded. "This is something I have to do. You see, for the last few years I've been breeding racehorses up in Taneytown. And each day, I've died just a little bit more. But now—now I feel alive again. You ever see combat, son?"

"No, sir."

"I hope you never do. You're scared right now. I'm scared, too. But when you're facing down the enemy, it's even scarier. It's also highly addictive. Do it enough times and you start craving that fear. I'm an old man. Only thing I feel these days are the aches in my joints. I need to feel that fear one last time. Can you understand that?"

"Yes, sir." His tone didn't sound convinced, but the Corporal nodded.

"Good. Then get me a bird ready. I want to be airborne in five minutes."

"Right away, Colonel."

"Dismissed." Livingston returned the young soldier's salute and then turned back to the wall of video monitors. President Tyler was on television, assuring the American public that they had nothing to fear.

Livingston thought maybe the American public needed to have something to fear. They needed to be afraid. Otherwise, the Clickers could win the day.

He picked up an outside line and called the farm in Taneytown. He'd expected the phones to be down and was surprised when it rang and relieved when May answered. She sounded on the edge of panic. Her family still hadn't arrived and there was no word on their whereabouts. He told her to arm herself with the 30-30 deer rifle in his gun cabinet, and command the upper floors of the house. "Keep the outside lights off," he'd said. "And stay inside no matter what you hear. Keep the cell phone charged up and on. I'll call you as soon as I can."

Then he told her something he'd never told her before in the time she'd been in his employment. He told her he loved her and that he hoped he'd see her soon.

Then he hung up before she could respond.

Stone Harbor, New Jersey
8:22 PM

Franklin Young was scared.

He was crouched on the floor on the third story of the large house on Newton Street as the rain pelted down and the wind howled outside. He'd volunteered to stay behind at the house while the rest of his extended family, which included his mother and sister, two aunts and three uncles and ten of his cousins, packed their belongings up and left. Mom had argued with him against staying but Franklin assured her he'd be fine. The house was old and built solidly, not like those million-dollar beachfront homes the out-of-towners bought and lived in for the summer. Those things were made out of cardboard compared to this solid brick home. It had survived more than its share of the handful of hurricanes that had blown this far north. Besides, somebody had to stay behind and salvage the place if looters decided to ravage the town. Mom had begged him to forget the house; there were those things out there, too! Franklin held up his Ruger .22 semi-automatic handgun that he'd gotten out of the safe in his room. "I'm a good shot and I have twelve boxes of ammunition and my Ruger. The house will be locked up tight and those things won't get in. If they're like normal crabs, they'll go by sight. They won't see me. I'll be fine. Now go!"

That had been the end of it. His family had left five hours ago and Franklin had battened down the hatches from the inside, dragging up the plywood paneling he'd been intending to use to remodel the basement and nailing them over the windows on the first floor. The town was deserted, of course, those things had either killed or chased off mostly everybody, and he had no idea where most of them had gotten to. He'd gone upstairs to his room and peeked out the window, looking for any sign of life on the streets below. He could see Second Street, Newton Street, and the beach two hundred yards away.

Deserted.

There were a few cars either sitting in the middle of the street or crashed into each other, their occupants dead and devoured. Franklin had been at the house when the things started coming from the ocean, and his cousin, Tim, was the first to run into the house to yammer the news. "There's monsters coming out of the water eating people!"

By some strange coincidence, most of the Young clan was at the house for lunch when the creatures struck. Tim and his sister Barbara had been at the beach when the things came ashore and they'd managed to make it to the house, but Barbara's friend, Mary, hadn't been so lucky.

Tim had to drag Barb up to the house with them as the things ate Mary on the beach. Barb had been hysterical. Franklin had felt a twinge of sadness at hearing this—he'd had a little crush on Mary, but he couldn't deal with that loss now. He'd had to act, had to let his training take over. Franklin was nineteen years old and studying to be an EMT in Lancaster, Pennsylvania. His family had owned the one-hundred-year-old brick house on Newton Street in Stone Harbor for twenty years and lived in it year round. The rest of the family lived near the Philly suburbs and came every summer to visit for days and weeks at a time. The house had six bedrooms, four on the second floor, two on the third, and sometimes there could be as many as twenty-five people crammed inside during one of their holiday excursions. It was like a big sleep-over. And it was a family tradition.

Now the family tradition was probably gone forever.

Hell had come to Stone Harbor, New Jersey.

It had come in the form of the giant crab-things with stingers, the things that Franklin saw attacking and eating people as they screamed in agony. It came in the form of chaos, death and destruction. It came in the form of widespread panic as people were killed by the creatures and by each other on accident as they raced away to safety. Franklin had seen dozens of people get hit by friendly fire as police officers and civilians alike shot at the creatures. He'd seen more get hit by cars, even more get trampled in their mad race to escape.

Uncle Ben had been at the wheel of his SUV when the first of the Young's left the house, and by then most of the surging crowd had pushed inland, leaving the streets relatively clear. They simply gathered everybody up and piled into the vehicles along with the few personal items they'd managed to fit inside with them. They'd been planning on leaving today anyway, but the kids wanted to get a few morning hours at the beach before they left. Besides, the hurricane wasn't expected to hit until late tonight.

Now Franklin was alone in the house. And the hurricane was approaching.

The wind had been picking up steadily all afternoon and by six it was dark outside. Franklin had been listening to the radio and the TV, monitoring both the storm and the news of the creatures attacking in other parts of the country. Franklin was astounded at first when he heard these things were popping up all over the place; it was a goddamn natural disaster. He remained glued to the news, unable to tear his attention away from it, until the power went out, halfway through the President's address.

Now the wind started to howl and the rain pelted the house. He looked outside. The sky was an ugly black. There was no way the ocean would come this far up, but it was possible the storm surges would push the fishing boats that were docked along the little bay nearby, spilling them and the Atlantic this far. If that was the case, the water could rise four feet. Which meant the basement would be completely flooded. The first floor of the house might be spared, but he couldn't chance that. And if those crab things came from the ocean they might float by and—

It was that thought which sent Franklin to the third floor with his gun, the TV and a radio where he was now sequestered against the corner.

Thank God they'd just replaced the roof.

Franklin hunkered down, still dressed in his swimming trunks and nothing else. The battery-operated radio droned on in the background.

He waited for hell to come to the Young family home.

York, Pennsylvania
8:30 PM

Rick headed west, and made it as far as York when the military cordoned off the Interstate and forced everyone towards the exits. He'd passed through a series of checkpoints, manned by nervous-looking troops, before being funneled into York and told he could go no farther. Now he was sitting in a motel room, staring at the monitor of his laptop. Through the thin walls, he heard a radio next door playing the tinny, honkey-tonk strains of Jeanne Pruett's "Satin Sheets." For some reason, the song made him think of Melissa. He wondered if she was okay, and what she was doing right now. Outside, the rain hammered against the motel room's big picture window. It sounded like someone was throwing handfuls of gravel against the glass. He wondered if the rental car would be okay, then decided he didn't care. He'd tried calling the rental company earlier, and extending his contract. He'd decided not to fly back home. He couldn't take it—couldn't handle that right now, so he'd decided to drive.

He felt numb. Shell-shocked.

His mother was dead.

Rick barely noticed the wind outside moaning around the motel's eaves. He hadn't bothered to shut the shades. The lights in the parking lot were out. The sky was dark, much darker at this hour than it normally was this time of year. It had been bright and sunny earlier. When he'd gone back into the hospital after his brother called him it had been a typical Pennsylvania summer; high eighties, with high humidity. When he came out an hour later the sky was already starting to darken, as if the atmosphere had sensed his general dreary mood.

The hospital …

When Rick arrived back in ICU, his family was in his mom's room, gathered around her. A nurse was monitoring a bunch of equipment that was hooked up to his mother's drained and emaciated frame on the bed. His father, his brother and his wife, Leslie, his sister, Patricia, and her husband Tom, were all standing around the bed. Pat was crying; his brother Bill was fighting the tears back. Rick had joined them, unable to take his eyes off his mother's comatose figure. Patricia was holding their mother's hand, crying and whispering to her, their father was standing over their mother softly stroking her forehead, and then a sudden sound broke the spell—the steady whine of the machine signifying flat-line.

Flat-line.

And Rick could do nothing but look down in numbing shock at his dead mother.

There'd been quiet tears, consoling words. Rick had retreated away from the group and looked out the window, memories of childhood flashing in his mind. He had no idea how long he was standing there until he felt a hand on his shoulder. "How you doing, little brother?"

And Rick had turned to Bill and before he knew it he was hugging him, letting the tears fall, letting the hurt seep through. He felt his brother's strong embrace, felt comforted momentarily by his big brother who, when they were kids, was always there for him, was always there to help him learn to ride his bike, always staying at his side to catch him if he fell off it; or who showed him how to bait a hook and go fishing; who taught him how to play baseball; who introduced him to the world of comic books, providing him his first copies of Spiderman and The Man Thing back when he was ten years old. He cried as the memories of their shared childhood rushed past him quickly, like a movie on fast forward. Tom had talked to the hospital administrators and they told everybody outside of the room an hour after Mom died, that the body would be released to Good's Funeral Home in a few days. If it wasn't for the impending arrival of Hurricane Gary it would probably be released tomorrow, but they didn't want to chance it. Bill had suggested everybody reconvene at his house and that's what they'd done. An hour later they were in Reamstown, gathered in the living room sharing their grief. Rick had been with them all, for once happy to be with his family, but then it had become too much for him and he'd excused himself and gone to his room.

He'd glanced out the window, saw a non-descript black sedan cruise slowly past. Moments later, it went by again.

He'd left within moments, hurriedly saying his good-byes, insisting he had to leave, that his presence in the house was endangering the others. His family had protested, but he'd done his best to explain. Then he drove to the airport, checking the rearview mirror during the entire journey. At the airport, he'd circled around through the parking garage, and then drove back out again, confident that he'd lost any tail he might have had. He'd driven through Lancaster County, passing by Amish farms and inner-city projects, and then had crossed the Susquehanna River into York County.

And had ended up stranded here after martial law was declared.

For a long while he'd tried to force himself to cry again, to feel the pain. To grieve. And despite the level of sadness he felt, for some reason the tears wouldn't come. It was like they were stuck, clogged up.

So he'd watched the wind whip the trees outside, and then sat at the motel room's desk, plugged in his laptop, and booted his computer up. The television was turned off. They'd warned him the cable was out when he checked in. In the room next to his, Jeanne Pruett had given way to Johnny Russell's "Rednecks, White Socks and Blue Ribbon Beer." Rick winced. Whatever the radio station was, it reminded him of where old country music songs went to die.

It was a habit of Rick's to check his email. He did it anytime he found himself in front of a computer. Sometimes, it took his mind off the still-powerful urge to write. He wondered if that desire would ever leave him. Probably not. Writing was in the blood, and it didn't leave you just because you were assumed dead and living under a bogus identity. Once or twice in the past few years, Rick had toyed with the idea of writing a new novel and submitting it under a pseudonym, but had ultimately decided it was too risky. Rick's style, while not literary, was distinctive, and he couldn't chance someone recognizing it.

He went through the tasks of logging into his internet account mindlessly, barely aware of what he was doing. There weren't many pressing messages to deal with. There was one from his current girlfriend, Janet, asking if he was okay. She'd seen the news coverage, obviously. And there was one from Ashley telling him their daughter was asking for him and telling him business at the bookstore was going good, and wondering if he was anywhere near the beach. Rick answered both of them, telling them Mom had passed away earlier that afternoon and that he was safe and that he'd call them tomorrow, as soon as the hurricane passed. Then he'd signed out of his email account and was now just blindly surfing the web.

Of course, he couldn't help but be drawn into what was going on. The net service was sporadic and slow. He couldn't get into CNN.com or Foxnews.com, so he tried alternate news sites.

The storm was coming. Water was coming. Rick didn't care. He should have. He was terrified of such things now, but it barely registered with him. Even the news that the Clickers had moved inland and were still on their onslaught didn't bother him or set him to absolute terror the way he thought it would.

His mother was dead.

Rick read a few of the online news stories of unrest in major cities due to the chaos, of giant Clickers attacking and devouring people by the dozens. He read about the Army amassing in various parts of the country, he read of the National Guard going in, he read reports that the things were being killed. But that didn't cure his pain.

He lurked on various message boards and news groups, and observed silently in chat rooms, trying to find something that would move him, make him feel. Rick read accounts of various posters' personal experiences. Some reported what the major news outlets were already reporting. Others were reporting stuff they were witnessing first-hand. Rick held his breath, spellbound as he read through these posts. Despite feeling terrified, despite wanting to shut down the computer and retreat, forgetting everything that was happening, he had to see how things were faring.

And it turned out things weren't faring well.

According to what he gleaned from the net, the Clickers were beaching themselves all along the East Coast, from Martha's Vineyard to as far south as St. Augustine, Florida. President Tyler had made some bullshit speech at the White House, saying they were calling in troops from across the country. The Clickers had killed hundreds of people, probably thousands, and were moving inland. There were reports of them traveling up rivers. Rick looked for any mention of the Dark Ones and had to resist the urge to warn people about them. He wondered if the government was monitoring the net right now. It seemed unlikely, but he couldn't chance it.

The wind picked up, howling like a train. The window rattled in its frame. Raindrops pelted the metal awning outside. Rick paused, thinking of Phillipsport briefly, and then turned back to the laptop.

He jumped in his seat as something exploded outside—a power transformer? A gunshot? He didn't know what it was.

The room went dark. He heard a muffled shout. His laptop blinked out. Next door, the radio stopped midway through a ballad by Stonewall Jackson.

Rick stood up, and carefully made his way through the darkness. Fumbling, he found the light switch and clicked it. Nothing happened. The power was definitely out.

Through the thin walls, he heard a man's voice in the room next door, speaking in reassuring tones. "Just wait. Just wait …"

Wait? Rick thought. The hell with that …

He could wait to see where the nightmare would take him next, or he could try to escape it. Rick chose the latter. After his eyes adjusted to the gloom, he packed up his belongings and crept outside into the darkness. The wind nearly tore the door from his fingers, and the rain whipped his face, stinging his eyes and skin. He was soaked within seconds, water dripping from his nose and chin and plastering his hair to his scalp.

Shivering, he pulled his keys from his pocket, pointed the remote at the rental car, and pressed the button to unlock the doors. The car chirped. The headlights flashed. Rick stepped off the sidewalk and ran for the car.

From the corner of his eye, he saw another man also running across the lot with a lopsided gait. He seemed to be limping, dragging one leg behind him. He drew alongside Rick.

"How you doing?" Rick shouted, facing the wind.

"Better now," the man replied.

Rick didn't notice the gun in the man's hand until it was shoved in his face.

7

Jennifer wrapped another strip of cloth around the technician's bleeding arm and urged him to be quiet. They were hunkered down in one of the public restrooms just beyond the lobby, hiding along with Richard inside a dirty toilet stall. The other two technicians and the security guard who'd comprised the emergency staff were now dead.

Jennifer supposed it was just a matter of time before they joined them.

It had all happened so suddenly. One moment, she'd been researching the species and waiting for Hurricane Gary, and then, over the intercom, she'd heard Richard screaming to get back inside the building.

Richard had tried walking back to the aquarium after the highways had become hopelessly snarled with traffic. He'd reached the waterfront just as the Clickers had crawled from the harbor and launched their attack. He'd made it inside the aquarium, but the creatures pursued him. Now they were inside, too. Claws clicked outside the door as the crab-things ransacked the lobby and gift shop. They could also hear the increasing fury of Hurricane Gary. Jennifer thought it might blow them further inland, maybe even as far as a hundred miles upstream.

"Keep pressure on this," she told the wounded technician.

He nodded, his eyes wide with fear.

Jennifer tried to calm him. "What's your name?"

"Duncan. Duncan Potter."

"We're going to be okay, Duncan."

"Think so?"

She nodded, afraid that if she spoke, her voice would betray her.

"You're Doctor Wasco, right?"

"Yep."

"Got a family?"

Her face clouded. "My parents. They're in Hunt Valley."

"Hope my wife and daughter are okay," Duncan whispered.

Jennifer tried to smile, and found she couldn't. Then, she sat back and waited. The space inside the stall was cramped, and her leg muscles grew taught with tension. She wished she could stretch them out, but in doing so, she would have kicked Richard.

"What was the extent of Dr. Ian Sinclair's research on Homarus Tyrannous?" she asked her boss. "Was he approaching it from a cryptozoological standpoint or as a paleontological one?"

"Paleontology, I would assume," Richard responded. "Why?"

"I just wonder how much he knew. How much he'd figured out about these things before his death."

"You think those things out there are Homarus Tyrannous?"

"Don't you? It seems obvious. I spent the evening researching them. Most of what I found comes from the archeological record. The reason I think this species is Homarus Tyrannous is due to rare reported sightings as well as other events which are commonly chalked up to urban legend. There were others, in addition to Dr. Sinclair, who seemed to know about them. A horror novelist and a waitress from Phillipsport. They died, too, supposedly in Phillipsport, although some say it was under mysterious circumstances."

"A horror writer," Richard snorted. "Well, isn't that fitting? Let me guess—he penned some of those cheap killer crab paperbacks from the Eighties?"

"I don't know what his books were about," Jennifer said sharply. "I don't read that stuff. But I'm telling you Richard, it all makes sense. Don't you see it?"

"Perhaps." Richard shrugged. "In truth, Jen, I haven't really thought about it. I was too occupied not ending up getting killed by one of them."

"You were outside?" Duncan asked. "How bad is the storm?"

"Pretty bad. The outer bands of Hurricane Gary were just starting to come ashore and already the damage is being done. We're safe where we're at, but I imagine the rest of the city is in a panic. It was heading that way when I arrived here. Clearly sliding into anarchy. And with those things ... what Jennifer thinks is Homarus Tyrannous outside hunting people down and killing them ..."

He shuddered.

"Were there a lot of them out there?"

Richard nodded.

"And now they're inside the aquarium," Duncan whispered. "With us. How, exactly do you think we're safe?"

"We're secure as long as we remain in this stall and stay quiet. There are no windows and only the one door. The creatures will go after easier prey—all of our attractions and exhibits. Indeed, if they stay inside, they'll move away from this area and into the aquarium itself, towards the tanks."

"And then the storm will rip the roof off and they'll find us anyway."

"Trust me; we're in a secure spot of the building. We've weathered a hurricane or two in here before. We just need to stay inside. Stay in this spot."

Duncan kneaded his injured arm. "Do we have weapons?"

"Weapons?" Richard looked surprised.

"Yeah. Weapons. Guns, knives—stuff like that?"

Richard shuddered again. "Outside, I saw a man fire several shots point blank into one of those things with no discernable damage. No, we don't have any weapons. And if we did, I don't think they'd do us any good."

"I think we're better off finding another place to hide," Duncan said.

"Don't you understand?" Richard whispered. "There is no place to hide. We're inside. The Clickers are inside. This place is like a buffet restaurant for them."

Duncan lowered his head. "And I guess the feeding frenzy has begun."

Richard didn't respond. He didn't have to. All of them knew that the young technician was absolutely correct. The hurricane raged outside, but at that moment, it was more dangerous inside the aquarium.

York, Pennsylvania
8:54 PM

"Where are we going?" Rick asked, trying to keep the fear out of his voice.

The Asian man lying in the backseat waved the gun at him. "Just shut up and drive."

"Okay," Rick said. "It's cool. I'm not arguing with you. You're in charge."

"That's right. I'm in charge."

"I'll cooperate." Rick blinked the sweat from his eyes. "Damn straight you will."

"But I need to know where to go, right?"

The gunman sighed in exasperation. His forehead creased. He glanced down at his bleeding leg and cringed. Closing his eyes, he lay back in the seat.

"Just anywhere. I don't care. Somewhere away from here."

Rick watched him in the rearview mirror. His eyes were still closed. If they stayed that way, maybe he could find a military checkpoint and they could help him. Then again, maybe the carjacker would shoot him before the military could do anything. Or worse yet, they'd rescue Rick only to learn his real identity.

"What's your name?" The man's eyes were still shut and the gun, while still in his hand and still pointed at the back of Rick's seat, rested beside him.

"William," Rick said, sticking to his false identity even during a moment of crisis. "William Mark. What's yours?"

His captor gritted his teeth, obviously in pain. "T ... tim."

"Your leg doesn't look too good, Tim. You want me to take you to a hospital? I promise I won't tell anybody what you did."

Tim shook his head. "No hospitals. No cops. And no more talking, man. Just drive."

Rick obeyed, focusing on the road. He had no idea where they were. Tim had forced him into the car at gunpoint and ordered him to drive down various back roads and side streets rather than taking Route 30, which was crawling with emergency services and National Guardsmen. Located approximately seventy miles north of Baltimore, York, Pennsylvania stood in the path of the hurricane as it came inland. However, despite that, an evacuation order had not been issued. It was believed the storm's strength would diminish before it made it that far. Heavy rains were expected, and flash flood and severe thunderstorm warnings had been issued, but no calls for mandatory evacuation. Still, between the steadily worsening weather and the fact that martial law had been declared, the streets were empty and York resembled a ghost town.

Decrepit tenement buildings and the skeletons of abandoned warehouses and factories surrounded them, adding to the gloom. Rain beat against the car's roof and windshield, and the wipers did very little to clear the torrent away. Rick's vision was severely limited and he drove slowly. He thought he glimpsed headlights ahead, but they'd turned away before he reached them. The pounding rain made him uneasy. It was like Phillipsport all over again.

"Can I turn on the radio at least?"

"Yeah," Tim said. "That's a good idea. Go ahead. Just keep it low."

Rick clicked it on. All of the local stations—those still on the air—were broadcasting local emergency procedures, so he switched it over to the car's satellite radio receiver. He dialed in one of the nationwide news channels and both men listened to several media pundits and scientists arguing over President Tyler's approach to the crisis and his State of Emergency address.

"—and then he said that we should disregard what so many of our colleagues are beginning to surmise, that it appears the

Brian Keene & J. F. Gonzalez

species is Homarus Tyrannous or a distant cousin of them ...
that they were thought to be extinct since the Mesozoic Period.
And that numb nut ..."

"Sir, need I remind you that this is the Commander in Chief
we're talking about? Show a little respect."

"You're right. He's not a numb nut. He's a damn fool. That
Jesus freak ... he had the nerve to say that he didn't accept the
scientific community's hypothesis ... he had the gall to say that
he was rejecting what the top scientists of the country were
saying because according to the Bible, the earth is only ten
thousand years old!"

In the back seat, Tim chuckled. "Yeah, I had the news on
before the power went out. The talking heads on TV are in a
tizzy over it. You should see what those lunatics on Fox News
are saying. They're scrambling like chickens with their heads
cut off. They put that little fascist commentator on ... that Sean
Hannity guy ... and he's spinning this story like you wouldn't
believe. Saying that all the so-called liberal media outlets are
now making a big deal about the President's religious beliefs
and that they're ignoring the real tragedy of the hurricane and
the goddamn things the fucking President refuses to believe in
that are killing people on the fucking street!"

Rick listened to him rant. His speech was rapid, his voice
high-pitched. Tim definitely showed signs of some sort of
mental duress. Rick changed the station to catch some of the
White House Press Secretary's babblings as Tim said, "And that
little douchebag has been spinning this story since it broke.
This administration makes the last one look like they were
goddamned saints!"

"You know what he always reminded me of?" Rick asked,
feeling a sudden kinship with his captor. "Remember those
pig-looking creatures in The Empire Strikes Back? The things
working at Cloud City? He looked like them."

Tim laughed. "You got that right."

They focused on the Press Secretary fielding questions from
an undisclosed secure location. "... was saying was it is up to
us to secure our homes, our businesses, and weather this storm
out. We have to help each other, look out for each other, and if

that means taking arms and taking some of the local wildlife out, then you should."

"Local wildlife?" Rick gripped the wheel. "He's calling the ... he's calling them the local wildlife?"

"Yeah. Unbelievable, isn't it? It's all so carefully orchestrated."

Rick didn't reply, but he was in silent agreement. He bet there were some respected journalists in the crowd, important questions ready to unleash from their lips, but they would go unrecognized, instead being passed over in favor of those who were in the Administration's pocket who would throw softballs at the Press Secretary.

They turned their attention back to the press conference. "... and when the military arrives at whatever town or community you live in, they will help you. In the meantime, all we're suggesting is to batten down the hatches and wait the storm out. A lot of people have already left the affected areas and that's a good thing. The National Guard and Army and other Federal Disaster Units are already working with State, Local, and the Federal Government in various relief efforts relating to the storm and the attacks. Once the storm has lifted the first thing to take care of will be those injured. There will also be a separate team dedicated to securing the affected areas of the attacks and killing the remainder of the wildlife species that have caused these attacks."

"It will take more than guns to kill them," Rick whispered to himself.

"How do you know that?" Tim sat up, clutching the gun. "Did you see one of them tonight? I thought they were near the oceans."

"They are," Rick told him.

"Then how do you know?"

Rick took a deep breath, and then told him.

The storm grew worse.

9:00 PM

Scenes from a slaughter:

From Florida to Maine, highways were clogged with traffic

as people rushed to escape the marauding Clickers. Once martial law was declared in several of those states, the traffic jams erupted into anarchy. As the Clickers headed inland, they came across the grid locked freeways and killed those who had set out on foot. Those who'd remained inside their vehicles fared no better as the creatures cracked open their cars like cans of tuna.

In Dade County, Florida, an alligator went head-to-head with a baby Clicker that wandered into a nearby creek. The creek turned red as the alligator spun into a death roll, trying to tear the dog-sized crustacean apart in its massive jaws. Minutes later the water turned black and sludgy with 'gator flesh as the Clicker emerged from the depths and began to feed.

In Fort Bragg, North Carolina, a trio of Clickers chased a twelve-year-old boy up a tree. He yelled for help for several minutes, throwing apples down at them, and then started to cry for his mother as the wind picked up.

When he finally fell asleep three hours later, his upper body resting comfortably in the tree's stout branches, the Clickers had already scampered off for better pickings elsewhere. He was jolted out of his light sleep with a great crack of thunder and almost fell out of the tree. Unable to see that the danger was gone, he could only cling to his safe haven and cry in frustration.

Baltimore's Inner Harbor area was deserted, except for the Clickers feeding on the dead and pouring into the National Aquarium where more captive prey awaited them in tanks. Debris blew in the city streets. The rain pelted down and the gutters ran with blood and gore. Further into the city, people were either at war with the Clickers—some were holed up in buildings and houses with various weapons, trying to fight them off—or had escaped town altogether, evacuating into Pennsylvania. The streets and highways were jammed with vehicles, some broken down or abandoned, others containing partially devoured corpses. Clickers dotted the city, scampering to and fro, pausing occasionally to nibble. The army arrived and fought back with heavy weaponry and mobilized infantry.

The nation's capital resembled a ghost town when a large force of Clickers crawled out of the Potomac River. They skittered across the mall, destroying national monuments and attacking anyone unfortunate enough to still be in the city. They gained access to the Smithsonian's Museum of Natural History, and engaged the fossilized remains of their ancient enemies in battle. The fossils broke apart and the creatures moved on. Back on the riverbank, more of the creatures slipped onto land.

The Susquehanna River fed into the Chesapeake Bay and hundreds of Clickers were migrating upstream. Communities along the river were unaware of this danger, however, as most people hunkered down to ride the storm out. An Amish man who had just stepped outside to make sure his barn was secure was cut in half as a monstrous Clicker bounded onto his property. More of the creatures slaughtered his livestock and family with equal fervor. Farther inland along the river, the staff at the Peachbottom Nuclear Power Plant hunkered down to weather the storm, unaware of what was creeping towards them.

In New York City, all points of entry leaving the city were hopelessly blocked. Most had given up hope and abandoned their vehicles, making their way over bridges and through tunnels on foot. They were turned back at the military checkpoints. Rioting broke out, and civilians battled armed forces in an effort to escape the city. Then the ravenous Clickers arrived and fell upon both.

Hurricane Gary, which had remained unpredictable and had stymied the world's best meteorological efforts to predict its patterns, made landfall, striking like a nuclear bomb.

Magog Bunker
The White House
Washington, D.C.
9:00 PM

"Your will be done, Lord," President Tyler whispered, tears streaming down his face. "Your will be done. On Earth as it is in Heaven."

"Sir?" Special Agent Clark Arroyo glanced into the room, his face etched with concern. "Did you need anything?"

"No thank you, son. The Lord provides me with all that I need. Please shut the door behind you."

"Yes, sir."

When he was alone, Tyler bowed his head in prayer and began to quote the Book of Jonah.

"But the Lord hurled a great wind upon the sea, and such a mighty storm came upon the sea that the ship threatened to break up. Then the mariners were afraid and each cried to his god. 'Tell us why this calamity has come upon us,' they cried."

His smile was grim.

"We know why this calamity has come, don't we, my Lord. Praised be Your name. But You will not let this mighty ship break up. 'But the Lord provided a large fish to swallow up Jonah so that he would not drown. 'You will save us, Lord. You will save your children. You will deliver us from evil and snuff the fires of Hell."

Dundalk, Maryland
9:09 PM

"Sir," the pilot shouted into the com. "We're getting batted around like a kite up here. I've got no choice but to set it down soon."

"Understood," Livingston hollered back, competing with the roaring winds and the whine of the helicopter's whirring blades. "Try to get us as close to the Inner Harbor area as possible. Radio Centcom and advise them of our status, then get a hold of our boys on the ground. Mark our position and have them send a welcoming committee. We're going to need it."

The soldiers aboard the chopper prepared for landing, checking their weapons and gear one last time, and making sure all essential equipment was stowed. Livingston reminded them to load armor-piercing rounds, rather than what they normally packed.

Several of the young men's faces were pale.

"Gentlemen," Colonel Livingston said, "welcome to Hell."

Below them, the feeding frenzy continued.

Interstate 83
Glen Rock, Pennsylvania
9:10 PM

Tony Genova drove as fast as he dared, given the hazardous road conditions. The highway was slick with rain, and the downpour obscured landmarks and road signs. Lightning flashed overhead, casting an eerie glow over the landscape for a second. Tony shivered. The whole day had been strange. One minute, they'd been sitting in Atlantic City, waiting to make the exchange with Frankie Spicolli. Then a bunch of crab-things straight out of a bad Sci Fi Channel movie had shown up and started killing people. Now here they were driving through the middle of a fucking hurricane near the Pennsylvania and Maryland border with a captive in the trunk and a briefcase full of top-grade heroin.

A thumping sound came from the trunk, barely discernable over Pink Floyd's Animals, which was currently in the car's CD player. The banging sounds got louder. The Greek was awake and pissed off. In truth, Tony couldn't blame the old fuck. The annual fireworks display, where they were originally supposed to nab him, had been cancelled because of the weather. Instead, they'd had to snatch the old guy from his home in Leader's Heights. The plan had been to drive him out to a secluded location near South Mountain or LeHorn's Hollow, kill him, and then drive him back to Roosevelt Avenue in York, where they had a man who specialized in body disposal. Killing him at Roosevelt Avenue was out of the question; too many neighbors equaled too many potential witnesses.

But now everything was going to shit. They couldn't get into York, couldn't get to South Mountain, and couldn't get to LeHorn's Hollow. Couldn't get anywhere, really. And now they were driving around, trying to figure out what the fuck to do, as Hurricane Gary ripped into town. So yeah, Tony could understand why the Greek might be angry. Kidnapped, knocked the fuck out, locked in the trunk of a car and driving all over Central Pennsylvania and the backwoods of Maryland.

And to top it all off, he'd missed the fireworks. Yeah, he had reason to be pissed. Tony couldn't blame him. He felt the same way. Tony's simmering anger grew stronger with every fruitless mile.

"For fuck's sake." Tony gripped the steering wheel harder, as a strong gust of wind battered the passenger's side, pushing the car onto the median. "We need to figure this shit out—and quick."

"We shoulda just dropped him on Roosevelt Avenue," Vince said. "I don't like driving around in this storm. It's scary."

"How were we supposed to drop him on Roosevelt when the road was closed due to flooding? Fucking National Guard was everywhere. What if they'd heard him back there? I told you to tie him up better."

Vince shrugged. The big man rummaged through a plastic bag at his feet and produced a package of Devil Dogs. He unwrapped the cellophane.

"You want one?" he offered.

"No thanks."

Tony veered around a downed tree, its trunk lying across part of the southbound lane. He heard the briefcase slide around in the backseat. They'd had no choice but to lug the heroin all the way from Atlantic City.

"Hey, Tony?" Vince sat up straight, looking puzzled. "What's a charade?"

"Huh?"

"In this song." He pointed at the CD player. "They say, 'ha ha charade you are.' What's a charade?"

"It's got two meanings. Like when you play charades? That's one of them."

"What's the other?"

"An absurd pretense."

"What's an absurd pretense?"

"This whole fucked up situation, man. This whole god damn day ..."

"... they're about nine, maybe ten feet tall and I want to say they're amphibious but they looked more reptilian to me, like giant Komodo Dragons that can walk upright like a man!"

Tim listened to Rick—who'd originally told him that his name was William. Tim forgot all about his wounded leg or the gun in his hand or the storm hammering their car. He was spellbound by the tale his hostage was spinning.

This had been a bad night, starting with the moment he'd decided to shoot his ex-wife, hoping to blame it on looters during the civil unrest breaking out because of the storm and martial law. It had gotten worse when he'd been shot in the leg by her new husband, worse yet when he'd killed them both, and had slid into madness when he'd hijacked Rick and his car in the parking lot of a nearby motel. His belly was already a gnawing pit of nerves. But this ...

What Rick was telling him was alarming. It was terrifying.

But it was also exciting.

"—hunt the Clickers! They hunt them! The Clickers are their natural food source. I'm sure they eat other things, they have to wherever the hell it is they're from, and for all I know maybe they're the ones responsible for all those lost boats out at sea or the occasional person that disappears on a sandy beach somewhere. Hell, maybe their range spans as far south as the Caribbean and one of 'em got that Natalie Halloway chick and ate her up right in front of those college kids who were busted for her disappearance! Remember that?"

Rick had opened up to his captor ten-fold, unleashing a torrent of built-up memories and emotions in the tide of information he was letting run forth. It came fast and furious and Tim listened to him with rapt attention. The story was so incredible, and to the average layman would probably sound like the ravings of a lunatic, but Tim believed him. How could he not? Especially with what was going on now, all over the east coast? He'd seen it himself on television.

"—years is what I figure. But get this. I've been reading up a lot on global warming and how ocean currents in the Atlantic—hell, all over the world!—are changing due to the rising temperature and the shifts in climate. I mean, you've got Arctic glaciers melting away, dropping chunks of ice in the ocean and that causes a ripple effect, you know? It's all physics, like that theory that the beating of a butterfly's wings in South America can upset the balance in the atmosphere enough to cause a hurricane in the United States. So this shit has been happening in the oceans for years now, and the underwater currents have been shifting because of it and it's bringing the Clickers and the Dark Ones to the surface on a much more frequent basis now!"

Rick finally stopped babbling and Tim spoke up.

"Who else besides you and this Melissa know about all this?" Rick had told him about he and Melissa escaping government custody in the days after Hurricane Floyd in 1994, but he didn't tell Tim where they'd traveled to or eventually settled down in; he didn't even tell him Melissa's new name, just that she was still alive.

"Nobody! Well, I told Colonel Livingston. He's the military guy I told you about who interrogated us in Phillipsport. I told him and another guy ... I forget his first name, but I remember his last. Richrath. Don't remember what rank or branch of the military he was. I told them, and I've been in contact with Livingston since then."

Not even realizing he was doing it, Rick turned off to avoid a checkpoint and squeezed the car down a narrow inner-city alley. The tires splashed through deep puddles, spraying more water up onto the windows.

"So what's your story?" Rick finally asked. "I've told you mine. You don't seem like a carjacker."

"I'm not." Tim checked his leg and saw that the bleeding had stopped. Groaning with pain, he leaned forward. "I'm a systems analyst at the Harley Davidson plant. I just ... had a bad evening."

"Want to talk about it?"

"Not really."

"Want to put the gun down? I mean, is it really necessary? Like I said, I'm on the run, too."

"Just keep driving, Rick."

They exited the alley and turned onto a side street that led out of the city and into rural farmland.

"Anywhere in particular you want to go yet? We can't just keep driving around, or we're going to get caught."

As if to punctuate his point, they saw the flash of red police lights in the rearview mirror. Tim immediately grew agitated. Rick pressed down on the accelerator. The lights faded, and then vanished.

"Are they gone?"

Tim turned around. "Yeah, looks like it. They must have been after somebody else."

"Well, we might not be so lucky next time. So you really should come up with somewhere to hide."

Tim paused. "Yeah. I know just the place. Take me there and I'll let you go."

"Where is it?"

"A little bed and breakfast in Shrewsbury, just above the Maryland border. My wife ... my ex-wife and I stayed there once, but it's been closed down for the last six months. Sits way back in the woods. Totally deserted. I'll ride the storm out there."

"And you'll let me go?"

"Sure."

"So how do I get there?"

"Take the next left. That will take us to the Susquehanna Trail. It runs alongside Interstate 83 the whole way down into Maryland."

"Susquehanna? As in river?"

"Yeah. Why?"

"I just don't like water is all."

After a moment, Tim laughed. "Yeah, I guess I can see why."

He leaned back in the seat, giggling to himself.

Rick was not laughing. Thunder split the sky overhead, and lightening flashed, bathing the countryside in blue-white light. Then the darkness returned.

They drove on into the night and the storm rocketed towards

them, leaving death and destruction in its wake—and bringing something else with it as well.

The sound of clicking claws echoed across the central Pennsylvanian landscape.

8

National Aquarium
Inner Harbor
Baltimore, Maryland
9:30 PM

They'd escaped from the bathroom and holed up temporarily inside an office.

Duncan glanced back at Jennifer and Richard. "Are you guys ready?"

"Of course we're not ready," Richard whispered. "Please reconsider this. It's a suicide run."

"You said it yourself, Doctor. If we stay here, they've got us trapped. No way we can barricade the office door against them. Our best bet is to flee on foot. Find another, more secure hiding spot."

"It's quiet out there," Jennifer observed. "Maybe they've left."

"Yes," Richard flicked his sweaty hair out of his eyes, "or maybe they're just waiting for us. I've seen them up close. They're much smarter than we give them credit for."

Jennifer frowned. "Then maybe we should stay here after all."

"I concur." Richard nodded. "It appears as if you've been outvoted, Duncan."

"Look," the technician sighed, "you two do what you want. I'm getting the hell out of here while I have the chance. Those things are probably busy with the tanks and displays. Hell, this entire building is one big captive smorgasbord as far as the

Clickers are concerned. While they're busy with the fish, I'm getting out. It's my daughter's birthday. She's seven. No way I'm gonna miss it. I've got to get home. If you're coming, then stick close to me and keep quiet. If not, good luck to you both."

"Where do you live?" Jennifer asked.

"White Marsh. Why?"

"Do you have a basement? Somewhere your family can take shelter from the storm? A place they can hide?"

"No." Duncan's bottom lip trembled. "That's why I need to make sure they're okay."

They both stared at the wounded technician. It was obvious that there would be no talking him out of this course of action. So instead, they steeled themselves. Richard and Duncan were both armed with makeshift clubs—legs they'd unscrewed from a desk. Jennifer wielded a long, pointed letter opener. It was shaped like a dagger and had a pewter crab on the hilt. Beneath the crab was the slogan, I GOT CRABS AT PHILLIPS SEAFOOD IN BALTIMORE, MARYLAND. The irony was not lost on her.

"Get ready," Duncan whispered.

Jennifer and Richard nodded. Jennifer's pulse raced in her chest. Richard's mouth went dry.

Duncan crept to the door. Slowly, he grasped the doorknob. With his other hand, he raised the desk leg over his head. Then, he opened the door.

A massive stinger punched into Duncan's stomach and erupted from his lower back. The crab-thing's appendage spurted long arcs of venom all over the floor, and the carpet began to smoke and burn. Impaled, Duncan squirmed, and then slid down the tail a few inches, trailing viscera like a slug trailed slime. The club slipped from Duncan's fingers and bounced off the monstrous Clicker's hard shell. Duncan opened his mouth to scream and vomited blood instead. Jennifer and Richard screamed for him. Duncan's hands closed around the base of the stinger jutting from his abdomen. Slicked with his own gore, he couldn't hold onto it.

The Clicker thrashed its segmented tail high into the air, and Duncan's head smashed through the drop ceiling. Shattered tiles rained down upon them all. The creature lowered its tail and whipped it back and forth. Duncan slid off the appendage with a wet sound. The hole in his mid-section bubbled and steamed. Parts of his insides still clung to the stinger. The creature raised its claws and charged. The pincers reminded Jennifer of a pair of maracas.

Click-click … Click-click …

The crab-thing made it halfway through the door before becoming stuck. Its shell gouged and scraped at the wooden doorframe. The creature hissed with anger. Duncan moaned once, and then lay still. Jennifer and Richard cowered against the office's far wall. The Clicker tried to force its way into the room, but couldn't. Held fast, it began ripping at the frame with its claws, tearing away chunks of wood and plaster.

"He'll be free in a minute," Richard said. "Get behind me. I'll try to—"

"Save the chivalry for later," Jennifer said. Her attention was focused on the ceiling. A ragged hole had been left behind in the tiles by Duncan's head. It revealed an air duct burrowing deeper into the facility. She followed the duct backward, and saw that it ran directly over their heads. All they'd have to do is remove the tiles and somehow get the duct open.

"Help me move the desk."

Richard blinked. "The desk?"

"Yes," she snapped. "Slide it over here. Even without the legs, we can stand on top of it and reach the ceiling. We can crawl through the ductwork. That thing isn't tall enough to reach us up there."

As if sensing her urgency, the Clicker's thrashings increased. It tore at the doorframe with frenzied rage.

Without another word, Richard shoved the desk over to where they stood. He grunted with the effort and his face grew red. Meanwhile, Jennifer glanced around for something to open the duct with. Her search was fruitless.

"Now what?" Richard asked.

Out in the hallway, they heard more Clickers arriving, attracted by their fellow crab-thing's struggle.

Jennifer clambered up onto the wobbly desk and studied the duct. There was no door or hatch on it, and no screw or vent—just a solid metal surface, smooth and seamless.

"Shit!"

"It's almost free," Richard exclaimed, keeping his eyes on the doorway. "Get it open."

"I don't know how," she admitted. "It always works in the movies."

Jennifer stabbed at the duct with her letter opener, and succeeded only in making a small dent.

"Come on." Richard grabbed her leg and urged her down. Then he led her to the closet. He shoved her inside and then slammed the door behind them. The emergency lights were still on throughout the aquarium, and a dim glow filtered through the crack at the bottom of the door.

"This is no good," Jennifer whispered. "It saw us come in here."

Richard didn't reply. Jennifer realized that he was crying.

She put her hand on his shoulder and moved closer to him. Then they embraced. She felt him tremble against her. Jennifer squeezed him tightly. He squeezed her back.

"When our daughter Susan died," Richard said, "Sarah didn't want to have any more children. I don't think she could handle the fear of losing another one. But in the time you've worked for me, I've come to think of you as a daughter, as well. I'm sorry, Jen. Sorry I couldn't save us."

Outside, they heard the loud splintering of wood, followed by a crash. The Clicker scuttled into the room. They heard its legs tapping on the floor. It paused, and they both wondered what it was doing. Then they heard the sounds of feeding and realized it had stopped to feast on Duncan's remains. A moment later, they heard more of the creatures enter the office.

"I guess this is it." Richard's voice rang with defeat.

Blinking tears away, Jennifer looked upward; making one last terrified plea to a God she didn't believe in.

An open grating on a ventilation shaft stared back at her.

Jennifer laughed. "Now that's how it happens in the movies!"

She removed her shoes and held them in one hand. Then she slipped the letter opener in her jeans. Quickly, Richard boosted her up. Jennifer crawled into the shaft. Then she tossed her shoes aside and reached for her boss. A tremendous blow rattled the closet door. Richard turned around, panicked.

"Hurry!"

The door shook again. The wood cracked. Richard turned back to Jennifer. She grabbed his outstretched hand and pulled. He was heavier than she'd imagined.

"Jen—forget about it. I'm too heavy."

"Richard, with all due respect, shut up and push!"

The door splintered. A crimson pincer thrust into the closet, grabbed a raincoat, and pulled it out. The creature hissed with annoyance. Richard let out a frightened squawk.

"One," Jennifer counted. "Two ... THREE!"

Richard braced his feet against the wall and pushed, as Jennifer pulled his arm. The desk leg slipped from Richard's hand. Jennifer cried out. It felt like her arm was going to come out of its socket. But then Richard's head and shoulder were through the narrow opening. He grabbed the sides of the shaft and pulled himself upward. Below them, the door buckled, then gave way completely and a Clicker forced its way into the closet, shredding everything in sight—coats, galoshes, a broom, and boxes of paper for the copy machine down the hall. The beast snatched at Richard's dangling feet, but he pulled them up into the duct just in time.

Camden Yards
Baltimore, Maryland
9:35 PM

Destruction rained down on the troops. The wind tore the roof off a nearby bar and dropped it on their heads. Livingston ignored the falling debris. He stepped forward, brought up his pistol and fired at an onrushing Clicker. The rain obscured his vision and the shot went wild. One of his men fried the creature with a flamethrower. Livingston wished for more firepower.

"Incoming," a soldier shouted into the com-link on his helmet. Before he could follow it up, a telephone pole snapped at its base and toppled over, crushing the unfortunate man.

Livingston grimaced. The kid was only twenty.

Another soldier rushed to help his fallen comrade, screamed for a medic, and then backed away as a Clicker emerged from behind a hot dog stand and tottered towards them. The soldier opened fire, forgetting all about the man pinned beneath the telephone pole.

"How far to the aquarium?" Livingston yelled over the cacophony of howling winds, gunfire, screaming men, and clicking claws—always that damned clicking.

"About eight city blocks, sir."

"Any word on our ground forces already in the area?"

"Delayed, Colonel. Sounds like they're taking heavy casualties."

"Squad leaders," Livingston shouted. "Move out!"

"But sir, these things are everywhere!"

"I SAID MOVE OUT!"

The young soldier was right, though. The Clickers were everywhere. Downtown Baltimore was far worse than Phillipsport had ever been. The creatures rushed from the stadium and lunged out of alleyways. They clambered over abandoned cars, crushing them like aluminum cans. The squad fought bravely. They did not buckle or back down. Instead, they took up positions and fought back against the onslaught. Regular bullets seemed to have no effect, but the flamethrowers worked magic. Within minutes, the air was filled with the smell of burnt meat.

"Steamed crabs, boys," a Sergeant yelled. "All we need is some butter and Old Bay seasoning."

"And a cold beer," another soldier agreed.

The Sergeant's laughter turned into a high, keening wail as a Clicker crept up behind him and sliced him in half at the waist. Men screamed.

Despite the pain from his arthritis, Livingston plowed ahead. He had the radioman call for Humvees, a tank, Jeep—any kind of motorized transport. He was told that none was forthcoming.

"We'll just have to commandeer something then," Livingston grumbled.

After another two blocks, they came to a desperate halt. An

overturned light rail train blocked their passage. Several cars lay on their side. The metal had been peeled back like the lid of a tuna can, and several large Clickers were perched atop the cars, leisurely pulling out the frantic commuters. Livingston safely guided his men around the wreck, and then called in an artillery strike. Minutes later, explosive shells detonated nearby—falling too short of the target. The radioman called in an adjustment to the coordinates. The whistle of the artillery shells was lost beneath the gale.

The explosions seemed only to draw more of the creatures onto their location. They began a running battle, desperately trying to reach the aquarium before their numbers dwindled to zero. All around him, Colonel Livingston watched brave soldiers fall, watched them get beheaded, disemboweled, watched severed limbs fall to the pavement, heard men screaming. Dying.

"Ought to just nuke the whole damned harbor," a soldier next to Livingston grumbled.

"Don't tempt me, son." Livingston fired at another Clicker. "Don't tempt me."

"Sir," the radioman reported, "estimated time of arrival for reinforcements is fifteen minutes. They'll meet us at the aquarium."

Fifteen minutes, Livingston thought. *If we live that long …*

Magog Bunker
The White House
Washington, D.C.
9:40 PM

Clark Arroyo had been with the Secret Service for over thirty years. He'd received numerous commendations and awards, and had served many Presidents. Currently, he was assigned to President Jeffrey Tyler's personal security detail. That meant he was with Tyler seven days a week, ten hours per day—and longer if they were traveling or if his relief called in sick. Arroyo had seen his fair share of danger in his time with the Secret Service, but he'd never been scared. Frightened. Uneasy. But he'd never known fear in the line of duty. He'd told his wife once, when they'd gone camping in the Shenandoah Mountains for their tenth anniversary, that he sometimes worried there was something wrong with him. He didn't know fear—not even when facing an assassin. But he did now.

Special Agent Clark Arroyo was terrified.

From behind the closed door, the President was singing an off-key hymn. Clark had never heard anything more disturbing.

"What a friend we have in Jesus ..."

He was familiar with the song. His great-grandmother had sung the very same hymn when he was young. He remembered sitting in her living room, watching her play the autoharp with her frail, thin hands. Her body had been fading, but her voice remained strong. It had always made him feel good. Filled him with comfort. Now, hearing the President's rendition, the hymn had the opposite effect.

Arroyo began to cry. He wept for his wife, her whereabouts unknown. He hadn't talked to her since the hurricane changed course. He wept for his daughters, both grown and married to husbands of their own. One of them lived in Nevada and was safe. The other lived on North Carolina's outer banks—and probably wasn't safe. He wept for the American civilians caught between the storm and these creatures from the sea. He'd seen the footage, just like everyone else.

But mostly, he wept for the nation. He loved his country. In this time of national crisis, America needed a leader more than ever.

The President continued singing, and Clark Arroyo's fear threatened to overwhelm him. Without realizing it, he reached for his sidearm.

National Aquarium
Inner Harbor
Baltimore, Maryland
9:50 PM

"Okay." Jennifer whispered as quietly as possible. She was worried that sound might travel through the ducts and somehow be magnified. "That's the fire stairs below us. All we have to do is get inside the stairwell and follow them down to the first floor.

"Or," Richard said, "we could just wait inside this ventilation shaft until help arrives."

"No way. You saw what they did to the rain forest exhibit. Not to mention all the other tanks they've smashed already. This place will be flooded in no time. If the water gets into the ducts, we're screwed."

The rain forest exhibit had been one of the National Aquarium's top attractions—its crown jewel. Situated on the top floor, it was a completely self-contained ecosystem, an actual mini-rainforest inside a greenhouse-like dome. It contained flora and fauna native to the Amazon basin. The marauding Clickers had destroyed it, shattering the glass and allowing the hurricane to breach the building.

"But what if they've accessed the fire stairs?" Richard stretched, trying to get rid of the kink in his neck. "I'd rather drown in here than end up as an appetizer for one of those things."

"It's doubtful they did. There's no prey in the stairwell, after all. Why would they bother with that when there are glass tanks all around them, filled with fish?"

"That technician, Duncan, didn't think there would be any in the office corridors either, and look what happened to him."

He shuddered at the memory.

Jennifer took a deep breath. "Richard ... Please. I know you're scared. I'm scared, too. But work with me."

It was hard to see his face in the darkness, but she thought he might be blushing.

"You're correct, Jennifer. I'm sorry."

She reached out, found his hand, and squeezed it. "It's okay. Don't apologize. Just stay with me. We'll be home in no time."

"Deal."

"Hold on to my legs so I don't fall."

They opened the grate and Jennifer lowered her head, glancing around the corridor. It looked eerie, bathed in the red glow of emergency lighting, but it was empty, save for two inches of water covering the floor. She listened carefully. From farther inside the building came the sounds of breaking glass and the squeal of a dolphin in distress. Jennifer fought back tears. The aquarium's dolphins had been among her favorites.

"What is it?" Richard asked.

"They've gotten into the dolphin exhibit."

"Which means that they're on the floors below us. Do you hear anything else?"

"No," Jennifer lied, not wanting to frighten him any further than he already was. But she did hear something else. She heard the clicking sounds. The hallway echoed with them.

Click-click … Click-click …

She took a deep breath and then climbed down from the ductwork. Richard followed her. Jennifer slipped her shoes back on and they both stretched their cramped muscles. Then they carefully pushed open the fire door and entered the stairwell. Jennifer clutched the letter opener. It made her feel safer. The door swung shut behind them. Water trickled down the walls, leaking from somewhere else inside the aquarium. The stairwell was silent; the thick concrete walls served as a sound buffer. Jennifer was grateful for the reprieve and began softly humming Depeche Mode's "Enjoy the Silence."

Richard frowned in concern. "Are you okay?"

"Sorry." Jennifer stopped humming and smiled instead. "Just happy to be out of that shaft."

"Me too. My knees and elbows are killing me."

"Let's exercise them, then."

They started down the stairs. Jennifer's heels clicked on the cement, and she had to take them off again. They reached the first landing, crept past the door, and went down the next flight of steps. Above them, they heard a fire door slam. The boom echoed through the stairwell. Both of them jumped. Jennifer held her breath. Richard leaned out over the rail and craned his head upward. A moment later, he leaned back.

"I can't see anything …"

Click-click … Click-click … CLICK-CLICK … CLICK… CLICK …

The sound filled the air, growing louder by the second.

Jennifer stifled a scream. Clawed legs tapped on the cement as the Clicker—if indeed, it was just one—started down the stairs.

Richard grabbed Jennifer's arm. "Run!"

They sprinted down the stairs, taking them two at a time and leaping around the corner for the next landing. As they did so, the fire door a level below them burst open. Two more Clickers lunged through the doorway and into the stairwell. The creatures cried out with a hissing-warble and the one on the floor above answered. Jennifer and Richard heard it coming down the stairs towards them.

"We're trapped," Richard gasped.

Braced for the worst, Jennifer yanked open the fire door on their landing. To her immense relief, the corridor was clear. The Clickers had been there. The carpet was sodden and torn, and the walls gouged by pincers. But there was no sign of them now.

Above and below them, the crab-things raced in for the kill. The stairwell thrummed with the noise.

CLICK-CLICK-CLICK-CLICK-CLICK …

"Come on." She pulled Richard into the hallway and slammed the door behind them. Desperate, Jennifer glanced around for something to block the doors with. The only thing in sight was a fire extinguisher. It was too thick to wedge through the door handles and not heavy enough to wedge against the doors.

"Forget it," Richard cried, guessing her intentions. "Just go!"

They ran down the corridor, rounded a corner, and then came to another service door. The door had a small window in its center. Jennifer glanced through it and saw that it opened out into the public portion of the aquarium, right in front of the shark exhibit. If they went through the door and turned right, they'd travel towards the dolphins. A left took them down into the shark area. Another popular attraction with tourists, the shark tanks took up two entire floors. A wide ramp cut through their center, so that visitors could literally walk through the middle of the tank and see sharks swimming all around them. Thick glass walls surrounded the four-level ramps like a reverse fishbowl. Jennifer remembered that at the end of the bottom ramp, there was an emergency exit door that led outside to the shipping and receiving department's loading docks.

"Almost there," she whispered.

And they were. All they had to do was open this door, run out into the aquarium itself, and flee down two stories worth of ramps through the middle of the shark tank. The tank itself was filled with over ten different species of sharks, as well as various small fish, stingrays, and other aquatic life forms. Due to its size and the abundance of prey, it would offer a tempting hunting ground for the Clickers.

Richard must have known this, too, because his eyes were wide and round and his skin turned pale.

"I can't do this," he said. "I just—"

Behind them, the fire door exploded inward and their pursuers darted into the service corridor.

"Changed my mind." Richard grabbed her hand and they ran through the door and into the main hall. Their progress was slowed by the amount of water on the floor; at least six inches and all of it rushing towards the shark tank's downward ramps. Richard's socks and shoes were quickly soaked, and his pace slackened as a result. Jennifer tossed her shoes aside. They waded to the top of the ramp. The Clickers hadn't yet made it that far. The tank's huge glass walls were still intact. A lone tiger shark swam over their heads, its shadow darkening the red glow of the emergency lights for a second. They splashed onward, mindful of the creatures pursuing them.

The water level increased as they plunged downward, slowing them further. Its depth had reached almost a foot. Jennifer tripped halfway down the second ramp and fell face-first into the water. She surfaced, sputtering and blinking the water from her eyes. It tasted foul—dirt and chemicals and fish and blood. Gasping, she flipped her wet hair out of her eyes. Jennifer caught a glimpse of a human finger floating by. She almost vomited.

Richard helped her to her feet. "Are you okay?"

Coughing, Jennifer nodded. They listened for the sounds of pursuit, but none were forthcoming. The aquarium was silent again.

"Maybe they went the other way," Richard suggested. "Let's

keep going while we've got the chance."

They continued downward, moving slower now and making an effort to conceal their splashing. They didn't speak. Richard held Jennifer's hand tightly. She wondered if it was for her benefit or to make him feel better, and then decided the reason didn't matter, because it worked either way.

Eventually, they reached the lower level. The water rose higher; trapped with nowhere to go. It was up to their necks, and they gave up trying to walk and doggy-paddled instead.

"Where's the exit door?" Richard gasped.

Jennifer pointed to the other side of the room. "Over there."

They swam towards it. Jennifer glanced at the towering walls of glass that surrounded them on all sides, and recoiled in disgust. A length of intestines floated by inside the tank. They were followed seconds later by a shark's tail. The rest of the shark was missing. She was just about to open her mouth and warn Richard that the Clickers were inside the tank when three of them appeared on the other side of the glass; two to their right and one to their left. Immediately, the monsters began pounding on the thick barrier with their serrated claws. The sound was muffled, but the power and violence behind the blows was clear.

"How thick is that glass?" Jennifer asked.

"There is no way they can break it," Richard said. "It was built to hold thousands of gallons of water, plus all the sharks. It can withstand an earthquake. Only thing that could break it is a direct hit with a rocket launcher at point blank range—and even then, it might just crack."

He sounded confident, but Jennifer did not feel reassured. Three more Clickers appeared, bringing the total to six. One of them was directly overhead. It hammered on the glass and she felt the vibration run through the water around her.

"Does that door open inward or out?" Richard pointed at the exit.

"I don't know. Why?"

"Because if it opens inward, we'll never budge it with all this water."

"Only one way to find out." Jennifer swam ahead, weaving

around the debris floating on the surface. She tried to ignore the Clickers, tried to ignore the muffled pounding, and found she couldn't. Each blow rattled the glass walls and reverberated through the water. As she reached the door, there was an awful cracking sound from behind her.

Richard said, "Oh no ..."

Jennifer turned and saw a spider web of cracks and fissures spreading throughout the surface of the far wall. The Clickers had grouped together in that section and were concentrating their efforts. The scientific part of her mind marveled over this apparent reasoning capacity. Who could have imagined the creatures possessed problem-solving skills? Then her survival instincts took over. She reached beneath the surface, found the door handle, and pushed. The door wouldn't budge. Richard swam to her side. Together, the two of them threw their weight against the door and shoved. It popped open, spilling both of them and the trapped water out onto the loading docks. Behind them, the shark tank exploded, showering the entire ground level with shards of broken glass, sharks, water, and six very angry Clickers.

Jennifer lost her footing. The rushing water slammed her against a green garbage dumpster. Richard struggled to shut the door behind them, but lacked the strength to push it against the tide.

"Here they come," he panted. "Jen, get up and run. I can't go any farther."

Jennifer tried to clear her head. She stumbled to her feet. Just then, a voice called out from behind them.

"Get out of the way!"

Jennifer and Richard didn't pause to determine who the speaker was. They obeyed the command, and ducked behind the dumpster. The first Clicker rammed through the doorway, hissing in anger, and was met with a deafening volley of automatic weapons fire. Jennifer put her hands over her ears and shut her eyes. Richard collapsed to the pavement and buried his head against the side of the dumpster. The gunfire continued for what seemed like a very long time; it was followed by an arc of flame, close enough that they could both feel its heat. The fine blonde hairs on Jennifer's arms were singed. The Clickers squealed in agony, and she heard their flesh sizzling.

When it stopped, they crept out from behind their shelter. The Clickers lay in a burned, congealed pile, along with debris that had washed out of the aquarium. Approximately three-dozen soldiers stood in the loading area, weapons held at the ready, watching all sides for further attacks. An older man in an officer's uniform stepped forward. Jennifer's first impression of him was that he was very handsome. Her second was that he meant business, and looked ready to kill someone.

"Do either of you know Doctor Jennifer Wasco?" His voice was stern and demanding.

"I-I'm Jennifer."

The old man's eyes widened and the ghost of a smile crossed his face. Then he stepped forward and shook her hand.

Jennifer was startled. "Who are you?"

"Colonel Augustus Livingston, U. S. Army."

"What are you doing here?"

His smile grew broader. "You're rescued."

9

The Dark Ones moved in silence. The hurricane was their harbinger; the winds whispered promises of the death and destruction they would soon rain down upon the surface. They drove the Clickers before them, not as prey, but as fodder. The lowly crustaceans provided a distraction, an exploratory force that would keep the humans busy until they could make landfall. Only then would the real slaughter begin. Their blood sang in anticipation.

Sixty feet down, they passed the shipwreck of the Hannah M. Lollis, which had sunk in 1882 with all hands and a cargo hold full of copper and fruit. The decrepit hulk fell apart as they clambered over its rotting, skeletal timbers. A school of yellowfin tuna that had lagged behind after all the other marine life had fled, scattered as they approached. The Dark Ones let them go, urged on by the promise of more exotic prey—and driven by an overpowering thirst for revenge.

The last time they'd ventured ashore, several years ago during a similar storm on the land's northern coast, the Dark Ones had taken shelter inside a cave. They'd prepared a nest for the season—feeding on the local wildlife and breeding. Then, weeks later, at the time of birthing, men had discovered their location. Flames followed—and death. The humans had weaponry like nothing they'd ever imagined; fire rained down from the sky. An entire generation of their species had been wiped out in the attack. The survivors escaped back into the sea, traveled far along the ocean floor, and told the rest about the tragedy.

Now they marched on man. Humankind had declared war. They would answer the challenge. The massacre would be avenged tenfold.

They emerged under the cover of darkness and waded ashore at Assateague Island. The beach and nearby tree line were littered with the torn carcasses of the wild horses that called the island home. The Clickers had already been here, and judging from the carnage, they had performed exactly as the Dark Ones had wanted them to.

The leader surveyed the carnage. A long, forked tongue slithered from his mouth and tasted the salt-air. He breathed through his reptilian nostrils, his gills slapping uselessly now along the side of his neck. The breeze tickled his green, scaled skin. He glanced up at the moon and wondered how long it would be until sunrise. Their kind had become more resistant to the light, but they would still need to find shelter before the dawn. All along the coast, from the warm southern climes to the northern coasts where they'd first emerged so many years ago, similar bands of Dark Ones would be seeking shelter as well.

Soon, hundreds of its kind amassed on the shore. Some of them sated themselves on horseflesh. Others stirred restlessly, anxious to shed human blood.

The leader smiled, revealing rows of razor-sharp teeth.

Soon they would get their chance. The slaughter would be unlike anything ever seen on land.

10

Never in a million years would Jennifer have believed she'd be squeezed into a military Humvee with several grim soldiers, a high-ranking Army Colonel, and her boss, all comparing notes on giant crab monsters while racing to stay ahead of the worst part of a major hurricane. The military motorcade swept on through the night, going as fast as their slowest vehicle so they wouldn't lose anybody: fifty-five miles per hour.

Jennifer was in the front seat, trying to see out the windshield. Water ran across it in sheets. This section of Interstate 83 was relatively clear of traffic or stalled vehicles. Livingston told them when she and Richard were ushered inside the vehicle, that the National Guard had cleared both lanes just north of the Beltway and directed traffic onto 795 and 70 heading east. Jennifer didn't bother to ask why. All she was concerned with now was comparing notes with Colonel Livingston, who seemed to have an uncanny grasp of the magnitude of what they were dealing with.

Both she and Richard had been given a cursory medical exam on the way, and Livingston had debriefed them. Jennifer found it a little disconcerting that the military had sent a team in just to extract her.

"So you have an idea of what's happening," Jennifer said.

"It's not just an idea. I know what we're dealing with."

Jennifer looked at him. Livingston's features were grave,

his jaw set in determination. The outer fringes of the hurricane were rapidly gaining on them, and Livingston was struggling to keep the Humvee on a straight course. The driving wind and rain buffeted the massive vehicle. Jennifer saw the speedometer needle creep up to sixty. The high beams were on, but even those weren't much help in seeing what the massive winds were blowing onto the highway. Twice Livingston had to swerve around chunks of debris—signs blown off overhead ramps, tree limbs. At the speed Hurricane Gary was approaching, the worst of the storm would probably be hitting within the next three hours.

"You must, since you knew where to look for me," Jennifer said.

"Thank God you got to us in time," Richard said from the back seat. He looked under the weather, tired, worried. "Those things would have gotten in if you hadn't—"

"We don't have much time," Livingston said, cutting Richard off. "So pardon me if I seem rude or disinterested in your ordeal. We've all been through a lot tonight."

"Yes," Richard agreed. "I suppose we have."

"How much do the two of you know about Homarus Tyrannous?"

"Not much," Jennifer admitted. "Just what's publicly known from the fossil record."

"Tell me about your work on invasive species," Livingston said. "Did it include any of your work on Homarus Tyrannous?"

Normally Jennifer would have hesitated before freely divulging such information, but Livingston had obviously done his homework. She sighed. "I've had an interest in invasive species for the past few years. Some of my research led me to what happened in Phillipsport. Naturally, that led me to the paleontological record and when I read about Dr. Ian Sinclair's findings I was astonished. I started drawing comparisons between Homarus Tyrannous and other specimens, most of them previously thought extinct. It was just a pet project, nothing I had the money to pursue seriously."

"I'm sorry to say, I originally thought she was off her rocker," Richard said from the back of the Humvee. "Especially when I peeked at her research material."

"When I saw what was happening today it brought everything back," Jennifer continued. "It made everything I'd studied official ... made it seem that all that time wasn't wasted. And when I was observing what was going on today, I came to the realization that the creatures we saw aren't being pushed onto shore from the hurricane. They're being driven out. Their movement is far more invasive than simply being driven out of the ocean from a hurricane."

"And that's what I've been wondering," Richard said. He wiped water from his forehead. After all this time, he was still wearing his white lab coat. It was bloodstained and torn. His glasses sat crooked on his face. "What the hell could be chasing them?"

There was silence for a moment. Jennifer knew that Colonel Livingston was silently agreeing with her hypothesis. After all, he'd told her he'd been in Phillipsport. He'd seen what happened there, had confirmed to her the reason why the military swooped in at the Aquarium to pluck them out was not to rescue them per se, but to consult with a leading scientific expert. Lucky she'd been that leading scientific expert, or she and Richard would be dead now. "They're being hunted by a species I've seen before," Colonel Livingston said. "Something that doesn't exist anywhere in the paleontological record."

"These things came ashore in Phillipsport too, right?" Jennifer asked.

Livingston nodded. "Yes."

"What are they?" Richard asked from the back seat. "For God's sake, Colonel, they can't be anything worse than what we've already seen?"

"They're far worse," Livingston said. He kept his gaze on the road, trying to pay attention as the memories from that last battle in Phillipsport flashed in his mind. "But that isn't what has me worried."

Jennifer watched Colonel Livingston. She noted the grave features, the look of fear in his eyes. This was a man who'd been through hell and lived to tell about it and his expression told her that something worse was in store. Jennifer found her voice. "So … what has you worried?"

"You're correct in saying that the storm isn't what's driving the Clickers up," Livingston said. There was a flash of sudden lightning, and for a moment 83 was lit up and Jennifer could see nothing but sheets of water pouring out of the sky. It was like God had a giant bucket of water and was pouring it endlessly down on the world. "Hurricane Gary will have something to do with washing some of them ashore and driving some up various rivers. But if you remember, they were beaching themselves in Jersey hours before Gary even shifted north. That didn't happen in Phillipsport."

Jennifer knew very little about Phillipsport, just what she'd learned from the few cryptozoology websites she'd visited. Obviously there had to be more than what the conspiracy theorists had postulated. "Yeah, I remember that. So what the hell is driving them up then, if not the hurricane? They're being hunted by something, is my guess."

"Your guess is one hundred percent correct," Livingston said. He took his eyes off the road long enough to catch her gaze, then turned back to the road. "They're being hunted by what I can only describe as Dark Ones."

"Dark Ones?" Richard asked. There was just the tiniest hint of disbelief in his voice. Jennifer wanted to smack him for it.

"Dark Ones," Livingston acknowledged. "That's what one of the survivors of Phillipsport called them."

"Rick Sychek?" Jennifer asked.

"Yep."

"And there was another one, too … Melissa something."

"That is correct."

"They're still alive?"

Livingston sidestepped the question. "I saw these things myself," he said. "And I want you two to listen to me very carefully. These things are going to be coming ashore any minute now, and when they do it is going to be utter fucking chaos."

"Tell me everything you know," Jennifer urged.

And when he did, she almost wished he hadn't.

Shrewsbury, PA
10:59 PM

Surprisingly, Rick remained calm as they drove down the lonely road running parallel to a creek that, according to his captor, fed into the Susquehanna River. Tim remained in the back seat, gun trained on him the entire time they were traveling. It was getting harder to see through the driving rain, and Rick realized with sinking dread that Hurricane Gary was going to hit them dead center. He'd tried to think of a thousand different ways to try to convince his kidnapper that driving into the heart of the storm was a bad idea, but each time Tim told him to shut up and keep driving. Rick remained silent the last ten minutes of the drive, his mind racing. They'd been slowly making their way south towards Maryland and the storm was growing stronger. Even worse than that was the scattered *click-click* of the Clickers; Rick pointed out the sound to Tim thirty minutes ago. "Fuck," Tim had said. "They're that big?"

"Yeah," Rick had said. He was leaning forward over the steering wheel, peering through his glasses out the windshield, trying to see the road.

"Goddamn."

"They're obviously being washed up the river," Rick said. He could feel himself beginning to panic now, all the bad memories from Phillipsport coming back.

"They won't find us at this B&B," Tim assured him. "It's in the woods, away from the river. We'll be safe."

Rick had been thinking about that over the past thirty minutes now as they reached an intersection. Tim told him to turn left. Rick turned, heading down another narrow back road. What Tim said bothered him. He'd told Rick almost two hours ago that he just wanted to ride the storm out, that once Rick dropped him off he'd let him go. But when he said that they'd be safe there, he was speaking plural. We'll be safe. Not he'd be safe, but we. Plural. Not singular. As in, the two of them were holing up at the B&B. As in, Tim had no intention of letting Rick go.

Rick's overactive imagination was what kept him from thinking about what was outside: the nearby river, the Clickers, the approaching Dark Ones. And what he was thinking was that Tim had something else on his mind. There was the possibility that what Tim said back there was a slip of the tongue, that he was now thinking of them as fellow Hurricane Gary survivors, but Rick didn't think that was the case. Still, he couldn't slip up now, couldn't show Tim he was nervous. He had to be calm and get Tim to the B&B, and then get the hell away from him when the chance presented itself.

Tim scooted up in the backseat. "We're almost there," he said.

Rick slowed down a bit, trying to see through the wind-blown rain.

A moment later the headlights of the car picked out a structure set back behind some trees. Tim motioned with the gun. "Turn here."

Rick made a right turn down a narrow driveway and the car's tires crunched wet gravel. He coasted down the driveway, and then they were suddenly in front of the building.

The bed and breakfast was an old Victorian house. With no lights on, the place looked like a haunted mansion. Rick didn't see any cars around. Tim had said earlier that it was closed down.

"Come on," Tim said. He had the gun pointed at the back of Rick's head again. "Let's go. Open the door and get out."

"Okay." Rick opened the door and stepped out. He was immediately soaked again by the rain.

Tim managed to get out of the back seat at the same time. Rick heard him hiss with pain. Rick shut the driver's side door. Tim was behind him, prodding him forward with the barrel of the gun. "Let's get inside."

Rick marched up the steps and a moment later they were on the porch. Tim tried the front door and found it locked. He pointed the gun at the doorknob and Rick winced as the shot cracked over the howling wind. The lock snapped and Tim barked, "Come on, get in, get in!"

Rick shoved his way through the door with Tim behind

him, and then they were inside the house.

In the dark.

Rick felt Tim behind him, panting as he closed the door behind them. "Hurricane's probably almost here. Baltimore ain't too far away, so we're still gonna get it pretty bad. We should probably head upstairs. River's maybe a mile or so away, and if there's a surge who knows how high the water will get."

"Yeah," Rick said. His throat was dry.

"Come on." Rick felt the barrel of the gun at his back, urging him forward. Rick took a step. He couldn't see shit, but his vision was slowly adjusting to the darkness. The drapes over the windows were drawn back, and what little light that came in from outside made the interior less dark. Rick could barely make out a staircase in front of them. "Upstairs," Tim said. "Let's go."

They made their way slowly up the stairs. Tim held onto Rick's arm. The Asian man was clearly in pain, but he was managing it well. Rick was trying not to be too scared; being close to the river was hard, and knowing the Clickers were out there was absolutely terrifying. Somehow, he was riding this out well. "You've stayed here before?" Rick asked.

"Yeah," Tim said.

"Upstairs?"

"Uh huh."

They reached the second-floor landing. "Down this hall," Tim said, steering Rick left.

Rick started heading down the hall, feeling his way through the darkness. The house was obviously well-taken care of. Rick moved down the hall slowly, making sure Tim was being guided towards his destination and paying heed to the barrel of that gun on his back. "Maybe once we get you in a room I'll look around for a flashlight, see how bad you're hurt."

"Here," Tim said, pulling on Rick's arm. "Stop."

Rick stopped. He heard Tim's palm tap on what sounded like a door, then felt movement and cooler air. The door to a room had just opened. "This way," Tim said. He steered Rick toward the dark room and urged him forward.

Rick's heart began to trip-hammer in his chest. "Listen man,

I don't think I should—"

"Just shut up and get inside!" Tim was right behind him, practically pressed against him. Rick could feel the man's breath on his ear.

Rick felt his way inside and all of a sudden he was more frightened than he'd ever felt in his life.

Tim was sporting a huge erection through his slacks. Rick felt it brush against the seat of his jeans briefly.

Outside, the winds howled.

Hunt Valley, MD
11:10 PM

"So where are we going again?" Richard asked.

"The Peachbottom Nuclear Plant," Livingston said. "It's right on the Susquehanna River, on the border between Pennsylvania and Maryland. In fact, some of the facility is on each side. Makes state regulations a big mess and causes a lot of headaches for the Nuclear Regulatory Commission."

"And tell me why you think that's a good idea?" Richard sounded sarcastic. Jennifer wanted to smack him again.

If Livingston detected Richard's sarcastic tone, he didn't show it. "Peachbottom is strong, secure, and sits very high up from the river. It's built to withstand a nuclear holocaust. A little Category Five hurricane like Gary should be no trouble."

Richard squawked. "Little?"

"Will we be able to get in?" Jennifer asked.

"With my credentials, yes," Livingston said. "I'm overseeing the current situation. They'll have no choice but to let us use the facility as a base of operations."

In the past thirty minutes they hadn't seen a single vehicle. When they passed Hunt Valley and got off the exit to head toward the river, Jennifer fought the urge to plead with Livingston to swing by her parents to pick them up. She hoped they were okay.

"What then?" Richard asked. "If these Clickers are being blown up the Susquehanna, won't we just have to—"

"I can get in contact with my units at Peachbottom. I

guarantee their power won't be out. Once I've made contact, I can have convoys dispatched when the storm begins to ease. I need to resume my command. I've got a mission to accomplish, and Peachbottom will not only keep us safe, it'll serve as a temporary base for me to direct my efforts in fighting these things. Plus, I'll have you two with me. Especially you, Dr. Wasco." Livingston glanced her way. "Your government needs you now."

"You sure about that? President Tyler sounded like he didn't want to even consider Homarus Tyrannous."

"President Tyler is a fucking idiot. Forget about him. And pardon my French."

"That didn't sound like French," Richard joked.

Jennifer suppressed a grin. It felt nice to be sharing a vehicle with a high-ranking member of the U.S. Military who shared her view of the Commander In Chief.

"Let's get to Peachbottom in one piece," Livingston continued. The wind buffeted the vehicle, making it shake slightly. "We've got another ten miles. We'll make it. Okay?"

Jennifer met Richard's eyes in the rearview mirror briefly. She saw the worry in them. Then she shifted to a more comfortable position in her seat. "Let's do it."

Shrewsbury, PA
11:23 PM

Rick finished dressing Tim's wound and sat back, surveying his handiwork. In the harsh light of the high-powered battery operated flashlight he'd found plugged into an electrical outlet, Tim's features looked strained, yet flushed. Rick was still high-strung, and he'd had to use all his will power to control the shakiness in his arms as he dressed Tim's injury, which was an ugly flesh wound in the thigh. He'd had to cut Tim's slacks away to get at it. Tim had watched with bated breath, still clutching the gun. Once again, Rick had performed well under duress.

Rick had been trying to tell himself for the past twenty minutes that what he'd felt had not been an erection as he worked at dressing Tim's wound. No sooner had he felt it,

Tim told him where to find the flashlight. "They keep battery-charged flashlights plugged in each room. There should be one directly in front of you at floor level, plugged into this wall." Sure enough, there was. Rick had unplugged it and turned it on. That's when he saw that Tim had directed them into a large room with a king-sized bed and a very large bureau. There was a large, antique-looking desk pushed against one wall and a loveseat at the foot of the bed. A bathroom was attached to this large room, and Tim had directed Rick into it for a first aid kit, which was in the medicine cabinet.

Tim had sat down on the bed, wounded left leg splayed out. In the glare of the flashlight, Rick got a better look at his captor now; he was probably ten years younger, stocky, his skin pale, most likely due to stress from his ordeal. His facial features suggested Chinese or Vietnamese descent. He'd held onto the gun, keeping it trained on Rick the entire time his wound was being tended to. Rick tried making conversation with Tim as he worked on the injury.

"So what happened to you?"

Tim shook his head. "You don't want to know. Everything turned to hell today. I didn't plan to shoot her, it … it just happened."

"Shoot who?"

"My ex-wife."

Rick tried to keep his voice calm and his expression neutral. "Got into an argument, huh?"

"I guess you could say that. Her new man, too."

"The other guy … he shoot you first?"

Tim didn't say anything for a moment. When Rick finished, he inspected his work. The wound was dressed and patched up good and tight.

"What happened was …" Tim said, wincing as he tried to bend his knee. "… it just shouldn't have happened. I didn't … things just didn't work out."

"I understand." Rick began replacing the first aid items, already deciding not to continue questioning Tim on the events that led him to be shot. If Tim wanted to tell him, he would. "You should probably lie down, get some rest."

Tim said nothing. He was sitting on the edge of the bed, slowly moving his wounded leg. In the glare of the flashlight, he could see the wound wasn't as bad as he'd originally thought it was. It appeared the bullet had put a deep graze in the meat of his left thigh. The wound hadn't looked that deep, and Rick cleaned it as best as he could with the alcohol he found in the medicine cabinet. Tim had gritted his teeth through the pain, and then it was done. Even with a graze like this, his leg was going to be stiff.

Rick closed the first aid kit and stood up. "I'm gonna go put this back."

Tim raised the gun. "No. Put it down."

Don't let him see you're afraid! Rick put the first aid kit down on the floor. "Okay, fine. I'll leave it here."

Tim scooted back on the bed. He motioned to Rick with the gun. "Get in."

Rick felt his stomach drop down an elevator shaft. "What?"

"Get on the bed!"

There was something different about Tim now. His eyes were dark, his features more menacing.

"Look, man, I brought you here, you said you'd let me go when we got here. We're cool, okay? I'm just gonna—"

The sound of a shell being loaded in the gun's chamber was loud, even amid the fierce storm outside. Tim's posture was more direct; his once pained features now taking on an element of cunning and evil. "I said, get in the fucking bed!"

Rick began moving toward the bed, his mind screaming no while his body obeyed the command. He was slowly easing himself into a sitting position when Tim barked another command. "No, no, wait … hold on! No! Stand up. Off!"

Rick got off the bed, confused and scared. Tim motioned with the gun, keeping the barrel trained on him. "Take off your jeans."

"Wh-what?" Fear overtook Rick, completely enveloping him.

"Get fucking undressed!" Tim screamed.

"Listen man, why do you want to—"

"Just shut up and get undressed before I fucking shoot you!"

Tim yelled again. His pale features were now slightly red with excitement. Rick saw with newfound horror that Tim had an erection again.

"Jesus, man!" Rick began to whimper.

Tim moved forward, grabbed Rick behind the neck with one hand and stuck the barrel of the gun beneath his jaw. His face was inches from Rick's. "You want to know why I shot my ex-wife? Here it is: I was just about to do her when her boyfriend came back. I had to shoot her to shut her up, and she was lying on the floor, bleeding and whining, and then that nitwit comes in. I had him for a moment, and I knocked him around a little bit. Fucking pussy started crying, so I thought, hey, why not fuck him first, and then I'll fuck the ex, you know? I'd just gotten his pants down and gotten all nice and hard for him when he pulled this fucking gun out of a bureau drawer by the bed. Can you fucking believe that? Fucker had a piece in the goddamn room! He shot me and I just pulled the trigger on him. Put all nine rounds into his sorry ass, and then I reloaded and finished off the ex. I didn't know how bad I was shot, so I got the hell out of there. That's when you came along."

Tim's hand bore down on a nerve in the back of Rick's neck. Rick was barely aware he was crying as Tim shoved the barrel of the gun into the hollow of his throat.

"I am going to get myself a piece of ass tonight, you got me? Now take off your fucking pants before I fucking shoot you!"

And trembling, trying hard to control his fear, Rick began to unbutton his jeans with shaky fingers.

Wrightsville, PA
11:30 PM

Tony and Vince eyed the bridge with apprehension. The hurricane had knocked down many trees, and a few minutes earlier they'd seen a barn roof lying smashed across the road. There was no telling what the winds would do to the concrete pylons beneath the bridge.

"I don't like it," Vince said. "Let's go back."

The Greek pounded on the trunk lid again, as if agreeing with his captors.

"We can't go back," Tony said. "That fucking storm is right on our ass. We cross this bridge and we're in Wrightsville. Cheri lives there. She's got a cellar. She'll put us up till the hurricane passes."

"Cheri? Is she the one what gave Tommy DiMazzio head on the pool table at the Broadway Café? Got them big, floppy pancake tits?"

"No. That was Sandy. Cheri dances down at the Foxy Lady."

"The one with the little girl that likes Winnie the Pooh?"

"Yeah." Tony nodded. "That's her."

"She seems nice. Her kid is cute. Made me sing songs to her once." Chewing his lip, Tony edged the car forward. A sudden gust of wind slammed into the driver's side like a freight train and pushed them into the ditch. Fighting the wheel, Tony got them back onto the road.

"Gonna have to gun it if we want to make it across," Vince advised. "Go slow on that bridge and the wind will pick us right up. We got a need for speed."

Tony hated to admit it, but his overweight friend was right. He floored the accelerator and the tires spun on the rain-slicked pavement. The car shot forward. In the back, the Greek let out a muffled, frightened squawk. Tony's lips moved in silent prayer.

As they flew across the bridge, he risked a quick glance down. The river churned below them, the foaming waters surging over the banks and flooding the surrounding countryside.

Vince screamed. Startled, Tony looked up in time to see the deer run out in front of them at the end of the bridge. A Clicker lumbered out of the woods in pursuit of the fleeing animal. He jerked the wheel reflexively, and the car spun out of control. They rammed the Clicker and their front end buckled. The creature's shell split open, splattering the windshield with gore. Then the car veered off the monster and spun again. Tony had enough time to shout at Vince to hang on, and then they slammed into the guardrail. The impact jarred them both. The airbags deployed with such force that Tony's cheek was burned. Vince bit through his bottom lip and blood filled his mouth.

Metal shrieked. Something groaned. And then, it was over as quickly as it had happened.

The car teetered on the edge of the bridge. Tony glanced in the back, looking for the briefcase. It wasn't in sight. Before he could find it, they heard the groaning sound again, and Tony realized that it was the twisted guardrail, buckling under their weight.

"Fuck." Vince pushed the passenger's side airbag out of the way and spat bright red. He wiped his mouth with the back of his sleeve. "Bit my lip."

Tony took a deep breath, trying to force himself not to panic. "You okay?" Vince asked.

"I'm fine," Tony said softly. "Vince, listen to me real carefully. Don't move. Don't even breathe heavy."

"We hit one of those crab things."

"I know. Did you hear me? I said don't fucking move."

Vince cocked his head. "Are my ears ringing, or do I hear a freight train?"

"That's the wind. Storm will be on us any minute now."

"Shit."

"Yeah."

Both men grew quiet. Vince mumbled the Lord's Prayer under his breath. Tony tried to stay calm.

"Look," Vince said, his tone changing to amazement. "Still got my Devil Dogs."

The big man undid his seatbelt and leaned forward to pluck the snack cake from the floor of the car. The vehicle groaned and slid another inch.

"Vince," Tony shouted, "I fucking said don't fucking move!"

"You ain't got to be mean, Tony."

Vince dropped the package and sat back in his seat, huffing petulantly. Tony sighed. They were in a bad position, and he wasn't sure what to do next. One sudden move and they'd splash into the river. If they didn't get out soon, the storm would push them off the bridge as well. But if they waited for help, their rescuers would find the heroin—and maybe the Greek, too. Or more of those crab things would show up. Tony closed his eyes.

"I need a fucking drink."

"We got a bottle of vodka in the glove compartment," Vince said.

Before Tony could holler at him, Vince leaned forward again.

Both men screamed as the car plummeted off the bridge and into the roaring waters below.

Magog Bunker
The White House
Washington, D.C.
11:35 PM

"Mr. President, Secretary Barker wants to—"

"Mr. President, your press secretary is—"

"—advisor says we—"

"—Mr. President—"

"—President—"

President Tyler had been holed up in his private prayer chamber since the press conference, and the Lord had assured him that they would all be delivered to safety. He'd been ignoring his staff's intercom communications and had prayed for them to surrender their will to God. It upset him that his staff, his key people who'd professed not only their alliance with him and his initiatives but their Christian faith, would fall away from Him so quickly. It troubled Tyler greatly. When Hurricane Gary was over, there were going to be changes made to his staff. Big sweeping changes. And their key constituencies were going to hear about their behavior. Oh yes, they would.

President Tyler had been on his knees in deep prayer, and now he rose to his feet. His joints creaked in protest. The intercom continued to squawk:

"—MSNBC is having a field day with this!"

"—the Prime Minister is very concerned. He's wondering if—"

"—the House Leader wants to call a special session tomorrow morning to assess damages made to—"

"—Livingston requested that I re-deploy troops from border patrol to the East Coast and transfer troops in Afghanistan to the United States to take over the border patrol duties. They can assist efforts here and I'm going to go by his recommendation."

Tyler's head snapped toward the intercom. He was across the room in a second, finger stabbing the button. "Barker, was that you? Barker!"

The babble of voices stopped, like a multi-vehicle collision. Barker cleared his throat, then said, "Yes, Mr. President. That was me."

"What's this about pulling troops out of Afghanistan?"

"Colonel Livingston has requested we transfer troops from Afghanistan, Iran, Iraq, and elsewhere. He says we need more in the homeland to fight what will be a second wave of—"

"No! You are to keep our troops where they are! Why do you think—"

"Um, pardon me, Mr. President, but in the interests of our country—"

"I am acting on the best interests of our country! And I have been chosen by God to lead this country! You will not go against my orders again, do I make myself clear!"

"Mr. President, please—"

"Do I make myself clear?"

In the background. "My God, he's insane!" It sounded like Clark Arroyo, one of the secret service agents.

"Arroyo, was that you?"

Hushed silence. Then: "Yes, Mr. President."

"You dare call me crazy, Mr. Arroyo? You dare call a man of faith, crazy?"

"I'm sorry Mr. President."

"You better be sorry, Mr. Arroyo, because you're fired!"

Another voice cut in. Donald Miller, his Political Advisor. "Mr. President, things are changing very rapidly up here. With all due respect, when you're finished with your prayers we could really use your guidance."

That was more like it. Donald Miller was the architect of his political career. Miller worked the kind of miracles only a true man of the Lord could. He'd miraculously turned public opinion around during the election, back toward the Republican Party and, most important of all; he'd strengthened the Christian base. He'd even gotten a high majority of the Catholic vote.

Hearing Donald's voice cut through the din of confused voices strengthened his own faith; thank God Donald was still with him.

Tyler sighed. "Thank you, Donald. I'll be up in a moment."

The voices began again, swarming over each other: "Mr. President, FEMA is requesting—"

"Mr. President, as the Secretary of Defense I must insist that we heed Livingston's advice and—"

"Mr. President, the American people want to be assured this isn't going to be another Katrina—"

"Mr. President the Department of Agriculture wants the authority to examine the specimens captured and—"

"Stop! Enough!"

The voices stopped. President Tyler took another breath, collected his thoughts, and continued. "First things first and one at a time.

Barker, you still there?"

"Yes, Mr. President."

"I will not tolerate you disobeying me. If you do it again, I will see to it that you are removed from office. The only thing I want you to do is to make it clear to this Colonel Livingston, whoever he is, that he is not to override your authority in any way. We are not pulling troops out of Afghanistan or Iraq or anywhere. Our military will use the resources they have here and nothing more. God will see us through this disaster. Do you understand me?"

Silence.

"Do you understand me?" More forceful now.

"Yes, Mr. President." Barker sounded defeated.

"Good. Regarding the Department of Agriculture, I want my speechwriter to prepare a statement from me. Donald, you there?"

"Right here, Mr. President."

"Get a hold of Eric as soon as possible. I understand communications are probably down right now, but get to him as soon as you can. Have him prepare a speech stating that the American people are not to trust anything scientists are saying about these so-called creatures."

Audible gasps. Among them, Clark Arroyo's voice. "Jesus, he really is a fucking whacko."

"Are there any other secret service agents in the room?" Tyler asked. The more he listened to Arroyo, the more annoyed he was getting with the heathen.

"Right here, sir. Carl Johnson."

"Anybody else?"

Another voice, more timid. "Here. Ken Bacon."

"Bacon and Johnson, I'd like you to disarm Arroyo and escort him out the building."

More sputters of protest. Ken Bacon's voice became shocked. "But Mr. President ... we ... we can't just escort him out the building! There's a hurricane—"

Clark Arroyo, in a tone of anger and defiance. "Hey, fuck you Jeff, I fucking quit!"

And at the sound of the dreaded eff word, Tyler became livid. He slammed both fists into the wall near the intercom. "Don't you speak to me like that again!"

Amid the excited babble, Barker's and Miller's voices urging everybody to "be calm" and "please, settle down," was Clark Arroyo's angry, defiant voice. "Fuck you, you fucking piece of shit, fuck you!"

The intensity of the voices escalated, and now it sounded like there was a struggle going on. Agent Bacon muttered, "Come on man, calm down," and Barker was saying, "Just get him out of here, and get him the hell out of this goddamn room now!" Arroyo yelled, "Get your fucking hands off me, motherfuckers!" A panicked scream—it sounded like Laura Ashcroft, the Federal Prosecutor. The struggle grew more frenzied briefly and then the more angry voices began receding; it sounded like Arroyo was being led away, still yelling and cursing. Tyler jabbed at the intercom button again. "Barker! Barker! Are you there?"

Barker, flustered. "Right here, Mr. President. Special Agent Arroyo is being escorted out."

"Don't you dare take the Lord's name in vain in my presence again. Do you understand me?"

"Yes sir, Mr. President."

"Is Arroyo gone?"

The sounds of the struggle had now ceased. Tyler could make out a few quiet murmurs, probably of relief, in the background. Then, Donald Miller's voice came through strong and clear, confident. "Agent Arroyo has been escorted out of the room, Mr. President. I will see to it that he is relieved of his duties."

"I want him out of this building now!" Tyler yelled. "Do you understand me?"

"Yes, Mr. President," Donald said. "It will be taken care of."

"Good." He closed his eyes, willing himself to calm down. It always unnerved him whenever he heard somebody so flippantly toss curse words around and mock the Lord, especially with that much anger. Tyler realized that a large portion of his fellow Americans wouldn't agree with him on this but if he had his way, the entire country would be run by Biblical law and heathens like Special Agent Clark Arroyo would be executed by stoning—according to the Old Testament—for the kind of crimes he'd just committed. Tyler prayed for the tide to turn for the United States to be run by Biblical law; it was a major reason why he'd run for President in the first place. Very few were aware of his vision, of his yearning to establish Biblical law as the law of the land, and the overwhelming majority of his staff had no clue. Donald Miller was the only one within earshot who was of the select minority who knew of Tyler's full plans. "I apologize to all of you for blowing up," he said. "I realize I'm under stress. I didn't handle that well. I'm sorry."

There were calm murmurs of acknowledgement. Tyler sighed, feeling better. Keep it up; keep playing them as you've been doing all along. "And now to get back to what we were talking about. The speech I want prepared should address that I do not believe the scientists who are now going on record as saying that these creatures are a previously-thought extinct species, that it is believed they died out millions of years ago. My Christian base will understand where I am coming from, but the rest of the country will obviously be upset. I'm sure the ACLU will scream for my head over it. But what I want Eric to write is that the scientists making these statements are not government scientists. I doubt if any of them have even examined specimens yet. Is that true, Miller?"

"That is correct, Mr. President. We've received no word yet on any testing from the private sector or from government-funded labs."

"Then time is of the essence," Tyler said. "I want Eric to write this as quickly as possible. I want it on record that these scientists haven't examined specimens, that they are basing their opinions on hearsay, and that we won't know anything until actual specimens are accounted for and studied. In the meantime, they are to ride this storm out to the best of their abilities."

"How about if I write the speech for you, Mr. President?" Donald Miller asked.

Tyler smiled. Donald was on his wavelength. God praise the man! "Even better, Donald. Even better."

"Mr. President, if I might make one observation." Barker sounded like he was getting his confidence back.

"This isn't about the troop situation again, is it Barker?"

"No, it isn't."

"Good. What is it?"

"Colonel Livingston submitted a report to the Joint Chiefs of Staff over ten years ago following a similar incident. Remember Hurricane Floyd? 1994?"

"Vaguely, and your point?"

"Here's the short version. New England got hit with a Category Five Hurricane that formed late in the season. One of the hardest hit areas was the coast of Maine. One of the towns there, Phillipsport, was basically wiped off the map. In addition to the National Guard, the Army was called in to provide assistance at various spots where the hurricane hit. Livingston wound up in Phillipsport and witnessed what we're seeing now with the Clickers."

"The what?"

"The creatures we're seeing on TV, Mr. President."

"That's what they're called?"

"That's what he called them, Mr. President."

"Is there a point to this, Barker?"

"The point is, Livingston arrived as the second onslaught was receding. He personally saw them, and he claims over a dozen of his convoy unit witnessed them. Only two people survived Phillipsport. They provided detailed descriptions on what really happened and it dovetails with what is happening now, only what we're seeing is on a much grander scale. They say that—"

"Hold on, hold on, what are you talking about? What is this about a second onslaught? What the heck are you talking about?"

Barker fell silent. For a minute, Tyler wasn't sure if the Secretary of Defense was going to continue. "The second onslaught was a race of creatures more vicious than what we're seeing now. He said they were reptilian, that they walked upright, that—"

"Oh my God, they've got you brainwashed with this evolution malarkey that these things are dinosaurs!" Tyler couldn't believe what he was hearing. It was absurd, and he had to stop it now.

"Please let me finish—"

"Enough! I don't want to hear any more of this drivel!"

Barker was insistent. "This is all in Livingston's report that he submitted to—"

"Why haven't I heard about this until now?"

Barker stopped. There were quiet murmurs in the background. "His report is marked classified, sir," Barker said.

"Is Livingston a Democrat, Mr. Barker?"

"Uh … I … I … I don't know, Mr. President." Barker sounded flustered.

Donald Miller came to the rescue. "Colonel Augustus Livingston is a registered Republican, Mr. President."

Tyler snorted in disbelief. He shook his head. He had to get things moving. "Enough of this about Livingston. I don't care what's in his report, and I wasn't made aware of it. Nobody at the Pentagon has called, have they, Miller?"

"Not that I'm aware of, Mr. President."

"Then we're going to go as planned. Miller, get my speech ready. I want to go before the cameras in fifteen minutes. As for the rest of you, you are not to speak a word of what just went on to anybody. Do you understand?"

Murmurs of agreement and acknowledgement sounded.

"Barker, you are still under my command. You will override anything Livingston says, or anything any of our other military advisors have to say. What is happening is a test. God is testing our faith as a nation. Dinosaurs are not going to attack this country because there are no such things as—"

"I didn't say these things were dinosaurs—"

"Do not interrupt me, Barker! These Darwin-polluted scientists think these crab-things used to be extinct, that they used to live millions of years ago and you and I both know that these same deluded fools believe dinosaurs lived back then. You and I know that is impossible, right?"

"Yes, Mr. President." The tone of Barker's voice suggested to Tyler that the Secretary of Defense wasn't so sure. *My God, have those godless evolutionists gotten to Barker, too? Barker, who was endorsed by the Christian Coalition?*

"If Livingston wants to live in his little fantasy world, more power to him. He just isn't going to give orders based on this fantasy on my watch. Understood?"

"Yes, Mr. President."

"As far as these so-called reptilian-things, they are obviously the product of more ... of more ... oh Lord forgive me for saying this ... they're the product of bullshit, okay? I want to know more about this Livingston character. Miller, when you're finished with my speech, get me everything you can on Livingston. I want to know everything about him, up to and including what he had for dinner last night."

"Right away, Mr. President."

"You're all dismissed. Remember, not a word about this to anybody. And is Agent Bacon back yet?"

Bacon: "Here, Mr. President."

"You stay here. I'm going to finish my prayers and then I will be right up."

Tyler sighed as he heard the shuffling sounds of footsteps retreating. A moment later there was silence.

He turned off the communications button, got down on his knees, closed his eyes and began to pray. He prayed for strength, for guidance, for wisdom. It was a quick prayer, direct and to the point, and when he was finished he was filled with a sense of righteousness. He was doing good. He was steering his flock in the right direction. Some were protesting, and others were violently hostile like Arroyo. Those people would be dealt with. For now, Tyler felt that the Lord had things in control. He would see them through this. All they had to do, as a nation, as a government, was to put their faith and trust in Him.

He sighed and rose to his feet. And he would have to watch Barker a little more closely. No question about it.

Now feeling calm and confident, President Tyler exited Magog and headed upstairs ready to take the reins for the Lord.

11

Rick had never received a blowjob from a guy before, and he kept his eyes closed the entire time Tim went down on him. Tim kept the barrel of the gun pointed at Rick's chest. Rick was so scared his penis wanted to retreat into his body rather than get hard. He shuddered.

Tim sat on the edge of the bed, Rick standing in front of him, jeans pooled around his ankles. Outside, the wind was howling and the rain sounded like buckets of water were being dumped on the house. Through it all, Tim continued to work his penis, trying to get Rick hard.

Rick had gotten his pants down with shaky hands and had been somewhat relieved when Tim ordered him to step forward. He'd gotten right down to business, keeping the gun trained on him the whole time, only pausing long enough to say, "I'm gonna get you all hot and worked up first, then I'll be hard and then your ass is mine!"

Rick had trembled and fidgeted the entire time Tim sucked him off. He wasn't gay, and he didn't consider himself homophobic at all. He'd had gay friends for as long as he could remember and never felt uncomfortable around them. What he was feeling now was violation, plain and simple. It was unwanted sexual contact and that constituted rape, and therefore Rick was nervous, scared, and angry. But with a gun pointed at his chest, he was terrified to do anything to defend himself.

"Fucker, get hard!" Tim glared at him menacingly. "I want you to have a hard on when I fuck you!"

"Oh man …" Rick begged. "Please …"

Tim moved the barrel of the gun into the hollow of Rick's throat. With his other hand he began stroking Rick's shriveled dick. "Get hard!"

And for five long minutes Rick was frozen as Tim continued to suck his shriveled penis, the barrel of the gun slowly descending down his throat to his chest. The wind continued to howl outside. Rick forced himself to calm down. There's got to be some way to calm this guy down. Got to be some way to distract him, get him to let down his guard. Got to be—

He was looking around the room, trying to think about how to get himself out of this when he saw the flashlight.

It was sitting on its side on the bureau beside the bed. It was still turned on, its beam the only source of light in the room. Rick saw it and began to think about Ashley Jacobs, his ex-girlfriend and mother of his daughter, Samantha. He thought about how much he missed Ashley, how he still loved her and wished he hadn't screwed things up between them. And then he began to think that if there would be one more thing he could do before he was raped and murdered by Tim, it would be to make love to Ashley just one last time. He began to think erotic thoughts of Ashley; how her mouth felt on him, how her lips felt when he kissed them; the feel of her breasts, the arch of her back, the skin at the hollow of her throat when he kissed her there. He thought those things and felt a stirring in his groin. Tim noisily continued to suck him, grunting in pleasure. Rick watched him, the plan suddenly dawning on him as he continued to think about making love to Ashley, letting himself get hard.

He reached out with his left hand toward the flashlight.

"Oh man," Tim said, pausing for breath. In his lust, Tim had lowered the gun; the barrel was now pointing toward the wall, the weapon dangling from his fingers. "I knew you could do it. Yeah, get it hard for me, baby." Tim dived back in.

Rick's body was a bundle of tension. Suddenly he wasn't afraid anymore. He knew exactly what he was going to do.

Tim stopped and moved back on the bed. The hand holding

the gun was planted on the bed, the weapon lying flat on the mattress. "Get on the bed!" Tim commanded.

There was a loud thump on the wall.

The noise startled both of them, but Rick saw the window of opportunity and went for it. Tim had jumped slightly from the sound, his gaze directed at the wall. "What was that?"

Rick grabbed the flashlight with his left hand and, just as Tim turned toward him again, he brought the front end down into his face.

The blow rocked Tim's head back and he fell on the bed screaming.

Rick swarmed over him and brought the flashlight down on his face again.

And again.

… again …

The adrenaline was running so strongly he was barely aware of the flashlight breaking apart in his hand as he smashed it into Tim's face, or that he was yelling at the top of his lungs. "Motherfucker, I'm gonna kill you I'm gonna kill you gonna kill you!"

The sudden ferocity of his attack was more than enough to catch his would-be rapist and murderer off guard.

Rick had no idea when Tim was beaten into unconsciousness.

He didn't remember stumbling back from the bed to trip over his jeans, which were still pooled around his ankles. Didn't remember getting up and grabbing the dead lamp on the bureau, didn't remember bashing the heavy base of it into Tim's head.

The next thing he was aware of was suddenly being warm. His arms hurt and he realized he was holding the ruined remains of a lamp, that his arms and face were coated in something warm and wet and then he realized he'd beaten Tim's head into an unrecognizable pulp.

He dropped the lamp and stumbled away from the bed. He became entangled in his jeans again and he fell down on his bare rump. He was suddenly aware of the howling wind outside, of another thump hitting the side of the building.

Ohmygodijustkilledhimjesusfuckingchrist!

And then once again he received another adrenaline spurt. He was on his feet in a flash, pulling his jeans up and fastening them as he ran out of the room, crashing into the wall and fumbling for the doorway before he finally found it, his fear propelling him out, his brain telling him to slow down, slow the fuck down, it's dark in here! And then just as his legs obeyed the command, he felt himself tumbling down the stairs. He reached out and gripped the banister, which slowed his tumble somewhat. He rolled down half a dozen steps and came to rest with his back against the banister, his breath coming out in gasps.

Rick didn't pause to assess his injuries. Forcing himself to slow down, he descended the rest of the staircase and stumbled blindly in the dark toward where he thought the front door was. He plunged forward like a blind man; arms outstretched, and felt his way around walls and through doorways until he reached the front door. He gripped the doorknob and opened the door; he was immediately blown back by the strong wind. At least it wasn't as dark outside as it was in the house. He struggled out to the porch, hunched over against the driving wind and rain. The last time he heard a weather report was well over an hour ago. Hurricane Gary was expected to make landfall in Baltimore sometime around 1:00 AM. What time was it now? Rick had no idea. He thought Tim had abducted him around 9:00, maybe 9:30, and it seemed like it had taken almost two hours to make the drive down to Shrewsbury. He couldn't have been inside the Bed and Breakfast for more than forty minutes. Which meant it was probably close to midnight and he had an hour or so to reach shelter before Hurricane Gary hit.

He staggered down the steps, the wind carrying him along. The rain drenched him and for once it was a welcome relief; it washed Tim's blood off him. Rick ran to the car and got in, slamming the driver's side door. He sat hunched over the steering wheel for a moment, trying to collect his bearings.

Oh my God, I made it, but I just killed somebody, but I made it, I made it, I'm fucking alive!

He had to get out of here. No way was he staying at this Bed and Breakfast, not with Tim's corpse upstairs. Fuck that.

Rick reached into his soggy jeans and pulled out the keys to the rental car. He got the vehicle started, turned on the headlights and began making his way back down the driveway.

There was another thump that sounded amid the wind and Rick caught a glimpse of what it was. The rising winds of Hurricane Gary had blown something against the side of the house. He recognized it right away; it was the size of a dog, and had a red shell. He'd seen them in his mind ever since Phillipsport.

He caught the barest glimpse of the latest Clicker as it scuttled along the ground at the base of the Bed and Breakfast and just seeing it, realizing how close he'd come to possibly running into one of those things as he'd rushed to his car, made him accelerate down the driveway.

The wind buffeted the car around, rocking it on its shock absorbers. He'd never driven in such a strong storm before. It scared him to think that this was only the outer fringes of Hurricane Gary, that the inner circle of the storm was probably only fifty miles away and rapidly gaining. Those winds would be strong enough to blow this car into a tree. He had to reach shelter, and he had to do it quickly.

He made a left out of the driveway and drove as fast as the weather would permit. He had no idea which direction he was going in; he'd become completely turned around during his ordeal with Tim. Surely he would come across another building somewhere.

He drove through the heavy winds and rain and he didn't see a single vehicle.

All he saw were woods.

Rick felt his panic rise as he strained to see through the blinding sheets of rain. He could barely see five feet in front of him.

Where the hell am I?

He counted down the minutes as he drove. One minute … two … three …

The woods cleared away on either side of him but he still couldn't see for shit. A gust of wind rocked the car slightly. Rick gripped the steering wheel, fighting to keep the vehicle on the road.

... four minutes ... five ...

The wind seemed stronger here and it was a struggle to keep the car on the road. Rick didn't realize he was holding his breath until he exhaled, releasing some of the pent-up tension.

... six minutes ... seven ...

The wind appeared to die down slightly. Rick kept his grip on the steering wheel. He knew he had to come across some form of civilization soon. Shrewsbury was the last town in Pennsylvania; Tim had directed him down a back road that apparently ran parallel with the river. How far away was the Susquehanna? Rick had no way of telling. He was completely disoriented. At this point he would pull into a dilapidated gas station if he found one. He didn't want to be stuck in his car when it was picked up and tossed around like a tin can.

There was something ahead of him in the distance. Rick squinted, trying to make it out. It looked like a light.

Headlights.

Oh God, please let it be a cop or something, hell it can be anybody just as long as they aren't crazy!

And as Rick kept driving, fighting to keep his rental car on the road amid the high winds, the headlights drew closer. He reached for his high beams and flashed them. The vehicle ahead flashed its high beams. Rick breathed a sigh of relief.

The headlights grew larger. Rick slowed down. It wasn't until he was ten feet from the vehicle that he saw it was a military Humvee.

And it was leading an entire military convoy.

"Oh shit ..."

The White House
Washington, D.C.
11:55 PM

Clark Arroyo was hunkered in a corner of a public restroom on the fifth floor of the parking structure adjacent to the White House. Overhead Hurricane Gary passed northward. The storm's fury was relentless. Twice, Clark cringed as debris crashed into the parking structure.

The restroom was the only place Clark could find refuge in. After being relieved of his duties and surrendering his service weapon, he'd been escorted to the main entrance by his superior, Ken White, who'd come up from the command center in the West Wing. Ken had been diplomatic. "I'll put you up in a room in the East Wing," he'd said. "You'll be safe there for the night." The East Wing of the White House contained rooms where staff members could catch some sleep should they need to during times of crisis or, in many cases, during times when business kept them at the White House for long periods of time. Clark was fine with that; he was pissed off and afraid for his country, but he was okay with spending the night in one of the rooms because he knew he'd be safe. But then Secretary Barker had come in and demanded in no uncertain terms that Arroyo was to be escorted off the White House grounds. Now!

Ken White had protested. "But sir … there's a Hurricane outside!"

"President Tyler wants him removed now!" Secretary Barker had growled at him.

And that's how Clark Arroyo came to be here, in the parking structure trying to take cover from the Hurricane in the most secure spot of the structure he could find—the men's room. Ken had waited while Clark gathered his things and then he and Barker had escorted him to the door. Clark was sure if Barker hadn't been present, Ken would have spirited him away to the East Wing for the night. But no, that asshole had accompanied them to make sure Clark was physically out of the building.

Now he was here. Afraid for his life.

Clark still felt the sting of embarrassment as he remembered begging Ken White and Secretary Barker to stay indoors while the Hurricane was raging. The howling of the wind was great, and Clark had been afraid that the moment he stepped outside the wind would carry him away. "Are you out of your mind?" He'd raged at Barker. "Look at it out there! I'll get killed!"

And the look on Barker's face. There was something there that told Clark that the Secretary of Defense was acting on orders, that he was finally buckling down under orders from President Fuckwad himself. For the past year, Clark had secretly been monitoring Barker's behavior and it had looked like the Secretary of Defense was still trying to retain some of his sense of honor and duty. All of President Tyler's Cabinet members had been that way. They'd been gung ho the first month or two of the administration, then their spirits had started to lag, probably when they began to realize what a bona fide lunatic the guy was. Clark had felt the same way, but had kept a stiff upper lip. Part of him actually hoped he was imagining things, that the so-called liberal media was wrong about their assessment of President Tyler. Tyler's advisor though, Donald Miller … that guy was creepy as shit. So were some of the other key cabinet members. The Attorney General, the guy who ran the Department of Agriculture, a few others. They were religious zealots, and they were scarier than those nutty Scientology whackos Clark sometimes ran into in Florida when he was on vacation. Everybody else had been blindsided by these people, Barker included. And now that push was finally coming to shove, he was seeing who was going to fall in line and who wasn't. Clark was one of the guys who was refusing to toe the party line, hence his expulsion. Barker didn't want to wind up out on the street, cast aside like garbage, so he was swallowing his honor and pride and doing whatever Tyler told him to do, even if it went against his personal ethics.

Even if it meant harm to the country.

Clark had put up a struggle, so much so that Ken had to bodily shove him out the door. Clark had caught a glimpse of Ken's face behind the double glass doors when he did this, and Ken had looked ashamed and scared. He also looked like he was sorry he was doing this. Clark knew that if Ken had stood his ground he would have been thrown out too, stripped of his job immediately. Ken had more to lose than Clark, especially financially. Ken and his wife, Sarah, had just lost a civil suit brought on to them by the parents of a man who was killed in a car crash that involved their son, who'd been the driver. Their son, Robert White, was drunk when the accident occurred. He was now confined to a prison hospital; medical bills were piling up. Robert White had been underage when the accident occurred, in a vehicle registered to his parents. They'd had to mortgage their house to pay for legal representation in the civil suit. Ken had told Clark that they were going to sell the house and their cabin in the West Virginia mountains to help pay for the damages incurred in the suit. Ken had even talked about cashing out his 401k. They were losing everything they'd worked for, and Clark knew that Ken was merely trying to hold onto the only thing he could now—his employment, which was his financial lifeline.

Clark didn't blame Ken White. If he were in his superior's shoes, he probably would have done the same thing.

Clark had clung to the outer wall of the White House for a few minutes as the wind buffeted him around, the rain lashing his face. Then he'd staggered along the east side of the building toward the parking structure when he remembered he could get there via a pathway that was somewhat protected from the elements. He struggled against the wind and rain, most of it blocked off from a roof that covered the walkway that led to the parking structure and then he was finally safe.

He'd made it up to the fifth level where his car was, planning to hunker in the backseat but then he thought, suppose something happens and the car gets blown out and I fall five stories down? That had driven him out of the car to seek more secure shelter in the men's room, which was in the middle of the parking structure. Surely being surrounded by four solid concrete walls within a massive parking structure would provide some protection, wouldn't it?

Before he left his car, though, he'd retrieved a handgun he kept stashed beneath his driver's seat. It was a Sig Sauer 9mm with a full magazine. Three spare mags were stashed in the glove compartment. He took those, too.

Taking the weapon and mags with him had been done on pure instinct.

And now as he sat shivering in the men's room, thinking of his wife and daughters, hoping they were okay, he began to focus on President Tyler again and how dangerous a man he was, and he wondered for the first time ever in his life what it would be like to assassinate a high-ranking political figure.

Shrewsbury, PA
11:59 PM

Before Rick could run, a bright spotlight flashed towards him. He felt naked in the beam. As if the soldiers in the lead Humvee could see inside him, see everything about him. He felt like they knew his real name and identity, his fugitive status—and the fact that he'd just been raped. The wind ruffled his clothing and rain beat at his skin.

Rick put his hands up and sighed in defeat. He was tired. Tired of running. Tired of this life. And as the convoy ground to a halt, and a soldier stepped forward, he felt a strange sense of relief.

Hope they just shoot me right here on the spot, he thought.

"Rick?"

The speaker was hidden behind the spotlight. Rick couldn't see him, but the voice sounded familiar. But it couldn't be him ...

"My name is William," Rick said. "William Mark. I need ... help."

The soldier stepped around the spotlight and walked towards him. "Rick. It's me."

Rick's eyes widened.

"Colonel? Colonel Livingston?"

The Colonel responded but Rick couldn't understand him. He suddenly felt like he was hurtling down a long, narrow tunnel. Something roared in the background. His mouth went dry. It was hard to swallow. Hard to breath. His ears rang and his skin felt hot and prickly.

"Rick?" Colonel Livingston ran towards him. "Are you okay?"

"I ..."

The Colonel caught him as he passed out.

"Get a medic over here, now!"

The rain pelted them all. A few miles behind them, the storm unleashed its full fury. In the darkness beyond the edges of the highway, they heard a chilling sound.

CLICK-CLICK ... CLICK-CLICK ... CLICK-CLICK ...
CLICK-CLICK ...

"Oh Jesus," Richard gasped. "They're all around us."

Jennifer closed her eyes as the sounds got louder. As a result, she didn't see the first Clicker waddle out onto the highway's shoulder. The rest of the group was not so lucky. It was a massive beast, fifteen feet in circumference, with pincers the size of canoes. It smashed through the guardrail and rushed them. The rest of the creatures swarmed from the woods and charged. The soldiers opened fire and the battle began in earnest.

Deep inside the tree line and hidden from view, the real enemy watched with inhuman eyes.

Part Two:
The Next Wave

12

July 4th, 2006
Rural Virginia
12:30 AM

When it was all over, after the Clickers had moved on and Hurricane Gary had hurtled farther north towards Pennsylvania, the survivors came outside to survey the damage to their properties.

The Dark Ones were there to greet them.

Justin Ramsey had retired from NASA two years before. He and his wife, Winnie, had bought a little place out in the country; a "Gentlemen's Farm" was what their friends called it. He had a chicken house and two female goats (named Thelma and Louise) and next year he hoped to raise bunnies as well. When he and Winnie emerged from their root cellar, the first thing Justin noticed was that the old oak tree which had stood in the center of their yard was now uprooted and splintered. It lay on its side, and had gouged a huge trench in the dirt. But what made Justin gasp out loud was what the tree had fallen on. The massive trunk had crushed one of the crab monsters that had run amok during the storm. He and Winnie had heard reports about them on their battery-operated radio, but in truth, Justin had only half-believed it. The whole thing reminded him of Orson Welles infamous War of the Worlds broadcast, and he wondered if this could be the same thing. If it was, the joke was in bad taste.

Now, staring at the squashed crustacean, he knew better.

"Oh," Winnie groaned, "the tree! That's a shame. I wanted

you to fix up a tire swing for the grandkids."

The rain had turned into a light mist. It felt good on their skin.

"Could be worse," Justin said. "River could have flooded over the banks and run right into the cellar. Then where would we be? Good thing we've got this elevated yard and high banks. Bet our neighbors didn't fare as well."

"You don't think that crab thing is still alive, do you?"

"Yes," he gasped in mock fear. "It's going to get you!"

"Justin Ramsey, you stop it right now!"

"Sorry, hon." He smiled. "Don't worry. It's dead. See? Its guts are spilling out. Look how bad the tree cracked its shell."

Winnie's nose wrinkled in disgust.

"Looks like the house is okay," Justin said. "A few broken windows. I see some tiles are missing from the roof. Gutters are hanging off. But it's still standing."

"Just like us."

Silently, they reached out and clasped hands. Then they began to walk towards the dead Clicker. The stench was horrendous, a coagulating miasma of rotten fish and brine and blood.

"Wish we had a camera," Justin muttered.

Winnie's grip tightened around her husband's hand. Justin winced.

"Who's that over there?" Winnie pointed towards the chicken house. It was then that Justin heard frightened squawking from within the coop.

"Hey, are you okay," he called. "You need some help?"

The figure did not move. It was hidden in shadow, and Justin couldn't make out any features. Whoever it was, he was tall and beefy. The figure had a full two feet over Justin—maybe more—and probably close to one hundred pounds.

The frenzied cries of the chickens increased. Justin felt a surge of apprehension.

"Hey," he tried again, "you okay, buddy? Come on out."

This time the figure complied. Slowly, it walked into the moonlight. Winnie screamed. So did Justin. Because it wasn't a man at all. It was a lizard, walking erect on two legs, its green body covered with scales, its hands clawed, its chest a mass of muscle, and its eyes—the eyes were the worst; yellow and unblinking and intelligent. Justin had no doubt. There was a deep, malevolent intelligence in those eyes.

The door to the chicken house swung wide, the rusty hinges creaking, and another lizard-man stepped out. Its face and chest was slick with blood and feathers. A dead rooster hung from one clawed hand. A long, forked tongue snaked from its mouth and licked the blood from its lips. It straightened its posture and rose to its full height. The creature was almost ten feet tall. Justin was reminded of Komodo dragons.

"Winnie, get back down in the root cellar!"

But even as they ran, the creatures fell upon them. The Dark Ones crossed the distance between them and their prey in a few quick strides. They seized the Ramsey's from behind and tore into them without mercy.

The flesh was flayed from Winnie's face. Justin's spine was ripped out, and the creature then whipped him with it as he collapsed.

First came the storm—and the Clickers. Now, there was something far worse. The Dark Ones proceeded up the river, which led to the seat of power according to their reconnaissance.

Justin and Winnie Ramsey were the first human casualties of the second wave.

They were not the last.

Peachbottom Nuclear Plant
12:35 AM

Moving Rick into the Humvee was easy—he'd fainted, and with the help of several enlisted men, as well as Richard Linnenberg, Colonel Livingston had gotten him into the back of the vehicle. They were only three miles away from Peachbottom when they came across him, and Rick remained unconscious until they were safe inside.

Escaping the storm had been fairly easy, too—if somewhat harrowing. They just needed to keep moving and stay ahead of the worst of it. Escaping the Clickers was a little tougher, but they'd accomplished that as well. They'd lost several more men during the battle, but the creatures could not stand against the flamethrowers and armor-piercing bullets. The Interstate was littered with dead crustaceans as the group sped away.

Gaining access to the plant was no problem. They'd called ahead, and the facility's supervisor knew they were coming. Livingston flashed his identification at the armed guard who was stationed in the tiny security booth at the gates. The storm was gaining strength and right behind them.

So were the Clickers.

Livingston shouted at the guard, "Get inside! It's going to get worse!"

Havoc ensued. The guard who secured their entry met with his superiors, who appeared disgruntled at the arrival of the visitors despite the advance warning. They grumbled about military intervention and the proper chain of command. Livingston quickly met with the evening's shift supervisor and once again went through the rigmarole of identifying himself and explaining his mission. He could have pulled rank—or a gun—easily enough; could have been a real asshole about things, but he wanted cooperation from the Peachbottom staff. The shift supervisor had two armed guards with him; both appeared ready to draw their weapons at the drop of a command. The shift supervisor's name was Jeremiah Brown. He looked pretty young to have such an important, high clearance position. He also appeared scared.

"If you require additional verification, I will be perfectly willing to radio in to my superiors in D.C.," Livingston said. His First Lieutenant, a thirty-ish officer named Tranning, flanked his immediate left.

Jeremiah examined the identification. He was a tall, wiry, African-American man. "That won't be necessary. We've been monitoring the police and military frequencies all afternoon." He handed the papers back to Livingston. "It's a good thing you made it here."

"Listen carefully," Livingston said. "I know this place can withstand the hurricane, but the enemy was snapping at our heels as well. How prepared are you for an assault?"

Jeremiah smiled. "If they come by land, the security fence is electrified. All we have to do is turn it on—provided the storm doesn't damage it."

"Good. They don't like electricity. What about the river?"

"We have thick concrete buffers, plus the dams and turbines, and our security measures. I won't say its one-hundred percent foolproof, but unless they brought heavy explosives, we should be able to withstand them."

"Let's hope so." Livingston turned to one of his troops. "I want men spread out all over this place. Soon as the storm passes over, take up positions along the perimeter. Let us know as soon as they try to attack."

The young soldier snapped a salute. "Yes, sir."

"Why would they attack?" Jeremiah looked confused. "Wouldn't they just move off in search of easier prey?"

Livingston shook his head. "Not necessarily. They're unpredictable. That's what makes the ugly fuckers so hard to exterminate. The storm will slow them down, but believe me, they'll be here."

One of the guards spoke up. "You brought a wounded man in; was he attacked by one of those things?"

"No, he just fainted. We ran into him a mile or two from your facility." Livingston said. "Some of my men have minor injuries as well. Is there someplace secluded where they can rest?"

Jeremiah directed one of his guards—his name was Bernie Coverdale—to assist Livingston. Within minutes, Bernie had directed Livingston's group to a lounge-like area deep in the bowels of the Plant. Rick was beginning to regain consciousness. He'd been kept separate from the rest of the wounded soldiers. Jennifer Wasco had cleaned the blood that stained his hands and, as Richard helped him up, she leaned close to Livingston. "He's not injured," she whispered. "And he won't tell me where the blood came from."

Livingston nodded. Jennifer was barely able to contain her excitement that this was Rick Sychek. He'd told her and Richard to keep it to themselves.

Once in the lounge, Rick began coming out of it. Livingston

noted the stark change in his physical appearance since the last time he saw him. Twelve years ago Rick had been a good-looking, somewhat muscular man. The man sitting before him on the lounge sofa looked twenty years older, was rail thin, almost sickly-looking. The only giveaway was his eyes. Livingston would never forget Rick's haunted, brown eyes.

Those eyes stared back at him now afraid. "What's going to happen to me?"

"Nothing," Colonel Livingston said. He nodded at Jennifer and Richard. "I need to be alone with him for a moment."

"Sure." Jennifer said. She and Richard left the room.

When they were gone, Colonel Livingston sat down on the coffee table by the sofa. His arthritic knees cracked and he grimaced slightly. "Okay, now that the formalities are out of the way—"

"Listen, man," Rick said, and he started babbling immediately. "I'm not who you think I am. I'm only—"

"I know, I know," Livingston said, his voice soothing. "You're William Mark. Who else could you be?"

Rick stopped babbling. He appeared momentarily stunned. "Um … I don't know."

"As far as I'm concerned, you're William Mark." Livingston leaned forward. "Just like you told us when we picked you up. But it's good to see you in any case.

Rick managed a weak smile. "Despite everything, it's good to see you too, Colonel."

"How you feeling?"

"Oh … Okay … I guess."

"You had blood on your hands." Livingston motioned to his shirt. "There's blood on your shirt. You hurt anywhere?"

"No." Livingston could tell Rick was evading his questions. Something happened to him that he didn't want to talk about.

"The girl who was in here, the doctor—she won't tell anyone who you are. She and her boss are the only ones who know. Nobody else knows you're here."

Rick licked his lips. "That's good."

"Nobody knows you're here," Livingston repeated.

"I know."

"Nobody knows you're here," Livingston stressed it a third time. "Do you understand?"

Rick looked at him. Their eyes locked briefly. Rick understood.

He looked down at the floor, nodded. "Yeah, I understand."

"Good. Nobody will find out, either."

Rick looked back at Livingston again. "Promise?" His voice was lowered, pleading.

"Yes."

Rick sighed. He seemed to relax. He slumped back on the sofa.

Livingston leaned forward. When he spoke, his voice was a whisper. "Have you seen any Dark Ones yet?"

Rick shook his head. "N ... no. No, not yet."

"Just Clickers?"

Rick nodded. "Yeah."

"Why are you out here?"

Rick sighed, his eyes flicking around the room. "God, it's a long story."

"Simplify it for me."

Rick's eyes darted around the room briefly, as if he were trying to find something hidden, then he began telling his story. He started by telling Livingston he was in Philadelphia because his mother had passed on. He skimmed on the details. He brought the story to a close by relating that he was trying to drive west but was forced off the highway in York, Pennsylvania and then was carjacked. "I had to defend myself," Rick said.

Livingston nodded. The blood was explained. He had no intention of finding out what happened to Rick's assailant. "Of all the things that could happen," Livingston said, shaking his head in astonishment. "This beats the cake. Carjacked and assaulted in the middle of a goddamned hurricane while those things are out there crawling all over the countryside."

"You said the woman's a doctor?" Rick asked. "What kind? And who's the guy?"

"Dr. Jennifer Wasco and Dr. Richard Linnenberg, scientists with the Baltimore Inner Harbor Aquarium. Wasco is an expert on invasive species." Livingston brought Rick up to date with his activities over the past twelve hours and when he was finished Rick looked less stressed, more relaxed.

"So they know everything?" Rick asked.

"Yes."

"Do they believe?"

"What do you mean?"

"In the Dark Ones."

Livingston thought about it for a moment. "Wasco does. I'm not sure about Linnenberg, although I wouldn't doubt it after what he's seen today."

"What are we going to do?"

Livingston rose to his feet. "We're safe here for now. Just waiting for the storm to blow over. Hopefully, our outer defenses won't be too badly damaged. We expect this area to be crawling with Clickers momentarily. Nothing we can do but wait—and make sure we're ready for them. Meanwhile, I need to establish a command center and plug back in, get briefed on the latest. I'm going to ask Dr. Wasco to prepare a report on the Clickers. Perhaps you can help. I could use your—"

Rick shook his head. "Uh uh, you said nobody would know who I am. If I talk about it with her and someone else overhears us, they'll find out who I am and—"

Livingston looked grave. "I'm going to be tied up directing operations. I need you, Rick."

Rick frowned. "My name's not—"

"Okay, okay, William." Livingston looked annoyed. "You have my solemn word that I will have you under protective custody. Dr. Wasco has been able to piece things together through research. She's not only a specialist in invasive species, she's taken a keen interest in Homarus Tyrannous and other species long thought extinct. She's a respected scientist and if we can get her on TV to positively identify these things, it will do a world of good. The goddamn President and his band of lunatics have been spinning this thing like crazy, in case you haven't noticed."

Rick sniggered. "No shit! They've been calling the Clickers 'local wildlife'."

"My point exactly. As far as I know, no reputable scientist

has examined them, nor do they have knowledge of them, so their best efforts are being downplayed by those fanatics at the White House. Jennifer is all we have in turning the tide here and she's going to need you." Livingston paused briefly. "Please."

Rick sighed. "Okay."

Livingston clapped Rick's shoulder. "Good. Thank you. Your country thanks you as well."

Rick sneered. "You'll understand if I don't feel too patriotic right now, Colonel."

Livingston rubbed his forehead. "You might be surprised. Our current administration is an abomination. They stand for everything I've ever fought against. But I'm too old to start a coup."

Rick got to his feet. Under the soft lighting of the lounge, he looked frail, weak. His long graying hair was damp. "I wish I could get a change of clothes."

"Let's see if we can get Mr. Brown to procure something for you," Livingston said.

Livingston led Rick out of the lounge and found Jeremiah, who was waiting at a guard station. "Any way we can get a change of clothes for Mr. Mark?" Livingston asked.

"That should be no problem," Jeremiah said. "Come this way."

Fifteen minutes later Rick was in a fresh change of clothes courtesy of the U.S. Government. Jeremiah had retrieved them from a stash of spare maintenance department uniforms. The blue coveralls were loose and billowy around him, but they would do. He cinched them around his waist with some bailing twine. Rick felt nervous as he was introduced to Dr. Richard Linnenberg and Dr. Jennifer Wasco, who were relaxing in the main command center of the plant. Livingston drew them both aside. "You have fifteen minutes for him to fill you in on his observations about what happened in Phillipsport," he told them. "Then I need you to prepare a quick statement. I'm going to arrange to have you give a statement to the press as soon as we can establish contact and gather them together. If the President and his cabinet refuse to get word out to people on the East Coast—word that can save them—then we'll do it."

Livingston could tell Jennifer was excited about meeting a firsthand witness to the Phillipsport tragedy, but she did a good job in keeping her enthusiasm subdued.

"Sure thing, Colonel. Thanks."

First Lieutenant Tranning approached. "Excuse me, Colonel."

"Yes, Tranning?"

"I contacted Washington to give them an edited status report on our position and Secretary Barker said that he must speak to you."

"Let's go deal with him, then."

He turned to Wasco and Linnenberg as he headed to the busy command center. "Go easy on him. He's had a rough night."

"We all have," Richard said.

When they reached the command center, Tranning picked up a secure phone line and dialed a number. He listened for a moment, and then handed the receiver to Livingston. A female voice said, "Please hold for Secretary Barker." Save for the static of television screens showing stations that had been knocked off the air due to the storm, the command center was quiet.

The other end of the line opened up and Barker came on. "Livingston? That you?"

"Yes, Barker."

"I'm sorry to have to do this, Colonel." Barker sounded embarrassed. "But I'm afraid I have to relieve you of your duties. You're—"

"What?" Colonel Livingston suddenly found it hard to breathe.

"—to return to Fort Detrick as soon as the hurricane is over. You will then be flown home immediately."

"Have you lost your fucking mind? We're at war, Mr. Secretary. What's the reason for this?" Livingston could barely contain his anger. He wanted to reach into the phone and strangle Barker.

Barker's voice trembled. "I'm sorry, but I have my orders."

"On who's authority?" Livingston yelled.

"On the President's!" Barker said. Now he sounded a little more authoritative.

"I don't understand," Livingston said. "I was reactivated because of my experience with what we're dealing with. Why am I—"

"You are being dismissed for disobeying my orders," Barker said. Livingston could now detect the faint tinge of superiority in the man's voice. "I issued a simple command to you to help secure order. You ignored me and began giving orders that run contrary to this mission. Commandeering one of our nation's nuclear facilities is just one example. You were not authorized to do that."

"We're at war," Livingston repeated, barely able to conceal his rage and disgust. "And your reason is bullshit. What's really going on?"

"Your continued promotion of illogical science and untruths of the wildlife that is currently causing temporary havoc is another reason why the President—"

"Oh, blow it out your ass, Barker!" Livingston fumed, and now the floodgates opened. "I see this for what it is. That jackass of a President you bow to finds it hard to accept that his little fantasy world is falling apart around him. That's it, isn't it? He can't accept the fact that there are creatures unknown to modern science wreaking havoc on our world because he can't accept the fact that legitimate scientists and not those numbfucks from … Bob Jones University or whatever bullshit college Tyler went to … he can't accept that legitimate scientists are unanimous in saying these creatures were previously thought extinct. That's it, isn't it, Barker?"

A pause, then, "I've got no choice. You have to understand …"

"Bullshit, you sniveling little worm. Forget politics for a minute. Our actions over the next few hours will affect millions of lives. Be a fucking man and grow some backbone."

"This conversation is ended. Our experts tell us the storm will begin to weaken within the next two hours. Report back here, directly to me."

"You want me so bad; you come on up here and get me

yourself. You're Tyler's dog. Fetch."

Barker's voice was strained. "If we don't see you by 0600 hours, we'll assume you've gone AWOL. We can spin it as treason if need-be."

"Spin it however you want, you little fuck. Like I said, if you want me, you'd better send your best men—and a body bag for each of them."

"There will be consequences, Colonel Livingston."

The line went dead.

"Goddammit!" Livingston slammed the phone down.

Tranning looked concerned. "Trouble, sir?"

"Yes, Tranning, there's trouble. President Tyler is losing his fucking mind."

"Losing?" The officer arched an eyebrow. "I thought he'd lost it a long time ago."

A head poked out behind a cubicle wall where a group of technicians were gathered around watching a computer screen. "Colonel Livingston? There's something you should see."

Curious, Livingston and Tranning made their way to an area that served as a bullpen. Four technicians were seated on chairs at various workstations, along with Jeremiah. There were computers and banks of electronic equipment and it overlooked a larger work area in the lower level that was now empty of people. "Report," Livingston said.

Jeremiah pointed at a large computer flat screen. "Obviously, the massive power outages are no problem for us. We've still got some internet access and dedicated phone lines. The cables are buried."

"What are we watching?"

"This is playing now on a live-feed across the networks and cable news stations."

President Tyler was giving another speech from a secure location in the White House. His once-youthful features were glazed, his skin pale. To Livingston, he looked like he was enthralled in some form of religious mania. "So when I say to you that the scientists who have been on all these shows saying that the creatures that are attacking people are related to dinosaurs, I'm telling you this is false. These are not government scientists. This is not the official White House stance on this tragedy. This is an attempt by our enemies in the media who wish to undermine our security and safety for a chance to strike a blow at this administration, which rejects all claims of—"

"Oh my God," Livingston said. "What the hell is he doing now?"

"This guy is something else, isn't he?" The tech said, shaking his head.

"—the contrary. Now there's a saying popular among many respected people in the scientific community, that the earth is billions of years old. But when the majority of the citizens of this great country are Christian, who believe in the Bible which offers no direct proof to the contrary ... which, by all evidence from the various books within the New and Old Testament suggests that the earth is no more than ten thousand years old ... and when so many people place—"

"I don't believe this," Livingston said. "Bad enough the country is under attack from the Clickers. Now it's besieged from within by a religious fanatic as well."

Jennifer, Richard, and Rick entered the room.

"What's going on?" Jennifer asked.

"Our fanatic of a President is losing his goddamned mind!" Livingston said.

"—Colonel Livingston has been relieved of his command. Yes, next question?"

Rick, Jennifer, and Richard glanced at him in shock. Livingston felt his ears burn.

"No," the President responded to another question from the press. "We cannot confirm or deny that a renegade outfit, led by Colonel Livingston, has seized a nuclear power plant. As I said before, Livingston has been relieved of his command. This is the Lord's will and He shall—"

Tranning cleared his throat. "Permission to speak, sir?"

"Permission granted." Livingston went rigid, half-expecting the officer to arrest him right there.

"Sir," Tranning continued, "there's a hurricane going on outside. I don't think we got that last transmission. Far as I'm concerned, you're still in charge."

Livingston pulled him aside so that the others gathered around the computer monitor couldn't hear.

"Tranning, we may need to make a command decision."

The young officer blinked, but said nothing.

"Do you understand what I'm implying?"

"I think so, sir."

"How many of our men would disagree with such an option?"

Tranning shrugged. "Hard to say for sure, Colonel, but I think most would side with us, given the situation."

Livingston nodded. "Good. Find out who would stand against us, and then lock them up somewhere on site. Same with the plant's staff and any other civilians."

"Begging your pardon, sir, but should we really take men away from the fight?"

"If they won't stand with us, then yes. I'm reluctant to do so, but this nation has other enemies to worry about now. It's no longer just the Clickers."

"I'll see to it, sir."

"Carry on, son. Carry on."

Tranning hustled off and the old man rejoined the others. For the next ten minutes all they could do was stand in stunned silence as President Tyler told the people of the United States not to listen to the most respected scientists of the world, that God would take care of everything, that the creatures currently causing so much havoc were not an unknown species and that very soon things would be back to normal.

And Colonel Livingston was left wondering if his plan to defend his country against enemies both within and abroad would work. Scowling, he turned to Jeremiah.

"You want to live?"

"Yes. Very much."

"Do you trust me, or are you siding with that limp dick on television?"

"I'm with you, Colonel. The Clickers are right outside. President Tyler isn't. You know best how to deal with them. He doesn't."

"Good. You said you have communications with the

outside."

Jeremiah nodded.

"Excellent. Invite the media down here. Get them on standby. We're going to deal with the Clickers. When that's over and the storm has passed, we're going to have a press conference. I think it's high time the American public found out about Phillipsport—and what's occurred tonight."

"Philli—" Jeremiah began, but before he could finish, Rick cut him off.

"Colonel, you can't! What about Melissa? They'll kill us."

Livingston faced him slowly.

"Ri ..." He caught himself just before he called Rick by his real name. "William, you're just going to have to trust me as well."

The Susquehanna River
Near the Pennsylvania/Maryland Border
12:48 AM

"Trust me, you fat fuck." Tony went under briefly, resurfaced, and spat out a mouthful of water. "You can do this!"

Vince's face was panic-stricken. His legs kicked wildly. "No I can't, Tony. I can't fucking swim. You gotta help me stay afloat."

"Just hang on to the log. Don't let go."

"Oh Jesus," Vince moaned. "Oh Jesus, Jesus, Jesus."

They clung to an uprooted tree as it rocketed down the river, tossed and spun by the churning water. Both men were soaked and their teeth chattered uncontrollably from the cold. Heavy rains lashed at them and their despair grew with every mile. Clickers lined both banks and they heard their claws, even over the thunder. Each time the lightning flashed, they saw more of them. So far, they hadn't spotted any in the water, but Tony wondered if they even would. Maybe the creatures hunted from the bottom. Maybe they wouldn't see them until it was too late. He readjusted his grip on the wet, slippery bark. The car was gone and with it, the Greek and the briefcase. Terrified as they were, Tony was more scared of what Mr. Marano would do when—if—they made it out of this alive.

"Tony? My arms are getting tired."

"Hang on, Vince. Just hang on."

A sudden bump jostled them both and nearly plunged Vince into the rushing water. The big man shrieked. Tony groaned as his stomach lurched.

"Oh fuck this shit," Vince cried. "Fucking stupid hurricane. Fucking stupid crab monsters."

"The water is getting rougher. That's all. Just don't let go. Ignore the crab monsters!"

"Ignore them? How the hell can I ignore them? They're all over the place!"

"Close your eyes and think about food."

Tony looked for landmarks but could see nothing in the spray and darkness. Nothing except the predators lined up along the riverbanks, watching them float by. He shivered and it had nothing to do with the wet or cold. The creatures' black eyes never changed—just bobbed around atop their long stalks, tracking the log's progress. And then he saw something else, something behind the monsters. It peered out from between two trees.

"The fuck?"

Tony wiped the water from his eyes with one hand. His other hand gripped the log tighter.

Vince had calmed down some, but his voice grew panicked again when he heard Tony's tone. "What's wrong?"

"Saw something. Out there, with those crab bastards."

"What was it?"

"I dunno. Looked like a guy in a lizard mask or something. Can't be, though. If there was someone out there, those things would rip him to pieces."

Suddenly, as if they'd been startled, the Clickers began to move towards the water. They rose up on their segmented legs and rushed into the river. For a moment, Tony saw their claws jutting up like shark fins. Then those submerged as well.

Oh shit …

"Vince, you still got your gun?"

"Yeah. Why?"

"We've got company." Tony pulled himself up onto the log. "Get your legs out of the water."

Vince tried to scramble aboard, but his legs kept slipping. "I can't! Help me."

Clutching his pistol in one hand, Tony extended his other hand to Vince. He kept his eyes trained on the water around them.

"I can't reach you."

Tony leaned closer, still focusing on the river. Dark shapes moved beneath the surface. A flash of light from the shore caught his eye. He glanced up and nearly screamed. A nine-foot-tall man-lizard emerged from the trees, followed by another, then six, then a dozen more. Several of them carried weapons—tridents, clubs, spears, and nets woven from some sort of metallic material. They drove the Clickers before them and took positions on the bank.

"Tony! Pull me up!"

Vince's cold, wet fingers clasped around Tony's outstretched hand and pulled. Tony nearly tumbled over the side. Grunting, he yanked backward with all his strength.

"Goddamn it, Vince, you've got to—"

Vince stiffened and his fingernails dug into Tony's skin. He opened his mouth and sighed. His eyes rolled up, showing whites. Then he began to shake. Frantic, Tony stuffed the pistol in his waistband and tugged with both hands. He heaved Vince's top half out of the water. The man's lower section was missing. He'd been cut in two at the waist. Retching, Tony let go of the dead man's arm. Vince splashed into the river and bobbed upward. Tony glimpsed his insides.

"Vince! Come on, man. You've gotta live ..."

In shock, he reached for Vince again, thinking that if he could just get him to a hospital, the fat man would be okay. Something whistled through the air and slammed into the log. Tony felt a sharp, icy pain in his hand. He looked down and saw a trident pinning it to the log. The weapon had impaled his hand between the wrist and his knuckles. More missiles zipped past him, embedding themselves in the log or splashing harmlessly into the water.

Massive claws erupted from the foam and clenched down on the log with their vice-like grip. The wood began to splinter.

Tony screamed.

The log disintegrated.

And on the shore, the Dark Ones laughed.

Peachbottom Nuclear Plant
1:15 AM

At the first opportunity, Colonel Livingston attempted to contact the battalion he'd left behind at Camden Yards in Baltimore. He managed to get a squad leader on a frequency that was still operational and asked for a status update. "What's that?" he yelled into the radio. The squad leader had responded but it was hard to hear what was being said due to the ferocity of the storm.

"… 've been … ed," was the response.

"What?"

Suddenly, the connection was clear. "Clickers were defeated, but now there's something else coming out of the water."

"Engage them."

"Begging your pardon, Colonel, but I received word that you were de-activated, sir. We're reporting to Colonel Allman out of Fort Bragg."

"Dammit!" Livingston paused briefly to collect his bearings, and then leaned forward over the mike. "Listen to me, soldier. Allman is a good man and a fine soldier, but he doesn't know what we're up against. He's—"

"I'm sorry, sir, but Allman has ordered us to fall back and await further orders, via command of the President."

"What?"

"We're moving out now. I'm sorry, sir."

"What about the—"

"I've been ordered to not communicate with you further, sir. Sorry." The connection was terminated.

"Goddammit!" Colonel Livingston almost threw the mike into the wall. He whirled toward the command center and was struck by how grave and terror-stricken everybody looked. Jeremiah Brown and his team were watching him with expressions of dread. "They've stripped me totally," he said.

"They've taken me completely out of the loop."

Jeremiah could only look at him. He'd briefed him on the basics; the man had a good head on his shoulders. He and his team had been monitoring the news and the security systems outside for the past five hours and knew first-hand what was going on outside. Jeremiah looked grave. "At least we're safe here. This place can withstand a category five storm. We have food and water. We're out of danger from the storm and the Clickers."

"But that's not everything," Livingston said, turning back to the communications center. After the brief feeling of euphoria he'd felt when he learned that he was being reactivated, that he felt needed and wanted for his expertise and knowledge, now he felt that this same experience was being used against him. It was a crude vendetta. "I only hope my unit ... the men I've already briefed ... what I've told them ... I hope they listen to wisdom and stick with it."

"We can only hope, sir," Jeremiah said.

There was a brief screech from outside. The howling of the wind had picked up in ferocity. Tranning ran into the room, breathless and pale.

"You've rounded up the dissenters?"

Tranning nodded, still trying to catch his breath. "Colonel," he gasped. "We've got Clickers in the perimeter."

"Engage!"

"Yes, sir." Tranning whirled and ran to relay the order.

Livingston frowned. "I think we might need to escalate my plan.

You have video recording equipment on hand?"

Jeremiah nodded. "Yes, I believe so."

"Get it. We can't wait to do a press conference. I need to get our message out now."

Various locations along the East Coast
1:20 AM

The Dark Ones had continued their onslaught all up and down the eastern seaboard. Some of them dragged old weapons on shore with them; tridents and spears rescued from long-sunken ships. They came ashore and made stealth attacks in remote locations. An old man who lived by himself on the outer banks of North Carolina was garroted by a trio of Dark Ones who dined on his corpse as the hurricane raged overhead. Between Jacksonville and St. Augustine, Florida, they made a stealth invasion on beachfront homes and ransacked those that were empty. The few people they found inside trying to ride out the storm were slaughtered mercilessly.

In Stone Harbor, New Jersey, Franklin Young was asleep on the top floor of his family's beach house when the Dark Ones burst into the flooded living room downstairs. The sudden barrage of noise woke him up and he fumbled for his handgun. The weapon was no match for the Dark Ones, however. They'd caught Franklin's scent from outside, and honed in on it. The .22 shells he fired into the creatures did minimal damage to the Dark One's thick, scaly hides and death for Franklin Young was mercifully swift.

In Mannheim, Pennsylvania a Mennonite businessman was holed up in his den, unable to sleep due to the ferocious storm when a trio of Dark Ones burst into his house. The roof's blown off, was his last thought before a dark, green thing towered above him and launched a maw of razor-sharp teeth into his head. The man bleated once, and then his skull was crushed between massive jaws as the Dark One began to feed. Within moments, the other two Dark Ones converged to lay claim on other portions. The Mennonite businessman was split evenly three ways down the gullets of the Dark Ones, who then set forth for more.

In New York City, Connie Stewart, Derek Brubaker, and Bob Ellison had found a secure spot in a storeroom upstairs, directly over O'Mally's bar. They'd watched in terror as the giant Clickers roamed up and down the street, occasionally mowing people down. When they saw the first signs of the Dark Ones, Bob Ellison reacted immediately.

"Get down!" They ducked beneath the window and Bob found an old quilt in the corner of the storeroom and draped it over them. Connie asked what the hell he was doing and he whispered: "My buddy told me about these things. If they're what I think they are, they rely on smell and this blanket will mask our scent." Fortunately for them, Bob Ellison's friend, who was into conspiracy theories but had never seen a Dark One, much less Bigfoot or a Chupacabra, was correct. The Dark Ones passed O'Mally's bar completely. Instead, they ventured across the street and proceeded to dine on stranded restaurant patrons who'd been holed up at Ray's Famous Pizza.

Peachbottom Nuclear Plant
1:31 AM

Jennifer stood off to one side, wringing her hands while Rick and Colonel Livingston argued. The old man was adamant that Rick should appear alongside him in the broadcast and Rick was steadfast in his refusal. Rick kept pleading that Livingston consider "Melissa," and accusing the Colonel of using him. Livingston stood behind a podium with the nuclear regulatory insignia on it. He pounded the top of the podium with his fist and the tips of his ears were red. Several of the civilian employees were angered as well. Apparently, Livingston had ordered several of them, along with a handful of soldiers, to be placed under arrest. They were currently being held in a locker room and armed guards had been posted.

"Colonel," a technician hollered, "the situation is getting worse outside. With all due respect, if you're gonna do this, do it now."

Fuming, Livingston dismissed Rick with a wave of his hand. Then he motioned for Jennifer and Richard to join him at the podium. They shuffled nervously through the crowd and stood beside him. Richard wiped his glasses on his wet, dirty shirttail and tried to smile. It wasn't convincing.

"I have to warn you both," Livingston said, "that what we're about to do is treason. I'm sure you both know the possible penalties involved. This is nothing short of a coup attempt."

"We know," Jennifer said. "But there's no other way. Too many people have died tonight. They didn't have to. We have to stop this now."

The old man smiled and patted her hand. Then he turned to Richard.

"And you, Doctor Linnenberg? Are you absolutely positive you want to go through with this?"

"I love my country, Colonel."

Livingston breathed a heavy sigh. "Okay then. Let's do it."

The technician called for silence, and then got behind the camera.

"Okay, and five … four … three … two … one."

He pointed at the Colonel and a red light went on. Livingston stared at the camera, frozen. Jennifer reached down and squeezed the old man's hand.

"It's okay. We're with you."

Colonel Livingston cleared his throat and then began to speak.

"Good morning. My name is Colonel Augustus Livingston, U.S. Army, retired. Yesterday, my country had need of me and I answered the call. I was asked to defend you; to defend your lives and your homes, and I did as I was asked. Today, the battle continues. My fellow Americans, we have all suffered losses. The situation is dire. As I stand here before you, our nation is beset by enemies on all sides; from the uncontrollable forces of nature, the creatures that have decimated our coastal cities all along the Eastern seaboard, and more insidiously, from within our own Capitol. President Tyler and his cabinet, in conjunction with other clandestine forces within our government, have conspired to cover up the truth about the events of the last twenty-four hours. They have assured you that the situation is under control. It is not. They have hamstrung the military and National Guard and both the local and federal emergency services—the very people who are supposed to protect you cannot do so because of our government's incompetence. Our leaders in Washington have only made things worse, and the cost was paid with American lives.

"Indeed, this didn't have to happen at all. It could have been prevented. Most of you will remember Hurricane Floyd. In 1994, it wreaked havoc on Maine's northern coast, killing over 1,800 people. The heaviest damage occurred in a town called

Phillipsport. What you didn't know is that most of the deaths in Phillipsport had nothing to do with the storm; they were caused by the very same creatures that have attacked us today. Our government knew about them then and conspired to keep the knowledge secret. Civilians who survived the 1994 attack and had knowledge of these creatures were threatened and forced into hiding for fear of their very lives. Sadly, I was part of this vow of secrecy because at the time I thought it served our nation's interests. However, I also warned those in command of a greater danger and of the absolute certainty that this would happen again. My warnings were ignored, particularly by the Tyler administration, and now we see the ramifications of it.

"With me are Doctors Jennifer Wasco and Richard Linnenberg. Both are renowned in the field of marine biology, and both can verify that the creatures currently attacking our nation—Clickers, to use the popular term—present a far greater danger than the President is admitting. Those of you watching this are probably wondering just what the situation is on the East Coast. Perhaps you've only heard scattered reports or rumors. That is because the President ordered a media blackout in the interests of national security. But those interests serve neither the nation nor its security. For you are our nation and you are in danger. The President did this to serve his religious ideology and the ideology of those who support him. You're not getting information because he thinks it will be detrimental to you. But not having the facts may very well cost you your life.

"I'm sure that our citizens in the affected areas can't hear me, but for the rest of you, here is what you need to know. The Mid-Atlantic region is currently suffering from the catastrophic aftermath of Hurricane Gary. In addition to that, the entire East Coast, from Maine all the way down to Florida, is under attack by these Clickers. They are predators and carnivores, and you should exterminate them on site. Believe me when I say they will not hesitate to do so to you. They can move about on both the land and sea, and can survive in salt water and fresh water. The Clickers are impervious to small arms and other weapons, but high caliber firearms and other projectiles that can pierce their shells can bring them down. They are especially vulnerable to fire. They are spreading farther inland, and it is possible that they may show up on our Gulf and Pacific coasts as well. Arm yourselves and make defenses. If you do not have access to heavy weaponry, then take shelter immediately. Most importantly, support your military, law enforcement, and emergency management officials. Help them help you, because our government is not.

"I mentioned that the creatures are moving inland. Doctor Wasco says this is not normal behavior for them. Normally they would not stray so far from their home. The reason they are doing so now is because they are being driven forward—herded if you will—by an even deadlier enemy. We've taken to calling this second race of creatures 'Dark Ones.' They are reptilian and walk erect on two legs. They are incredibly intelligent, have reasoning capabilities equal to that of mankind, and can use weaponry. Some of you might be thinking that this sounds like a bad movie. Trust me when I tell you I have never been more serious.

"It is my belief, and the belief of my associates, that these Dark Ones set the initial attack in motion in an effort to throw our nation into chaos and disarray so that they might then launch a second attack. They have achieved this with remarkable results, aided by both the hurricane and by the ineptness of our President. His sheer arrogance and ignorance has aided the enemy and Americans have paid the price.

"I call for President Tyler to step down. I call for his cabinet and supporters to also step aside. If no one will guide this country and do what must be done to protect it, then by God, I will. I, Colonel Augustus Livingston, am calling for a national show of no confidence in our leadership. I'm asking all American citizens, be they military or civilian, to stand beside me and defend this nation from the forces both within and abroad. I'm asking that our allies come to our aid, as we have done so many times in the past for you. My fellow soldiers, I'm asking you to disobey your direct orders and do the job you enlisted for. Protect your country.

"The President has demanded my resignation. It is not forthcoming. I will not step down. I will not retire. I will continue to fight until every one of these creatures is either dead or running back to the sea. Join me. Help me defend our country by defending yourselves. Thank you."

Jennifer wiped tears from her eyes. The emotion and earnestness in Livingston's tone had moved her. She noticed that Richard was sniffing as well.

"I don't think," Richard whispered to her, "that I've ever been prouder to be an American."

Livingston stepped away from the podium and Rick moved through the crowd towards him. They shook hands.

"Thank you," Rick said.

Livingston turned to the technician. "Getting that out to the media and any other sources you can is our number one priority. Right away, before anything else happens. Now, if you'll excuse me, I need to see how our defenses are holding outside."

Falls Church, Virginia
1:44 AM

The leader of the Dark Ones surveyed the scene ahead from the safety of a deserted building. Behind him were hundreds of his kind, temporarily sated on horseflesh and the occasional human. Thousands more of their kind were making headway all along the seacoast. The main forces were pressing onward to humankind's seat of power—Washington, D.C.—and would surround it on all sides before pressing forward with the main assault. They knew there were other human nations, but it had been this one that declared war, and thus, this one would pay the price.

The need for vengeance was instinctual, primal. It burned within them all. Acting as a single, cohesive unit, they'd driven the Clickers up from their deep-sea enclaves, making special efforts to drive out the elders, which were more massive and destructive than their younger and smaller counterparts. The elder Clickers had communicated with their own kind, sending subtle signals beneath deep-water trenches and the result had been a chain effect that rippled along the seacoast. Havoc had spread among humankind, making them more vulnerable for the Dark Ones and their final invasion.

What then, once the plan was completed?

The leader wasn't sure. That was for the elders to decide. But he tasted victory on his forked tongue. Ingrained in their memories was the taste of victory from centuries ago, before the lands above had been heavily populated with humans. There had been long centuries of relative peace when humankind and the Dark Ones coexisted. The Dark Ones rarely came ashore; when they did, it was to forage for the Clickers that were driven up by undersea currents. The few times they'd come across humans, they'd dined extensively. All that changed with the last rising, which had not been so long ago. There were many more humans now, so many that it seemed they'd taken over completely. Had the humans not annihilated them in that cave, the Dark Ones might have remained hidden in their underwater enclaves.

Humans had started this war.

It wouldn't be the first time they'd fought against the Dark Ones.

The leader's forked tongue tasted the air. Among the many legends passed down among their kind was one involving a company of humans that sailed over to the northern parts of their territory. This family of humans was lighter in skin and hair color than those normally found on these shores and they were more hostile. They'd come in large ships, the first ever the Dark Ones had seen, and they'd bore large, heavy weapons made of iron: swords, sabers, tridents. Some of them wore heavy iron over their chests, and others wore an iron-like covering over their heads—some of the coverings had the horns of bulls or rams on them. The Dark Ones had never come across humans like this.

Humanity had made that first strike without warning and the Dark Ones had been forced to defend their own. They'd driven the fair-skinned humans away, had killed and consumed most of them. Centuries passed before they saw humans like this again.

Now they were everywhere.

The Dark Ones had attempted to live out of sight of this

newer breed of humans, and had done so for a few hundred years. Then they'd come ashore during the height of a storm much like this and acted on instinct, as they always did. The settlement they'd struck was one they'd sacked centuries before, back when the land was still fertile. It was still relatively remote from other humans.

They did not expect to rile up the humans. Did not expect to be hunted themselves.

They did not expect to be slaughtered so ruthlessly in that cave.

The leader yearned for the wisdom of the Great One, who had been killed during that last invasion. The leader had found the body himself, when the Dark Ones were retreating into the ocean. He and some others had taken the Great One's remains to their watery abode and laid him to rest.

During the retreat, other Dark Ones were killed but their kind always managed to whisk the bodies of their fallen brothers away. Only one had been unaccounted for.

That fallen brother was the reason why a party of Dark Ones had been sent ashore after the initial retreat. They'd made a home in a remote cave, a large family of Dark Ones, and were slaughtered by a surprise invasion of humans.

The message this attack brought was simple.

The humans knew who they were now.

The scent of the humans was everywhere in this place above the sea. The leader had learned to recognize the scent from the scant underwater invasions they'd undertaken in the few years since the massacre. As the leader, he'd communicated with his kind to stay hidden, to let the humans search and find nothing. The leader and the other elders of their kind would plan an assault that would wipe out the humans and eliminate the threat once and for all.

Now that time was here. The storm had blown over, just in time for their own storm. They rose en masse and intended to end the threat of mankind forever.

Peachbottom Nuclear Plant
1:57 AM

Livingston listened to the incoming reports. Outside the nuclear power plant, the storm had begun to abate slightly. But even as the hurricane's force lessened, the Clickers' assault reached full strength. So far, his troops had managed to hold them back and without suffering heavy casualties.

From behind them in the technical bullpen, one of the techs said, "We've just lost our internet connection."

Jeremiah turned to him. "That's it. Now we're cut off entirely."

Livingston felt cut off, too. Cast aside. Set adrift.

Once again, alone.

"Did we manage to get that transmission out to the public?"

The technician who'd filmed the speech nodded. "Yeah, it's out there. Whether the media will grow some balls and broadcast it or keep kissing Tyler's ass is another story."

"They'll show it," Livingston said. "They feed off situations like this, same way those things outside feed off us."

The lights flickered, went out, and then came back on.

"Don't worry," Jeremiah told Livingston. "We've got all sorts of backups and generators. It's inconceivable that this facility could lose power."

Then the lights went out.

And stayed out.

"Not a problem," Jeremiah whispered. "The emergency lighting will kick on in just a second."

A second passed. Two. Ten.

The corridor stayed dark.

Jeremiah's voice sounded very small and afraid.

"Colonel, perhaps we have a problem, after all."

Just within the secured perimeter of the Peachbottom Nuclear Power Plant, in what was formerly a locked room before the cable that supplied power to the security system was pulled, a dark shape fumbled with something. There was a horrible bleat of frustration and then the outer lights dimmed, flickered briefly, and then went out entirely. The thing backed out of the room and rose to its full height.

The Dark One grasped a conductor in its spade claw and threw it to the ground. It had breached the high concrete fence that guarded the nuclear power plant unseen and took down the cables that fed the security cameras. Then, while the Clickers and the soldiers had done battle, it managed to sneak through the fray and enter the facility, slaughtering several soldiers at their posts in the process. It had found the room where the backup generator was located and destroyed the unit completely. In doing so, the Dark One had not only taken down the electrical power of the facility, it had effectively neutered the backup system. Deeper inside the massive facility, a separate power source was keeping the nuclear reactors humming along smoothly, despite the power outages. Should that source go down, there was another one buried well beneath the facility that would take over. That was the last line of defense. If that one failed and the reactors malfunctioned, the result could range from nuclear seepage to an all out meltdown that would affect the entire Mid-Atlantic region.

The Dark One smiled. All was going according to plan. It only hoped that its brethren in Washington, D.C. were having as much luck.

13

The White House
2:08 AM

Clark Arroyo hid inside a closet and tried to figure out what was going on. All around him people were running and shouting. He heard footsteps pounding down the corridors and voices crying out in frustration and anger. He wondered what the cause of all the alarm was. It couldn't be the hurricane. The worst of that had passed now. It couldn't be the Clickers. No way those dumb beasts could breach security around the White House, and even if they did it was inconceivable that they'd gain access to the Magog bunker. He pressed his ear against the panel door and listened.

"—wants his fucking head on a platter. It's a fucking coup attempt, plain and simple."

"We could dispatch Delta Force. Have them secure the plant and take down Livingston and his forces."

"Call in the Airborne."

"Can't. They've broken off contact, too. Sworn allegiance to Livingston."

"I'm telling you, send in Delta."

"No, activate Black Lodge. At this point, I'd say this is more up their alley anyway."

"Tried. They say they're busy elsewhere."

"There has to be some way to recapture the plant."

"What about the reactors? If he wanted to, Livingston could—"

The speakers hurried off, out of Clark's earshot. The air

inside the small closet was stifling. He wiped the sweat from his brow and tried to think. A vein in his head throbbed from the stress. What the hell was happening? Livingston—that was the Colonel they'd reactivated earlier to deal with this crisis. Had he gone rogue? Was he defying a Presidential directive—an order from his Commander-in-Chief? And what had they been saying about a reactor?

Clark Arroyo had been hiding in the closet for the past thirty minutes. He'd left the men's room of the parking structure over an hour ago and, braving the hurricane-force winds, managed to make it to the outer perimeter of the East Wing of the White House where he'd gained access via his key card, which Ken White had failed to confiscate when he was thrown out of the building. Once inside he didn't waste time. He slipped into an empty room and hunkered in the closet. He knew it was possible that the storm hadn't knocked out the security cameras and if so, armed guards would be coming his way shortly. He'd waited in the closet, gripping his Sig Sauer tightly, and waited.

Nobody came.

He waited for fifteen minutes, battling a rush of emotions. Fear for his wife and daughters. Anger at his mistreatment and the disrespect shown to him. Most of all, he felt fear for his country. All these conspired in him to take action: he would gain entry into the White House and, if he wasn't caught, he would sneak inside and either gain enough valuable insider information that President Tyler was off his rocker and was jeopardizing the nation due to his ineptness and religious zealotry or, if the opportunity presented itself, he'd take the bastard out along with those closest to him.

When he was positive that his fellow Secret Service agents hadn't been tipped off by the building's security system, he'd let himself out of the closet, opened the door to the hallway and peered out. The coast was clear.

He'd spent the next forty minutes moving deeper into the recesses of the White House. Hiding in empty conference rooms, crouching beneath desks, and hiding in closets.

He'd concealed himself in his latest hiding spot when he heard the commotion ahead of him.

He had to get out of there. Sneak out of the White House, find his wife, make sure she was safe, and then get clear of Washington. But if the Clickers were still running rampant he wouldn't make it a block, let alone all the way home. Still, he had to try. The power in this place was crumbling. President Tyler wasn't just dogmatic or pious—he was downright insane. Now it sounded like even his own men in the field were turning against him.

Carefully, Clark edged open the door and peered through the crack. The dimly-lit corridor was empty. He crept out of the closet and headed for the nearest exit. He heard several distant shouts. The sound of running footsteps pounded towards him. Quickly, Clark turned and headed back the other way, towards the bunker entrance. More footsteps came from that direction as well. He ducked back inside the closet and drew his weapon.

"Shit," he whispered to himself. "What now?"

The lights blinked, and then went out. Red emergency lighting clicked on automatically, illuminating the corridor.

Then the screams started.

Peachbottom Nuclear Plant
2:17 AM

Rick wanted to do nothing more than recline on a sofa in the lounge and fall into dreamland. He was dog-tired, but the events of the past day had done a number on him. His mind was wide awake, turning everything over, processing it. And what he was processing wasn't very reassuring.

The Peachbottom Nuclear Plant had lost all emergency power, including that of the backup generators. All remaining power was being channeled to the reactors to avoid a meltdown. Everything else was dead. That could only mean one thing.

The Dark Ones were here.

He'd whispered this warning to Livingston in panic shortly after it was discerned that the generator had, indeed, come on briefly after the power went out but then shut down. The techs had been scrambling to find out why the backup generator failed, and Jeremiah Brown had worked with another team to insure that the generator powering the reactors was functioning properly. Livingston had pulled Rick and those two scientists aside and told Jeremiah they were retreating to the lounge. "Under no circumstances are you to go out to the main generator," he'd said.

"Why not?" Jeremiah replied. The bullpen was dark. The techs were babbling in frustration, trying to get things back up. "We can't work in the dark!"

"Get flashlights," Livingston said. "In the meantime, don't set foot outside. The reactors will be safe."

"But—" Jeremiah had sputtered in protest.

"I'm ordering you to stay inside!" Livingston thundered. "Tranning? Secure the bullpen exit."

Rick had heard Tranning make his way to the exit of the bullpen. Some of Jeremiah's staff members muttered. He heard one of them say, "They're just as fucked up as President Tyler!" Rick wanted nothing more than to bitch-slap whoever said that.

"Gentlemen, you saw the Clickers outside," Livingston said, his voice commanding. "Correct?"

Jeremiah and his team murmured that, yes, they'd seen the Clickers. "But this plant is secure!" Jeremiah said. "Even giant crustaceans can't—"

"I don't have time to provide you with a history lesson, men," Livingston continued. "But like I said in the broadcast, in addition to the Clickers, Hurricane Gary, and the ineptitude of President Tyler and his followers, we have another threat to take seriously. That threat is a race of creatures called The Dark Ones. Not much is known about them, but they're extremely dangerous. In fact, they're more deadly than the Clickers and they possess a cunning that is deceptively frightening. I witnessed these things over a decade ago in Phillipsport, Maine. These creatures are—"

A flashlight was turned on. One of the techs was holding it, and he placed it on the desk. Rick saw Lieutenant Tranning was holding his rifle in a stable position, ready to deploy.

"Good," Livingston said. "Do we have any more flashlights on hand?"

"Hold on." Another tech fumbled along his desk and

brought out another flashlight. Once turned on, the bullpen was illuminated with more light.

The bullpen looked even more frightening with the flashlights turned on, especially with the howling of the storm so audible from outside. It gave the room a haunted, bleak appearance, filled with shadows.

"As I was saying," Livingston said. "These creatures are extremely deadly. They hunt the Clickers for food. Part of my mission in this operation was to lead efforts in educating the military on their threat and coordinate efforts to destroy them and protect the American public. I've spent the last ten hours trying to do so, to no avail. Make no mistake, these things will make the devastation Hurricane Gary and the Clickers are causing look miniscule by comparison."

"How could these Dark Ones ... or whatever you call them ... how can they breach the security of this plant without being spotted by your men?" one of the techs asked.

"There's a battle going on outside. They could have stampeded the Clickers in this direction and then snuck in while my men were fighting them."

"And these things are smart enough to take down the backup generator?"

"Yes."

"How else do you explain it?" Rick said. It was the first thing he'd said to the Peachbottom Nuclear Plant staff since arriving. "I saw the Clickers themselves before the Colonel and his team rescued me. You guys all saw them ... right?"

There were murmured acknowledgements.

"If the electricity is out and these Dark Ones are out there, will that allow them easier access to us?" Jennifer Wasco asked. She sounded deathly afraid. "I mean ... aren't the outside entrances manned by a security access card?"

"The backup generator that powers the reactors also operates the security of the building," Jeremiah said. "The doors are securely locked. And if for some reason the generator that powers the reactors and the security system fails, there's a secondary backup generator that's underground. No way that can be breached unless the things get in here, and that ain't gonna happen."

Rick couldn't help but think he was trapped in that Lucky Supermarket freezer again with Doc Jorgenson, Melissa Peterson, Janice Harrelson and her son Bobby and the others. Trapped with few options, few weapons, a deadly storm raging and an even deadlier presence waiting to take them down should they so much as step outside. "Colonel Livingston is right," Rick heard himself say. "We have to stay inside. The Dark Ones are out there, and if you step outside to check out the generator you're just going to give them a way in here."

"Have you seen these Dark Ones?" Jeremiah Brown asked Colonel Livingston.

"Yes."

For a moment they were locked in a silent standoff, Colonel Livingston and Lieutenant Tranning on one end, Jeremiah Brown and his two security guards on the other. Rick noticed that Tranning had flicked the safety off his Assault Rifle.

They heard the rise and fall of the wind and rain outside.

"Enough of this," Livingston snapped. "Every moment we waste talking, those things get deeper inside the facility."

Jeremiah dropped his gaze. "Okay. We stay here. It's too risky to step foot outside anyway. The battle is still underway. We'd just be asking for trouble, Dark Ones or no Dark Ones."

Tranning flicked the safety back on his assault rifle.

Rick noticed the change come over Livingston immediately. He took control like the high-ranking Colonel he was, ordering Jeremiah's security guards to take Tranning's command. One of the techs found a few pairs of short-wave walkie-talkies and distributed them to Tranning and the security guards. Tranning briefed them and within moments each man headed to various locations to ensure the security of the main interior of the plant. Livingston nodded. "I'll be in the lounge with doctors Linnenberg and Wasco. Mr. Mark will get some sleep there."

And then they'd retreated to the lounge.

Livingston had taken one of the walkie-talkies with him and it sat on a coffee table. Rick was stretched out on one of the sofas, opposite Dr. Linnenberg and Dr. Wasco, who were sitting in easy chairs. Colonel Livingston was pacing the room.

Rick wasn't sure if he could trust Wasco and Linnenberg, but Livingston had told him they were okay, that they could be trusted, so he'd told them a little about what he'd been through. He hadn't been able to tell them much, though. He'd been curious to hear their stories and as they told him, each scientist taking turns, Rick was spellbound by what he was hearing. He was especially shocked and surprised by the sheer size of the Clicker's they'd seen.

"They were as big as cars?" Rick asked.

"Well … yeah …" Jennifer said. "Those were the biggest ones. Most of them were smaller."

"The ones I encountered twelve years ago were about as big as a medium-sized dog."

"The one that came after us at the Aquarium was about the size of a small car," Dr. Linnenberg said. "It had a stinger that was … it had to be two or three feet long."

"Jesus!" Rick said.

"Jennifer and Richard are lucky they made it out of there," Colonel Livingston said. He stopped pacing and joined them in their little huddle amid the sofas and chairs in the center of the lounge. "I was just as shocked as you, Rick, when I saw the size of some of these things. The ones we came across in Phillipsport were nowhere as big as these."

"Do you think that's their normal size?" Rick asked Dr. Wasco, who was sitting across from him.

"It's hard to say," Jennifer said. She sat in the chair cross-legged. She looked exhausted.

"Do you think it's possible for crabs … or lobsters or whatever … to get that size?" Rick asked.

"Spider crabs get pretty big," Jennifer said. "They have a leg span of about eighteen feet."

"Eighteen feet," Rick said to himself. He remembered reading about Spider crabs years ago in high school.

"These … Clickers … or whatever they're called," Jennifer continued. "They appear to have a totally different structure than a spider crab or any other crab or lobster I've observed."

"No shit!" Rick snorted. God, he just wanted this nightmare to be over with!

"They're perfectly proportioned," Jennifer continued. "The big ones we saw had a total body mass of about seven or eight feet in length. About the size of a small car. Their legs are in proportion to their body mass, and at first glance they resemble a giant Neopetrolisthes ohshimai, or the Anemone Crab, but they have the hind structure of a common lobster with a tail like a scorpion. Their claws are about the size of their thorax, which in the case of these big ones is about four feet."

"I could've sworn the one that got Duncan was bigger," Dr. Linnenberg said.

"We aren't going to know for sure until we can get a dead one to study," Jennifer said. She turned to Colonel Livingston. "Did the government retrieve samples from the Phillipsport incident?"

All eyes turned to Livingston, who regarded them calmly. He checked his sidearm and returned it to its holster.

"The Clickers might be bulletproof," he said. "But the Dark ones aren't. If they make it this far, we'll be okay."

Then he lapsed into stone silence again.

"You totally ignored my question," Jennifer pointed out. "Your art of subtle reflection needs some work, Colonel."

Rick thought, you fucker, now's not the time to play this classified X-Files bullshit! Fucking tell us!

Livingston sighed and for the first time he looked tired. He rubbed one weather-beaten hand over his face. "This doesn't leave the room. If it gets out and … my name is mentioned … I'll deny it vehemently. Do you understand?"

Slow nods around the room. All eyes were on Livingston.

Colonel Livingston straightened himself up from his position on the end of the sofa and leaned forward, elbows resting on his knees. Linnenberg and Wasco sat up straight, their attention wholly directed at Livingston. Even Rick moved himself up, eager to hear what Livingston was going to say.

"I do know that discarded Clicker specimens were gathered and the remains were studied in a government laboratory," Livingston said. His voice was low, and they all had to strain to hear him. "I was briefed on the findings and there wasn't much new that paleontologists hadn't already guessed. The species was identified as Homarus Tyrannous, and all indication that the species was extinct was laid to rest right there. Testing was done on the venom it produces and as far as I know, experiments are still being done on it. That wasn't the highlight of the lab's findings, though. No, the highlight was the Dark One that Rick and some of the other Phillipsport survivors killed."

Rick's mind instantly went back to the Lucky Supermarket freezer and that ferocious but brief fight with the Dark One that got inside. He'd thought about that creature ever since; wondered whatever happened to its remains.

Now he was going to find out.

Livingston's gaze was directed at him. "You remember?"

Rick nodded. "Yeah."

"Well, don't keep us in suspense, tell us what happened?" Richard Linnenberg asked.

"Mr. ... Mark here ... as you know, was one of half a dozen people who holed up in a supermarket freezer during the last invasion of the Clickers," Livingston said. "Something happened, though, and a Dark One got inside."

"We left the freezer to see what was going on outside," Rick said. He remembered the events as if they'd happened yesterday. "I saw a ... I saw a family get ... get mauled by those things."

"A couple others saw these things outside and the creatures caught their scent," Livingston continued. "They were chased back into the freezer. Only one of them got in before the steel door could be slammed shut. It killed ..." Livingston turned to Rick for clarification. "... one of you, correct?"

"Yeah," Rick nodded. "It did. It got a guy named Lee. Bit his head right off. I picked up a rifle and took a shot but Janice Harrelson ..." Even now, thinking of Janice brought a sting to the back of his throat "We were smart and lucky enough to stockpile that freezer with weapons. Janice and I brought some with us from the sheriff substation. One of those weapons we brought was a rocket launcher; one of those little shoulder mounted ones. Janice grabbed it and fucking blew that thing's head clean off."

"They left the Dark One in there when they finally made their escape," Livingston resumed."Mr. Mark and one of the other survivor's, Meliss ..." He paused, unsure of Melissa Peterson's assumed name. "... told me about it a few days later when I questioned them. I sent a team of soldiers out to retrieve it. It was whisked away to the lab and ... to this day ... I have no idea what became of that research."

"What do you mean?" Rick asked.

Livingston sighed again. He looked defeated. "For the first six months or so I was briefed at every opportunity. The government did a good job in keeping what happened at Phillipsport covered up. I supported the cover-up, but I did not support the clandestine effort to have all of you witnesses driven underground." He glanced at Rick. "I ... I was able to divert their attention away from you in several cases, all the while continuing to work the file and be briefed on the scientist's findings. The Dark One was unique. It was confirmed to be a totally independent species. It was something that ... well, it was something totally unknown to modern science. It looked like a reptile, but it was adaptable to both the deep sea and land. Its respiratory system was complex—the thing had lungs and a pair of gills! And its brain ... it was much larger in size than that of a regular reptile or amphibian. In fact, its structure seemed to suggest that it ... well, that it was of a higher intelligence."

"It had a brain like us?" Rick asked.

"Somewhat."

They let that sit for a moment, turned it over in their own minds.

"Naturally, we wanted to find more of them," Livingston continued the narrative. "More Clickers, more Dark Ones. When the initial reports came back on both species, two teams were dispatched. One was a diving expedition that performed a series of maneuvers from Massachusetts all the way up into Nova Scotia. That operation wasn't conducted until the following Spring, when the weather conditions were better. A second operation was conducted closer to Phillipsport. This one was based on another mission that was carried out right after search and rescue had come in and our own unit had done its mop-up. It consisted of a tracking team, which managed to verify that the Dark Ones had gone back out to sea. Further searches by various teams were conducted and when one of them turned up missing in March of the following year, a second search and rescue team was dispatched. This one was equipped by the U.S. Military, though. And what they found ..."

"What did they find?" Rick asked.

Livingston sighed again. His eyes looked haunted, as if he'd seen the horror himself. "A ... a whole bunch of these Dark Ones had made a home in a cave. Just south of Falmouth. The missing team came across it and was massacred. The first man that entered the cave was ... well, he was killed outright. Report I read said that something came out of the cave and pulled his head clean off. The unit commenced firing and they basically blasted their way inside." Livingston cast his haunted gaze across all three of them. "It was a massacre."

"They wiped them all out?" Jennifer asked. She looked spellbound by the story.

Livingston nodded. "Yes, they did. Four soldiers were killed. The unit dispatched twenty-three Dark Ones."

"My God!" Richard Linnenberg muttered.

Rick Sychek was appalled. "They killed all of them?"

"What did you expect?" Livingston said, turning to Rick. "You expect us to capture them alive?"

Rick didn't know what to say.

Livingston shook his head. "During the mission, the team found a nest ... a lair, if you will. About five or six females were found, and all of them had eggs that were on the verge of hatching."

"So they are like reptiles and amphibians, then?" Jennifer asked.

"In that respect, yes." Livingston's features were clouded by the memory. "I was going through a rough time when this happened. What I saw in Phillipsport ... well ... it haunted me." He turned to Rick. "Mr. Mark here will probably be able to relate. What I saw was something that nobody had ever seen before. It ... it made me realize ... with much greater ... with much ... shit, I don't know how to explain this, but—"

"It made you realize there are more things to this world than we'll ever know or understand," Rick said.

Livingston nodded. "Yeah. But it's more than that. I went through those feelings, plus I saw men get killed. Men who served under me. Men whose families I knew, who I trained, who ate dinner at my table and I at theirs. Good men. I saw them massacred, cut down by things we still don't have a firm grasp on even understanding what they are and ... and I was ordered ... I was ordered ... to not only keep a lid on it ... but ... I was ... I was ..."

All eyes were on Livingston now. Rick thought that the Colonel was having a hard time expressing himself. He felt a flutter of fear at the look on his face. *He's scared to death,* Rick thought.

"None of this leaves the room," Richard said quietly.

There were subtle nods and murmurs of acknowledgement of this from Jennifer and Rick. Livingston regarded them all, seemingly a little more relaxed at this reminder. "Yes," he said, his voice lower still. "Thanks for reminding me of that."

There was silence for a moment.

Rick thought he knew what Colonel Livingston was going to say. He was tense with anticipation.

"I wanted not only a full investigation into Phillipsport, I wanted a full investigation into the Clickers and the Dark Ones," Livingston continued. "I made my case in a report I filed to the Joint Chiefs of Staff in April of 1995. I pressured them into a meeting that was classified. I shouldn't be talking to any of you about this, but fuck it. They've made a mess of it, so I don't give a shit anymore." He sighed, rubbed his face. "They kept stalling me. A couple of independent, secret investigations were carried out by the FBI and the Department of Agriculture, and I was briefed on some of their findings for awhile. But then at some point I was brought in to a meeting with a high-ranking government official. To this day, I don't know who this guy was. It was like something out of the X-Files. It was just this guy in a black suit. A guy about my age, probably five, ten years older. He had a folder with him. Two folders, actually. One folder contained paperwork pertaining to my upcoming retirement, which I hadn't even planned on taking for another ten years. I looked at this file, noted that everything was filled out correctly, that … well, basically, I was being forced into retirement. I looked at this guy and I have to admit, I was confused. I didn't understand what was going on. Then he showed me the other folder, told me to look at it, and basically said that if I don't retire now … if I don't retire and if I say anything … to the wrong people … or if I let certain classified information about what went on in Phillipsport and the … the Clickers and the Dark Ones … if I let that out …"

"He threatened your family?" Rick asked.

Livingston closed his eyes briefly, rubbed his forehead as if he had a headache. Then, he resumed: "My marriage with Julie produced no children, but we were happy. We'd been married fifteen years at that point. She was the perfect example of a military wife. She knew all the high-ranking government and military officials, was friends with many of them. They all liked her, and she liked them. What they … what a lot of people didn't know about, not even Julie, was that I'd fathered a child out of wedlock with my high school sweetheart. This was a long, long time ago. I was just a kid … my last year of high school. I … we were going to get married but never did. I knew I was going to have a career in the military, was going to be a soldier, and … she said she'd wait for me to come back … that once I returned from basic we'd get married and live on base. We'd be a family. That never happened. My son Josh was born that October while I was at basic training and when I came back eight weeks later … Patricia had hooked up with another guy. There … there was almost a bad scene. I was so enraged I wanted to beat the hell out of both of them, but I didn't. Instead, I ran straight back to base and dove into military life and never looked back."

"You never saw your son after that?" Jennifer asked gently.

"I saw him again," Livingston replied. "Patricia and I kept in touch … and I paid child support. It wasn't arranged through the courts at all. I felt it was my obligation to support Josh, and I did. But I never told anybody, not even my superiors. I just made an effort to see my son whenever I had leave. I'm sad to say that my relationship with him was never very good. I was away most of the time, and I had to watch him grow up from afar."

Rick felt himself go livid with anger. "That spook had info

on your son, Josh? That's who he threatened?"

"No." Livingston looked at Rick. "But you're close. He said nothing about having Josh or Patricia killed.

Instead, he said that if I was to keep pressing this issue ... if I let anything leak out ... it was possible that ... an accident ... would happen to my grandchild."

There was stunned silence.

Richard said, "Oh my God."

"I hadn't seen or heard from Josh in five years," Livingston said. "We'd ... sort of drifted apart when he was a teenager. I ... I didn't know what this guy was talking about at first. But then he mentioned Josh by name, told me that my son was now married and the father of a four-year-old and ... that's when I learned that I had a grandchild for the first time."

Rick didn't know what to say.

"That's how they were able to guarantee my silence for the past eleven years," Livingston said softly. "I assured the man who visited me that their secret was safe, that I would be glad to accept full retirement. And I did. I exited military life and became a civilian for the first time in over thirty years. I did it because I had to. I did it not for the sake of my country, but for the sake of a child I still haven't even met." Livingston regarded all of them. "Do you understand?"

Rick, Jennifer, and Richard nodded.

"I tried to enjoy retirement," Livingston continued. "I really did. But Julie ... she became bitter ... saw that something was bothering me and insisted that I tell her about it. She could always see through me, and when I refused she became even more bitter. I couldn't tell her. I couldn't risk it and she should have known this, but for some reason she chose to ignore it. The last year of our marriage before she passed on was unhappy, I'm sorry to say." For the first time it looked like Colonel Livingston was on the verge of breaking down; his stony veneer crumbled just a tad, then he regained his strength. "She finally passed on ten years ago. Breast cancer."

"I'm sorry," Jennifer said quietly.

"And that's how our government has kept the Phillipsport incident under the radar from the mainstream media,"

Livingston said. He regarded them all again. "I have no idea what they did after I retired. I have no idea what further research was conducted, what was learned. The men I served with in Phillipsport … well, there weren't many of them. Richrath was one. You remember him, Rick?"

Rick nodded.

"Those of us who served in Phillipsport and saw things were, as far as I know, visited by the same gentleman. We were all given generous retirement packages. With the exception of one man, we've kept our part of the bargain."

"What happened to that one man?" Jennifer asked.

"Most of the men who went into Phillipsport were Army Reservists," Livingston said. "Many of them were either killed or wounded horribly by the Dark Ones and Clickers. Those that survived … many of them remain in military hospitals, locked away in psychiatric wards. Others have deteriorated into madness … they live on the streets; their families have been convinced that they've simply gone crazy. Some have disappeared, if you catch my drift. The one man I'm talking about, Chief Lieutenant Marshall Smith, headed a squad that entered Phillipsport from the north. His team played a part in securing that supermarket and retrieving the remains of the Dark One Rick and the others killed. He was given the same talk, given the same retirement package as the rest of us."

"How many of you were there?" Richard asked quietly.

"My guess was no more than a dozen," Livingston answered. "Smith kept quiet for a while and then five years later the vehicle he was driving went off the road near his home in Montana and crashed into a rock. The vehicle exploded, killing everybody inside, which consisted of his wife, Alice, and their teenage children, Kathy and Cody." Livingston paused. "An hour later, about fifty miles away, in a little town called Middletown, a house burned down. The blaze killed a family by the name of Dobbs. Marshall Smith and his family were returning from the Dobbs' residence when they crashed."

"You think Marshall Smith let it leak to the Dobbs family?" Rick asked, his mind racing. "And that … somehow those spooks knew about it when it happened?"

"I don't know," Livingston said. "But the coincidence is strange and frightening. I didn't learn about the connection until years later. I simply did my part and stayed silent. I didn't even poke into it or the Phillipsport incident. Instead, I got into breeding my horses and that became my obsession. It was a matter of survival. I had to obsess over something. If I didn't have that to occupy my time, I'd probably be dead now from an accident." He paused. "If you know what I mean." Rick mentioned the black car he thought he saw outside his brother's house. Then he said, "I've always wanted to ask you this, but I was afraid to."

"I have to admit every time you called me, Rick, I'd get paranoid."

"I'm William, remember?"

"Right, okay. William!"

"Why the hell did you get paranoid?"

"There was never a tap on my phone, but I know that it's easy to pull phone records," Livingston said. "And I was always afraid that somebody, somewhere, would put two and two together and not only track you down, but think I was leaking information to you or withholding something. I was always afraid for Danny, my grandson. So after you called, I would get in touch with Josh to relieve my fears."

"What black car are you talking about?" Jennifer asked Rick. "Were you followed?"

"He's been wanted by our government since Phillipsport," Livingston said. "So has Melissa Peterson. I imagine the same clandestine government agency that paid me a visit with my retirement papers and the friendly warning is also the same one that has been trying to find him all these years."

"So they have been trying to find me?" Rick asked. "Even after all this time?"

"You better believe it."

"But why?"

"It's a matter of national security."

"What kind of bullshit is that?"

"Lower your voice," Livingston warned.

Despite being exhausted, Rick's mind was awake. He was

scared and furious. "I knew we were wanted early on, when Melissa and I left. You told me so yourself when we first called you when we were on the run. That's why we disappeared. In the years that passed, we basically kept our heads down and didn't draw attention to ourselves. I figured if we even tried to see if we were still wanted, something would happen to make us a target."

"That is correct," Livingston said. "Even an internet search on your names would have alerted the proper organization."

"Even now after all this time?"

"It's become more complicated now, but yes. Granted, your name does turn up on Google searches due to your former career, and that has been taken into consideration. But believe me, that kind of information is monitored. You've done a good job in remaining underground."

"Apparently I haven't done that good a job," Rick said, trying to control the shakiness in his voice. "Or something happened that tipped them on to me but … I could've sworn that before I left my brother's house I saw a black car cruise around the house. It freaked me out. I've been real paranoid about that shit since Phillipsport, you know what I mean?"

"Oh yes, I know exactly what you mean," Livingston said.

"That's why I took off and started heading west. I thought I would lose them somewhere, but instead I wound up in York with some fucking psycho!"

"No need to go where you don't want to go, William," Livingston advised.

Rick was cognizant enough to realize Livingston was giving him an easy out. The Colonel probably realized Rick had either seriously injured or killed somebody in self-defense and was encouraging him to let it alone, bury it. He also had a hunch. "You never told anybody that I was calling you?"

Livingston's gray eyes locked with Rick's. "No."

"Not even when you were still active?"

"No."

"Why?"

"Like I said. I had a feeling they would do to you what I saw them doing to my men, that you would be detained in secret, whisked away to some secret location. Maybe even disappear."

The hunch was proven correct. Livingston had been covering for him the past twelve years.

"Why would the government want to cover something like this up?" Richard Linnenberg asked. "I would think in the name of science ... of human safety ..."

"I can't answer that question," Livingston said. "I have no idea why such a tight lid was clamped on this. My initial thought was it was a matter of avoiding a nationwide panic."

"This government agency ..." Jennifer asked. "Who are they?"

"I don't know the code name, but they work independently of the FBI and the CIA. They don't take orders from either political party or any branch of government. They were formed during the beginning of the Cold War to keep certain things under wraps, and they do so indiscriminately. They know things about our past ... about certain current events, that our current legislative and executive branch know nothing about."

"Kind of like the whole Men In Black myth," Jennifer said.

"Yes," Livingston answered. "Very much so."

Jennifer's features changed to a slow dawning of terror. "Oh my God!"

"What?" Rick asked.

"If the Dark Ones are as intelligent as they ... as they think they are, maybe this organization knows about it ... maybe they're afraid of this information getting out. Maybe they—"

"Maybe they think the Dark Ones might be capable of emotional thought," Rick said, catching Jennifer's epiphany. "Which would enable them to—"

"Seek revenge for what happened in 1994," Colonel Livingston finished.

The four of them looked at each other, a sense of horrific comprehension now stitched through all of them.

Outside the lounge came the faint sounds of men screaming in horror and pain.

The White House
2:30 AM

Things were happening within the White House and Clark Arroyo felt powerless to stop it.

No, he thought. Not things. Things weren't happening. Shit was happening. Things were what was causing the shit. Those crab things …

He was still inside the cramped closet, still clutching his Sig Sauer tightly, and he knew in no uncertain terms that he couldn't escape now.

It would be impossible.

He could hear the dim sounds of scattered gunfire coming from outside. He didn't know what was happening, but his guess was that those creatures were heading toward the White House and government sharpshooters were beginning the process of picking them off. He wondered if they'd gotten anywhere on the White House grounds, or perhaps breached the interior of the building. The power outage could have been due to the storm, but it could have gone out from other nefarious means. Clark had to keep those options open.

He was just beginning to plan how he might escape the closet when he realized something.

As a Secret Service agent, Clark Arroyo knew all the ins and outs of the White House grounds, buildings, and the various secret bunkers and tunnel networks within the proximity of the District of Columbia, Maryland, and Virginia. The Magog Bunker was just one such secret underground complex largely unknown to the general population. What a lot of people didn't realize was that the White House itself had secret rooms and passageways that snaked through various sections of the building.

Clark took a step back and began moving his hand along the wall of the closet. Despite being a little disoriented from everything that had happened, he was fairly certain this closet had a hidden panel that opened onto one of the secret corridors.

His palm rubbed against a section of the wall and he felt it slide back automatically. Cool air touched his back, indicating the passageway behind him.

Feeling relieved, Clark stepped into the hidden passageway, now completely hidden inside the White House.

Various locations across the United States
2:30 AM, Eastern Standard Time

Eric Lansdale had insomnia, and as he sat up channel surfing late that night in his Nashville, Tennessee, apartment, he came across CNN.

The anchor was broadcasting from Los Angeles. "We've just received this communication from our Wire Services," the female anchor said. "And we're broadcasting it as our duty to keep you, the viewers, informed. As you know, the East Coast is currently being bombarded by Hurricane Gary, a massive category five storm. As some of you may also know from scattered reports on CNN and elsewhere, a species of giant crustacean have been discovered; literally hundreds of thousands of these creatures have been beaching themselves along the East Coast from northern Florida to the coast of Maine, and there have been reports of human fatalities as a result of these giant creatures. Some scientists have taken to calling them Clickers. Shortly after we began reporting on this, CNN corporate headquarters in Atlanta received an order by both the Department of Agriculture and the Department of Homeland Security to stop reporting this story, so we complied. However, in light of what we are about to show you we've decided to air this clip and let you decide for yourself whether President Tyler's speech, which CNN has just broadcast live, is yet another smokescreen attempt at concealing the truth from the American people or if he is, indeed, telling the truth."

Eric was intrigued. He sat up on his sofa, hands on his knees, wondering what it was this time the government was trying to cover up.

The feed cut to an interior shot. An older man who looked like a high-ranking military official was standing behind a podium. Flanking him was a middle-aged man with short dark hair and glasses wearing a tattered white lab coat, and a woman in her early-thirties with shoulder-length auburn hair who looked like she'd been awake for too long.

"Good morning," the military official said. "My name is Colonel Augustus Livingston, U.S. Army, retired. Yesterday my country had need of me and I answered the call. I was asked ..."

Eric Lansdale sat spellbound as Colonel Livingston made his plea.

Five minutes later, Eric was on the phone with his best friend, Donald, in Cookesville to see if he'd heard about this. His friend hadn't. Furthermore, his friend was fast asleep and was pissed off at him for being woken up. "I gotta go to work tomorrow," Donald said.

"Turn on the news," Eric said.

"The fuck for? Asswipe!"

"Just turn on the fucking news!"

"This better be worth it." Donald said. Eric heard Donald fumble with something, and then he heard the TV click on. Then silence.

Five minutes after that, both men were calling friends and family across the country. Only a few were aware of the Livingston speech. Most of them were asleep and expressed irritation at having been woken up. That irritation quickly gave way to disbelief when they heard what Eric and Donald had to say.

It turned to outrage and fear when they turned on the news for themselves and saw replays of Colonel Livingston's speech.

"Tell everybody you know," Donald said to one friend, Barbara Thompson, a woman he'd dated a few years ago who he was still friendly with. "This is some major shit."

"I'm calling my mother," Barbara told him before hanging up.

And so it went.

In Ottersville, Missouri, a middle-aged couple named Dave and Annette Murray were up late watching Fox News when the anchor cut in with the story of the Livingston coup. "I wonder how Washington is reacting to this?" One of the anchors mused.

"I wouldn't be surprised if this administration brings him

up on charges of treason," his co-anchor, Robert Feldman replied.

"What are they talking about?" Annette asked. She yawned. It was 1:30 AM and they'd just finished watching one of the Left Behind movies on DVD.

"I don't know," Dave said.

"To give you an idea of what is being played now on CNN and MSNBC, we're running an excerpt of a tape our affiliates in Nashville picked up from the wire service not too long ago," the anchor said. "Take a look."

Portions of Livingston's speech played. Dave Murray watched in stunned silence. "This is … this is …"

"Terrible!" Annette finished for him.

"What a … how …"

"Outrageous!" Annette finished his thought again. Her tone had taken on an edge of anger.

"How can … I don't …"

"Believe I'm hearing this," Annette finished for him again. They were both looking angry now.

"Calling our President a religious fanatic?"

From Annette: "How dare those … those …" She was so angry, she could barely speak.

"Heathens!" Dave finished for her. He stood up from the sofa. His face was red.

"So is that what we are then?" Annette asked. "Religious fanatics? Because we're doing what the President says and waiting for the official government scientists to make their statements on this hurricane and those so-called creatures?"

"We should have known something foul was up," Dave said. With a look of disgust, he switched to the Trinity Broadcasting Channel. "I never liked Fox News anyway."

Annette looked at her husband in amazement. "You never liked Fox News? You? When did this happen?"

Dave thumbed the volume up on Pat Robertson. "Since three minutes ago when they started streaming this crap from the liberal media."

At Camp Pendleton Marine Base in San Clemente, California, First Officer Lance Pearce was hanging out with his buddies

Steve Gerald and Henry Lee Weinrib in their barracks, playing cards, drinking Lone Star beer, and shooting the shit. Pearce was in the hole to Gerald for a hundred bucks and Weinrib was in the hole by about twice that when Private Jerry Petty stormed into their room.

Jerry looked excited. "Turn the news on!"

Henry looked up from the game. He was holding a straight. "What's up?"

Jerry darted for the remote control. On the TV, a DVD of a live Motorhead show that Henry had gotten from a bootlegger at the Orange County Flea Market a few weeks ago was playing. He switched quickly to CNN. "You guys are gonna shit when you see this," Jerry said. He was so excited his voice was cracking.

The rest of the guys stopped the game and turned to the TV. Outside, other enlisted men crowded into Weinrib and Pearce's room. One of them, a tall, lanky black guy named Jamal, said to another man, "... that's the shit I was tellin' you about, man!"

Colonel Livingston: "—asking all American citizens, be they military or civilian, to stand beside me and defend this nation from the forces both within and abroad. I'm asking that our allies come to our aid, as we have done so many times in the past for them. My fellow soldiers, I'm asking you to disobey your direct orders and do the job you enlisted for. Protect your country."

Henry said, "What the hell's going on? We under attack or something?" Behind him he could hear his brothers raising ruckus. Off in the distance he could hear Lieutenant Southard barking orders. "Briefing on CNN and MSNBC! Attention, major briefing on CNN and MSNBC, all soldiers tune in to CNN and MSNBC and await further orders!"

"Jesus, what the hell's going on?" Steve said.

One of the soldiers that had come into the room with the initial overflow from outside said, "They've been running this as a loop for the past fifteen minutes. They'll replay it again."

From CNN: "Help me defend our country by defending yourselves. Thank you."

From outside, the sound of vehicles, of weapons being assembled, of troops being gathered.

Henry felt a spike of adrenaline rush through him. It was unlike anything he'd ever experienced before. It wasn't even like the rush of adrenaline he got while in the midst of heavy fighting in Fallujah, in the heart of Iraq just last year. "Whatever this is," he said to himself, "this is big."

Somebody nearby said, "They're replaying it again!"

All eyes turned to the TV screen. Henry saw an older man dressed in military fatigues flanked by a guy in a white lab coat and a woman in a stained T-shirt and jeans. The guy in military garb began his speech again. "Good morning. My name is Colonel Augustus Livingston, U.S. Army, retired. Yesterday, my country had need of me and I answered the call. I was asked—"

There was silence inside and outside the hall of Henry Weinrib's barracks room as he and his fellow soldiers were briefed by Colonel Augustus Livingston. Outside there was the sound of orders being given from what sounded like Colonel Harrison. "… we go up at twenty-four hundred hours!"

When Colonel Livingston's speech ended again, Lieutenant Southard was outside their room. "Assemble on the field, soldiers. Move out, move out!"

And for Henry Weinrib, the war started at that precise minute.

Peachbottom Nuclear Plant
2:35 AM

It was a war zone—and like all war zones, it was hell.

The original soldiers under Livingston's command who arrived at Peachbottom with him were thirty-six strong. A dozen were added through Peachbottom's Armed Security Team. That brought the count up to forty-eight. Eight of those men were now incarcerated in a locked storage room for admitting they would not join in Colonel Livingston's coup. That left forty soldiers and a handful of civilians to battle the Clickers and any Dark Ones who might come near the plant.

Upon arriving within the gated perimeter of the complex, weapons had been carted safely within the bowels of the structure. Guards had been posted outside, manning various spots along the high concrete fence. When the Clickers arrived, those guards commenced firing. Lieutenant Tranning had gone outside, bearing Livingston's order to engage, and backup was swift as the rest of the soldiers stormed outside. Private Paul Rodriguez was in one of the guard towers when he saw something that looked like a man waving its arms. He raised his weapon at the figure and it wasn't until he had it within his sights that he realized the figure really was a man, and that he was in the river, clinging to a tree branch that had been lodged against the Plant's damn. The man was waving and gesturing at him.

Private Rodriguez barked a command into his shoulder-mounted radio. "I have a civilian outside the plant, at the damn, and we're free of Clickers. Can somebody get out there and bring him up?"

Private Atkins answered him. "Northwest corner, Rodriguez?"

"Affirmative."

"Private Jones and I are making our way out. Our troop is covering."

"Report back in three."

Rodriguez watched as Atkins and Jones scurried out of the gate and headed to where the man was. He could see troops covering them from various points along the wall. They'd mowed down a bunch of the Clickers when they arrived, and now as he watched Atkins and Jones help the man out of the river, he thought he saw movement about one hundred yards out. "You're going to get company in a minute!" Rodriguez called out.

The man almost fell back into the river, but Jones and Atkins were there to stop his fall. The man was on his feet quickly, Jones and Atkins helping him along as they hurriedly escorted him to the gate. A moment later, the shapes in the distance became more easily identifiable: Clickers.

Rodriguez saw the three of them make it to safety. "Get him to Livingston!" Then he commenced to engage with his fellow soldiers.

The plant was besieged from the south and the east by the

Clickers as they swarmed up the swollen riverbanks. High caliber ammunition rent through their shells, pulverizing them. For the most part, the soldiers were safe; many of them were in secure locations, firing from atop guard towers or from the rooftop of the building. Thanks to the heavy wind and rain and the ferocious battle that was raging, some of them that were within close proximity did not see the dark shapes that moved in the shadows. Nor did they hear the sound of screaming as one of their own, a young soldier named Kenneth Reinheimer, was eviscerated by the sharp claws of a Dark One within the perimeter of the large concrete wall that surrounded the plant.

Kenneth Reinheimer was to have guarded the south exterior of the building. While most of the fighting was going on to the east and north, a skeleton crew of troops remained stationed along the other perimeters to stand guard. Kenneth was one of those, keeping a position on the ground right behind the South Guard station.

When the Dark One jumped over the concrete fence, Reinheimer gave a shout and swung his weapon toward the creature. He squeezed off several shots before the monster was on him, disemboweling him with one swoop of its claw. The creature crunched into Kenneth's head like a child biting into a candy apple, blood and brain matter squirting between its teeth. Within moments, most of Kenneth Reinheimer was down the Dark One's gullet. When it was finished, it ripped a metal door open and sauntered inside the plant.

It caught the scent of another human nearby and turned its head, trying to catch sight of the human, seeing him as the soldier called out, "Ken? Ken, where are you?"

That was all the Dark One needed. Relying on scent and sound, it dove toward the source of the voice and neutered it with slashing claws and snapping teeth.

The soldier went down in a spray of blood.

More Dark Ones slithered down behind the wall and joined it. The Dark One bleated softly, motioning toward the interior of the plant. Two of them entered the building. It then motioned around the corner of the building and two other Dark Ones crept along the wall, heading to the East side.

Scattered gunfire from the north. The Dark One listened, pleased with itself.

The man's name was Tony Genova and he was bleeding profusely from a leg wound; he also had a nasty puncture wound in his hand. "Damn crab thing got me," he said as he sat on one of the chairs in the lounge, dripping wet. His accent was a bizarre compendium of Brooklyn, Jersey shore, and Pennsylvania Dutch.

Jennifer tended to the wounds as Livingston, Jeremiah, Dr. Linnenberg, and one of the technicians from the bullpen, crowded around them. Only Rick remained where he was, huddled on the sofa, watching with interest.

Livingston looked agitated. "What did you say happened again?"

"The storm blew me off the road," Tony said. He was Caucasian, of medium build with short dark hair wearing the tattered, wet remains of dark slacks, a white dress shirt, and black shoes. "I was trying to leave Baltimore, trying to get to my sister's house in Lancaster, Pennsylvania when it happened. I sat in the car until the floodwaters came, then I got out and that's when I saw those things. They chased me, but one of them got me with its claws. Oww!" He flinched as Jennifer applied a dressing on it. "Shit, that hurts."

"When did you say this happened?" Livingston asked. Livingston had been manning the communications outside when he heard Rodriguez give the news that they'd just rescued a civilian from the river. Apparently, he'd been clinging to a floating scrap of wood and the current had slammed him into the power plant's dam. The Colonel sent Private Tom Schellenger out to meet them and escort the man inside. It was weird that the guy was out there; he should be dead, given the number of Clickers marauding across the area. The new arrival seemed nervous and evasive. He wasn't sure if it was from his ordeal or something else, but the Colonel took an instant disliking to him.

"I don't know, man! It was like, a few hours ago." Tony watched Jennifer as she tended to his wounds. "Damn things

... I've never seen anything like them."

"Neither have we," Jeremiah Brown said.

"You're lucky," Livingston said, appraising the newcomer. "It could have been a lot worse."

Tony snorted. "You're telling me."

Rodriguez came on the line. "Colonel Livingston! We have Dark Ones at two o'clock on the West side of the building!"

Livingston drew away from the group huddled around Tony Genova on the chair. "Engage them! Give them everything you have! Kill them!"

The White House
2:45 AM

Donald Miller was adamant that President Jeffrey Tyler and a pair of Secret Service Agents go with him back to the Magog bunker. "It's too dangerous for you to be here," he told the President. The creatures were now reported to be swarming through the capitol. Alexandria and Georgetown were already overrun with Clickers—and something else. There was some confusion in the initial reports as to what the second race of creatures actually was. Privately, Miller wondered if Livingston could have actually been right.

They had taken up command in one of the conference rooms on the third floor of the building. Ken White informed Donald that the building would withstand the hordes—it was designed to withstand not only hurricane force winds, but most kinds of military attacks. There were dozens of underground rooms below the White House for the specific purpose of military planning during the event of a nuclear war, but Tyler hadn't wanted to retreat there. He'd insisted that one little storm wasn't going to send him cowering with his tail between his legs.

Instead, he'd remained in the conference room with Ken White, Secretary Barker, Kathy Hayden, who was the Secretary of State, and Donald Miller. Kathy told them that the head of the Department of Agriculture, Wayne Keane, was working on a press release to explain the mainstream media's reports on the so-called Clickers that everyone was so worried about. Barker

informed them that communications with Livingston had been
cut off, probably due to the storm. "I've ordered Colonel Allman
out at Fort Bragg to get to Peachbottom and place Livingston's
convoy under arrest. His troops can secure the site."

"What about the possibility of other dissenters?" Tyler had
asked.

Tyler had been livid when he learned that Colonel
Livingston's press release was leaked to the media. For the first
time in Donald Miller's tenure with President Tyler, he'd been
afraid for not only his job, but his life. When Miller broke the
news to Tyler, the President had already retreated to a private
area to pray. At first Tyler had not wanted to come out. Miller
had to tell him through the intercom that Livingston had
committed treason.

Donald rubbed the bruise over his left eye from the punch
the President had landed on his face. Tyler had been furious.
When he stormed out of the bunker the first thing he did was
take a swing at Donald, who'd been unprepared for the blow.
Tyler would have beaten the crap out of him had the two Secret
Service agents who were guarding the door to the Magog not
been there. It had taken all their strength to subdue Tyler, who'd
been in a violent frenzy. "I want Livingston dead, do you hear
me! I want his fucking head brought in on a platter!"

For the first time, Donald Miller had been afraid of President
Jeffrey Tyler.

It had taken Tyler a good half-hour to calm down. His anger
was raging, and it had needed an outlet. The Secret Service
agents had pulled Tyler off of Miller, probably saving his life.
While one of them helped Donald to his feet, the other one
walked Tyler down the hall, trying to calm him down. "Let's
just walk away from this and try to calm down, Mr. President,"
the agent said.

"Fuck!" Jeffrey yelled. Then he took a swing at the Secret
Service agent who was trying to calm him down.

Like Donald Miller, the agent was unprepared for the
sudden violence. The blow caught him in the face. Unlike
Donald Miller, the Secret Service agent reacted instinctively.
Primal rage overrode years of conditioning and training. As

President Tyler came at him again with another blow, the agent deflected it and, in a quick martial arts move, got the President's arm behind his back. The agent had his service weapon out and was placing the tip of the barrel against the President's head when Donald Miller shouted. "Stop it, Nathan!"

President Tyler struggled. "Get your filthy hands off me!"

Nathan holstered his weapon. He kept his grip on Tyler's arm. "Calm. The fuck. Down, Mr. President."

"Let go of me!"

Donald shouted at Nathan to let the President go. He then had to defer to the President's authority to turn his back on what was to happen next. "I'm still pissed the hell off and I need an outlet," Donald heard Tyler say after he ordered both Secret Service agents to disarm themselves. At first Donald had been confused; surely Tyler was just going to fire both men himself. He was unprepared for what was to happen next.

"You two, get out," Tyler had told Donald and the other Secret Service agent, a man with ten years on the job named Hal King. "Now!"

Donald had seen the crazed look on Tyler's face and knew that if he disobeyed the order his political career, if not his very life, was in mortal danger.

Hal King had tried to talk some sense into President Tyler. "Mr. President, with all due respect."

"If you don't get the hell out of here in the next ten seconds, I will make sure you will never work anywhere ever again." Tyler thundered. "Do you understand? You won't even be able to get a job at Burger King!"

That left Donald Miller and Hal King with no choice but to walk away.

When Jeffrey Tyler emerged from the Magog Bunker a few minutes later he was out of breath, his coat was rumpled, but he looked more calmed down. He straightened his appearance in the mirror in the outer hallway of the main building as Donald Miller and Hal King waited calmly. "He'll be fine," Tyler had said. He rubbed the knuckles of his hand on his coat, smearing blood on the garment. "He took his lickings like a man."

Donald Miller had been silent. He didn't know what to say.

"Let's adjourn to the main conference room," Tyler said once he was finished inspecting his features.

And now here they were.

Miller still didn't know how badly Tyler had beaten up Nathan Howard, but Ken White assured him that it wasn't that bad. "He has a broken nose and he'll need stitches on his face," Ken had told him in a whispering tone before the meeting kicked off. "He's resting now in the infirmary."

"I agree with Barker," Miller now said, banishing Nathan's injuries away to be dealt with later. "Livingston and his men are to be rounded up and arrested immediately."

"Any chance we can get Black Lodge in on this?" Tyler asked.

"It would be incredibly risky," Barker admitted. He looked beat. The top two buttons of his shirt were unbuttoned, his tie loosened slightly from his neck. "They'd have to be airborne as soon as we get word that Gary has been downgraded to a category two."

"What category are we at now?" Tyler asked.

Miller answered. "National Weather Bureau has downgraded Gary to a Category Four and weakening."

"So we can have Black Lodge at Peachbottom by dawn," Barker said.

"Let's do it." Tyler turned to Miller. "We need to deal with the press. We need to get Black Lodge to CNN, MSNBC, and Fox as soon as possible."

"I agree," Donald Miller said. "The problem is going to be their affiliate stations and local news outlets."

Tyler looked as if he was going to lose control of his emotions again. His features twisted into a grimace as he slammed the conference room table with his fists. "Call in an order to military bases in other parts of the country. Order them to send troops to all local news stations and order the programming managers to cease transmission of that footage. Anyone that refuses is to be shot."

Donald Miller didn't even blink, but Secretary Barker gave a short gasp. He quickly regained his composure. "Yes, Mr. President." He rose from his seat and went over to a phone on the other side of the room to get a secure line.

Various locations across the United States
2:50 AM, Eastern Standard Time

Colonel Nicholas Nave never gave a rat's ass about doing what
was politically correct. The minute his wife, Becky, woke him
up to tell him the news he was on the phone to his subordinates
at Fort Bliss in El Paso, Texas.

He had Lieutenant Sanchez on speakerphone as he got
hurriedly dressed. "Report I got says Hurricane Gary should
be downgraded to a Category 2 by the time our Black Hawks
reach the Pennsylvania state line," he said, buttoning his shirt
as he spoke. "It's supposed to die out over Ohio. I've been on the
phone with Colonel Armstrong out of Kansas and Colonel Slade
out of San Antonio. Slade's sending fighter planes to D.C. He's
also sending a team of birds to act as an offensive to Colonel
Allman's troops."

"Allman's in Barker's command?" the voice coming out of
the speakerphone asked.

"Affirmative." Colonel Nave had been stationed at Fort Bliss
for twenty years. He was in his late fifties with a strong, lean
build. He'd quickly suited up and was psyching himself up
for his ride, which was due to pick him up at the house in two
minutes. "And I want to be in the air at 0200 hours."

"Yes, sir," the voice on the speakerphone said. "We're getting
birds ready now. We have ground troops assembling, too."

"Good. Any word from Livingston personally?"

"Not yet, sir. Communications in that area are still down,
but we should have it re-established at 0200 hours."

"Excellent!"

While Colonel Nicholas Nave prepared to lead his troops
out of Fort Bliss into battle on the East Coast, this scenario was
being repeated at no less than three dozen military bases across
the country, most of them from areas unaffected by the storm
and the creatures. One retired Army Colonel, a man named
Dallas Bradbury, who'd served with Livingston in Vietnam,
was watching CNN at his home in Las Vegas when the footage
came on. He called the nearest Army base a minute later,

identified himself, and when he learned they were assembling troops to make the trip to the East Coast, told them he wanted to accompany them to Maryland. "But sir," the young grunt on the phone said. "If you're retired we can't just reactivate you!"

"I don't want to be reactivated, son," Bradbury said. "I'm volunteering."

In Lexington, Kentucky, a firefight erupted between two squads of soldiers. One group had been assembled at the command of their drill Sergeant, Alfred Rossington, who was gunning to kick some righteous crustacean ass over what he'd seen on the news. They were confronted by base Sergeant Michaels, who had a life-sized poster of Secretary of Defense Barker on his office wall and a signed photo of President Jeffrey Tyler in a gold-tinged frame on his desk. Michaels had a core group of soldiers who hung on his every word, and when he ordered Rossington's troops to cease their mission, Rossington gave the order to ignore it. The resulting firefight killed eighteen men and wounded a dozen, Rossington and base Sergeant Michaels included.

Soon, dozens of fighter jets and Black Hawk helicopters equipped with soldiers, weapons, and ammunition were winging their way to Washington, D.C., Baltimore, Maryland, and the Peachbottom Nuclear Plant in Pennsylvania. Other planes and helicopters bearing troops were heading toward affected areas from Maine to Florida. Depending on their area of departure, arrival time was estimated at forty-five minutes to two hours.

The only good thing about that was Hurricane Gary was, indeed, weakening.

But the armies of the Dark Ones were getting stronger.

Peachbottom Nuclear Plant
2:53 AM

Tony glanced around at the other civilians and wondered what the fuck to do next. He'd managed to escape the Clickers in the river by diving all the way down to the bottom and letting the current speed him away. When he could no longer hold his breath, he'd dart back to the surface, grab a lungful of air, and then go under again. He kept this up until hitting the dam, after which the troops had pulled him from the water.

The muffled sounds of rapid, automatic gunfire echoed outside, along with screams and shouts. Nobody spoke. The technicians and employees were sprawled out on chairs and across the floor. The two marine experts, who'd been introduced to him as Jennifer and Richard, sat off to one side. The woman had her eyes closed, and the older man was reading a day-old newspaper. The other guy, William Mark, kept staring at him, and it was making Tony paranoid.

The chances of William Mark recognizing him were unlikely, but not impossible. Tony studied his face. He certainly didn't recognize him. Guy didn't look like he belonged to anyone's crew. But even still, he was hard. Tony could tell that. Mr. William Mark might not be a criminal, might not be in "the life," but he'd faced down death a time or two. It was easy enough to see, if you knew what to look for; the signs were there in his posture, the lines on his face, and the haunted look in his eyes.

He was staring at Tony again.

Tony stared back, unflinching.

Mark broke the gaze, letting his eyes wander over the sleeping woman's form.

Tony's paranoia grew.

He wished he still had his gun.

Doug Wath had been a janitor at Peachbottom for almost thirty years. He was looking forward to early retirement in another five, provided he lived through the night, of course. He'd bought a little piece of land in West Virginia and built a hunting cabin on it. With nothing to tie him down, his wife now an ex-wife and his kids long grown with families of their own, he couldn't wait to move there permanently and hunt every day. Maybe sometimes he'd let his best buddy, Dale Murphy, come hunt, but then again, maybe he'd keep it all to himself. Game was abundant around the cabin; deer, pheasants, wild turkey, and bears.

Nothing like those things outside, though.

He wondered what it would be like to hunt one. As the siege began, he'd asked one of the soldiers if they had any extra rifles, and if so, could he lend a hand in the fight. The soldier, barely old enough to shave, had dismissed him with a shake of his head, telling him to stay inside and out of harm's way.

Anxious and needing something to occupy his time, Doug had decided to clean up the blood all over the floor in the vending area. One of the soldiers had been wounded and they'd brought him in there temporarily. Doug didn't know where he was now; maybe back on the front lines or maybe dead. But scarlet traces of the wounded man remained, and the way he saw it, if they wouldn't let him fight, he might as well do his job.

Deciding to retrieve his mop and bucket, he opened the door to the janitor's closet and a dead man fell out. Doug gave a frightened yelp and shrank away. The dead man's head sounded like a melon as it hit the floor and cracked, but there was very little blood. When Doug rolled him over, he saw why. There was a neat little bullet hole in the guy's forehead about the size of a dime.

"Holy shit …"

He knew the dead man. His name was Mitch Johnson, and he was—had been—a boiler operator. The man's uniform was missing and he'd been stripped naked, his hands and feet bound with duct tape, and his underwear stuffed in his mouth.

Doug had listened when Colonel Livingston had addressed Peachbottom's personnel. He knew about the Clickers and the Dark Ones. He knew that the Dark Ones were smart and deadly and could use weapons. But the Colonel had insisted the Dark Ones didn't use firearms, which meant that someone else had killed Johnson.

As he knelt by the corpse, a shadow fell over him. Doug started to turn and then something hard smashed into his face. His mouth erupted with pain and filled with blood.

"Nothing personal," a voice said. "You just happened to come across something that was none of your business."

A second blow crashed down upon his head, and Doug Wath's vision went black.

Rick was growing paranoid.

His imagination was running wild due to the sounds of the battle outside and with the constant flashbacks to Phillipsport, 1994 replaying in his mind.

Being stuck in this lounge reminded him of being stuck in that supermarket freezer at the height of Hurricane Floyd.

And with that, his mind was playing tricks on him.

He was hearing noises.

Something had breached the walls of the Power Plant.

He was lying on a couch in the lounge. He couldn't sleep—how could he sleep knowing what was going on outside? Livingston was standing near a table where some weapons had been laid, communicating with his troops outside via walkie-talkie. Rick could hear the battle over the squawk of feedback and static.

And he could swear he was hearing a noise from somewhere outside of the command center in the plant.

After Jennifer tended to Tony's wounds, she'd retreated back to her chair near Richard. Tony had flexed his wounded leg, gritting his teeth. Rick had watched him warily from his perch on the sofa. Maybe he was being paranoid, but something about that guy just wasn't right.

Livingston had ordered a handful of men to remain just within the perimeter of the building to guard the interior. Perhaps it was their footfalls he was hearing outside the lounge. That's what he kept trying to tell himself.

Besides, another employee had just entered the room a few moments ago; a maintenance guy or something, judging by his coveralls. The name stenciled on his uniform said "Mitch." He'd glanced around the room and then taken a seat in the corner, not speaking to anyone. But if there had been something out in the corridors, it would have slaughtered him.

Unless it had let him slip by, hoping to trap them all together …

The area they were currently sequestered in was on the ground floor of the plant. There were three floors above them consisting of administrative office space. The ground floor housed the command center where the general daily activities of the plant were directed from as well as building security, the operations and maintenance areas, the building cafeteria and the IT data center. The basement level housed more of what was in the command center—machinery and computers that operated the nuclear reactors.

What Rick was hearing outside the area of the command center, which consisted of the bullpen that overlooked the basement command center and the lounge where he and the other civilians were, was akin to what he'd heard twelve years ago when he was trapped inside the freezer at the supermarket in Phillipsport.

It was the stealthy slither of large, reptilian claws clicking on linoleum floor.

Tony was sitting upright on the chair, flexing his leg. He was surveying his surroundings. "It's pretty nice in here," he said.

"Yeah, it is," Richard said, looking up from his newspaper. "You're lucky you were so close. Those things almost killed us."

"I bet," Tony said. His hands brushed the sides of his suit coat. "They ran me off the road."

Behind Rick, he could hear Livingston talking to his troops via walkie-talkie. It sounded like the battle outside was growing worse. He also felt Livingston's gaze directed at them as he talked, as if he were watching them.

"How long were you out there?" Richard asked Tony.

"A couple hours."

Rick felt a chilly finger run down his spine.

If he was out there for a couple of hours, why didn't Livingston's convoy pick him up when they arrived? Surely he would have seen them from where he was … right?

Unless he approached Peachbottom from another direction, the voice of reason shot back to counter Rick's growing paranoia. Maybe nobody knew he was out there because there were no guards out there at the time. And if we showed up on one side, there's no way Livingston and his troops would have seen this guy, much less—

Peachbottom's Security Team would have seen him if he'd shown up anywhere within the perimeter of the plant. They were expecting us because Livingston called ahead. If this guy showed up before we did, or even around the same time, they would have seen him and either shot him or hauled his ass in here with us.

What if Tony Genova was really with the government? An assassin. What if they'd sent him to kill Rick, or even Colonel Livingston—or both?

Rick held his breath. The sounds he thought he was hearing grew closer. They weren't his imagination. He hoisted himself up into a sitting position. Jennifer was scrunched up on one of the chairs on his right; she opened her eyes and looked over at him.

"You hear that?" Rick asked.

Jennifer cocked her head to the side, listening.

Richard sat up. "What do you hear?"

Jennifer held up her hand for silence.

The four of them were still for a moment.

Colonel Livingston noticed the exchange and shut off his walkie-talkie. He stood at his corner of the lounge, silent.

When the sound came again all four of them heard it this time. It was unmistakable.

Something very large and heavy was traversing the hallways of the power plant's interior.

"They got in," Livingston said.

Rick was on his feet in an instant. "Holy Jesus fucking Christ, now what?"

His outburst disturbed the rest of the civilians. All of them were instantly alert, babbling in excited confusion.

"Stay calm," Livingston said. He slung an assault rifle over his shoulder. Then in one swift motion he drew his side arm and pointed it at Tony. "Mr. Genova, will you get on your knees with your hands on your head, please?"

Jennifer looked at Livingston with shock. "What?"

Rick felt his heart race, the paranoia he felt toward Tony justified.

Tony looked calmly up at Colonel Livingston. "What for? What's wrong?"

"Just do as I say, now!"

What happened next occurred in what seemed like slow motion to Rick. He watched as Tony turned away from Colonel Livingston and began to do as he was told. He slunk down onto the floor of the lounge on his knees. As he did so, Mitch, the late arrival, snaked his right hand into the pocket of his coveralls. Rick wasn't sure if it was the retort from Livingston's sidearm or the gun by Mitch's body as it fell to the floor. Jennifer screamed; Richard yelled in surprise; the other civilians scrambled out of the way; and blinking in surprise, Tony pissed his pants. Rick wasn't even aware that he'd scrambled off his safe position on the sofa and was standing with his back against the wall of the lounge until Colonel Livingston stepped over Mitch Johnson's prone body and pumped a second bullet into the man's head. Then he turned to Tony.

"My apologies, sir. I assumed you were the one at first."

Tony grinned. "No sweat. I like your style."

"What the fuck are you doing?" Jennifer screamed. "You just killed that man."

"I did, indeed. He would have done the same to us."

Jennifer shook her head. "You're insane."

"Colonel Livingston," Richard said slowly, hands held out in front of him, "while we appreciate all of your efforts tonight, I believe you owe us an explanation. I will not sanction nor be party to cold-blooded murder."

Livingston bent down and picked up a black handgun that had fallen out of the dead man's hand. He ejected the magazine and checked the chamber. "A Glock. Round already chambered. Here's your man in black, Rick."

"You guys thought I was some government assassin?" Tony asked.

"Yeah," Rick admitted. "You've got to admit that it was awfully weird how you just showed up out of nowhere and made it in here alive."

Tony shrugged. "What can I say? I'm a resourceful guy."

"Who are you, really?"

Before Tony could answer, footsteps pounded toward the lounge and the door was wrenched open. Jeremiah Brown and two of his security guards were there, firearms out and ready.

"What happened?" Brown asked. "Is that man dead? And why is he wearing Mitch Johnson's uniform?"

"Just a minor inconvenience," Colonel Livingston said as he whisked the Glock away. He looked at Rick. "I had a gut instinct about this guy the minute I laid eyes on him. He's from the same agency that forced me into retirement and has been after you and Melissa."

"How the fuck do you know that?" Jennifer was clearly upset. Her eyes were wide, panic-stricken. "You barely talked to the guy!"

Livingston shoved his hand into the dead man's pocket and extracted his wallet. He flipped it open and found what he was looking for. He held it out to her. "Does this satisfy you?"

The ID on the badge identified "Mitch Johnson" as Harold Bronski, a member of the Central Intelligence Agency.

The thought that he'd just escaped certain death was not lost on Rick, but it wasn't the first time he'd been through this tonight. He remembered the sounds he'd heard in the corridor.

"Mr. Brown," he asked, "did you see anything else in the hallways when you rushed in here?"

Jeremiah frowned. "No. Why?"

A sudden burst of static from the walkie-talkie and Tranning's voice came on the line, breaking his thoughts. "This is Four Actual calling Command. Colonel Livingston, sir? Do you copy?"

"Right here, Tranning!"

"There's dozens of these things, sir, and they're breaching the walls!" Amid the static was the sound of gunfire and screams from the battle outside. "They're climbing up the walls and we're getting a lot of them but ... holy shit, one of them just got over. Oh fuck!"

"Four Actual, repeat that. Four Actual? Tranning! Tranning! Do you read me! Tranning!"

A burst of static erupted from the speaker, followed by Tranning moaning. And then ... CLICK-CLICK ... CLICK-CLICK ...

Then the transmission ended.

"Team Two, did you copy that?"

There was no response.

Livingston sprinted out of the make-shift command center he'd set up for himself in the lounge and ran into the bullpen, brushing past Jeremiah and his security team.

"Shit!" Rick muttered.

"What are we going to do?" Jennifer sounded scared.

"Come on," Richard said. He headed out of the lounge to the bullpen. Reluctantly, Rick and Jennifer followed. The other employees waited for Brown to tell them what to do.

"Tell you what," one of them joked. "I'm gonna bring this up with the union."

Jeremiah and his security guys had followed Livingston out to the bullpen and they were in deep discussion with the technical team. "We need to retreat to a secure location," Livingston told the group. "Now!"

"We're going to have to go to the bunker," Jeremiah said. "Near the reactors."

Richard turned pale. "What about the radiation?"

"We'll still be shielded. Wouldn't want to live there, but our exposure should be at a minimum, provided the assault doesn't last for days. I assure you, it won't be lethal."

"A dosage of radiation or getting eaten by a Clicker," Jennifer said. "Tell me my life isn't working out."

"Let's do it," Livingston said.

As Jeremiah Brown gathered his security crew and technicians, Livingston herded Rick, Jennifer and Richard back into the lounge. He'd previously set a small cache of weapons on a table that rested against the far wall of the lounge—some pistols and high-caliber semi-auto assault rifles and boxes of ammunition and magazines. Livingston waved his hand in the weapons' direction. "Take your pick."

Rick picked up a handgun—a Sig Sauer 9mm—and found the correct mags for them. Richard picked up an AR15 assault rifle.

Livingston arched an eyebrow. "Do you know how to use that, doctor?"

Richard patted the weapon. "I once spent a week in a survivalist camp. It was for one of those corporate team-building exercises. Are you familiar with those?"

"Yes," Livingston said. "We called it Vietnam."

Richard blushed. "We just shot at bales of hay."

"Well now you'll get to shoot something more." Livingston turned away.

Tony selected a Kimber 1911 and an extra magazine. Just holding the pistol made him feel more confident again. The pain in his wounded leg vanished. He aimed the weapon at the wall and checked the sight.

"First one I kill is for you, Vince," he muttered under his breath.

Something thumped in the corridor.

"You'd better pick a weapon," Rick told Jennifer.

She shook her head. "I've never handled a gun before in my life and I'm not about to start now. And the Colonel—he just shot that man without even thinking about it."

"That's what he does. That's who he is."

"Well, that's not me."

Rick silently accepted this reasoning as he stuffed the Sig down the front pocket of his coveralls and joined Colonel Livingston at the door to the lounge. "You heard that, right? Outside?"

"Yes," Livingston answered. "Sounds like it's on the other side of us. Probably a few doors down."

"There's a locked door between us and that section of the building, right?" Jennifer asked.

"I think so."

"I wonder if the power affected it?"

"I guess we'll find out." Livingston opened the door to the hallway slowly.

Jeremiah and his team were ready. "Let's go." He began leading them out of the command center via the back way when there was a heavy crash from behind them. They all spun around.

Two very large Dark Ones had just torn the locked doors out of the wall. They pulled the pulverized metal down and one of them roared. It swiped out with one clawed hand and ripped through the face of the nearest man, shearing his flesh down to the bone. Rick felt his legs turn to rubber.

He pulled the Sig Sauer from his coveralls pocket, but couldn't get a clear shot. The power plant's employees were in the way. And they were being slaughtered.

"Get in the bunker!" Jeremiah screamed. "Get in the bunker!"

As the security team ushered the technicians ahead of them, along with Jennifer and Jeremiah, Rick, Richard, Tony, and Colonel Livingston opened fire. The high caliber shells did considerable damage at such close range. Rick was briefly satisfied when one shell pulverized one of the creature's faces.

As the Dark Ones went down they heard the squeals and roars from their own kind within the building along with another sound.

Click-Click! Click-Click!

"Goddamn," Rick muttered as he ejected a spent magazine and slapped in a new one. "They brought their fucking pets along, too."

"Come on! Come on!" Jeremiah Brown was already twenty yards down the hall, waiting for them at the doorway to what looked to be a secure area. "Move, move, move!"

They ran.

As they ran down the maze of corridors with the Dark Ones and Clickers in hot pursuit, Rick heard Livingston yell into the walkie-talkie he was still carrying, trying to get word on what was going on outside. "Team Two, report! Four Actual. Bravo Six! Anyone?"

Nothing except static, gunfire, and screams.

As they fled down the stairs to the lower section of the plant, Rick was babbling hysterically. "They've gotten in, Colonel. They've gotten in the fucking building! Jesus fucking Christ!"

"Goddamn it, I know they got in the building!" Livingston yelled.

"How can they get in?" Tony asked. "And what the fuck were those things back there in the lounge? They looked like snakes with legs."

"They're called Dark Ones," Rick told him.

"Can they get down here?"

Rick brushed past him. "You better fucking hope not. And if they do, you'd best save a bullet for yourself."

Jeremiah took charge, sauntering past Livingston once they reached the bottom floor. He swiped his key card through the card reader and there was a click as the lock was disengaged on a heavy steel door. Jeremiah opened it and they streamed through. When he slammed the heavy door behind them, Livingston felt a little relieved.

Jeremiah was panting, out of breath. "This way," he said, as he led them down another hall. It was well-lit. They ran down what seemed like an endless maze of hallways with white walls and floors and soft fluorescent lights until they came to another heavy steel door. Jeremiah swiped his key card, waited a beat, and then pressed the pad of his index finger on a black device on the card reader. A moment later there was a beep and another clicking sound as the lock was disengaged. Jeremiah opened the door. "Come on! Nothing can get through this door."

As they streamed through, Livingston noted the thickness and strength of the door. It was easily four feet of heavy steel and was controlled not only by key card access but by fingerprint recognition as well. "How strong are those locks?" he asked as Jeremiah shut the heavy door behind them.

"They're able to withstand ten tons of pressure," Brown said. He was standing in the center of the hallway, looking down two corridors that flanked his left and right. "That way is where the reactors are. You need security access to get there, too. And over here," he motioned to his left, "is a command center for emergencies. The backup generator is down here, too, and thanks to our quick thinking earlier when the first backup generator was destroyed, this one should be humming along perfectly."

"Maybe I can re-establish contact," Livingston said as they started down the hallway toward the command center.

"Do you think the outside world is reacting to your transmission," Jennifer asked. "Will they listen?"

"God, I hope so," Richard said.

"Me, too," Livingston agreed.

They reached another door and once again, Brown swiped

his card and placed the pad of his index finger on the reader to unlock it. He ushered them into a wide work area that was well-lit with plenty of desks, computers, and other electronic equipment that appeared to be fully functioning. Jeremiah dived for one of the workstations and got right down to business. "Bob, get on ten and give me a report. Clive, I want a report on the systems and Dave, give me a report on security."

Livingston retreated to a corner of their new command center. He thumbed the communications button on his walkie-talkie. "Team Two, report. Team One, what's your status? Bravo Six? Four Actual?"

There was no answer.

"Tranning?" Livingston's voice cracked. "You there, son? If you can't respond, just key your mike."

Static.

"Shit!" Feeling Tranning's loss would come later. In the brief time they'd spent together, Livingston had built an instant rapport with the young soldier, one that could have solidified into a good working relationship had he been twenty years younger. He was sorry that Tranning was probably dead, but he couldn't think about it now. He had to establish contact with the outside world.

He reached for the cellular phone on his belt clip and turned it on. He waited a moment while it powered up.

Jennifer Wasco was standing by him and saw the LED readout on the phone as the device went through its powering on stage. "Come on," she urged. "Please give us a signal!"

The LED readout read SEARCHING FOR NETWORK.

"Come on!" Livingston urged.

The readout changed to NETWORK FOUND.

Along with four bars of power.

"Son of a bitch," Tony said. "I really need to change service providers."

Livingston thumbed the controls on his cell phone and navigated to where the phone numbers were stored. May had pre-programmed the numbers for him and taught him how to use it. Livingston flipped down to the letter R and hit the Connect button when Colonel Gary Richrath's name came up.

He brought the phone to his ear and listened as it rang.

Livingston hadn't seen or spoken to Colonel Richrath since shortly after Phillipsport. He'd made no attempt to contact him since his visit with the government spook that day in 1995, and he'd heard through the grapevine that Gary was living a quiet life in his own forced retirement somewhere in Illinois.

The line on the other end was picked up on the third ring. "Augustus Livingston." Richrath sounded wideawake and ready, as if he were expecting his call.

"No need to explain why I'm calling," Livingston said. "You obviously saw my statement on the news."

"Affirmative; it's generated a shit storm, Augustus."

"How so?"

Richrath sighed. "You do realize that this isn't a secure line, Colonel?"

"Does it really matter at this point?"

"No, I suppose not. I doubt there's anybody left to listen in."

"That bad?"

"Casualties in the millions. That's the estimate I'm hearing."

"And my transmission?"

"I'm leaving my son's house in Champaign," Richrath said. "I just dropped my wife off there. Kevin and his family are pretty well armed, and they've barricaded themselves in the house. I knew Kevin's place would be safe until I could get out of town."

"What are you talking about?"

Richrath's tone of voice was grave. Livingston had a hard time telling if his fellow Army Colonel was angry at him or simply angry at the current situation. "Carol and I saw the first airing of your statement. It was very powerful and it evoked strong feelings and emotions in me. I acted on them and readied myself up. An intruder outside the property activated my silent alarm and I quickly armed myself. I caught the guy at the side of the house and took him down with a headshot. There was one other, and I brought him down with a shot to the back. He was still alive and I was forced to end his suffering. He was assigned to the CIA. It appears that the President seems to have an extreme prejudice towards us now."

"Damn!" Livingston wondered how many of those spooks were out there, seeking to tie up all the loose ends. Couldn't Tyler see how pointless it was now? There was no way to keep this quiet, not with so many Americans dead. Not with so many Clickers littering the nation's landscape.

"I established contact with Fort Campbell," Richrath continued, "found out they were heeding your message, and headed over there after getting Carol to Kevin's house. I'm in a Black Hawk now about forty minutes away from Peachbottom."

Livingston felt the breath whoosh out of him. "Do you know how many reinforcements you'll have?"

"Over two thousand strong by the sounds of it," Richrath said. "I've been in contact with various military bases on the West Coast and the Midwest. All of them are sending troops to the affected areas. North Carolina is sending every single Marine they've got."

"Is there any word from Barker?"

"Barker has called in orders for your arrest and is sending troops from Fort Bragg. They're loyal to the President. They should be reaching Peachbottom in thirty minutes."

"Peachbottom is overrun with Dark Ones and Clickers," Livingston said. "Do you copy me? I've lost over half my troops and a good portion of Peachbottom's Security team. The rest of us are holed up in the subterranean portions of the building. Is anybody on Barker's side?"

"From what I'm seeing, not many." Richrath's voice changed a little; it sounded like he was smiling. "There's a lot of in-fighting amongst the troops right now, but our side seems to be coming out on top. Like I said, the Airborne out of Bragg, and a few others here and there are still taking orders from Tyler and Barker, maybe the Seals and some Marine and Army battalions, too. But all in all, I'd say we outnumber them five to one, Colonel."

Livingston felt further relief. "That's good to hear."

"Colonel Eastman out of Kansas is leading the offensive for us," Richrath continued. "And Colonel Nave out of Fort Bliss has assumed command of the Air Force. Nave has ordered fighter jets in the air and the first wave of them should be reaching the coast of North Carolina shortly."

"What about Washington?"

"Nave has given orders to engage Barker's forces over Washington if it comes to it," Richrath said. "Eastman and Nave conferred with me due to your original report to the Joint Chiefs in ninety-four and I recommended Barker and Tyler be taken out. Several of your men out of Fort Detrick went AWOL under Allman's command and are heading to Washington now to carry that order out."

Jesus, Livingston thought. He felt a strange sense of pride that his briefing of the Clickers and Dark Ones had not been lost on his men out of Fort Detrick. He also felt an odd sense of detachment at the news that orders had been given for the President's assassination. We're fighting a civil war, Livingston thought to himself. We're at war not only with these creatures, but with our own government. All because they were acting in their own self-interest and let their personal ideology override common sense and reality. What a damn shame.

"I should warn you," Richrath continued, "that intelligence on the ground indicates that the main enemy force is converging on Washington. That may very well be the main battleground."

"First," Livingston said, "I'm going to need as many men as you can send to Peachbottom. Ground troops will be necessary to flush out the Dark Ones that have breached the perimeter and interior of this plant. We'll need troops that can penetrate the interior and do a clean and sweep. Meanwhile, send our armor and heavy weaponry into D.C."

"Affirmative. You'll get your rescue team, Augustus. Just hang on."

"One more question, Colonel Richrath."

"What's that, spider-soldier?"

Livingston grinned. He and Richrath had served together in Southeast Asia. One night, while bedded down in a banana grove, their platoon had been besieged by tarantulas. Livingston had gone crazy, running around and stomping on the arachnids. Since then, Richrath had occasionally called him "spider-soldier." The nickname stuck in the dozen times they came across each other over the intervening years. It was nice to hear that Richrath hadn't forgotten it.

"What is the civilian and media reaction to my statement?"

"Like I said before, it's raised a shit-storm. There's still a few staunch conservatives defending Tyler's Administration and some of the more reactionary conservative bloggers have been quick to label you everything from a traitor to a commie liberal—"

Livingston snorted in disgust. "It figures! As you know, I'm anything but that, Richrath."

"I know, sir. Some have taken to calling for your execution. But an overwhelming majority of people—Democrat and Republican, Liberal and Conservative—are in our corner. We've even got civilian volunteers heading to the affected areas. The Vice President is somewhere in Nebraska trying to hold Tyler's Administration together and failing miserably. Half of Congress is in disarray; they're holding an emergency session now via speaker phone and internet from various secure locations in and around Washington."

"They were evacuated, correct?" Livingston asked.

"Yes, but there were a lot of them out of town for the weekend, back home with their constituencies. They're running around like decapitated chickens."

Livingston chuckled at that. "Good! Carry on, soldier. Carry on!"

"See you soon, Augustus."

"One more thing," Livingston said slowly. "Have a bird circling Washington. Serious payload."

"What?"

"Just in case."

"It won't come to that, Augustus."

"Just in case," Livingston repeated.

"We'll be there in thirty minutes." Richrath signed off. "Keep your ass down and your powder dry until the extraction team arrives."

Livingston folded the cell phone back up and turned to the group, who had paused in making sure the systems were running smoothly to listen to Livingston's side of the conversation.

Rick studied the Colonel. "Is the cavalry coming?"

"Help is on the way," Livingston said. For the first time since this second wave had started, he felt a glimmer of hope.

Whitman Air Force Base, Missouri
3:00 AM, Eastern Standard Time
A B-2 Stealth Bomber soared into the night sky. The pilot, Cariaga, repeated several "Hail Marys" as he set course for the East Coast. His knuckles were white and he gritted his teeth hard enough to give himself a headache. Cariaga had flown missions and sorties over Iraq and Afghanistan, but he'd never been more terrified in his life than he was now.

The clouds parted, and the plane shot across the horizon.

14

Banks of the Potomac River
Washington, D.C.
3:08 AM

It was so big that it stuck out of the water, its red, barnacle-encrusted shell breaching the surface like a shark's dorsal fin. Water streamed down its ridges, splashing into the river below. The hull of a boat, unmoored and destroyed by Hurricane Gary floated by. The massive creature seized the wreckage in one giant claw and crushed it to splinters. Then it continued on its way. Its pincers clacked together, and the sound carried across the land, audible a mile away.

CLICK-CLICK … CLICK-CLICK …

The giant Clicker's smaller brethren fled in its path, and its masters, the Dark ones, kept their distance, watching the monster's progress from afar. The creature pushed its bulk from the river and lumbered onto the shore. The muddy riverbank collapsed beneath its weight. The Clicker squealed in frustration and heaved itself onto land again. Its segmented legs sank into the storm-drenched earth, and the ground trembled with each step.

Cautiously, the Dark Ones emerged from hiding and jabbed at it with their spears and tridents. With a roar that sounded like a herd of elephants, the Clicker swiped out with one massive claw, knocking several of them aside. The others danced out of range, also being careful not to get too near its pulsating tail; venom dripped from the bulbous appendage and splattered the ground.

With much prodding and stabbing, they managed to alter its path and send the Clicker stomping off across the city.

Its path would take it directly towards the Capitol—and the White House.

Peachbottom Nuclear Plant
3:21 AM

They sat and they waited. Livingston had positioned everyone with a weapon at various points around the room, guarding all entrances and exits. Jennifer and the other unarmed individuals sat in the center of the bunker. Jeremiah and his technicians worked feverishly, trying to ignore the sounds coming from outside the reinforced walls; wet sounds; screaming, shooting, tearing, ripping—clicking.

With the air conditioning out, the temperature inside the room had crept steadily upward. Rick wiped the sweat from his eyes and readjusted his grip on the pistol. Tony tapped him on the shoulder, and Rick turned to him.

"So we cool?"

"Yeah," Rick said, sticking out his hand. "Look, I'm sorry we doubted you. You've got to understand, I've been on the run so long, and I don't know how to interact with people anymore."

"Why'd he want to kill you, anyway?"

"Because of what I know; it's a long story."

Tony shrugged. "No worries. Every man's got his secrets."

"What about you, Tony? I asked you once before, but you still haven't told me. Who are you, really?"

Tony paused before answering. "I'm a deliveryman. Me and my associate, Vince, were making a delivery. We got caught in the storm and the Clickers ambushed us on a bridge. We went into the water. I came out. Vince didn't."

"My condolences. I guess we've all lost people tonight."

Rick's thoughts turned to Melissa. He wondered if she was okay, if she was even alive. He hoped her identity hadn't been discovered by the government, that she wasn't in danger of being assassinated by the same spooks that had tried to kill him earlier. Then he thought of his mother. In a strange way, he was glad she'd passed on before all of this. Strange, how things turned out. Yesterday he'd been at her deathbed. Now he was barricaded deep inside a nuclear power plant, making a desperate last stand against the very creatures that had separated him from his family in the first place. In between, he'd been raped, hunted, and chased by enemies on all sides.

Jennifer stood up and walked over to Richard. Her superior had aged during this ordeal. She could see it etched in his face. He smiled at her reassuringly and Jennifer tried not to cry.

"We're going to make it," he said.

"Do you really think so?"

"Yes, I really do. Livingston said help is on the way. They'll get here in time. The Hurricane is gone so that won't slow them down."

"Even if we do survive, what then?" Jennifer asked. "What about our loved ones? While we're in here, what do you think is happening to them? They were at ground zero, Richard. What's the point of surviving if it's only to bury them?"

Richard put his hand on her shoulder and squeezed. His voice was soft, but stern. "Don't talk that way. Don't you dare. I know Susan, and I know she'd want me to keep on fighting. Your parents would want the same. Remember when we were trapped in the aquarium, right before Livingston arrived to save us? I figured we were done for. Thought that was it; we were dead. But we weren't. You just have to rely on the human spirit. We're a tenacious race. Humanity always prevails."

Wiping away a tear, Jennifer leaned up on her toes and kissed his cheek. Richard blushed.

"Susan is a very lucky woman, Richard."

"And one day, you're going to make someone a very lucky man, Jennifer."

She started to respond when the walls vibrated. Everyone in the room jumped, and Richard almost shot the door.

"Steady," Livingston ordered. "Maintain control."

Something was pounding on the walls and doors, trying to get inside.

"I thought nothing could get down here!" Rick muttered. He checked the mag on his Sig Sauer; fully loaded.

"Nothing should be able to get down here," Jeremiah said, his eyes darting around the bunker. "But we're dealing with the extraordinary here."

There was another loud pound on the wall, along with shuffling.

Jeremiah sipped cold coffee from a cracked ceramic mug and sighed. "Well, I guess this is it."

"Bring it on you cocksuckers," Tony shouted. "We got something for your ass."

"Enough," Livingston yelled. "Keep silent and stay ready."

"And then what?" Tony smirked.

Livingston turned back to the door. "And then we live ... or we die."

The White House
3:37 AM

Ken White looked horrified. "I still can't believe that you're going to have members of the press executed. It's madness ..."

"Got a problem with that, Mr. White?" President Tyler seemed like an entirely different man now. Gone was the youthful, clean-cut, wholesome American image that had wooed voters yearning for honest change in government. That image had been replaced by total insanity.

White stammered. He was pale, his hair in a messy disarray from the late night and the long hours. "I just ... what's the purpose of suppressing information that might save people's lives?"

"The Lord is going to save people's lives!" Tyler thundered, slamming the conference room table again with his fist. Everybody seated around the table jumped, startled at the sudden outburst. "The American people have to put all their faith and trust in the Lord! Not a bunch of atheist Darwin-polluted Godless scientists!"

"But ... what's happening is ... what they're reporting on is really happening?" White stuttered.

Tyler shot out of his chair. "When have you seen Dinosaurs roaming down Pennsylvania Avenue, Mr. White? Huh? Tell me!"

From across the room, Secretary Barker was at the red phone giving orders to the military: "Um ... Mr. President?"

Tyler whirled around to face Barker. "What?"

Barker could only look out the large triple-paned plate glass window that overlooked Pennsylvania Avenue and point outside.

"Well, what the hell is it?" Tyler asked. He was growing frustrated.

Before he knew it, Donald Miller was out of his chair with the others and standing at the windows overlooking Pennsylvania Avenue. Kathy Hayden gave a sharp gasp. "Oh my God!"

Tyler joined them. "What are you gawking at?"

Miller felt his faith shatter at what he saw.

Fifty yards away from the White House along Pennsylvania Avenue, what could only be described as large reptilian creatures were making their way up the front lawn of the White House. They walked on their hind legs. One of them was carrying what looked like some kind of spear. Another clutched the handle of a large golden trident—the sharp end of which was impaled in a Secret Service agent's chest.

"My God, they're real!" Ken White breathed.

Through the howling wind of the storm they heard the sharp reports of automatic gunfire from government sharpshooters, who'd been ordered on the roof of the building before the storm hit. Some of the bullets found their mark, tearing through the creatures' thick hides and dropping them. Scattered among the creatures were the Clickers, their claws clacking together, paying their reptilian masters no heed.

And beyond them, in the distance, looming over the building across the street, something else moved. Something big; its shadow covered all.

"Oh my God ..."

From somewhere nearby—inside the building—Miller thought he heard the sound of a man screaming.

"They're storming the White House!" White had his service weapon out and headed out of the conference room.

A Secret Service agent was at President Tyler's side in a flash. "We have to move you to a secure location, Mr. President."

But Tyler wasn't paying attention. His attention was riveted to what was going on outside, on the lawn of the White House.

Miller, too, found it hard to tear his gaze away.

There were hundreds of the creatures. They were spread all across the White House lawn, crawling up the steps.

It grew darker outside as whatever was moving across the street drew closer.

The ground shook beneath its heavy tread. Miller could feel the floor vibrate beneath his feet.

They heard the commotion of Secret Service agents in various parts of the building yelling at each other in frightened voices. There was the sound of more automatic gunfire, from another portion of the building. More screams of pain that were quickly cut off.

Secret Service Agent Nate Walpow stepped back away from the window. "Oh my God, what is that thing? Look how big it is!"

Secretary Barker's face was white, pale as a ghost. "They're like an army."

One Secret Service agent was trying to pull President Tyler away from the window. "Mr. President, we have to get you to a secure location now!"

Somewhere within the building came the sound of breaking glass. Gunfire followed, accompanied by screams of agony.

Tyler could only look shocked.

Miller knew how he felt.

It was all true. Everything the scientists said ... it was all real.

And if it was true ... if the creatures outside really were a race previously thought extinct ... if they were really what Colonel Livingston said about them in his classified report eleven years ago ...

God help them all.

"Mr. President, I think we'd better do what Agent Smith advises," Miller said softly.

President Tyler turned to look at his closest advisor. It was hard to read the look on his face. "I send my VP out to Nebraska to our safe spot so he can maintain some semblance of order to our administration while God's house is under attack, and the minute Satan's minions storm His house you want to retreat?"

Those words had a chilling effect on Miller. He felt an icy finger down his spine. Is he not seeing what's going on outside? Hell, I didn't believe them myself, but they're here right in goddamn front of us and I can hear men in this building yelling and screaming in fright! Even if they are Satan's minions, shouldn't we do something about them?

"We are not leaving!" President Tyler said, jabbing an index finger at Miller. "Do you hear me? We're not backing down from Satan! God is testing our faith!"

Secretary Barker was looking at the President with a look of horror. "Are you out of your mind? Look at what's happening out there!"

From below, the sound of carnage, gunfire, and more screams.

Tyler's voice rose. "I do see it, Barker! I see that Satan has clouded your vision! These things are the product of the Imp! Don't you see that?"

The sounds of carnage on the floor below them grew more frenzied. There was the sound of shattering glass, frenzied yells, and more gunfire. Somebody on the lower level of the White House started screaming, "Oh my God, Oh my God, ohmygodddddd!"

"Fuck this; I'm getting the hell out of here." Barker sprinted for the door.

"Smith, shoot him!" Tyler barked.

Special Agent Smith had drawn his weapon at the first sound of disturbance from outside. He looked panicked, confused. Miller could tell that Smith's instincts were commanding him to secure order in the room, but President Tyler's order ran contrary to that, tugging at his loyalty.

Barker reached the door to the hallway.

Tyler screamed at Smith, "I'm the Commander In Chief, goddamn it! Shoot him!"

Agent Smith raised his weapon and fired.

The shot hit Barker square in the center of his back. It pushed him out the door into the hallway, where he slid down the wall leaving a smear of blood.

Tyler was still screaming orders. "Shut that fucking door!"

Another gunshot blasted through the room and Special Agent Smith dropped like a stone. Kathy screamed.

Ken White turned to the remaining people in the room— Special Agent Walpow, Kathy Hayden, Donald Miller, and President Tyler—his weapon drawn. "This fucked up shit is stopping right now!

Special Agent Walpow drew his weapon and pointed it at White just as White drew a bead on him.

The two men stood facing each other. Standoff.

Miller's heart was racing. His legs wanted to propel him out of the room and out of this mess, but he was afraid of being struck down himself or—even worse—of losing President Tyler's respect. So he forced himself to stay rooted to the spot.

"Drop your weapon, Walpow," White said.

"Walpow, I want you to shoot Mr. White!" Tyler screamed.

"Walpow, I am your superior and I'm telling you right now to drop your weapon!"

"I'm the Commander In Chief! God has called me to this position! You are in no position to be challenging God's authority!" Tyler was yelling so loud, veins were bulging from his forehead.

"Walpow, please listen to me!" White pleaded.

The sounds of carnage continued and were joined by an even more sinister sound. To White, it sounded like the creatures were making their way up the rear stairway.

Outside, there was the sound of concrete and steel hitting the ground as a building was crushed by the giant thing outside.

A spark went off in Miller's mind. "Wait a minute! We don't need to do this. We can all get out of here. Isn't there a panel hidden in this wall that contains a secret stairway that leads to the bunkers beneath the White House?"

"Yes, there is," White said, not switching his firing stance.

Miller moved away from the window toward the interior wall. He started feeling along the wall. "We need to find it and get in there before whatever is happening downstairs finds its way up here."

"Miller," President Tyler shouted, "you have to trust in the—"

Donald Miller whirled to face him. "'When you go to war against your enemies and see horses and chariots and an army greater than yours, do not be afraid of them, because the Lord, your God, who brought you out of Egypt, will be with you. That's from Deuteronomy, Mr. President. We are not retreating, we need to reconvene so we may do battle with the forces of evil. If prayer is going to help us, President Tyler, then we all need to get to Magog bunker so we can pray for the Lord's strength and guidance. Most importantly, we all need you to lead us in prayer and we can't do that here with Satan's minions out there destroying our men. It's distracting, and to put ourselves in jeopardy would be defeating God's purpose. Now let's arm ourselves and get about the business of fighting the good fight."

Miller's words had a profound effect on President Jeffrey Tyler. His eyes lit up with righteous fury. "Now there's a man of the Lord! Let's do it!" He broke away from the window and joined him at the wall. "Special Agent White and Walpow, drop your weapons. Let's retreat to Magog for prayer."

Walpow watched Tyler join Miller at the wall and lowered his weapon. Ken White did likewise. Kathy Hayden closed the door to the conference room and locked it. She leaned against it, panting, her face damp with sweat.

From outside the hallway came the sound of an animal-like roar and heavy footsteps. Whatever was making those sounds sounded large. They could all hear a clicking sound that accompanied the footsteps, as if whatever was coming down the hallway had sharp claws.

Kathy screamed and rushed toward President Tyler and Miller at the wall. "They're getting closer!"

"The panel's right here." Tyler said. He pressed the wall and a compartment began to open.

From out in the hall, the sound of the Dark Ones outside the door to the conference room grew louder. There was a heavy pound on the door.

"Shit, open up, hurry!" White screamed as the frenzied pounding continued outside the hallway, accompanied by more bleats from the Dark Ones.

The compartment door opened to reveal what appeared to be a closet.

Special Agent Clark Arroyo stepped out of the compartment brandishing a Sig Sauer 9mm handgun. He raised his weapon, squeezed off one shot, and dropped Walpow. Then he turned the weapon on President Tyler and grinned.

"Time's up, Mr. President."

The entire building shook. It sounded as if something was tearing the roof off.

"Arroyo ..." Tyler backed against the wall and fought to keep his balance. "Stand down, now!"

Clark smiled. "I don't think so. You know how you guys are always going on about Judgment Day? Well, it's upon you. Reap what you fucking sowed, you son of a bitch."

Tyler screamed.

Clark laughed.

Then the door to the conference room burst open and the Dark Ones rushed inside.

Peachbottom Nuclear Plant
3:38 AM

Incredibly, the heavy steel door buckled under the force of the tremendous blows hammering it from the other side. The hinges groaned, and the bolts fastening them in the wall began to bend.

"Oh fuck ..." Rick took a deep breath and held it. His hands trembled. "You said those locks could withstand ten tons of pressure, how the fuck can these things—"

"If there's more than one, they can probably muster the strength," Jennifer said, her voice grim.

"All of you form a line," Livingston said, his voice steady and calm. "Right here, next to me, so that you don't catch each other in the crossfire. They're coming in through this door."

"Ya think?" Tony shook his head in derision, but shuffled

forward. "This is a hell of a way to die."

Richard had to raise his voice to be heard over the pounding. "Would you quit saying that, please, Mr. Genova? I think we're all frightened enough."

"I hope you are," Livingston said. "Because that's what it's going to take to get out of this. Now get ready."

Jeremiah Brown stepped out from behind the control console. "Colonel? What can me and my men do to help?"

"Do you have any other weapons in here? Mop handles, bleach or other hazardous chemicals? Anything like that?"

"No."

"Then all you can do is pray. That might help."

Jeremiah glanced down at his feet. "I'm afraid that I'm an atheist."

Livingston grinned. "So am I—except in situations like this. Then I become a believer."

The door buckled again, and the top hinge tore free of the wall. The door fell inward a few inches, and Rick glimpsed a Dark One through the gap; the muscles beneath its green, scaled flesh rippling in the glow of the red emergency lights. Worse, he could smell the creature—a fishy, briny stench. Although he couldn't see them, he heard the familiar sound of the Clicker's claws.

It sounded like there was an army of them in the corridor.

He supposed that was pretty accurate.

He watched as Jennifer, tears in her eyes, stepped forward and kissed Richard tenderly on the cheek. Then she stood up on her tiptoes and did the same to Livingston. The old man's cheeks turned red, and he looked surprised. Then it was Rick's turn to be surprised as she slid beside him and did the same.

"Good luck," she whispered in his ear.

"You, too," Rick swallowed the lump in his throat and then concentrated on the door, his pistol held in both hands and at arm's length from his body.

"Where's mine?" Tony asked.

"Sorry," Jennifer said. "I don't know you well enough yet."

"Maybe after this is over?"

Despite her fears, Jennifer smiled. "Sure."

"Well then, let's kill these mother-fuckers."

"Colonel," Richard said, "I can get a shot through that crack at the top of the door. I can see part of a Dark One out there."

Livingston nodded. "Do it."

Richard crept forward and thrust the barrel of his gun through the crack. Before he could squeeze the trigger, the weapon was seized by a clawed hand. As he grappled with the Dark One, another of the creatures thrust a spear through the opening, piercing his shoulder. Richard screamed and let go of the gun. The Dark one yanked the rifle through the crack and Richard sank to his knees. The battering started again, the noise deafening.

"Get him out of there," Livingston shouted. "Get ready!"

Rick watched, stunned, as two of Jeremiah's employees ran forward and dragged Richard to the back of the room. Jennifer knelt beside him. Blood spread out across his shirt. The spear was still sticking out of him, the sharpened seashell tip jutting from his back. Richard clutched the blood-slicked shaft and groaned. His eyes fluttered. His lips turned blue.

"You're going to be okay," Jennifer gasped. "You're going to be fine."

"Don't pull that spear out," Rick advised her. "Just try to keep him still."

If she heard him, she gave no indication. Rick turned back to the door just as the Dark Ones succeeded in breaking it down.

"Fire!"

Livingston's weapon sang out and the others followed his lead. Rick, Tony, and Colonel Livingston stood shoulder to shoulder, determined not to let the creatures break through their line of defense. Brass jackets bounced off their shoulders and chests and clattered onto the floor like hail, and the room filled with smoke and screams from both the humans and the invaders. Behind them, many of the technicians backed up against the far wall, pressing against it and either closing their eyes or staring as death crept closer.

Two Dark Ones fell in the doorway, bullet holes riddling their massive forms. A third swiped out with his arm as Tony shot it in the face. Even as the pulped remains of its head splattered onto the creatures behind it, the Dark One's talons slashed across his chest, drawing blood. Grimacing, Tony took a step back.

"Hold the line," Livingston yelled over the gunfire. "Stand your fucking ground!"

Shaking his head in frustration, Tony locked his knees and drilled another Dark One.

Suddenly, Jennifer ran to the front of the room and joined them, the last spare rifle in her hands. She closed her eyes, squeezed the trigger, and jerked backward at the report. The shots went wild, hitting the ceiling. Undaunted, she opened her eyes and fired again. This time, she had a more firm grip on the weapon and her shots hit closer to her target.

"Cover me," Rick said, and quickly changed magazines. His trembling hands were numb from the rapid fire, and he had difficulty sliding the fresh mag into the pistol. As he worked, a small, dog-sized Clicker darted forward and lashed out at his foot with its tail. Rick sidestepped and kicked it. Pain shot up his toes. It was like kicking a fire hydrant. Hissing, the Clicker stabbed at him again. The magazine clicked into place. Rick pushed the barrel against a groove in the creature's shell and squeezed the trigger. Yellow goo gushed out of the wound.

"Not so bulletproof after all when we're this close, are you, you little motherfucker?"

The attacking hordes drew back around the corner and the hallway was suddenly empty, except for the corpses of the Dark Ones and Clickers they'd slain.

"Everybody okay on ammo?" Rick asked.

"I don't know," Jennifer admitted. "How do you tell?"

While Rick showed her, Tony parted the torn fabric of his shirt and checked his wounds. Livingston turned to Jeremiah and his men.

"See if we can get this door back up and in place."

"Why bother, Colonel?" Jeremiah said. "We don't have anything to brace it with. None of these office chairs are heavy enough."

"He's right," Richard groaned. "What's the point?"

Livingston stepped into the doorway and stared down the

empty corridor. "The point is that we fucking survive."

"Oh, the hell with this," Rick snapped, striding after him. "They're right, Colonel! What's the point? Even if we kill these things, more will come. And even if by some miracle we managed to escape, what then? The government will still be after us. We'll still have to watch our backs. Trust me—I've lived on the run, and I'm fucking tired of it. I'm sick of looking over my shoulder, sick of feeling the crosshairs every time I go outside, sick and tired of living on borrowed fucking time. And all of it is these things' fault!"

He shoved past the startled Colonel and into the corridor. As he stepped over the bodies of the Dark Ones, they all heard a sound from around the corner.

CLICK-CLICK ... CLICK-CLICK ... CLICK-CLICK ...

"Rick," Livingston whispered, "get back here."

Ignoring him, Rick walked on. His pace did not slow.

"I mean it. Get back here right now."

Rick raised his pistol and pointed it into the shadows at the end of the corridor. "Come on, you son of a bitch."

The monster answered the challenge. It rounded the corner and filled the hallway with its form. The Clicker was so huge that its shell scraped against the walls and ceiling and dug furrows in the drywall. The sound of its pincers slamming together reverberated down the corridor, drowned out only when Rick opened fire. He walked towards it as he fired, aiming for its legs and eyestalks. Cursing, Livingston ran after him.

Jennifer, Tony, and Jeremiah ran to the door and watched in dismay and horror as Rick ran out of ammunition. He seemed not to notice and continued walking purposefully towards the onrushing Clicker, still squeezing the trigger, oblivious to the fact that he was empty. Enraged, the Clicker raised its claws and closed the distance between them.

"Rick," Livingston shouted, "drop!"

If Rick heard him, he didn't show it. Colonel Livingston tried to draw a bead on the giant crustacean, but Rick was in the way. As it loomed over Rick and prepared to seize him in its claws, there was a loud explosion from farther down the corridor. Plaster rained down on them and thick smoke filled the hallway. Hissing, the Clicker tried to turn around, but its massive bulk got stuck. Thrashing, it squealed in frustration.

Taking advantage of the distraction, Livingston raced forward and grabbed Rick by the shoulder, shaking him and spinning him around.

"What the hell is your problem?"

Livingston was so furious that his spittle landed on Rick's cheek. The dazed man didn't seem fazed by it. Shoving Rick behind him, the Colonel drew a bead on the beast. Before he could fire, another explosion rocked the corridor. It was followed by the sounds of automatic gunfire.

"Fire in the hole," a voice warned.

Livingston cheered.

"Fall back," he shouted, running into the bunker and pulling Rick with him.

"What's happening?" Jennifer asked, confused.

"Richrath's reinforcements have arrived," Livingston told her. "Cheer up, Doctor Wasco. You're rescued—again." He motioned to Jeremiah. "Have your people get against the far wall and stay there."

"Well how about that," Tony said. "And here I was beginning to feel like General George Custer."

"No," Colonel Livingston said. "That's for our President. Soon as our situation improves, I'm going to personally deliver his Alamo."

"I don't think," Richard groaned from the corner, "that your analogy matches up, Colonel. Custer wasn't at the Alamo."

"Then here's another analogy for you, Doctor. I'm going to give him his very own Hiroshima."

The White House
3:39 AM

The Dark Ones poured into the room, leaping over Agent Walpow's still twitching corpse and charging them. Distracted, Clark spun around and fired at the onrushing invaders. The lead creature drew back its arm and flung a trident. The missile flew through the air and struck Kathy Hayden in the stomach.

She slammed into the wall and the trident held her in place, impaling her. Her screams turned to a sharp gasp. She fumbled with the shaft jutting from her abdomen.

President Tyler and Donald Miller both ducked down behind a long, rectangular conference table. Both men scrambled for the pistol that Walpow dropped when he was shot. Miller grabbed the weapon, but Tyler struck him in the temple with a right hook. Growling like a beast, the President tore the gun from Miller's hands and then crawled away.

Ken White and Clark both stood their ground, selecting their targets as more Dark Ones swept into the room. For every one of the creatures they killed, two more took their place. The Dark Ones' speed belied their size. Ken pulled the trigger again and was met with an empty click. He paled.

"Oh God ..."

Snarling, two of the creatures crossed the room in four quick strides and towered over him. Ken fell to his knees, dropped the empty pistol, and clasped his hands together in prayer.

"Please ... please ... please ..."

The largest of the creatures reached out and grasped Ken's head between its scaly hands. Then the Dark One began to squeeze. Ken's pleas turned to a low whine. His mouth formed an "o" shape and his teeth cut into his cheeks. His eyes bulged from their sockets. The creature applied more pressure and Ken's skull cracked.

Miller shrieked as another Dark One knocked him to the floor, and then grabbed his legs. It swung him through the air, repeatedly slamming him into the bookshelves. His spine shattered. His head burst. His bowels vacated. His body went limp. The creature tossed him aside.

Taking advantage of the confusion, President Tyler crawled to the secret passage that Clark had entered the room from. He slipped through the doorway, then stood up and fled. Clark emptied his magazine into the Dark Ones as they tried to surround him, then darted through their ranks and took off in pursuit of Tyler. He slammed the door shut behind him, plunging the passageway into darkness. Clark engaged the lock and crept forward. His eyes hadn't yet adjusted, and he had to rely on sound. He heard Tyler's footsteps ahead of him, running away. Outside, the Dark Ones flung themselves against the door. Razor-sharp talons lashed at the wood. They'd be through it in no time at all.

Clark ejected the spent mag and slapped in a fresh one. He fired one bullet into the darkness. It whined down the passageway, and the momentary flash of light made his night vision even worse. He didn't care. President Tyler's frightened scream was worth it.

Somewhere outside, something shook the building. Clark was momentarily knocked against the wall from the force of the shaking structure.

Something was out there. Something worse than the Dark Ones and the Clickers.

But that wasn't going to stop him now.

He ran after his prey, while the Dark Ones clawed at the door.

Peachbottom Nuclear Plant
3:50 AM

Colonel's Richrath and Livingston shook hands and embraced, slapping each other on the back.

"It's good to see you, you old war horse."

"You, too," Livingston replied. "Thanks for pulling our asses out of the fire."

Richrath shrugged. "It's what we do."

"What's the sit-rep?"

"Enemy has been obliterated. We control the plant. Site is secure. How about the reactors?"

"Brown?" Livingston turned to Jeremiah. "Any chance of a meltdown?"

"No, Colonel. We're fine."

"We'll get medical attention for your people," Richrath said, watching Jennifer and Rick helping Richard and Tony. "You okay, Augustus?"

"I'm fine. What's the situation across the country?"

"Civil war. Your coup was greeted with open arms by many

people across the spectrum. The Clickers and those other things have pretty much been defeated, or at least driven back into the ocean. Damage is in the billions, of course, and the loss of life is staggering."

"Any estimate on casualties?"

"Millions."

Livingston scowled. "All because of that sniveling Bible-thumper Tyler."

"Washington is still overrun. The enemy seemed to concentrate their forces there, almost as if they knew it was the seat of our power."

"They do know that," Rick said from the corner. "They're smarter than you think. As smart as us."

"That's William Mark," Livingston explained. "He's an expert on these things."

Richrath stared at Rick. He recognized him after a second; remembered him from Phillipsport. He winked and nodded, indicating the secret was safe. Then he turned back to Colonel Livingston.

"So what now, Augustus?"

Livingston paused. "The enemy controls this nation's capital. And I'm not just talking about the ones from the sea."

"Yeah?"

"Open a comm link with that bird we have in the air. I'm going to call in an air strike."

The color drained from Richrath's face. "Augustus, you can't be serious …"

"I've never been more serious."

"What's he talking about?" Rick asked.

"A nuclear option," Livingston explained. "A surgical strike, designed to take care of all these bastards once and for all."

The room fell silent, and then everyone began talking at once. Rising to her feet, Jennifer approached the officers and put her hand on Livingston's shoulder.

"Colonel, I know we've been through a lot tonight. And not just with the Clickers. You were betrayed by your country. We all were."

"Tyler is holding this nation hostage." Livingston pulled

away from her. "And it has always been this nation's policy not to negotiate with terrorists."

"But this isn't the way. Don't you see? There's been enough devastation tonight. Enough death. Our country will be permanently scarred by all that's happened tonight. Don't make it worse just to make it better."

"What do you suggest we do?"

"Richard said something to me earlier, when we were trapped in here. He said that sometimes you have to rely on humanity."

"Meaning what, Doctor Wasco?"

"Meaning that we have to count on the American people to do what's right. Let them handle Tyler. You've fought enough tonight."

Livingston considered his options. Then he turned to Richrath.

"Order more ground troops into Washington immediately. Divert all personnel not involved in rescue and cleanup operations."

"And the bird?"

"Call it back. Tell the pilot to stand down."

Richrath smiled, and then saluted. "You're doing the right thing, Augustus."

Livingston didn't respond. Exhausted, he wondered if his farm was still standing.

He wondered if he could ever return to it.

Washington, D.C.
3:51 AM

Specialist Terry Wright had wanted to operate a tank since she was a little girl, when she and her older brothers used to play army in their back yard as children.

That was years ago, and now Terry was grown up and in the Army for real. She was in her third year, serving out of Fort Detrick, and when she was discharged she was going to college for a degree in nursing.

Terry had taken to the tanks almost instinctively. She learned to drive them, service them, and operate the cannon. Now she was in an M1A2 Tank, positioned in the gunner's station, her target sighted in the two-axis view piece.

She called down to her driver, Private First Class Barry Moore, via her shoulder-mounted radio. "Enemy sighted. Hold back."

She felt the tank slow down a bit. She maneuvered to the left, the massive Clicker dead center in her sights. It was gigantic; it had to be well over a hundred feet in length and probably twenty or thirty feet in height. A bunch of those lizard creatures had been herding it toward the White House, and as Terry pressed the trigger she felt a sudden burst of adrenaline as her shot caught the giant Clicker dead center in the middle of its eyestalks.

The explosion was loud, even amid the scatter of gunfire and the sound of the creatures. The shot pulverized the Clicker, sending exoskeletal matter and white, gooey crap everywhere. Terry saw the thing was still standing, its top half bearing a giant hole in the center, and she lowered the cannon to aim at its mid-section. "Shit, I hope this thing takes the shot. It goes through, I'll be taking out half the White House."

"Blow it the fuck up!" Barry shouted in her earpiece.

Grinning, Terry drew a bead on her target and fired.

This time, the shot took the creature down for good. She saw its mid-section blow apart, spraying gunk over the lizard creatures and the smaller Clickers, and then the giant was down for good.

It was hard to tell if that last shot did any damage to the White House, but that wasn't the point. She'd obtained her objective. She'd blown the fuck out of that giant Clicker.

She never knew firing a real tank would be so rewarding.

Potomac River banks, near D.C.
3:55 AM

The leader seethed in anger.

It was forced to watch from its safe vantage point in the abandoned warehouse as the humans began making headway in their defense. The Dark Ones had been stealthy in their attack, and had killed an untold number of humans, more than enough to take revenge for the slaughter of their kind in the caves. The goal to eliminate the threat once and for all, though, was now in serious danger.

Herding the Clickers had been genius; finding the Queen of the Clickers had been even better. The leader was aware of her presence, knew she often dwelt in deep trenches in the ocean, hardly ever surfacing. To drive her out of the ocean, onto land, would wreak terrible havoc on the humans.

The leader had hoped to use the Queen of the Clickers to destroy the building where the humans had their central government. That was his intention. He hadn't anticipated the slow movement of the Queen, nor her restlessness. The leader lost a dozen of his brothers to her claws and the Dark Ones had kept a safe distance from her, being sure to stay in her blind side as they herded her toward their destination. As they guided her, they allowed the Queen to destroy other works that the humans had built—mostly buildings and cars. And when their goal was finally in sight, the leader had watched while the Queen crawled up to it and began tearing into the structure with her sharp claws.

He hadn't anticipated such a heavy attack from the humans, not this soon. The storm was still in force, but it was weakening. He was hoping the storm and the general confusion they'd caused with their attack would have been enough to scare the humans away long enough to take out their infrastructure once and for all.

But that wasn't to be.

The leader roared in frustration as he watched the Queen get blown apart by the green thing that blew fire. Infuriated, the leader swept a car off its tires, hurtling it over on its side.

It stopped. Now wasn't the time to go on a rampage. If he wanted to live to fight another day, at another time, he had to retreat now. And he had to save as many of his brothers as he could.

Calling out a signal to retreat, the leader roared its message across the Potomac. He waited, his hearing poor, but his senses tuned to the vibrations of his own kind's vocal cords. What came back was a roar of acknowledgement from his brethren: they'd received his message and were heeding it. The message was being relayed to the others. They were retreating.

With one last grunt of dismay, the leader leaped down from the parking structure and began making its way toward the black waters of the Potomac, away from the humans.

Hopefully, not all of his army would be slaughtered.

The White House
3:58 AM

They moved in darkness; hunter and prey—and the things chasing them both.

When the echoes of the President's footfalls suddenly faded, Clark halted and then crept forward with caution. He rounded a corner and there was a loud crack and bright flash from ahead of him. The bullet slammed into the wall, inches from his head. Clark aimed at the flash and fired two shots. He heard a shout, and then the sound of someone pulling the trigger on an empty weapon.

Grinning, he stepped around the corner and approached his quarry.

President Tyler lay slumped against the wall, bleeding from a gunshot wound in his stomach.

"It takes a long time to die from a gut shot, Mr. President."

"I'm not afraid of you," Tyler gasped, his voice slurred. "Flesh is weak. The soul is eternal. Kill me now and I'll stand before God, and be welcomed into the kingdom."

"Give him my regards."

Clark placed the barrel of his gun against the trembling man's head. Moaning, Tyler closed his eyes. A dark stain appeared on the crotch of his slacks.

"The Lord is my shepherd ..."

Before he could pull the trigger, Clark heard a noise; talons clicking on the corridor's tiled floor. The Dark Ones—closing in on them. He pulled the gun away. Tyler opened his eyes in surprise and stared up at him.

"You see, Arroyo? It's still not too late for you. You can find redemption. Pray with me. Ask that He forgive your sins and wash you in His blood."

Clark grinned. "You think that if I kill you, that you'll go to Heaven?"

"Of course I will."

"So you'll miss out on Hell? The demons can't touch you?"

Snarls and hisses drifted down the corridor as the Dark Ones became aware of their location. Padding footsteps turned into a run.

"Y—yes," the President said. "Clark, please. We have to ..."

"Guess what, Mr. President? You're wrong. The demons are coming for you right now."

He turned and fled down the corridor, plunging ahead into the darkness.

Behind him, President Tyler screamed.

Then came the ripping sounds.

Clark Arroyo navigated the secret passageways and eventually he emerged onto the White House lawn. The entire area was teeming with troops, and the bodies of the dead lay everywhere. Lying dead near the front lawn of the White House was a giant Clicker, its shell pulverized. Clark saw with a sense of numb amazement that part of the White House itself had been demolished. There was a large gaping hole in the building. Dusty smoke hung in the air, which reeked of brine and fish.

"Are you okay, sir?" A soldier approached him, concerned.

"I'm fine," Clark said. "But the President ... Those things got inside. The President is dead."

The soldier appeared shocked and fumbled for the proper response. Clark interrupted him.

"Should we take shelter? Are there more of the creatures out here?"

The soldier brightened. "No sir. This area is secure now."

"Then we've won. It's over."

"Yes, sir, I believe it is."

"President Tyler," Arroyo said, interjecting sorrow into his voice. "He's dead. Those things got him. There's still some in the White House."

The soldier spoke into his shoulder-mounted microphone. "Prepare to enter the White House. More of them are inside."

And as a battalion of soldiers began making ready to storm the White House with heavy weaponry, Clark Arroyo smiled as he made his way to a medical station and waited for the dawn.

Various Locations along the U.S. East Coast
5:00-9:00 AM

As fast as hell came to earth, it settled down with almost equal quickness.

As Hurricane Gary weakened and military personnel from across the country swept into the affected areas, the scales began to tip. Tanks obliterated Dark Ones. Troops bearing high caliber automatic weapons mowed down Dark Ones and Clickers alike. The National Guard assisted, beginning the task of performing mop-up duties and maintaining law and order in a few areas that had begun to slip into civil unrest. As if the Dark Ones and Clickers knew the tide was turning, they began to retreat; the Clickers appeared to sense that the currents were changing and migrated back into the ocean. Most were destroyed by heavy gunfire. Likewise, the Dark Ones heard the call of their leader and almost immediately began relaying the message along the Eastern Seaboard. Within minutes they were racing to the shore, diving into the watery depths. Many of them made it to safety; many others were slaughtered mercilessly.

In New York City, Connie Stewart peeked her head over the windowsill of the storage room over O'Mally's Bar where she, Bob Ellison, and Derek Brubaker had taken refuge. The three had kept each other awake all night out of pure fear and necessity. When Connie saw powerboats equipped with military personnel come charging down the still-flooded Seventh Avenue below her, she reached down and shook Bob Ellison out of a light doze. "Hey, I think I see military out there!"

Bob and Derek were up in a flash as more speedboats roared by. "Those are Navy guys," Derek said, excited. "Thank God, I hope this is over!"

As military, law enforcement, and civilian volunteer rescue

teams began the effort of locating victims and helping to evacuate people, they were greeted with cries of relief and shouts of victory. People emerged from storm shelters, basements, attics, amazed and sad at the carnage. In Baltimore, a homeless man (the same vagrant that Richard had met earlier during his attempt to reach the aquarium) stepped out into the morning sun from his second-floor refuge of an abandoned house as the last clouds of Hurricane Gary broke apart, grinning gap-toothed. He was carrying a large fishing net and was scooping up small dead Clickers by their legs, throwing them inside. "Gonna have me a big 'ol crab feast tonight. Hell yeah, jus' gotta get me some butter and some Old Bay and I'm there!"

At a makeshift command center outside of the Peachbottom Nuclear Plant, Rick talked to Melissa Peterson on his cell phone. Despite being tired, he felt a sense of relief ... it felt like something had been lifted off his shoulders, that for the first time in over a decade, he could feel free and relaxed. "—I just wanted to make sure you were okay," he told her, after sighing in relief when he heard her voice. "So much has happened that you don't ... well, it'll take forever to tell you about it."

"I've been worried sick about you," Melissa said. "How are things down at ground zero? Anything like before?"

Rick shook his head. He had seen some of the news footage, which was being broadcast all over the world now. Despite hearing verification of President Jeffrey Tyler's death and Vice President Danny Bower's slide into the position of President, the political talking heads were already doing a number on the Tyler Administration. "They're over," one of them said. Rick could only grin at that.

"Naw. It's nothing like Phillipsport. For one thing, we really won this time."

"Seriously?" There was a sense of doubt in Melissa's voice. Rick didn't blame her one bit.

He glanced over at Colonel Livingston, who was fielding questions from reporters about fifty yards away from him. In the past few hours, Livingston had become the de facto leader of the country and everybody knew it except the surviving fragments of the Tyler Administration. Rick had heard Livingston make a call to the CIA to put in the order to cease Project Phil, the code name for eliminating all the Phillipsport witnesses and survivors. He was made aware of the code name fifteen minutes ago from a CIA defector who used his security clearance to get to Peachbottom. Normally, the CIA would not take orders from a high-ranking military official, but their displeasure toward the Tyler Administration was the deciding factor. Besides, the whole world knew about Phillipsport now. There was nothing left to cover up.

Rick told her this. Melissa was silent for a moment. Then: "What does that mean for us?"

"We're free, honey. We're free."

Melissa's voice cracked. "I wish I could believe that."

"Believe it." Rick closed his eyes, suddenly feeling tired from his ordeal. "I'm flying back home as soon as possible. I want to get on with my life. I want to see my daughter, want to try to patch things up with Ashley. I've spent the last twelve years running, Melissa. I'm tired of running. I ran away from Ashley when things started going bad between us, and I want to make things right if I can."

"And if you can't patch things up with her?"

"Then I'll feel better knowing I at least tried. At least I can still be a part of my daughter's life."

Thirty minutes later, Colonel Livingston was on the phone with his housekeeper, May. "I'm so glad to hear you're okay," he said.

"You too, Colonel," May said.

"And your son and his family?"

"They made it over here an hour after you left."

"Good." Colonel Livingston was relieved to hear that. "May, I have a favor to ask of you."

"Yes, Colonel?"

"In the bottom right-hand drawer of my bureau in the bedroom there's a spiral bound phonebook. Under the letter "W," you'll find a listing for Josh and Maryann Waggoner. Can you read that number off to me?"

"Sure, Colonel, just a moment."

And as May headed to his bedroom to retrieve his

phonebook, Colonel Livingston looked up at the blue sky overhead and hoped that he would get to see his grandchild, that his long and frequent absences from his son's life had not proven to be a disaster.

Epilogue

BOMBARDMENTS CONTINUE

Tod Sylva
Associated Press
July 12, 2006

Military operations continued today along the Eastern seaboard of the United States as the American Naval and Coast Guard forces destroyed further breeding grounds and dwellings of Homarus Tyrannous ...

DEEP SEA CAVERNS DISCOVERED

Val Lann
Associated Press
July 30, 2006

Military operations and marine biologists today discovered a catacomb of underwater caverns that extend from the Chesapeake Bay to the Maine coast that is believed to be the entrance to the breeding ground of the species that are now referred to as "Dark Ones."

Marine Lt. Robert Brennan told the Associated Press today that a full-scale search and destroy mission was underway. "We've got a number of dead specimens in our possession now that we're studying. It's through those findings that we were able to discover the entrance to these caverns."

It's not known how large these underwater caverns are,

or how many of the creatures may be hiding inside them. But Robert Brennan says that extreme caution is going to be made in eliminating the creatures. "We can't afford to sit idly by and let these Dark Ones have a chance to become a threat again."

SYCHEK'S BIOGRAPHY DEBUTS AT NUMBER ONE

Kelli Datlow
Hellnotes.com
September 22, 2006

As clean-up and humanitarian efforts continue across the Eastern seaboard, one of the principal players in last July's disaster got some good news today. Author Rick Sychek, who spent several years living under an assumed identity and on the run from clandestine government forces, saw his autobiography debut at number one on The New York Times bestseller list. A Conspiracy of One, which details Sychek's ordeal, was released this week by New York-based publisher Diamond Books. Movie rights have been optioned by Hollywood producer John Boucher ...

MIDTERM ELECTIONS BLOWOUT

Mark Jennings
New York Times
November 6, 2006

As a result of the fallout with the Tyler Administration over Hurricane Gary and the Clickers/ Dark Ones catastrophe, voters sent a clear message to Washington—the United States is no longer represented by corporate interests or ideologues. It is clearly, we the people.

House Republicans lost over half their members, with the new seats being taken up by a mixture of seasoned Democrats, Independents, and what is looking to be a new breed finally gaining voice in the Republican Party comprised of Senators and Congress people who explain they were never comfortable with Jeffrey Tyler's extreme right-wing brand of government in the first place ...

WASCO NAMED NEW DIRECTOR

David Howison
The Baltimore Sun
January 10, 2007

Dr. Jennifer Wasco was named Director of the National Aquarium in Baltimore today during a retirement ceremony for Dr. Richard Linnenberg. Linnenberg and his wife recently adopted a child and plan to live in ...

BOWER RESIGNS
FORMER SECRETARY OF THE TREASURY
ALAN DOWD SWORN IN AS PRESIDENT

Naomi Peterson
The Washington Post
January 30, 2007

In a stunning move right before impeachment proceedings were about to get underway, President Bower, who ascended to the Presidency in a smooth transition following the death of Jeffrey Tyler during Hurricane Gary and the Clicker/Dark Ones invasion, announced his resignation. Secretary of the Treasury Alan Dowd was sworn in as President when Vice President Moore, Speaker of the House Garrison, and President Pro Tempore of the Senate, James Conway declined the position ...

LIVINGSTON WINS!

Staff reports
Associated Press
November 1, 2008

With sixty percent of the nation's precincts reporting,

experts are predicting that retired U.S. Army Colonel Augustus Livingston has won both the popular vote and the electoral college, and will be named as the next President of the United States ...

BARGE MISSING, FATE OF CREW UNKNOWN

Trent Simmons
Newport News Intelligencer
March 19, 2009

The crew of a missing barge is feared dead after a third day of searching by the Coast Guard and other authorities turned up nothing ...

About the Authors

J. F. Gonzalez (1964-2014) was the author of over a dozen horror and dark suspense titles including *Primitive, The Beloved, Fetish, Survivor,* and is the co-author of *Clickers II: The Next Wave,* and *Clickers III: Dagon Rising* (both with Brian Keene). His short fiction is collected in *Old Ghosts and Other Revenants, Maternal Instinct, When the Darkness Falls,* and *The Summoning and Other Eldritch Tales.* In addition to these, he wrote non-fiction, screenplays, technical manuals and other corporate communications, and the occasional ghostwritten writer-for-hire novel.

Brian Keene is an American author and podcaster, primarily known for his work in horror, dark fantasy, crime fiction, and comic books. He has won the 2014 World Horror Grandmaster Award and two Bram Stoker Awards.

Curious about other Crossroad Press books?
Stop by our site:
http://store.crossroadpress.com
We offer quality writing
in digital, audio, and print formats.

Printed in Great Britain
by Amazon

38406266R00172